Web of Intrigues

Web of Intrigues

Betty Hogg

AMHERST

ISBN 978-1-903637-51-7

Printed and bound in Great Britain by
Biddles Limited, King's Lynn, Norfolk

First published in the UK in 2008 by

Amherst Publishing Limited
Longmore House, High Street, Otford, Sevenoaks, Kent TN14 5PQ

To Evelyn, Georgie, Derek, Wat, Helen, and all the
younger ones and their young ones – and all my friends.
Frances and Alan Hobkirk for their continued interest
– Karen and Ann and Rhona for keeping asking.
Aileen in Selkirk, who has had a hard time lately.
Mr Fiddes, my headmaster of old, who is now ninety-seven.

Thanks to Carol White for her information about London.
I didn't know what a nippy was until she told me.
Thanks to Andy for teaching me how to work the
computer over the phone. All the way from Leeds.

Chapter One

'Steady lad, steady,' Barbara Fairburn patted Peacock, her hunter's neck as he careered from the road onto the grass verge, scared, as an ambulance with sirens blaring, shot passed them, screeching its way round a corner and out of sight. A police car followed, emitting an equal amount of racket.

Barbara cursed. She didn't know the urgency of this call, but surely a horse deserved a bit of consideration on the main road. Peacock side-stepped and pranced. She couldn't get him to settle. The excitement of a morning's cub hunting, still heated his blood.

Two miles on, a side road wound towards Hawthornside farm, her home. At the stables, she dismounted and handed the reins to Tony, her groom. His face was white and he wouldn't meet her eyes.

Refraining from questioning him, she turned to go. She was tired. The many hours in the saddle were beginning to take their toll. She knew it was most unwise to be galloping round the countryside so far into her pregnancy, but what the hell – life was for living. Even her love life had not in any way diminished. With Dan Sykes, the local plumber, and Bert Wilson, her gardener, as lovers, she was no saint. Her husband, Peter, only when inebriated, made a move towards her in bed. Mostly, she feigned sleep, but when she did comply, to keep a fragment of peace, she lay like a statue until it was over. This irked him. 'You're a cold blooded bitch, Barbara,' he grumbled. 'You're like a trout in the river; only it can be eaten and enjoyed.' Inwardly, she smiled.

If only he knew, she mused. Or did he? Was his habitual drunkenness his way of glossing over the fact?

'Ma'am.' Her reverie was broken as Tony spoke.

'Yes, Tony. What is it?' Barbara saw his gaze leap over her head and turned. Two policemen plodded with big feet towards her.

'Mrs Barbara Fairbairn?' the tallest one asked.

'Yes.'

'Can we go somewhere quiet. I'm afraid we have some bad news.'

'Bad news? What?' Even as she spoke, she noticed the absence of Peter's car – and knew. The ambulance – the police car. It all tied up.

'Is he – dead?' she whispered.

'Yes madam. I'm sorry.'

The ground seemed to dance dizzily round her. She hadn't been in love with him for years; yet it was still a shock.

Today was his funeral. She shed no tears. He was gone, and that was that.

'Ashes to ashes, dust to dust,' The minister's voice cut the silence cloaking the drizzly, dank air. The cords slithered over the edges of the grave. Soil, flung from Barbara's gloved hand, rattled with a clunk on the coffin.

Friends bulged the cemetery. He had been well liked. Barbara stood with head lowered, her black coat barely hiding her state of pregnancy.

'She'll never be short of a man,' said Pete, the butcher, as the long line of people paying their respects trooped along the chipped road from the cemetery.

'No, she's like a bitch in heat when there's a man around.' Fred Marshall's words were loud, travelling to all and sundry above the crunching footsteps. Smugly, he continued his bawdy diatribe, knowing his listeners' avid ears were soaking up every word like sponges.

'Watch what you're saying about the lady, you sod,' a voice

interrupted from behind. An angry hand grabbed his shoulder. An even angrier face, pressed close to his. It was Dan Sykes, red jowled and indignant.

'Alright, alright, keep your hair on. I'm only saying what everybody else is.' Fred buttoned his lips and hastened his steps. Dan Sykes shouldered past him in a flurry of rage.

'They say he pays her a visit,' said Fred when Dan was out of earshot. 'Bert Wilson as well.'

Tom Garrick, in the procession of mourners, heard this altercation and ensuing remarks. He was numbed. Poor Alice, he thought. Surely Bert would have more sense. Tom wasn't a man who indulged in local tittle-tattle. He enjoyed talking about farming. Anything pertaining to the land. The news imparted by Fred, scratched against his brain all night. Dan and Barbara, he could swallow, but Bert – that was hard to take in.

Next day, the hunt met at Tom's parents' farm. His dad, in his wheelchair, watched from the front door. Tom played host, handing out the traditional drinks.

Placid hounds, tails wagging with joy, mingled round horses' feet. The horn echoed over tree tops and hedges; then they were away. Barbara Fairbairn was there. With verve and style, she jumped everything in sight. She was fearless. Some admired her. Others didn't.

'She shouldn't be hunting in her condition,' said Mary Marshall. 'What if she has a fall? It might kill the bairn.' The morning was cold, causing her eyes to water and her nose to run. She sniffed. Rummaging in her pocket, her hand emerged with a white hanky. Vigorously, she wiped and rubbed until her nose was red. A final sniff held at bay another drip. 'Huh!,' she continued. 'Her kind get away with anything. She'll maybe rue the day yet, though. There's a time for everything!

'Aye, she thinks she's God, that one. HE'LL be the only one that knows who the father is,' said her friend Jane. She sniffed too. It seemed to be catching.

'Well, it's not a miraculous conception, that's for sure. It's a foregone conclusion, the way she carries on,' cried Grace.

They all laughed and wound their way homewards. Great cackling guffaws, that subdued even the baying of the hounds.

The object of their disdain rode wilfully on. She was a very attractive woman. Today, the speed of the gallop flicked her hair into streams of russet. Tight jodhpurs clung like a second skin to her well rounded buttocks.

'God, look at that.' Tom moved his gaze from Barbara's shapely bottom and fixed it on Dan Sykes. 'What a view. It puts a heat in the blood on a cold morning like this.'

'Get your own woman, Tom.' Dan's eyes flashed with fury. 'Hell, you should be married with a few kids by now.'

'Sorry, old chap.' Above the pounding of hooves, Tom shouted an apology. Dan's response made him fully aware of the truth in the rumours. Most likely it was true about Bert too, he thought. It saddened him to think how Barbara used his friend. How she used all men. She'd get her just deserts some day, that one.

An early frost had formed a crust on a ground still soft underneath. It nipped the cheeks and smoked the air with every breath and word. A haze swirled round the rugged outline of Ruberslaw's peak. Clods spewed from galloping hooves and mud sprayed intent faces. Tom's mare was keyed up. Foam flecked her neck where the reins touched. Tom was fired up too, but his feelings stemmed from anger, not excitement.

Damn that Barbara,' he cursed, vowing to keep himself well out of reach of her clinging clutches. Attractive widow, or not, she was not for him No one knew his innermost thoughts. Ever since Bert had returned from working up north, bringing Alice with him as his wife, Tom's heart had been stolen.

'Meet the wife,' Bert had said. 'Alice, this is Tom.' He had looked into those quiet grey eyes, his heart somersaulting in his chest; his throat tight; his 'How do you do?' alien even to his own ears. If Alice guessed, she kept it to herself.

Feeling dispirited, he retired from the chase early. The mare wanted to go on, and her strong mouth tugged at his arms, but he pulled her up and turned for home.

'You're back early, son.' His father looked up in surprise, his eyes peering over the thick frames of his glasses.

'Yes, my heart wasn't in it today, somehow.' Tom avoided his dad's alert gaze and escaped upstairs to change his mud splattered clothes. Splashing cold water on frost chafed cheeks, he descended the stairs and strode into the room.

'Woman trouble is it, lad?' Norman's concerned eyes scanned Tom's face.

Tom raised a hand and drew it across his brow.

'It's that bitch Barbara. She plays with men like a cat does with a mouse. She's even got Bert ensnared in her callous clutches.'

'Mmm, it's best to avoid the likes of her if you can, lad.' Shrewdly, Norman assessed his sensitive son. Stocky, fairly tall, dark haired, hazel eyed. At the moment, he was solemn, but when he smiled, the warmth of it lit up his face like a lamp. He was a very presentable chap.

'Don't worry, you'll find the right one. When you do, it'll hit you like a dose of diarrhoea. You'll know all right, son.'

His father chuckled, crows feet crinkling his eyes into slits of memories. Memories of his first meeting with Jean. Now what did he have? Stuck in this bloody wheelchair. No legs. What use was he to her like this? Christ, diabetes had a lot to answer for. He shook these thoughts from his mind. Tom was the one that mattered. It was his happiness that was important. In silence, he continued to scrutinize his disenchanted son.

Grabbing the racing paper, Tom hid behind its welcome pages. He hoped his dad couldn't see into his mind. All he would see was a picture of Alice. Embossed for eternity. His Alice, yet not his. Tom sighed. She was beyond his reach. Married to his best friend – and she was pregnant.

He rubbed his eyes. He could do with a drink. He'd see if Bert was at home. He picked up the phone. Bert answered.

'Hello, Bert. Would you like to go for a drink, later? I'll come and pick you up.'

'I'd like to, Tom, but Alice isn't feeling too good. Better not risk it. Come over, though. I've got some bottles of ale in the pantry.'

'Right, thank you. See you, Bert. Bye.' Suddenly, Tom felt more joyful. He would see Alice. His heart was a traitor to his mind. Yet – would his mind always be the victor? His inside squirmed at such dangerous thoughts.

His family's farm was adjacent to Hawthornside, where Bert worked. In light of what he had heard at the funeral, Tom felt like giving Bert a cautionary word, but it was Bert's business, not his. He'd give him the benefit of the doubt. He turned his attention to his father.

'I'm going out later, dad. To see Bert.' He listened for noises in the kitchen. It was silent. 'Where's mum? Tom looked at the clock on the mantelpiece then at his dad.

'Away to a meeting. Something to do with the kirk. She'll be back soon.' His father spoke flatly, a dull look in his eyes.

'Would you like a turn round the steading before nightfall? We've got the cattle in.' Tom watched his father's face light up. 'Good, that's settled then.' Carefully, he eased him into a thick, tweed jacket, tucked a travel rug round his thighs and little bits of stumps - all that was left of his once strong legs - and whirled him outside.

Curious heads swung in their direction as they walked down the alley between the cattle courts. Steam clouds flew from glistening nostrils. Black eyes gleamed.

'They look in fine fettle,' said Tom's dad. 'That's a good Hereford bull. He'll leave some nice calves.' His gaze wandered over the sturdy beast with interest.

Two farm cats jumped from the manger under the rack. They stared up at Tom's smiling face. 'You're too early pussies. Milking time isn't for a while yet.' They rubbed against his legs, tails up, backs curved, purring.

They didn't believe him.

The Land Rover was at the door when he and his dad returned. His mother was stirring something in a pan on the cooker. A half smile tilted the corners of her mouth.

'Hello, mum. What's your secret?' said Tom, having noticed her smile.

She glanced up, startled, a flush creeping across her cheeks.

'Don't look so worried, I was only joking,' he laughed.

Along the passage, he continued, stopping at the sitting room door. With expert hands, he twisted the wheelchair through the space. Six strides took him to the warm fire blazing in the hearth.

Harshly, his father spoke.

'She spends far too much time doing work for the kirk. That minister should get himself another wife; and Jean should act her age. I hear her jabbering away in the kitchen when her friends are in. Gordon said this, or Gordon said that. Gordon did this, or Gordon did that. Hell, it makes me sick. It's not as if he's giving her the eye or anything. What does she think he's got under that cassock of his – a bloody magic wand?'

Norman's chest wheezed in sympathy with his feelings, his eyes glinted like steel.

Tom looked in amazement. His dad had never given such a harangue, or vented his spleen in such a fashion before. Poor dad. Jealous – of the minister.

He stepped to the kitchen door. His mother still stirred with circular movements at something in the pan. Still with that same half smile sitting on her face like a fixture. Maybe dad had a point. He thought of his own liking for Alice. Would folk recognise the signs that HE tried so hard to hide? Hugging this notion to himself, he stalked out, banging the door behind him.

Time escalated. Autumn's energy was spent, and now winter held the reins. Tom had just fed his dogs, and was about to take them to their kennels, when the phone rang. Giving a huge sigh, he retraced his steps to the kitchen and picked it up.

'Hello, Tom Garrick here. Oh, it's you, Bert.' A long torrent of words on the other end, stilled Tom's tongue. He could make out Alice and doctor. The rest was just a gabble.

'Hey, steady on, Bert. Start again, but slowly this time.'

'It's Alice. Her pains have started. Can your mother come, Tom?' Bert seemed at his wit's end.

'Of course she will; I'll drive her. We'll be there in ten minutes. Legs feeling suddenly weak, he approached his mother. 'Bert's just phoned. Can you help Alice? The baby is on its way.'

His mother's earlier years of nursing, flamed her mind into action. Instantly, she took charge. 'Tell him to hunt out some old sheets. Tell him to talk calmly to her. Tell him not to panic.'

Relaying this information to Bert, Tom flung down the phone and picked up his keys. 'Come on.' He stared at his mother. 'Alice seems to be in a bad way.'

'We'll have to get someone from the cottages to see to your dad.' His mother threw the words at Tom, as quickly he shot to the car. 'We might be gone for quite a while.'

'Don't fuss, Jean.' Norman jerked his head towards the door. 'Get Isa, she likes a game of dominoes.' He felt the draught from the open door hit his neck. 'Hell, you'd think they'd been born in a field,' he muttered to himself. Then he thought of Isa and cheered up. She'd give him a piece of that chocolate sponge normally forbidden in his diet. Diet, be buggered, he fumed. It wouldn't bring back his bloody legs.

Tom revved the engine. Twisting round in her seat, his mother reached for the door and clicked it shut. She looked at Tom's hands, white knuckled on the steering wheel, and a curious expression crossed her face.

She knows, thought Tom. Well – it was snap. He knew her secret too.

Darkness was beginning to pull its blinds over the land as

they set off. Trees, stark, skeletal shapes, silhouetted the fading sky. To the right, up a narrow road, golden glows peeped from cottage windows. A hastily opened door, splashed beams of light onto the step and stony surface beyond it, as Tom's car crunched to a standstill. Bert filled the doorway, his face as white as his shirt. 'Man, it's good to see you, Tom. You too, Jean,' he cried.

'Will I take her to hospital?' Tom's voice was tight.

'No, she's left it too late. She managed to make it to the bedroom, but her pains are bad. Come on Jean, I'll take you up.' Bert looked worried. It's a blessing that Barbara installed a telephone,' he puffed, as on shaky legs, he stumbled up the stairs.

'I'm away to get Isa to look after dad,' said Tom. 'Will be back before you know it.' He saw the look of anguish on Bert's face, and fled.

On the bed, Alice drew up her knees, trying to squash the terrible pain. A moan escaped her dry lips. Her hands clutched crumpled sheets, and her eyelids screwed into tight folds over her eyes as she pushed.

'That's right, Alice. Push down – hard. Take a deep breath. It will make it easier. Come on, you're doing fine.' Jean was trying to inspire her into making a greater effort, but Alice was listless. Jean grew anxious. All the signs proclaimed a long night.

A breathless Tom returned. Downstairs, Bert and he heard the shouts – and the silences. The silences were worst. More ominous. Tom fidgeted from chair to chair. Bert chewed nervously at his nails.

'You'll have to go up, Bert. She might be needing you.' Tom's voice was hushed.

'No, I can't. You go. You're used to cows calving and ewes lambing. Maybe you can help. Do something, Tom, for Christ's sake.'

With thudding heartbeats, Tom climbed the stairs. At the bedroom door, he paused, then slowly entered. His mother stood at the bedside. She looked up when he came in.

'Hold her hands, Tom, I think she's given up. She needs encouragement.'

He crossed to the bed. Alice lay with splayed legs, her face taut, her hair damp and straggly, her eyes shut. Gently, he clasped her hands. They were clammy with sweat. 'Alice, it's me – Tom. You've got to try a bit harder. Come on, you can do it,' he whispered.

As if from a distance, Alice heard his voice. Like the sound of a stone hitting the bottom of a well and echoing its way back up again. It triggered a response. She pushed. A loud 'oh' filled the room. Then it was there, the baby, all slimy and gooey.

'It's a girl.' Jean picked up the tiny bundle with an awe reserved only for babies. A quick slap on the bottom, aroused a loud roar. 'Hello, to you too, little lass,' she said. Her voice was quiet; soothing. Quickly, she wrapped the baby in a blanket and placed her in her mother's arms.

Alice's eyes slid over the perfect features of her child, then shyly crept to Tom.

A lump the size of an orange, filled Tom's throat. What he had witnessed was special. It would stay with him always; a bond, holding them together like a lover's knot; and he knew she cared. Just a bit.

Still hovering by the bed, was his mother. 'Once she's cleaned up, I'll give you a wash too, Alice. Then you may feed her. Tell Bert he can come up now, Tom.'

Sheepishly, Bert tip-toed into the room. As he peered down at the tiny face, he was filled with wonder. Such perfection – and he had helped make her.

Alice kept her face averted; her eyes closed. She didn't want to see her husband. The very thought of him brought bile to her mouth. If it wasn't for her nosy neighbours, she would buy single beds, but they would see them being delivered. All she needed was their gossipy tongues wagging; telling everybody about her and Bert's bedroom arrangements. She sighed; snuffling in that blanket, lay a new life. A life that needed her.

Drowsily, she wondered if Barbara Fairbairn had been delivered of her baby yet. In her dazed state of mind, it seemed of the utmost importance.

And indeed, in a hospital some miles away, Barbara had given birth to a baby boy. As she gazed with pride at her son, Barbara's heart was full. His plump, little hands clenched and unclenched. His fingers were long, with a grip like an octopus.

'You'll be as strong as Hercules,' she said softly. 'Now, let me see the rest of you.' Her gaze landed on his legs – then down to his feet. 'Oh, God!' The cry flew from her lips. Her hand shot to her mouth.

He had webbed toes. In circles, it ran through her head. Webbed toed, webbed toes, webbed toes. How the hell had she bred a son with webbed toes? To any other mum it would have been a minor thing, but to Barbara, 'twas as if he had two heads.

She knew it must be a hereditary thing. Her husband had certainly not had them. So who then, was the father?

She thought of Peter, her late husband; his booze inflamed fumblings the last time he had his way with her. It came to her like a record playing in her ears.

'Come on, Barbara, you're my wife. You cannot deny me,' he slurred. The staleness of his breath, filled her with revulsion. A leg stretched over her, followed by his leaden bulk. 'Let it be swift,' she prayed – and it was. Relief spread over her as, with a sigh, he rolled onto his side. Minutes later, he was asleep.

Her mind jolted to the present. Her face was sombre. Surely she hadn't conceived then? Not after nearly four barren years? She'd begun to think he was infertile. Or she was. Her thoughts swung to Dan Sykes. Mousy coloured hair, eyes pools of passion, she awaited his visits with a body as eager as his.

Then there was Bert. Fair haired, blue eyed Bert, who made love like he was tending the garden, pouring all his affection into the act. He loved her, she knew, but love was too complicated a thing for a woman like her. She let out a long breath and laid back her head.

Rich, auburn hair splashed the pillows with streaks of fire. Her eyes, lifeless as a stone, stared at her son as if at a chimerical thing, then they swirled towards a nurse standing by her bed.

'If any of you speak of my son's abnormality beyond the hospital premises, I shall have you dismissed. I have a lot of clout in this locality, I'll have you know.'

'Och, Mrs Fairbairn, What are you worrying your pretty head about?' the nurse admonished. 'He's a lovely boy. It's what's inside that counts, not nature's faults. Not that they are faults,' she added crisply. A rustle of apron, a squeak of shoes, and she was gone.

'Rotten, selfish bag,' she muttered under her breath as she strode purposefully up the ward. Poor little mite, having a mother like her.' Then she smiled. He had everything a male needed, that lad. It didn't matter a docken if he had webbed toes.

Barbara looked at the small face and conceded that he was indeed handsome.

'Who are you like?' she murmured. At the sound of her voice, he opened his eyes. They were a dark shade of blue, but would change to brown, like her own did. He snuffled and gurgled into his fist. 'You don't care, do you?' she said, in a subdued tone, 'but I do.'

The genetic linkage regarding the webbed toes was to cause distress in the lives and relationships of many, with tragic consequences. Yet, a ray of light shines in an unexpected way.

Chapter Two

The following week, Dan and Emma Sykes became parents to a baby girl. They called her Beth. Weeks later, with baby warmly clothed in pink, Emma traipsed down the village main street. She espied an evasive Barbara, blustering along, her pram wheels looking as though tuned up for a Grand Prix.

No one as yet had set eyes on her offspring. This brought to the air, a kind of mystery.

'She's frightened we think he looks like one o' her lovers.' Mary Marshall's lips smacked the words out with glee.

'Well, they say a bairn always fathers itself. So time will tell.' Grace Stuart tossed her head, her eyes following the pram's progress along the pavement.

With this in mind, Emma honed in on a scarlet faced Barbara; blocking her path, forcing her to stop.

'Oh, hello, Barbara,' she cried. 'Let's have a look, then.' Green eyes peered at the child no one had seen. 'Ooh, he's gorgeous. What's his name?'

'John, after his grandfather from my side. He's dead, though.' Barbara fidgeted, trying to get away, but Emma held her back.

'You know – my Beth and your John might get together one day. They came into the world about the same time; surely that's an omen.'

Emma giggled.

'Then there's Cathy. She and Beth will be fighting over him

when they're a bit older.' She threw a wicked look in Barbara's direction. 'I wonder which one will win?'

Neither of them, if I get my way, thought a furious Barbara. Definitely, definitely not. With unseeing eyes, she swept passed Emma.

Unconsciously, her thoughts wandered to Cathy, Bert and Alice's daughter. Her brow wrinkled with concern. She would do her best to keep them apart. Someone higher up the social ladder was her aim for John. Also, another worry teased her mind. The what if – kept running in never ending circles inside her head. The faces of Dan and Bert ran with it, but which one would stem the tide?

Her resolve to keep John and Cathy apart had an enemy from the start. Fate. It beat her at every turn. Ever since they could toddle, a hole in Barbara's hedge had brought them together.

'Hello,' said John, as he scraped through the thick, privet hedge that divided his garden from the road which led to the cottages where Cathy lived. 'I'm John. What's your name?'

'Cathy.'

'Are you coming to play?'

'Yes.'

'I've got a water pistol.' He held it out. 'Would you like a shot?'

'Oh. yes please. You can try my yo-yo. Here –' Shyly, she passed it to him.

That was the start.

Sometimes, they ventured into the farm buildings, finding magical pleasures in every corner. Mostly, they went to the stables – to see Tony as he tended Peacock, Barbara's bay gelding, and her mares, Cleopatra and Sunny Dawn.

Tall, slim and only seventeen, Tony lived with his parents in Torwell, the nearest village. Brown haired and blue eyed, he had the pick of the local lassies.

Often they followed Dave Hart, as he went about his work on the farm, their short strides stretching to match his giant steps.

Dave was farm manager. He was big, black haired and brawny, with merry, brown eyes and a double chin. His dogs, Spot and Bess, followed him everywhere.

The children loved him.

'He's my bestest friend next to John,' said Cathy to her mum and dad.

'Best friend, Cathy, not bestest,' reproved her mother.

'Yes, he's my best friend.' Cathy beamed a smile to her mother. But John is my bestest, bestest friend in the whole world.'

Bert laughed loudly. Alice frowned; the art of grammar forgotten, as her thoughts veered to the future. She hoped they would never be anything stronger than bestest, bestest friends.

Next day was extremely cold. Fred Marshall was ploughing. He sat huddled into his winter coat, the collar raised to stave off the wind. On his head, was a grey Balaclava helmet, and on his hands, he wore home knitted mitts. Even wrapped as he was, the chill seeped through the many layers he wore to combat its bite.

Back and forth, the tractor chugged. Dark soil crumbled into straight furrows as the ploughshare sliced its way along the field. Gulls whirled with greedy eyes. Fred's neck craned sideways in order to see. One needed eyes both back and front, for this job.

John, Cathy and Dave, eyed the spectacle with rapt, eager faces.

'I mind fine when the horses did the ploughing,' said Dave. 'It was a bonny sight. The most gentle of creatures they were, for all they were that big.'

'Where are now?' John gazed up at Dave's florid face.

'Sold.'

'Did mum sell them?'

'Aye, that was a sad day that. Like losing best mates.' Dave lowered his eyes, a melancholy expression clouding his handsome features. 'That's progress for you, laddie. It's fair sabotaging the country.' His hand swept the air. 'All this will be yours one day. Take good care of it, son.' Abruptly, he turned. 'Come on, Maggie had scones in the oven when I left the house.'

'I'll race you,' cried John to Cathy. 'First one there gets one of Maggie's scones.' They looked at each other and laughed. They knew they'd get one anyway.

Maggie's slim figure stood in the doorway. She'd heard their voices and was waiting to greet them. 'Mighty me, you're in an awful hurry this morning, bairns.' She winked as, wide eyed and breathless, they slithered to a stop at her newly scrubbed step. 'Has he been bribing you with my scones?'

Two heads nodded, mouths smiling.

Cups of milk and plates of scones filled with Maggie's home-made raspberry jam, were placed before them. Amid dogs, cats and screens of washing, they sat on the rug before a blazing fire and partook of this yummy feast.

An extreme antithesis to Dave, Maggie was petite, mousy haired and quiet, and Dave adored her.

Barbara was lucky to have him as manager. His insight regarding stock and the land, made him an invaluable asset. His animal magnetism had not escaped her either, but any fluttering of mascara covered lashes, met with complete indifference.

Bert was different. He was like putty in her hands. Dan used her, as she used him. Dave rose above them. Strong and steadfast, he was loyal to that mousy wife of his.

Barbara was envious.

As she rouged her cheeks and added a dash of lipstick to her pouting lips, Barbara gave a gloating smile. The mirror above the mantelpiece, flung back her image. A pleasing image, she knew. This fact she cultivated; luring paramours like the pollen covered flowers that attract the bumblebees and bees.

She had an eye for men, Barbara. Even the minister's visage tweaked its way into her thoughts. He was nice looking for a minister. Not that ministers were woven from a different cloth, they weren't.

'Oh well,' she murmured. 'At least he's free.' Her lively, somewhat dubious lifestyle, would put the kibosh on any such association, though, she thought. Not that she had inclinations in that direction, she hadn't.

You never know – she picked up her brush and drew it slowly through her hair. He might be a tiger in bed. Then again, he might say, 'get you behind me, Satan,' just when he was about to capitulate; the bible taking over his baser instincts. What a waste of a fine man.

Relationships should be more than just sex though, she reflected; surprising even herself with this disclosure. He was a nice man though, Gordon McKenzie. How had he managed to escape the clutches of another woman all those years? He had plenty admirers. Yet he remained aloof. His wife must have hurt him terribly when she ran off many years ago.

Barbara's eyes glittered. She pulled her jumper over her hips and patted her hair, then with a final pout, blew all thoughts of him away. She had other fish to fry.

Her salvation was Dan, but even his visits lately were sporadic. She challenged him the next time he came.

'What's wrong, Dan? Have you tired of me?' Her voice caught the teeth of her concern, and Dan looked at her, then quickly away.

'No, it's not that, you know it isn't. We just have to cool it for a while.'

His hands caressed her breasts, then slid down her body. She moaned and pulled him close. Their love-making was silent, except for the creaking of springs and a clock ticking. Ticking away their precious time together. All too soon, it was over. Dan feasted his eyes on her as if for the last time. 'God, you're lovely, Barbara. How am I going to do without you?'

'Then why —?'

'Shush!' A strong finger held back her anxious words. 'It's Beth. She's at school now. Children pick things up. What if she tells Emma?' His arms tightened round her pliant body. 'Look, I'll come when I can, Barbara. I can't promise, though.'

Hell, Dan, she's only five years old. She would never understand.'

'Of course she would – and so would John.' Dan's peaty eyes bored into her's like x-rays. 'I'll find a way. Say once a month. That's the best I can do.' Releasing her, he stood up. His clothes were scattered on the floor. He bent to pick them up.

Barbara watched from sex sated eyes as he plunged first one leg, then the other, into brown corduroy trousers, struggled into his shirt, stuck stockinged feet into stout working boots, then disappeared down the stairs. She heard his steps fade, then peter out altogether.

Funny, she thought. Their meetings had been so much easier since John started school. How ironic that Dan had suddenly developed a conscience. Still – she had Bert. Life was not all doom and gloom.

Time sped at an ever increasing pace. Years touched other years, with fingers of friendship, or knuckles of strife. Cathy was on her way to meet the gang.

'I'm away to play, mum.' She stepped through the door and half turned.

'Well, don't be too long.' Sternly, her mother spoke. Sad grey eyes, looked into big blue ones. Blue as the sky, Cathy's were, with lashes of a slightly darker hue than her fair hair. Cathy didn't know why her mother was always so solemn. Although sometimes she did seem happier. When uncle Tom was here. He wasn't really her uncle, but he came so often, and was so nice, she adopted him as such. Her pretend uncle. Anyway, she didn't appear to have any real uncles or aunts. Not even a granny or grandpa. If they existed, they were never mentioned.

Tom was here today. On an errand. He was just about to go. The prying neighbours were out in force; propping up the edges of the walls framing their doors. A strange lot they were, dissecting every look and action; ears straining for snippets of conversation; minds printing their own scripts.

'Cheerio, uncle Tom; see you next time.' Cathy tilted her face as he leaned his broad bulk to her level and brushed her cheek with warm lips. Half way along the path, she turned to wave. Her mother stood, still as a tree. An air of breeding emanated from her. Living in a row of cottages, the workers and their wives knew everything about everybody, but not about Cathy's mum. To them, she was enigma.

'She's hidin' something, that one. Sure as eggs is eggs,' said Grace Stuart.

Heads nodded. Folded arms leaned on apron covered bosoms. Cigarette smoke rose in hazy puffs. The day was raw, but they didn't feel the harshness of it. The heat of a good gossip kept them going.

Their aversion to Cathy's mother was born from a latent jealousy.

'Just look at him. Standing there like the bloody Laird o' Cockpen.' Mary Marshall's chocolate gaze was full of venom. One hand flicked fag ash to the ground. The other was stuck in the baggy pocket of an unbuttoned cardigan.

All eyes swivelled towards Tom as he stood in silent contemplation at Alice's door.

Uttering a quiet, 'Bye,' to Alice, he strode away, his anxiety curving his body like a high wind. Inwardly, he seethed. How could he not fancy one of the lassies that frequented the dances and pubs? Bugger!' He aimed a foot at a stone, putting all his frustration into the kick.

Cathy scuttled off. Something was not quite right. It wasn't like uncle Tom to be angry. Thoughtfully, she skirted Barbara's garden, and came to a halt on the gravelled driveway.

'Hello, Cathy.' John scooted round the corner on his new bike. 'I'm going to see Carma, are you coming?' Cathy nodded.

'Jump on, then.' Laughing, he helped her onto the seat, straddled the bar, found the pedals, then with a 'wheeee,' they were away.

Carma, his pony, stood, head down, eyes closed. On hearing them, her ears pricked and her grey head rose. She whinnied.

Using his feet as brakes, John drew up beside the fence. From his pocket, he withdrew a fistful of sugar lumps. With brisk steps, Carma trotted to get her treat.

'Here, you give her some.' John handed Cathy a few. 'Always remember to keep your hand flat. You might get bitten, otherwise.'

'Oooh, it tickles.' Cathy giggled as Carma's soft nose tickled her outstretched hand.

Companionably, John and she grinned. Picking up his bike from where he'd flung it, he beckoned Cathy to follow him to the house. They still spent a lot of time together, but played with the other children from the cottages also. A varied bunch, their playmates. Boys manifestly outnumbering girls.

Harry, with red, spiky hair and blotches of freckles running across his nose and cheeks, was a veritable cheat. A mixture of personalities, good traits and bad, fighting for supremacy. Always the leader. To the river, the barn. Play this, play that. Harry was the decision maker.

Together, they played all the usual games. Rounders, hide-and-seek, tig, football and marbles. On rainy days, the barn was their refuge. Many hours, they spent clinking each others' precious marbles circled on the ground. A shiny mass of colour, that every strike, blossomed into kaleidoscopic patterns.

Harry was unpredictable. Even now, taking part in a game of marbles while sheltering from the lashings of a heavy shower, he was creating havoc.

'Hey, you shoved that,' he shouted. 'You're supposed to just flick it with your thumb.'

'I never.'

'You did.'

'Well, I'm not playin' any more.' Cohn plonked his marbles into a cloth bag, kicked the opposing ones with scuffed shoes, stuck out his tongue in a show of bravado, then fled.

'You little twerp,' shouted Harry as they all scrambled for their prize marbles now scattered over the ground. Red faces cast angry looks at the retreating figure.

'Are you away for a sook at your mother's paps, you big baby?' Harry taunted him.

'Shut up.' Halting in his tracks, Colin flung his words across the taut space. 'My mother's paps are better than your mother's. Hers are as flat as pancakes. My cat's got bigger ones.' In earnest now, he raced; not stopping until well within reach of his mother's kitchen.

'What's up?' His mother rested her hand on the edge of a basin in which she'd been stirring and looked at him.

'Nothin'.'

'It must be something. You've been bubblin.' She held on like a terrier with a rabbit, trying to get to the bottom of it. 'Has that Harry been fighting with you? If he has, I'll clout his lugs.'

'No, we were just arguing.' Colin peered at the creamy contents in the basin. 'What are you makin' mum?'

'Pancakes.'

Colin thought of what he'd said to Harry and a fit of the giggles overtook him. Tears forgotten, he rushed out to tell the others. At first Harry scowled. Then he saw the funny side of it and joined in their hilarity.

'Oh, well,' he stated. 'Dad likes them flat. He's always touching them when we're not lookin'. So there.'

Cathy smiled. Unusual they may be, her pals, but she liked them. Elsie and she quite often had arguments, which ended with Mary Marshall shouting abuse at Cathy's mum. Her mother was wise. She kept her own council and stayed within. This only poured petrol on Mary's wrath. If Jupiter shook the universe with a turn of his head, then Mary, with the force of her tongue, shook the tranquillity of those living in the row of cottages.

The men had different attitudes. In spite of Mary's continual antagonism to Alice, Bert and Fred still remained on friendly terms. The children too. Any disputes were left to hunger in the night. By morning, they were dead.

John, Cathy, Elsie and Beth, joined Raymond, Alf and Harry at the local high school, which they had been attending for a year. It was now the weekend and the countryside basked in the arms of a scorching sun. Dave's dogs lay at the door, panting. The corrugated roofs on coal bunkers, were red hot to touch. The kids mooched about. Listless.

'Come on,' Harry exclaimed. 'Let's go to the pool above the bridge at Denholm for a swim.'

'Wait till I get John.' Cathy stared imploringly at Harry.

'Oh, all right.' Harry screwed up his face. It was lined with the impatience he was feeling. 'But hurry up, the sun'll no' shine all day.'

'Thank you, Harry.'

'See you, then.' Suddenly Harry felt flustered. Being with lassies did all sorts of funny things to him nowadays.

Converging at the steading, they set off to walk the few miles to Denholm bridge. Laughing, they threw sticks over the side, dashing quickly to the other side to see whose appeared first under the arches.

'There's Minto Crags,' pointed Harry. 'In the olden days, nobody could get up there. It was the stronghold of a notorious Border reiver.'

Shading their eyes with flattened hands, they all gazed at the rugged rocks impregnated with trees and bushes that necklaced the high face known as Barnhill's Bed.

'That's Fatlips Castle you can see half hidden amongst the trees We'll have to walk there some day.'

'You're a walking encyclopaedia, Harry,' said Colin. 'You should be a teacher.'

'What, and try to teach dunces like you?' Harry swerved as Colin swiped at him with his towel.

They started to run; down through the wee gate and along the path. Breathless, they reached the current carved bank of darkish soil that sank its feet into the sighing water. Grass, burned golden brown with the sun, was crisp and jaggy on their bare feet. Discarding their clothes, except for their pants, one by one, they slipped into the cool depths of the river.

John stood on the bank.

'Come on, sissy,' teased Harry. 'Get your shoes off.'

'Feared you stand on a thistle, are you? Or a cow pat?' Harry laughed. 'Imagine him wi' green feet, lads.'

Taunted enough, John jumped in; shoes still on.

Cathy and Elsie sat on the bank, watching.

'Harry says he's done it with Jean Dixon,' said Elsie to Cathy. I heard him tellin' Raymond last night. I bet he's only sayin' it to make himself look big.'

'Some boys like to boast.' Thoughtfully, Cathy looked at Elsie. 'Probably he only kissed her.'

'Aye, probably.'

All was quiet. The boys lay on their backs, languid strokes keeping them afloat. Then, with pants clinging, bodies goose-pimpled and dripping, they plodded heavy legged to the bank.

'See me, I'm a bullfighter.' Harry gave some dancing steps and pretended to cast his towel away, like goading a bull with a cloak.

Cathy blushed and turned her head the other way. She knew he wouldn't do it – but one never could tell with Harry – and she'd never seen that part of a boy's anatomy before. It made her curious.

She nudged Elsie's arm.

'Are they all the same size? You know – boys' thingies?'

'I'm no' sure. Jean's cousin is nineteen. She's been with loads o' laddies, we could ask her.' Elsie laughed. 'She'll think we're as green as grass, but I think I'd rather be green than have the lads say I'm easy. Would you not?'

'Yes.' Cathy peered at Elsie. 'Do you think she's had sex?'

'Aye,' Elsie nodded. 'Raymond says she's like a cow wantin' the bull.'

They giggled. It was the first time they had broached this subject. A new awareness enveloped them, their innocent minds, riding the waves of the unknown.

Monday dawned. Another beautiful day, that stretched fields and woods to a cloudless sky. As usual, Harry larked about on the way to the school bus. Head at an angle, imaginary mike in his hand, he aped Alan Whicker, one of the reporters on the television programme, 'That Was The Week That Was.' His good natured banter was infectious and had them all laughing.

First period for Cathy's class, was English. Their teacher, tall, thin, youngish and craggy faced, had a lopsided grin and a square jaw. Strict, but fair, he was well liked by most of the pupils.

Today, they were getting poetry. The lady of Shalott, one of Tennyson's poems. Cathy was entranced. Fancy seeing life through the eyes of a mirror. Poor lady, doomed if she looked down to Camelot.

Don't look down, don't look down: her mind shrieked as the teacher continued. But the lady WAS doomed. She DID look down.

As the teacher's gravelly voice drew the poem to its conclusion, his gaze flicked over the raised heads and came to rest on Cathy.

'Well, Cathy, you seemed to be interested. Why do you think she left the loom and looked down to Camelot?'

'Because the knight was handsome, sir. I think she fell in love with him.'

Behind her, some of the boys tittered. Cathy flushed a deep red. At break time, they teased her mercilessly.

'I think she fell in love with him, sir,' they parodied. Over and over again, until their cruel delight nearly had her in tears.

'What do you know about love, little miss fancy pants?' said Beth Sykes. 'Do you love John? Hey, everybody, Cathy loves John.'

Scornfully, Beth stared at Cathy. 'You'll never get him. He will want me before he wants you. My father has a business. Your dad is only a gardener.'

A real snob Beth was turning, thought Cathy. All the same, it disturbed her, making her see John in a new light. With his dark hair, fair skin and eyes the colour of chestnuts, he was a handsome lad. Taken aback at this thought, Cathy withdrew from him. Beth was right. Why would he choose her? Her parents were not rich. Beth's dad had lots of men working for him. He must be loaded. Yet – in spite of not having great riches money-wise, Cathy knew that she was wealthy in other ways. She was much loved. In her dad's outgoing way – and in her mother's more restrained affection. Bottled there inside her, she let it escape in tiny flashes of warmth. Also, she had John's friendship. Yes – her life was threaded with riches.

'So – Beth Sykes, you can take a run and jump,' muttered Cathy. 'Into the deepest part of the river, I hope.'

October scolded the countryside with onslaughts of rain, wind, then frost. Leaves changed to russet and gold. Frosts nipped them, and trees bared their teeth and let them fall.

A new moon brought about a change. Clouds clung together. Black. The horizon had swallowed a watery sun and darkness was beginning to fold over a mottled sky.

Cathy shivered. It was Saturday. John had been in town shopping. Now, they idled about wondering what to do.

'You're cold. Let's go to the stables to see Tony.' John's gaze flipped sideways. 'You're awful quiet.' His worried eyes studied her. 'You've been avoiding me lately, too. Are you well enough?'

'Yes.' Cathy blushed. She felt awkward. Since Beth's outburst at school, things had never been the same. She felt a great antipathy towards her now.

Tony's whistling stopped when he saw them. The smell of leather hung in the air. He was rubbing oil onto the reins and girths to make them soft and supple. His body straightened when they entered; his smile as cheery as the tune his lips had just relinquished.

'What's going on with you two, then?' His gaze raked over them like he was raking straw across the loose-box floor.

'Oh, we've just come to see you, Tony.'

John and Cathy looked at him and grinned. With legs dangling, they sat on the long work table soaking up the heat from the coke stove.

'Are you going to the dance next week?' John crossed his legs and looked at his friend.

'Aye, I'll be there.'

'Have you a girlfriend?'

'No, I just set a lassie home now and again. I want to enjoy life a bit before I settle down.'

'Are your parents going, Cathy? Or you?' John's eyes held a probing interest.

Cathy was confused. Her mother wasn't one for going to village activities. An extremely private person was her mum. Always pleasant. Always courteous. Yet a void, wide as an ocean, kept others at a distance.

Visions of Beth waltzing round the hall in John's arms, swamped her. She felt like crying.

'You can come with us. There's to be stovies at half-time. Bill Jenks and Dan Sykes are providing the music. Say you'll come, Cathy. Please.'

A bird took flight in Cathy's heart, winging it upwards; lifted with words of hope. She didn't know what kind of hope, but something clawed away there trying to get out. It puzzled her.

'That would be nice,' she said; mustering a dignity akin to her mother's. Her eyes glued to her feet, she missed the look of pride marching across John's face.

Stretching his arms, puffing out his chest and breathing deeply, Tony exhaled in a long whooo – then grabbed his jacket. 'Well, I'm finished for the day. See you the morn.' The squeaking of his bike, accompanied by the renewed whistling of an old Jim Reeves song, faded as he pedalled along the road.

'I'll have to go too. Mum's making shepherds pie. It's our favourite.' A farewell flick of her hand, and Cathy was gone.

Next day dawned windy, but dry. John, Cathy and the others, went to seek conkers. Tall and stately, the tree stood. Golden leaves covered the ground under it. Some still clung tenaciously, as if not wanting to let go of life. Fallen conkers mingled with grass and leaves. Some were round and prickly. Unbroken. Others were split. Nestling in their cases, lay shiny, brown conkers.

'Wow!' shouted Harry. 'Here's a whopper. Look!'

'It's not always the big ones that are best,' said Colin a bit peeved at not having seen it first.

'Is that you on about willies again, Colin? I bet it takes you half an hour to find yours, it's that wee.'

'Shut up, you big pillock. We're here for fun, not to argue with you.'

'Yes, behave, Harry.' John gave him a withering look.

It worked. Peace reigned. Quiet except for the rustling of leaves beneath their feet. Soon, pockets bulged. They had enough.

'If we go to the forge, Eddie might give us some horse-shoe nails,' cried Cathy. 'They're great for making holes in chestnuts.'

'Aye, come on.' A unanimous shout in favour arose.

Eddie was busy shoeing a horse when excitedly they poured into the blacksmith's work place. With interest, they watched as he placed a red-hot shoe onto the horse's hoof. It sizzled and smoked. He coughed and blew at the smoke so that he could see. A smell of singeing pervaded the air. Only when he'd hammered the shoe into shape and onto the horse's hoof, did he look up. Letting go of its leg, he creaked to a standing position. Sweat dripped from his nose and down his cheeks and clung to eyebrows and eyelashes.

'We wondered if we could get a loan of some nails please, Mr Taylor,' said Cathy.

'Sure, lassie. Take as many as you like. I used to do the same thing when I was a lad.' He coughed again and pounded his chest with a clenched hand. 'This'll be the death o' me one o' these days, but I'll not give it up.'

'Are the horses not awful heavy when you lift their legs, Eddie?' asked Alf.

'No – but sometimes I'll get one that's lazy a bit and leans on my back. Most o' them behave, though.'

'Thank you, Mr Taylor,' said Cathy. 'We're going now.'

'Aye, thanks, mister.' Harry spoke for the others, who were already boring holes in their chestnuts, faces intent, minds thinking theirs were best. The lad holding the horse had not uttered a word. He was only a nipper, but in no time, had boarded the broad back, and the horse, proud of its new shoes, clip-clopped happily homewards.

Eyes held in a time zone, Eddie watched the children, enjoying the vigour with which they did everything. He was one of them. A youngster again. Pointing to the sign above the door, he spoke.

'I've no son to carry on the business, so if any of you lot want a job when you leave school, then come to me. I'll learn you the trade.' He rubbed under his nose with his hand. 'Mind you, with Clydesdale horses no longer in use, blacksmiths are reliant on hunters and ponies and a few bits of agriculture work. It's not so rosy being in this line of work now.'

The kids looked at the nails then at him. They hoped he and the forge would be here for many years yet.

At school next day, Colin's wee chestnut beat Harry's big one. Colin was jubilant. 'I told you wee ones were best,' he cried. 'Here's to the champ.' Proudly, he held aloft the winning conker.

The school bus dragged to a standstill at their road end. At the cottages, they parted and dashed indoors. Those whose parents had acquired a telly, to loll about on the couch watching their favourite programmes, For Cathy, a book, and the calming tone of the radio.

Before entering his house, Colin turned on the step with a stare of victory. 'I'm away to frame my cheggie,' he quipped. 'I'll see you, Harry.'

'That was just a fluke. Meet me out here later and I'll knock that wee one o' yours for a six.'

'Huh! in your dreams, Harry. Mine'll beat your one any day.'

'You come home with me, Cathy. We'll leave that pair to it.' John grinned. 'I'll show you my catapult.'

On quick feet, they pattered up the drive to his house.

'Hello, mum, I've brought Cathy home.' John's voice shocked the stillness. His eyes beamed warmly at Cathy. 'She's about here somewhere. Have a seat.' Strong hands pulled a blue leather covered stool towards her.

Fascinated, she stared at his hands. Nearly grown-up hands, they were. Help! What was she thinking about hands for? What was wrong with her nowadays?

From a crystal bowl, he passed her an apple, then seated himself on a similar stool beside her. Fishing in a drawer, he withdrew a catapult. 'Look, it's a beauty, isn't it?'

'Yes, it's well made.' Cathy let her eyes roam round the kitchen. It was massive. Her mother would die for a cooker like that. Theirs was paraffin. Smelly and fumey. The stink clung to clothes and blackened the ceiling. Her mother despaired of it. Sometimes she cooked on the fire. It was on all day anyway. It heated the water.

Barbara appeared dressed in red slacks, white roll neck jumper and red shoes. 'Hello, Cathy,' she mumbled. Her eyes assessed Cathy like radar. Something fluttered inside her as she viewed the girl's lovely face. Trying to separate John and Cathy had been abandoned years ago. Now, a new resolve bit into her. Like frost. The question of John's parentage reared its head again. It stuck like a gramophone needle in a groove.

An identical fluttering filled Cathy's heart. Her mother adopted the very same look Barbara had sometimes. Only this morning, she'd asked. 'Why do you always play with John? Do you not have friends at school? Lassies you could bring here?' Her tone of voice had suggested dark disapproval. A frisson of fear had assailed Cathy. What had her mother been hinting at?

'There's Sheila from the pub, but she goes around with Beth Sykes. I don't like her. Anyway, I like playing with John. We play with Elsie and the lads as well.' Feeling mutinous, Cathy had jutted out her chin, determined to defy her mother on this.

Tight lipped, her mother had turned from her, thumping the iron with extra force along Bert's checked shirt. 'Has he any pals, then?' she'd asked; emphasizing the HE in a scolding manner. The ironing had stopped. An intake of breath had frozen, awaiting Cathy's reply.

'Yes, he has mates at school. They go to the cinema now and again,' Cathy had felt bound to say.

An expression of relief had blazed across her mother's features and the ironing had continued, but smoother this time. Cathy had pondered on this for ages afterwards. Now, she recalled the incident as she returned Barbara's cold stare. Virulent, more like, but why? Why also, was her mother so against John?

'Come on, Cathy. Why the solemn face?' John's voice broke her thread of discomfort. He rose and guddled in a drawer on the cupboard. Stuffing some peas and a handful of pebbles into his pockets, he made for the door.

'Ammunition,' he said. 'I've been collecting them. Follow me, Cathy.'

Even his voice was different, thought Cathy. How had she not seen this happening? Until now? Harry, Raymond and Alf, almost a year older, already had men's voices. Like buds opening into leaves, boys' vocal chords seemed to go through dramatic changes. Their bodies too. Openly, they spoke about it at school. The girls heard snatches of it and giggled; not really understanding.

'It'll make you go blind,' said one lad.

'It will not. I read in a book that that's just a load of rubbish. My father's a doctor. I'll ask him,' said his mate.

'Well, I'm not blind yet.' Little Tom Reid stared with stubborn intensity at the others.

John listened, but did not participate in such personal conversations.

We are growing up, thought Cathy. I wonder if Elsie has noticed?

Elsie had noticed. At least her mother had. As soon as the slightest of swellings showed through her vest, her mother had taken her in hand.

'We'll have to get you a bra. It's not decent goin' about like that.' So one Saturday, they ventured to the co-op in town. Umpteen different styles and sizes, Elsie tried on. A cups. B cups. Black, white, pink. Finally deciding upon a white, cotton B cup, size 34. Jumper back on, she looked in the mirror from all angles. Heck! she was like a pouter pigeon. Red faced, she went home, feeling shy for the first time in her life.

Harry grinned, but kept quiet.

She was his sister.

Cathy was still flat chested. She didn't care. Boyish of build, slender of leg, with an ethereal beauty already visible, she was stunning – and didn't know it.

John noticed it. Hot flushes crept up his cheeks every time he saw her. All kinds of new feelings invaded him. Often he had wet dreams. He wondered if girls had them. Did Cathy ever dream about him in that way? He blushed beetroot, at the thought. Hell, this growing up lark was difficult, sometimes.

Chapter Three

The night of the dance was a hive of activity. Stovies, reaching the tops of two black, iron pots, simmered slowly. Intermittently, someone stirred them to prevent them sticking. The appetising aroma wafted through the hall in savoury whiffs of onions and potatoes. Bowls of trifle stood on a table by the kitchen door where it was cool.

Harry sprinkled a chalky substance on the floor to make it slippy. The children slid across the whitened surface, making it even more slippery.

Pete, the butcher, sat taking the money at the door. Coins clinked onto a plate on a green topped table beside him.

It began to snow. Big, fat flakes, that glistened in the glow of an overhead light. People rushed in, brushing them from hair and shoulders. Soon, the hall was a hubbub of voices. Men stood in groups at the bottom, or sat opposite the ladies. They observed them with eager eyes, seeking one they fancied or would like to dance with.

Rap, rap, rap. Gordon, who was officiating, thudded the platform with a spoon. 'Will you take your partners for a waltz. Everybody up, please.'

Bill Jenks's fingers danced over the pearly keys of his accordion. A few chords. A warm up. Dan Sykes scratched his bow along the strings of his fiddle. Minds locked together, he and Bill let the notes of 'I Belong To Glasgow' fill the hall.

A rush of feet took the men and lads to the female of their choice. Bert's gaze lingered on Barbara. He was undecided. Alice was standing beside him and he should really get her up. For a while he waited.

'May I have this dance, Alice?' It was Tom's voice from behind him.

Good, thought Bert. That let him off the hook.

Barbara saw him coming and put on her best smile. A taffeta dress slunk sinuously down her body. Red hair framed her face; fiery, and dramatic against the green.

A sidelong glance to Dan on the stage, caught him viewing her as well. He looked tense. With alacrity, she jumped up, taking Bert's hand even before he'd asked her to dance. The fiddling stopped a moment, then continued.

Dan was troubled.

Serves him right, thought Barbara. She didn't take kindly to his long absences.

Bert pulled her close at every turn, thinking no one would see, but they did. Especially the women.

'See them,' said Mary Marshall. 'You couldn't get a razor blade between them. He presses her against his thighs every time they whirl. They'd just as well be havin' sex.'

'Aye, all them hormones flyin' around. I hope my man catches some o' them.' Agnes Gibson gazed with envious eyes. Her husband was in the employment of major Townsend at Manor farm.

'Is he hard worked there?' asked Mary.

'Aye, he is. It's a hard life being a shepherd. There's the lambing, the clipping, the dipping, and lots o' other jobs forbye. They work all the hours God sends.'

Her eyes swung upwards, as if seeking divine aid. He's fair knackered the now – and that's before the lambing. Just turns on his back and snores like a pig. See that Bert? The job he does is easy in comparison. No wonder he's full o' energy.'

Does he not get any help?'

'Help – that major wouldn't give you a whiff o' his breath; even if you needed the kiss o' life.' Her gaze shifted back to Barbara and Bert. 'They must be on pep pills or something. It isn't normal the way they behave, is it?'

Agnes peered at Mary from under thick, black bushy eyebrows that were badly in need of a pluck. 'Maybe their ancestors were rabbits,' she added, her bosoms nearly laughing themselves out of a low cut neckline.

The very opposite, were Tom and Alice, who danced silent and dreamlike, not daring to let their bodies touch. Tom willed the music never to stop, but it did. With his hand on her elbow, he guided her to a seat. He wondered if the trembling inside him could be transmitted through his fingers. Mind in a turmoil, he thanked her for the dance and walked away.

Next dance was a quickstep. Maggie Hart was sitting alone. Tom's swift steps took him to stand in front of her. 'Would you care to dance, Maggie? I see Dave's away to the pub. I'm no great shakes at dancing, but we'll give it a try.'

Does Dave always go for a drink during a dance?' he asked as they skimmed round the hall.

'Sometimes. He'll be back for the last dance, though. He always does.' She smiled. It transformed her face, and Tom could see how Dave worshipped her. Their mutual trust in each other was evident. How he wished to be enveloped by a love like that.

'Dancing brings a magic to my feet, Tom. It's the music. Dave says I dance like a linty. I'm sure he means sings, because a linty sings. It's a bird. That can't be right either, 'cos I sing like a crow with tonsillitis.'

Tom gave a hearty laugh. 'You're a tonic, Maggie. Dave's a lucky man.'

'What about you though, laddie? Have you not found a lady friend yet?'

'No, I'm a born bachelor, Maggie. Set in my ways. No woman will take me on.'

'Wheesht, man. Look at that lassie Townsend. She's fair salivating with staring at you.'

'Let her salivate for somebody else, then.' Tom chased her made-up face from his mind. In its place, he fixed Alice's noble one. Always Alice, he thought – and she could never be his. He looked round. His mother floated by in Gordon McKenzie's arms. Others watched with envious eyes.

'How does she always get a dance?' said one.

'Och, Jane, he dances with everybody.' Jenny Taylor, the blacksmith's wife. was quick to defend him.

'She's always first, though. Mind, she is smart. There's money there too. Maybe that helps oil the wheels a bit.'

'Oh, money isn't everything. Not when it comes to happiness.'

'She can be uppity sometimes.' Mary Marshall had to have her say.

Silent now, they gazed, their imaginations interpreting every action to fit in with their lurid thoughts.

'They make a good couple just the same,' said Netty Shaw, the butcher's wife.

'Yes, but she'll not get him.' Evelyn Hood, who ran the Post Office, spoke like a clairvoyant.

'What makes you say that?' Nettie was curious.

'I just know. What more can I say?' Evelyn liked to keep them guessing.

They fumed. Their eyes again seeking between the milling dancers for the pair in question.

An Eightsome Reel was in progress. John had Cathy as a partner. Whirling, laughing and whooping, they joined in the fray; red faced with the exertion of such a rumbustious dance.

A tight feeling restricted Alice's breathing as she observed them. Her thoughts gave her no peace. The incident sparking this unease, had stamped itself on her mind forever. She relived it now, in her head.

She was taking Bert his flask. He'd forgotten it. Making her way into the garden, she gazed along the numerous paths and neatly weeded beds, seeking him. Daffodils splashed their golden beauty in rows and clumps. Crocuses, deep purple and yellow, peeped from the borders, piercing the soil in uneven groups between the sadly wilting snowdrops.

Nowhere could she find him. Hesitantly, on quiet flat shoes, she stepped into the empty conservatory, along a passage, then to the sitting room. The door was ajar.

She peered in. The sight she beheld rushed her hand to her mouth, stifling a gasp. On the fluffy white rug by the fire, lay Bert and Barbara, lost in their own licentious world. Rhapsodic words of love spilled from Bert's lips. Words never uttered to her. Ever.

Dinner that night was made in a raging mist. Ironically, it was his favourite, Shepherd's pie.

Back home, Bert stopped in the porch. He was late.

In the hall, he relieved himself of his boots. The linoleum was cold. On stockinged feet, he padded to the sink in the kitchen. Habitually, he dried his hands on the towel behind the door. If the air held a strain like a clamp, he was unaware of it.

Alice retired early to bed. She was upset – and sleep evaded her. Wide awake still when he came into the bedroom, she visualised with closed lids, the usual ritual. Shirt, trousers, vest, socks – all flung haphazardly onto a chair. Socks – something in her mind clicked the picture on. Socks, wrinkled to the ankles. Bert's buttocks. Barbara's legs wound round them.

Alice squeezed her eyes tightly together, trying to blot the scene out, but it won its way through.

Now undressed, Bert made for the bathroom. Very fastidious with his ablutions, he lathered himself all over. Barbara's scent still lingered. He hated washing it off, but did so. A vigorous towelling heated his blood. He wanted her again.

Alice would have to assuage his desire instead. He slipped under the sheets.

'Get away,' Alice mumbled, as he laid a tentative hand on her thigh.

Her refusal stunned him and inflamed in him a greater urgency. God, he'd have her, he thought – by force if necessary.

On her back Alice lay, hoping he would give up, but he didn't. He was like a man possessed. Heaving himself on top of her, he prized her legs apart.

'No, no,' she gasped, her hands pummelling his chest. She was a wild cat, but he was strong and held at bay her attack and was more amorous than he'd ever been. In his mind – she was Barbara.

For a long time afterwards, Alice lay staring through the gloom of the curtained window. His seed was inside her. Without any doubt, she'd be pregnant.

That was how it happened all those years ago. She gazed now at the fruit of that plundering. Her beautiful Cathy. Fresh as new mown hay; oblivious of the friction that shrouded every day like a cloud.

Focussing on John now, the sight of Bert's infidelity fluttered in her head. Tormenting. Always tormenting. Like flies plaguing sheep. She hoped against hope, that she was wrong; for Cathy and John's sake. Like the sword of Damocles, that little word 'if' hung over them.

But how would she ever know?

Alice sighed. She couldn't risk letting their relationship blossom.

She tried not to think of Tom. Hazel-eyed, kind hearted Tom. Always there for her – for them all. She knew he liked her. The feeling was reciprocated – in her heart. His ever tender looks, melted the ice covering that pounding part of her.

The workers and their wives talked. Well let them. That avenue was blocked. A snowplough big enough to clear that pathway had not been invented.

On the platform, Bill Jenks unhooked the straps of his accordion, squeezed the bellows together with a wheeze, and laid it down. Reverently, Dan Sykes put his fiddle in its case and stood up. It was half-time.

'I could sink a pint, Bill.' Dan's eyes scanned Bill's kindly face. 'Let's go to the pub. We need a breather, anyway.'

'Aye, I was thinking the same thing. My throat's as dry as ashes.'

With creaking knees, they stepped from the platform. A raised hand to Jean, signalled their departure. 'We'll be back in a while. Keep some stovies for us, Jean,' roared Dan.

Steaming stovies were already being distributed. A queue snaked from half way down the hall to the door of the kitchen. Returning to their seats, they tucked in with gusto to the heaped platefuls given to them by the helpers. Eating halted the chatter. Filled bellies were more important.

Snow blanketed the street and pavements when Bill and Dan emerged from the warmth of the hall. Flicking up the collars of their jackets, they made for the White Swan, which was nearest. Smoke met them and stuck to them. Heat from the fire enveloped them. Flames hit their splayed hands as they bent before it. Shadows flickered over damp faces.

Pleasantly warmed, they made for the bar. Froth topped pints, gurgled down parched throats. 'I'll have another pint please, Daisy.' Dan held out the money. His eyes came to rest on Dave Hart leaning on the bar beside him.

'Hello, Dave. Are you not going to the dance?' Dan eyed the robust fellow with interest.

'Aye. I'll be there later. In time to give my wife the last waltz.' Dave returned his gaze. He knew the rumours regarding Dan's affair with Barbara. His wife seemed to be the only one left in the dark. Bloody shame.

'I suppose I should do the same.' Dan twisted round towards Bill. 'You'll have to play on your own for the last dance, Bill.'

Really, Dan wanted to give Barbara that dance, but he daren't. His mind tossed in the waves of a turbulent sea. Jealousy burned inside him as he thought again of Bert and her dancing. Close as a kiss. Christ! he missed that woman. He'd a good mind to pay her a visit tomorrow. This once a month stipulation was no bloody good. It was killing him. Bert didn't work on Saturdays. John would most likely be out. He'd chance it.

The plan devised, Dan felt exhilarated. All those yacking busybodies were not going to deprive him any longer. Suddenly, all bonhomie, he slapped Bill on the back. Have another drink, Bill. Daisy, give Bill here a dram.'

'A dram. You're surely feeling generous tonight, Dan. You on a promise, or something?' Bill winked at Daisy, whose shining eyes met his over the half empty glass on the bar. She was nice, he thought. Polite too. He hadn't seen her before. She must be new here.

A cold gust hit the heated room. With it, came Tom. Solemn faced, he made for the bar. 'A pint please,' he shouted above the babble of voices.

'Hello, what brings you into this neck of the woods, Tom?' Dan eyed him speculatively. Why had he left the dance? he wondered. Single. No ties. Hell, he'd give a lot to be in such a position.

'Escaping,' replied Tom. 'Like you, probably.'

'Ha, ha. Very funny. You are wrong, though. Bill and I are on our way back' Downing his drink in a gulp, Dan shot Tom a withering look and clanked his glass on the bar.

'Cheerio, Daisy,' his voice boomed. 'I'll see you the next time.'

Bald, full lipped, black eyed Bill, made his exit too. Feeling full of himself, he flung Daisy a special look. A look that told her he'd be back. Oh, well, he mused, he could always try.

Daisy washed his look away with a sweep of her long lashes. From under the black shade of them, she studied Tom. Unhappy, he was – and brooding, that was obvious. Handsome. Charismatic too, if he cared to unleash it. Daisy's brain rattled on, feeding on the information her heart was sending to it.

'Another pint for Joe, please.' He pointed to a small chap who'd come to stand beside him. Low and friendly, his voice carried its message through the din.

Self-consciously, Daisy averted her gaze. She hoped he hadn't noticed her close examination of him. Blushing, she lifted a glass and slowly pulled his pint.

'There you are.' She handed it over the counter. 'Tom, did I hear them call you?'

'Yes, Tom Garrick. My folks have The Spinney farm.' He held out his hand. 'How do you do?' His smile was warm and friendly.

'How do you do too, Tom.' It was like acting out a scene in a play. Her hand burned in his. A little flutter tickled somewhere in her tummy.

Have you another name then, Daisy?'

'Davies.'

'You don't sound local. Where are you from?'

'Cheshire. My folk have a tea room in Chester.' Quizzically, he scrutinized her. He didn't often come to this establishment. The Red Lion was his usual haunt.

Something told him this would change.

People were clamouring to be served. Friday nights were busy. Tom decided to leave.

'Bye, Daisy.' His eyes sought hers between the medley of heads.

'Bye, Tom. See you again, I hope.' Oh, how she hoped.

Snow swirled in savage gusts as Tom opened the door and escaped into the night. Daisy watched him go with a light heart.

'Hurry up, Daisy. You seem miles away the night. That was two lagers and a rum and coke.' Voice after voice, ordering, demanding. Just when she wanted peace. Time to savour her new feelings.

'Yes, Daisy, you do appear to be up in a cloud tonight.' Doreen her boss, blonde and petite, eyed her with curious eyes. 'Anything wrong?'

'No — Yes — I mean no. Oh, Doreen, do you believe in love after only one conversation?'

'Love! Huh! I loved once. Never again. The toerag ran off with the bar boy. Flipping heck! Talk about being hoodwinked. No, Daisy, you can believe in your knight in shining armour. The gentle eyes, the passionate lips, the loving arms and God knows what other drivel, but don't expect me to.

'Mind you, I could make an exception if some Adonis caught my eye.' Doreen rubbed a damp cloth along the shiny bar. 'Yes, you go for it, my lass. You point him out next time he's in. I'll give him the once-over. See if he's up to scratch.'

Outside the pub, Tom, unaware of the interest in him, hunched his shoulders and bent to meet the wind. Music wafted in brief bursts into the night as he walked towards the hall. The stirring sounds of the 'Primrose Polka,' met him as he entered. White, blue, striped and cream shirts blended with dresses of every hue, as round and round, the couples danced. In this maze, his eyes found Alice; dancing with Harry.

Something hit him like a hammer – right in the solar plexus. That lass in the pub. That's who she reminded him of – Alice. Quiet, mannerly and dignified; just like she was.

'I haven't betrayed you, Alice,' he said to himself. 'You've got to believe me.'

As if by telepathy, her answering gaze held on to his. 'You have,' it seemed to say. Her steps faltered. Her legs felt heavy as lead. The dance ended and everyone made a dash for their seats. She waved to him across the hall. Slowly, he went over.

'What's wrong, Tom? You looked as if you'd seen a ghost when you came in.'

'I did, but it was quickly doused.' He frowned. 'The snow plays tricks with us sometimes.'

With raised voice, the minister announced the last dance. He rallied forth amongst the youths, urging them to get up. 'Harry, you get Beth up. John you get Cathy. Raymond, don't run away;

ask Elsie.' Soon, he had most of them paired off. Even Colin managed to find a partner. Alf, pipped on the post for Elsie, stood at the door.

'The Northern Lights Of Old Aberdeen,' swayed the dancers round the slippery floor. Some danced cheek to cheek. Some smooched round the hall, clinging like limpets.

'Would you like to dance, Alice. Bert seems to have disappeared.' Tom's hand reached for hers.

'Yes, thank you, Tom.'

Tom's body stilled as he faced her. Grey-eyed, sweet natured Alice. His for the duration of the dance. The image of Daisy came unbidden. He felt guilty. Why?

Alice felt his slight withdrawal. A tiny, inner sixth sense telling her so. Whatever had happened out there tonight, had stunted something special between them.

Grabbing Gordon, some ladies from the guild shoved him to the front. 'Right everybody, quiet please. Let's have three cheers for the minister. Hip, hip, hooray. Hip, hip, hooray. Hip, hip, hooray. Now, it's your turn, minister. Speech, speech.'

'Umm. Right. Thank you all for coming. It's been a grand night.' He held up his hand. 'See you on Sunday in church.'

'Boo — boo —' Amid lots of hilarity, some boozy lads sought to intervene.

'Ssssh – let him speak. Carry on minister.'

'Thank you, Nettie. All right, all right. If you're not too hungover. You've got a day to recover.' Gordon's eyes raked across the hall. 'See you on Sunday.'

'Fat chance.' Drink ignited lips had the last word.

A mad rush had them hunting for their coats, gloves and scarves, then everybody made a beeline for the door. An exodus of people, pouring like a river into the night. The hall door banged shut, leaving an echo of memories.

Tom's thoughts did cartwheels as he negotiated the twisty road. Windscreen wipers scratched back and forth. Visibility was bad. His arm itched to stretch out to Alice sitting demurely beside him. Time flew when he wanted it to drag. Already, they were nearing the cottages. Drawing to a stop, he sprang out. Crossing to the passenger side, he opened the door and helped her out.

'Here you are, Alice; home safely.' Angrily, he noted the dark windows. Bert must still be with that brazen faced Barbara. Good friend that he was, Tom felt he could belt the daylights out of him.

'How do you stand it, Alice?' he whispered.

'For Cathy's sake, Tom. She loves him.'

'Where is she, by the way?'

'Staying the night with Beth Sykes. They seem to have settled their differences. John is staying over too. At his mate's house. So Bert will have his dear Lady Muck to himself.' Alice paused and looked up at Tom's face. 'They're growing up, Tom. I fear for them sometimes.'

'But why, Alice?' Tom's face was serious. 'They are sensible kids. You have nothing to fear.'

'Oh, but I have, thought Alice. And now – even if he didn't know it, he was slipping away from her too. One doubt was bad enough. Two – unbearable.

'Bye, Alice.' His gaze plunged into hers in the darkness; his words almost a valediction. God, she was getting morbid. Her hands fumbled for the key, the handle, then the switch. 'Click.' She blinked, dazzled by the sudden brightness.

In the room, the fire was a dull glow in the grate. A few thrusts with the poker brought it to life. She straightened. Level with her eyes on the mantelpiece, was a framed photo of Bert. She picked it up.

'You're a cad,' she shouted. 'A dirty, rotten cad. If I'd left you years ago, I'd have been happy now. With Tom.'

Full of pent up fury, she flung it against the far wall. A feeling of satisfaction shot through her. Leaving it lying, she went to bed.

Chapter Four

Gordon McKenzie flicked through the paper. He was restless. Not even Jesus could have calmed the heaving waves inside his head. No peace be still, to quieten the sea. No female to stroke away the tension torturing his body. No nothing.

Eighteen years now, he'd been without a partner. His lovely, auburn-haired wife, with emerald eyes, enticing lips and slender body, had vamoosed.

He'd thought she'd liked living here in Torwell village. The rural tranquillity seemed to suit her. Who could not but appreciate country life. The wonder of each season unfolding. The ever-changing scenes, but festering deep inside her, was an intense hate of it, and he had never known.

A passing parishioner saw her go; saw the taxi arrive at the manse door. Bags of belongings and crammed suitcases packed into the boot; baby daughter in her arms; she'd slid into the hearse-like taxi, then she was gone.

The minister recalled that day. Relived it.

Back from a hospital visit, he stepped inside his home. It was cold. A strange uneasiness struck him. 'Maureen,' he called. 'I'm home.' Worried eyes roamed the room. Ah – the pram was there. She must be somewhere. Quick strides drew him to the pram. It was empty.

'Maureen, where are you?' The quivering inside him escalated. To the kitchen, the dining room, the study, he went, but there were no traces of her; nothing there to show she had been, or was coming back. Frenzied steps flung him up the stairs. Empty drawers hung open. The mirrored wardrobe front reflected his face. Taunting him. 'Open me, open me,' it seemed to say, but he was afraid of what he might find. Tentative fingers found the handle and pulled. Her clothes were gone. Only his dark suits hung – like scarecrows.

His gut twisted. Head in hands, he sat on the bed. His hurt mind accepted she was gone. What he could not accept, was that Caroline, his precious daughter, was lost to him also. How could Maureen be so cruel? Why did she not say she was unhappy?

Even after all those years, it still racked him. 'Hell,' he swore vehemently. He, who preached every Sunday to forgive and forget and turn the other cheek. What a lot of twaddle. Why should he forgive her? Never even left a note, the bitch.

Where was that God he prayed to?

His faith was draining away like water down the plug-hole; drip, drip, drip until his body felt weakened. The creed of life pulverized. Tears skimmed his cheeks in salty streams. Supposed to bring release. Some bloody release. He felt worse.

A frantic knocking on the door, filtered through the fog clouding his brain. 'Hold on, I'm coming.'

His voice was a whisper. He did not want disturbed from the doldrums attacking him The crushing weight. The thudding of stone that was his heart. How could stone thud? Surely, he was dead. He felt dead. Shackled like Lazarus lying stinking in his grave.

Would someone come and resurrect HIM?

Persistent rattling echoing through the house, unbound his bonds, activated his mind, and forced his feet towards its source. On the doorstep stood little Bobby Telfer. Blue eyes flooded with tears, he stared up at Gordon.

'You've got to come, minister. My dad's lyin' on the floor and he's no' able to get up.'

A much used sleeve swept under his nose, adding to the dried contents of numerous other wipes.

Immediately, the minister came to life, thoughts of himself forgotten. Following the spindly ankles with stockings fallen round them in wrinkles, the scuffed heels, the thin body, his heart smote him. Poor lad, having a father who drank most of his wages on a Friday night, drank on tick on a Saturday night, and a mother whose only hope of a better life had been drowned years ago, was enough to break the most stalwart of spirits. Yet, he came regularly to Sunday school. Had a cheery disposition, and was as bright as a button.

Four houses down, they entered a green door. Paint flaked off in places and bulged in others. The bottom had dents in parts where Arthur, Bobby's father, had vented his anger.

Elma, his mother, beckoned Gordon along a dreary passage to the sitting room. The fire was out. Cold clutched everything. He shivered.

'Elma. What happened?' he asked gently. 'He fell, minister. Tripped on the rug. Bumped his head on the fender.'

'Let's have a look.' Kneeling beside the still form, his fingers felt for a pulse. There was none. 'You'll have to phone a doctor, Elma.' Gordon turned to face her. 'I'm afraid he's dead.'

Elma's hands wound round each other. They couldn't keep still. Her eyes, usually a dull grey, now seemed to acquire some semblance of life. Was this then, the birth of hope for her? he wondered.

'I'll telephone for an ambulance. You get some clothes together and send Bobby to the manse. I'll contact the undertaker.' Several ideas scudded along his brain. A plan began to formulate; skittered away, then presented itself again. It would keep, though. Until after the funeral.

'Have you any relations?' he asked.

'Aye, a sister in Durham, but she has nine bairns and a man without work. She'll not be able to come.'

'What about Arthur? Has he any kin?'

'A brother in Australia, but they didn't get on. He'll no' come either. I haven't much money, maybe the stingy old blighter will send me some.'

Gordon withdrew from his pocket a ten pound note. 'Here, take this. Buy some food. Anything you might need. I'll keep Bobby at the manse until you get things sorted out.'

'Thank you, minister. That's awful kind of you.'

'I'll be back later to see about the service. What hymns you would like and so on.'

'It's sacrilege singing hymns for him, but I'll do it – for Bobby's sake. If I had my way, I'd let them drop him down the hole without a box and let the worms feast on him. Beggin' your pardon, minister, but he was a right cantankerous bugger.'

The minister gazed at Elma with the hint of a twinkle in his ginger eyes. Half an hour ago, they'd been bleak as a desert. Seeing the revival of spirit in Elma's grey ones, his own had sparked to life too. Maybe his faith was not so severely dented after all.

Word of Arthur's demise spread like wildfire, and soon Elma's house was swarming with well-wishing neighbours. People who only gave a grudging hello, a tight smile, a sidelong glance, or swanned by without any sign of recognition at all, now came to offer their assistance.

'You sit down, dearie. We'll soon have your house spick and span,' said Vera from next door.

A pail of water, a bit of carbolic soap, an old cloth, followed by the magic of Mansion polish and dusters torn from a threadbare sheet, and the linoleum took on colours unseen for many years.

The fire was now alight. Elma sat beside it, bemused and shamefaced. How had she let things slide into such a decline? How could she thank the many kind people who had worked like ants; beavering away for hours without fuss or grumble?

Steam rattled the lid of the kettle. A cup of tea was set in her hand.

'Phew!' said Vera. 'We'll all have a cup. Jenny, you run down to Baird's shop and get some biscuits. I just can't drink without eating.'

'OK.' Small, dimply cheeked Jenny, lifted herself from the chair. Her eyes shone, fleeing into crinkles when she smiled. Her hair, black, streaked with silver, fell into a smart bob. Her husband was the village blacksmith. His appearance was deceptive. Though his arms were thin, he managed to cope with the heavy work needed to be done in the forge.

Tucked behind the Red Lion pub, it was a regular meeting place for the retired men of the village. With lots of time on their hands, they congregated there for a natter. As they chatted, he busily worked. The fire glowed as he pumped life into it with huge bellows. Old implements filled dark corners. Cobwebs clung to rafters and walls. The smithy had a character of its own.

At the manse, Bobby sat by the fire, gazing round in awe. A meal of gigantic proportions swelled his tummy, inducing a tiredness in his underfed limbs.

He yawned.

On a neighbouring chair, Gordon tenderly watched, as gradually the brown lashes drooped over Bobby's eyes. In one of the rooms, he'd made up a bed, and a bottle stole the coolness from cotton sheets. Rising, he crossed to the boy's side and gently shook his bony shoulders.

'Don't go to sleep, Bobby. I'll take you upstairs. You can have a bath, then off to bed.'

'A bath. Oh, minister, I've never had a bath before.' A smile stretched the taut skin of his face, making him seem all mouth.

'Tomorrow, we'll go shopping. Get you fitted with some new clothes for your dad's funeral and school. Your old stuff is beyond redemption, we'll just bin it.'

'Mum gets all my stuff from jumble sales,' Bobby mumbled. 'I've never had new clothes.'

Never had a bath. Never any new clothes – and never a full belly. Gordon felt humbled; like the blind man in the bible, whom Jesus had cured.

'I was blind, now I can see,' the man said. Gordon knew exactly how he felt. Bobby's plight had pulled the scales from his eyes.

He felt reborn.

The day of the funeral was dismal. A drizzle draped woods and fields and buildings. Bobby looked at the hole into which the coffin had been lowered.

'It's awful deep, mum,' he said. 'I bet he'll no' get any drink down there.'

'No, son, he will not. At least if he does, he'll not bother us any more.'

'I'll never drink when I'm big, mum.' His blue eyes held her gaze, willing her to believe him.

Gently, she patted his arm. 'Let's get back to the house. A few o' our neighbours are comin' for a bite to eat.' She daren't say – and drink. The lad would understand one day.

Everyone had gone except the minister. Elma seated herself on the rickety chair. She was shattered.

'Elma,' began Gordon. 'I would like to talk to you about Bobby. Would you be willing to let him come to the manse to live on a permanent basis? He has very great potential. Perhaps I could help him. See he gets a better chance in life.'

Elma was flabbergasted. She stared at him as though at a raving lunatic.

'There'd be work for you in the house, should you want it.'

'Thank you kindly, minister, but I've been offered a job in the butcher's shop. Bobby will be pleased as a dog with two tails, though.'

Stepping forward, Gordon twined his arms round her slender body. 'Thank you, Elma. You won't regret it, I promise.'

So a new life opened itself to her – and Bobby. Within a week, a wonderful transformation had taken place. As instructed by his mother, Bobby had dropped his broad dialect and spoke properly to the minister now. Full of lively chatter, he arrived home from school every day. He couldn't believe his luck. His home. Here, in this house. Full of exuberance, he tossed his satchel onto the couch and dashed to the kitchen.

Dinner was ready. Alice Wilson took off her apron and made for the door. Saying 'cheerio,' she hurried away as Bobby appeared. She felt the draught of his lightning speed as he entered and laughed. Gordon had found a real livewire in this young scamp.

Ladling mince and tatties onto plates, Gordon placed them on the table. Being a minister, he quietened Bobby's gush of words to say grace, then picked up his knife and fork. Bobby did likewise. For a while, they sat in silence.

Bobby spoke first, breaking the stillness.

'Colin Stuart farted at assembly this morning,' he said artlessly. 'It was really loud. We all had a good laugh. The teachers' faces were all screwed up like they had constipation. Harry did it when he left for high school. Said he wanted to go out with a bang.'

Changing a cough to a chuckle, Gordon fled upstairs. In the sanctity of the bathroom, laughter bubbled from him like lava.

'Have you got diarrhoea, minister?' asked Bobby when he returned to the table.

'No.'

'You disappeared awful quick, then. The beer used to make dad run like that.'

A huge beam spread across Gordon's face. How glad he was that he had taken this young lad in. Bobby would have to learn that some words were rude, though.

Fart was one of them.

Chapter Five

Excitement infected everyone as Christmas drew near. John, Cathy and the rest of the gang, went holly hunting.

'There's a tree in the wood next to the smithy,' said Harry.

'We'll need scissors to cut it. I'll get a pair from mum.'

John turned to go.

'I've got a pocket knife,' Colin piped up. 'It's really sharp.'

'Oh, well, I'll not bother with scissors. The knife will do fine.' John retraced his steps and joined the laughing boys as they shoved and pushed each other; teasing and mock fighting.

'I'm Sir Gallahad,' said Raymond, plucking a stick from the hedge and furiously brandishing it. Swiping the air. Cutting it in swathes, like his father scything the copious thistles that spread across the meadow and fields.

'I'm Sir Lancelot,' cried Harry, swishing an even larger stick dangerously close to Raymond's head. Clash, clash. Thud, thud.

'Hey, we should be on the same side,' cried Raymond, angry and a bit afraid, as he warded off Harry's wild thrusts. 'We're all King Arthur's knights. You're a big spoil-sport, Harry.'

Forcefully, Raymond chucked his stick onto the white, frost stiffened grass. 'Come on, let's go for that holly.'

Dark and shiny, the holly branches bunched outwards and upwards.

'See how the leaves are spiky low down and smooth at the top.' Harry pointed enthusiastically. 'That's to protect them from animals. Cattle especially. They love holly.' In amazement, they stared at him.

'How do you know that?' Colin looked at him with something akin to respect, their dispute now forgotten.

'Read it in a book,' mumbled Harry. 'Anyway, it's just common sense.'

Underneath that unruly, carroty hair, Harry was quite knowledgeable. It was on occasions like this, that it shone through.

Silence reigned as they set about plundering the leaves from the bushy evergreen. Later, arms prickled to death with bountiful bunches of red berried holly, they made for home.

'Mum's getting a Christmas tree,' said John. 'There are plenty in the woods. Spruce fir. She's getting Bert to saw one down. He does it every year.'

'That's not all he takes down.' The veiled words were side-mouthed from Harry to Raymond.

'I heard that.' A puzzled John swung round to face them. 'What do you mean?'

'Nothin'.'

'It must be something. Come on, tell me. If you have anything to say, out with it.'

'All the workers talk about it.'

'About what?'

'About Bert shagging your mother.'

'That's a lie. Take it back or I'll smash your nose in.' Suddenly, the day turned sour.

Cathy stopped, her lovely eyes blank with hurt. It couldn't be true. Her beautiful dad doing that with John's mother.

'You're a dirty, rotten fibber, Harry. You should be ashamed of yourself,' she cried.

'I'm not. They say you could be half brother and sister and you shouldn't get too close.'

An awkward silence held them together like an invisible rope, all the way back.

Harry passed John a subdued glance from under lowered eyes. 'Look, it might not be true. I'm sorry.' The apology blurted from regretful lips, but the damage was done. Tiny seeds planted; already taking root.

At the door, Elsie placed a comforting hand on Cathy's arm. 'See you the morn, Cathy, and don't worry. It's probably just gossip.'

Dry-eyed and solemn, Cathy gazed at her friend.

Changed from a snivelling tell-tale, Elsie was maturing. The contours of her pale face were filling out. Greeny eyes and light, reddish brown hair, both shone. A promise there, of not beauty, but a certain attractiveness. Also, and much more important, thought Cathy; developing inside her was a caring nature. Impulsively, Cathy gave her a quick hug. The holly in their arms, pricked their chests.

'Ouch!' they yelped and jumped apart, laughing. On this note of bonhomie, they parted company. In for the night. Doors closed. Except the door to Cathy's thoughts. The words, thick as porridge, stirred by Harry, were many times to be swallowed and regurgitated in a numbed recess of her mind.

'Oh, John,' she whispered. 'What if it's true?'

Alice noticed her wan expression as she came in, but didn't mention it. So they've had a rift, she thought. Good. Too close they were getting by far.

'You've got some holly, then?' Alice looked up from her book.

'Yes.'

'We'll put it up after dinner.'

'Right.'

No enthusiasm; no smile; nothing. It must be serious. Alice wondered what had happened.

At dinner, Cathy observed her dad from under fair lashes. He didn't look any different. He was just her dad. Her knife fiddled about on her plate with a chop. It was well done and difficult to cut. Picking it up with her fingers was not the done thing. Not etiquette. Very strict her mother was regarding manners.

If you can conduct yourself at the table, you can mix with any company, was her thesis. Her dad was more down-to-earth. Never shouted; never complained; never said no – and she loved him. She loved her mother too. In a subdued way. Her mother's way.

Very abashed her mother was at anything of a personal nature. All Cathy's friends at school had been informed about the facts of life when their periods started. On the day of Cathy's first menstruations, her tummy had ached.

'Have you got a hot water bottle, mum? My tummy is hurting.' This was her way of letting her mother know. The reaction was instant. Alice stood statued; silent and embarrassed. Cathy was a woman now.

In body. Yet, at thirteen – still a child.

John was maturing faster and nearly a man. Her hand swept aside a stray strand of hair. Fine and fair, it slid back. Her gaze lingered on the epitome of elegance standing before her. Long legs. No bust. Boyish, but breathtakingly beautiful.

Alice knew her mind was overreacting. She couldn't help it. Life was different now. Children were given more scope. She gave herself a mental shake.

'If you look in the top drawer of your dressing table, you'll find everything you need. Take care Cathy, my lass.' That was the nearest to the facts of life Cathy had received. She knew most of it anyway; from listening to others at school. Self-consciously, a bulky sanitary towel hooked to a narrow strip of a girdle, she went to play. A pair of slacks hid the bulge. She hoped. Some of her friends use Tampons. They were less obtrusive. She might get some.

The magic of Christmas; everything connected with the festive period, gladdened people's hearts. Mums hunted out old decorations. From corners to ceiling centres and above dangling light shades, the colourful creations were draped. Pieces of holly graced mirrors, pictures and clocks. Any mistletoe was strategically placed above door lintels.

It was Christmas Eve, and spirits were high.

Shivering in the cold night air, Cathy and Elsie made their way to John's house. In mittened hands, they each carried a gift. A whistle from Elsie. A gent's hanky with his initials embroidered on it, from Cathy. The ground glittered with frost. They stamped frozen feet on the mat at the door.

'Well – here goes.' Cathy gave Elsie a nudge and knocked loudly on the outer door. The sound seemed to vibrate through the whole house. Standing back, they waited. 'Ooh, it's spooky here,' Elsie whispered.

A light streamed out as the inner door opened. Dark eyes peered at their shapes in the doorway.

'Hello, if it's John you want, you'd better come in.' It was grudgingly said and the girls hung back, uncertain. A rush of warm air, coming out, was extinguished in its tracks by the cold air going in, as hesitantly they stepped inside.

Wearing wine coloured slippers, John appeared from the kitchen. 'Oh, it's you Cathy – and Elsie. Come on through to the room.' Waving them to a chair either side of the fire, he sank between them onto a green, leather pouffe.

Glittering decorations festooned every wall. In one corner, stood the biggest Christmas tree they'd ever seen. Baubles of all colours ranged up and down and round it. On the floor under it were lots of meticulously wrapped parcels.

'What a muckle tree,' Elsie gasped. 'It's even bigger than the one in the village and the kirk.'

Cathy nodded. She knew her father had got it, and remembered Harry's horrid remarks the day they went seeking holly, and quickly looked away.

On the way out, a stag stared from a large painting on the passage wall. Stared, not at them, but over their heads, as if overseeing some lofty terrain. Eyes, daring anyone to tread on his territory. Majestic, like a king. Rightly named 'The Monarch Of the Glen.'

'Isn't he beautiful?' breathed Cathy.

'Yes. It's by Landseer. Only a print, though.' John pointed to a smaller painting nearer the door. It was a mare and foal, entitled 'Mother And Son.'

'That's a print as well. The original is in the Tate Gallery. I love paintings.' John's gaze flowed over Cathy and Elsie. 'Do you?'

'I've never seen any like this before. We've just got photos on our walls.' Elsie looked awed. She giggled. 'If I get married to somebody with plenty money, I'll get him to buy a few.'

'Same here. We have two prints by a local artist. Mum bought them at a jumble sale.' Cathy turned to go. 'Thank you for the present, John. See you at Elsie's house on Boxing Day.'

Barbara had remained out of sight. She didn't present herself to say goodbye, nor did she wish them a Merry Christmas. Well, good riddance to bad rubbish, thought Cathy. For the life of her, she couldn't understand what awful deed she'd done to warrant such hostility.

Once outside, joyfully hugging their presents, the girls trod the icy path homewards.

'She's not very friendly, John's mother, is she?' said Elsie.

'No, she's a bitch. I think she hates me.' Cathy sighed. 'I don't know why.'

'Maybe because John likes you. Mothers are strange.' Elsie laughed. 'I wonder what she would think of the bold Beth Sykes? She has designs on John too. She's not his type, though.'

Once more, Cathy was astonished how sensible Elsie had become. Her perspicacity.

'What makes you think Beth's not John's type?' The beats of Cathy's heart accelerated as she awaited Elsie's answer.

'Och, she's far too pushy. Like a leach, she'd be if she got a lad. Quite nice she can be at times, but I wouldn't trust her with any o' my boyfriends.'

'Do you fancy anybody?'

'Aye, I quite like Alf.'

Small, tubby Alf. That was a turn-up for the books. Cathy smiled inwardly. She must try to get them fixed up with a date.

'I heard Harry tellin' Raymond that Alf's done it with an older lassie who works in a shop. If he tries it on with me, I'll biff him on the jaw.' Elsie grinned. 'I'm savin' myself. There's no laddie gettin' his fingers inside my breek legs.' Walking backwards, Elsie looked at Cathy's face illuminated into a haunting loveliness by the moon's glinting rays. 'When do you think we'll lose our virginity, Cathy? He'll have to be really special before I do it.'

'I don't know. Never, if mum has anything to do with it. She'd have me in a chastity belt. Especially when John is around.'

Cathy sniffed, then sighed.

'Och, we're young yet. Anyway, I read in a woman's magazine that you can lose it riding a horse or a bike.' 'Elsie puckered up her lips and closed her eyes in mock ecstasy. 'I think I'll kiss Alf under the mistletoe when he comes on Boxing Day.'

On these enthusiastic words, the girls linked arms and ran, their youthful laughter filling the night.

A happy Christmas song met Cathy as she went into the room. It was faint. She went to turn up the volume. Even at full tilt, the sound was weak. Blast! the battery must be flat. Just at Christmas too. The others in the row had television sets. Why could her mother not let them have one? Cathy felt tears prick her eyes.

'The battery's flat, mum.' Her face solemn, Cathy looked at her mother. 'Will the garage be open on Christmas day? I could take it in the morning.'

'Yes, usually Mike stops open for a bit, but the battery has to be charged, so we're stuck anyway.' Alice rested her hands in her lap and looked at Cathy.

On the old horsehair couch lay Bert, legs stretched, ankles crossed, green socks showing from beneath grey flannel trousers. Giving a slight cough, he sat up, swung his legs round and stood red-faced, staring into the fire. Suddenly galvanized into action, he sped through to the kitchen.

He wriggled his feet into shoes; brown brogue; his best. His breathing quick, he bent to tie his laces.

Shrugging himself into a checked jacket, he gave a fleeting glance in the mirror above the mantelpiece, then made for the door.

'I'm away,' he said. I'll be back shortly. The Land Rover is at my disposal over the festive period, so I'll take the battery to the garage.' He put on a spurt. He had an urge to see Barbara. She could be as acid as the battery at times, he mused. Yet at other times, her loving drove him to heights of pleasure never before attained. She was under his skin; like a virus. An itch that needed to be forever scratched.

At her house, he laid down the battery and stepped inside the porch. Giving a quiet knock on the inner door, he waited. After several minutes, it opened.

'Bert! what brings you here? Come in.' Her voice was velvet; seductive; with an underlying invitation. Her eyes glowed, black as a wild cat's. He'd never seen her look so beautiful. A stab of lust shot through him. God, he loved this woman.

'John's away to see Dave and Maggie. We'd better go upstairs in case he should return.' Taking his arm, she led him to her bedroom. Divesting himself of his trousers, Bert drew her to the bed.

'No,' she cried. 'We'll go on the rug. You're my rug man, Bert.'

The bed was reserved for Dan. Always. A brief jab of contrition pierced her, then with deliberate slowness, she peeled off her clothes.

Gently gathering her in his arms, Bert pulled her to the floor.

Later, in the kitchen, face rosy with lovemaking, he told her of his errand. He laid the razor thin, gold rimmed cup gingerly on its saucer, scraped back his chair, and stood up to go.

She rushed to stall him. Wait a minute, Bert. John has an old radio stashed away in his cupboard. You may have it.'

'How will I explain it to Alice, though?' His eyes clung to her slinky bottom as softly she stepped up the stairs. She emerged with a steely-grey radio. A long flex dangled from it. It looked almost new.

'It's electric. Here's your Christmas present, Bert. Well – a second Christmas present.' Barbara gave a throaty laugh. 'I enjoyed mine. So very unexpected too. Good night, Bert. Just tell Alice the truth. About the radio, I mean.' Again that throaty laugh. Hell, she was a tempting bitch of a woman.

A melting kiss, sent him winging down the road on singing feet. When he was home, he remembered the battery. He'd left it in Barbara's porch.

Alice squinted from half-lowered eyes as, having discarded his shoes, Bert padded on quiet feet from the hall. Head lowered, he stepped into the room. His body spoke of sex.

Bastard, she thought. He's been at it with her.

Could he hear such words circling in her head, he'd be dumbfounded. She even shocked herself at times. The old Alice suppressed. Frozen over.

He spoke now. Looking more at the floor than at her. Tanned hands held out the radio.

'This is for you and Cathy. It belonged to John. He has a more modern one now.'

Three stilted sentences that corroborated her fears. He HAD been with her. Probably John had been at Dave's place. She could smash the radio over his ego inflated head. Knock that smug look off his face, but what was the use. Anyway, there was Cathy to think about. Swallowing her pride, she took the proffered gift. 'Thank you,' she said. 'I'm sure we'll enjoy it.'

Feeling strangely euphoric, Bert plugged it in the socket by the fire. This Christmas might turn out better than expected.

In many homes, the excitement of Christmas Eve sent young ones early to bed. The mystery of Santa Claus; silently coming; silently going. Parcels of all shapes and sizes, left on the bottom of beds and under festive trees, filled their minds. With eyes big as moons, they lay awake; too worked up to sleep. And when at last, the touch of Morpheus fanned their lids, they slept, and dreamed.

In the morning, Cathy's hopes were more than fulfilled. She was overwhelmed. A radio for Christmas. Her dad singing a festive tune. The aroma of a chicken cooking. Oh – she couldn't believe her luck. With shining eyes, she hugged her dad, then her mum. Thank you, dad – and mum,' she exclaimed. 'This is the bestest Christmas I've had for years.'

For once, Alice refrained from correcting her grammar. Next day at the Marshall's house, a party was to be held. Bobby Telfer had received an invitation.

Gordon's thoughts battled within him Would there be drink? he wondered. Or smoking? Would their mums and dads be there? Would there be girls? If so, might there be – dare he think it – sex?

No – he discounted that thought. Nevertheless, it rained torrents inside his head, falling in huge drops of uncertainty. God – he was turning into a fusty old fuddy-duddy. The lad had to have a normal life. He was in his teens now; ready to spread a few feathers.

Maybe the time was ripe to enlighten him about a few things. Now was as good a time as any. On Christmas day. Celebrating the coming of one baby into the world, and trying to tell him how to prevent another.

On the newly acquired telly, the news was on. Gordon stood up and switched it off. Making for the comfort of his chair, he sat down and took a deep breath.

'Can I have your attention a minute, Bobby. I want to discuss something with you.'

'OK, fire away, minister.'

'Do you know about babies, Bobby?'

'Of course I do. I know about kittens and pups and lambs and calves as well. How?' Bobby's blue eyes held a question mark.

The minister tried a different tactic.

'Do you know how babies are made, Bobby?'

'Aye, with having sex.'

Gordon ran his finger round his collar. Suddenly, it felt tight. This was going to be more difficult than he had anticipated.

Scarlet-faced, Bobby met the minister's earnest gaze. Fancy a minister asking that. He watched the different expressions scurry like waves across his face and sensed with a jolt that he was embarrassed too. Oh, well – he'd better put him out of his misery.

'All the boys talk about it at school. Some of them have done it. Have you done it, minister?'

Cough, splutter, choke.

The minister's tonsils gargled his throat. His cheeks turned puce.

'Well – er – um – it's you I'm asking, Bobby.' Gordon coughed again. A nervous cough. Why on earth had he broached this subject? He'd have to get down to the nitty-gritty now and get it over with.

'Do you, umm, know about condoms, Bobby?'

'Aye, they call them French letters at school. Harry Marshall found some in a drawer in his dad's bedroom. He filled one with water and threw it at Colin's cat. He said he'd done his dad out o' a jump.'

'Now, now. Don't be vulgar, Bobby. I'm asking you because you are growing up. Not that you'll be needing to use them for a long time.' Gordon winged a silent prayer heavenwards. But boys must have advice on such matters. Also, condoms prevent diseases. Like aids and syphilis. They help keep female troubles at bay; like cervical cancer, and – importantly – they stop females getting pregnant. So use them when the time comes, Bobby.' Gordon stopped, his resources empty. What else could he say?

Standards were forever changing. In his young day, relationships were different. Sitting in the back row of the pictures. Sweating buckets at the idea of reaching across to hold a girl's hand. A few kisses if the film wasn't up to much, but when it came to fondling and touching breasts or any intimate parts, he had been far too bashful to attempt such familiarities. As for doing it? Well – he had only done it with his wife.

His eyes rested on Bobby, sitting as innocent as a new born lamb. Or was he? At that age HE had never heard of condoms. Maybe he'd led a sheltered life. All he wanted for Bobby was for him to be happy and secure. He looked at the ceiling, then at the floor and ended up examining his hands as if they were sprouting horns. His mind was drained.

Gosh, he wasn't half getting his knickers in a twist, thought Bobby. He saw him inhale deeply. Oh, no, he thought. He's not starting again? He saw his mouth forming the word 'so' and sighed with relief. He was finishing.

'So,' concluded the minister. 'You'd better behave yourself at the party tomorrow night.'

'Whoopee, you're letting me go. Thank you, minister.'

Wiping his brow, Gordon sank back in his chair. He hoped their little tête-à-tête had given Bobby something to mull over. A guideline on how to care responsibly for the needs of the opposite sex – and himself.

A new day dawned. Party day. As the minister drew to a halt outside Harry's house, dropped Bobby off, heard the racket permeating air and sky, he u-turned both car and mind. Misgivings stamped his foot harder on the accelerator, killing the night with noise and fumes.

'The minister's no' half puttin' his foot down the night. Is he in a bad mood?' Harry looked at Bobby.

'No, he'll be away to pray. He knows I haven't any condoms with me. I've just had a long lecture about birth control. Folk his age must think we're all sex mad.' Grinning widely, Bobby went to join the others in the room.

'Here, drink this.' Harry handed them glasses, filled to the top with his dad's home made beer, cool as ice from the larder. 'Down the hatch, lads.' Head back, he took a long drink. Half finished, he stopped to breathe, patted his stomach and burped.

They all laughed.

Soon, eyes began to sparkle and aspirations rise. They felt they could conquer anything. Sail the hungry seas, like Columbus in his endeavours to reach new lands. Climb Mount Everest. Swim the English channel. Fly to the moon.

All this, they could do with the heat of beer in their bellies. Knowing it was forbidden helped add to their enjoyment. Gripping his glass, Harry stepped towards the room. He beckoned the lads to follow.

'We'll join the lassies now,' he said. 'Bring your drinks with you.'

Sidestepping the others, John made his way to the source of the music. It belted out in squeaks and scratches from an old gramophone standing on a cloth covered kist in a corner.

Elsie and Cathy whispered near the door. Elsie was a burning fire; anticipation stoking the flames.

'Alf, come here a minute.' Excitedly, Cathy waved him over.

Feeling important at being singled out, Alf made his way towards them. Like a fly to a spider's web, he came to a standstill at the exact spot their scheming minds had contrived.

A step, a lunge, and Elsie's lips found their target. Yells of 'more, more,' urged Alf to retaliate in kind.

Sweeping her into his arms, he kissed her passionately. Cathy giggled.

Elsie looked dazed.

'It's my turn now.' Before Cathy could utter a word, John's arms held her in a vice-like grip. Like in her dreams, his mouth sought hers.

How can this be wrong, she wondered? How could she feel as she did if they were related? But in the deep waters of thought, already surfacing like The Loch Ness Monster, was the doubt.

Was it true, or untrue?

Unbidden, her mother's face swept before her, the same doubt written over it. With an anguished 'no-o-o,' she pushed him away.

As though she'd slapped him, John stepped back; overcome by something out of his control, no way of proving or disproving.

Helpless, the gang watched. Silence held them together like glue. Beth Sykes, quick to assess the situation, seized John's elbow. She felt for his hand. It was stiff, as though rigor mortis had set in.

'She'll come round, John. You'll see. Come on, I'll walk home with you.'

A fluttering of excitement filled her. She looked at the sombre expression on his usually cheery face and a stab of pity engulfed her. So dark and handsome and sensitive he was as he plodded quiet as a shadow beside her.

She peeped sideways. Stilted steps, dragged him along. She touched his arm. 'We'll go the long way home,' she whispered.

This was her chance, she thought, and nothing was going to spoil it. Diverging from the normal route, they turned right. A narrow path led them to a small coppice behind the stables.

'Let's stop here.' Beth swung her body to face his. 'Do you want to kiss me, John?'

He nodded, not knowing what he wanted, but needing something to take away the zombie-like feeling.

The nebulae of night, sometimes luminous, sometimes shadowed, tricked the evening sky. An owl hooted from its lofty perch on a tree. Across the dark divide, another answered.

An eerie magic wrapped round Beth and John. They savoured the intensity of a first kiss. For Beth, it was as awesome as the night. She knew he didn't feel the same. He still fancied Cathy, but she blocked this from her mind. Tonight he was hers. Whatever happened in the future, she had this.

Forever, it would run inside her head. Clear as crystal, like a burn rippling down a mountain side; singing to the rocks, the trees, the sky, and the silver minnows darting and diving in the deep pools gouged by nature's hands.

'It's getting late. We'll have to go.' Beth lifted her head from his chest. They uncoiled from each other and with coy looks, retraced their steps and made for John's home.

Barbara was watching television when the door opened. Two figures stood at the entrance, then made their way into the room. Astonished, Barbara bounced from the sofa.

'Mum.' John put his arm round Beth and drew her forward. 'I'd like you to meet Beth Sykes.' He glanced at Beth. 'Beth, this is my mother.'

A dreadful dawning hit Barbara's eyes. Her gaze cut across Beth's face like a whip. God almighty – first Cathy, now her. The very ones whose fathers she was having relationships with. One of which was without any doubt, John's dad. Oh, the tangled webs of life. She was sure they would spring into the grave with her. Her mouth closed into a thin line. Teeth bit into her bottom lip. Blood salted her saliva.

'What's wrong, mum? You look faint.' Troubled eyes stared at her. From past experience, John knew that look. It didn't bode well for him.

'I'm fine.' Jellied legs sank her back onto the sofa. Like a chiselled carving, she sat, never letting her gaze waver from Beth. Hair like Dan, mouth like Dan, brow like Dan. She brought his very presence with her.

As for John – he didn't resemble anybody. He was just John. Except – a sharp breath escaped her throat, expelling itself to join the mist curling round her.

Except his webbed toes. The words were twisted tree trunks in her head. Her eyelids closed, pulled by the weight of her thoughts.

'Has your mother been at the bottle?' whispered Beth as they installed themselves in the kitchen, safe from her hate filled eyes.

'No, I don't know what's wrong. She was the same with Cathy.'

'Oh.'

Cathy's name hung between them like a flypaper. It dangled between glances. It dangled between lips too scared to move lest the name be uttered again. It filled the space between the stools on which they sat, knees nearly touching. She felt it slide over her like a snake. Abruptly, she stood up.

'I'll have to be going. Will you phone my dad, please, John?'

'What's the hurry?' He crossed to the unit with an anxious expression on his face. Picking up the phone, he dialled, then handed it to Beth.

At the other end, Dan heard his daughter's message with mounting anger. Christ! this was all he needed. The route to Barbara's boudoir was difficult enough without Beth courting John. She would never be away from the place. He groaned. His hands held his face, as if trying to stem the flow of his worries.

He gathered his brow into furrows. The clock shouted ten o'clock. Stupid blasted cuckoo clock. His hands itched to strangle the bird every time it popped out.

Lifting his jacket from a hook on the wall, he grabbed the van keys, pulled his deerstalker hat over his thick, mousy hair and stomped outside.

A toot, toot, signalled his arrival. He wasn't going in. Barbara would understand.

At the door, John touched Beth's arm. 'Will you see me again?' he murmured. 'Tomorrow?'

'Yes.' The word breathed from her in a rush, in case he might change his mind.

That night Beth had a dream.

A raven hovered over her. Big and black, its span of wings was like a huge cloud. It changed and took on the appearance of a dove. The dove was light grey with a tinge of pink. As she gazed from the haze of her dream, it flew down with a graceful swoop and laid a twig on her bosom.

It told her the way was clear. It told her the flood in John's heart had dried up. It told her to cultivate the soil and harrow it with love, but the soil was filled with stones and the harrows stuck. From the centre of a vast field, big as a desert, a signpost rose. It had three signs. They pointed in different ways, but were blank. The dove stood on one of them. Its feet were chained – and only she had the key to set it free.

She awoke sweating, clothes half over the bed. What a peculiar dream, she thought. So vivid. So real. Did it mean anything? Was it an omen?

In his narrow bed, John lay staring into space. Sleep evaded him. The events of the night swept over him. He had enjoyed being with Beth. He'd never touched a girl before. Cathy still lay like a lump in the pit of his stomach, but she'd refused him. He knew why and understood. His thoughts swam in the current of a new found well-being. Beth and he would go to see her tomorrow. It was most important that they remain friends. He sighed – and at last slept, but unlike Beth, his sleep was long and dreamless.

Chapter Six

The new year let go of last year's strings. It welcomed the snowdrops. Clumps and clumps of glistening jewels, studding hedgerows, bankings and woodlands.

It said goodbye, as the graceful heads faded and folded back into the soil; nature holding the reins of power; rocking earth's cradle; setting them off to months of slumber.

February passed.

Dave Hart knelt on the muddy ground. His expert hands explored inside a lambing ewe. She needed help. The lamb was big and wrongly positioned, but something else was wrong, thought Dave. Eyes glazed with pain, the ewe moaned. After much tugging, the lamb slipped out. It was lifeless. Dave felt around to see if she had another inside. She hadn't. He swore under his breath. He'd have to put a spare lamb on to her.

Setting the ewe onto her feet, he manoeuvred her along the field. The unstinting help of Spot and Bess, made it easy. As essential as arms and legs, were his dogs.

Bruce Tait was shifting bigger lambs and their mothers to another field. His waterproof leggings swish, swished against each other at every step.

Bruce liked working with sheep. He liked animals. Had an affinity with them. He felt like Solomon; regarding the life of his beasts before all else. He wasn't religious, but realized that only someone of great omnipotence, could create a little lamb.

His eyes followed the passage of a red van. Glimpses of it flashed between spaces in the hedge. It was easy to follow. Bruce knew whose it was – and its destination.

Rumours abounded. Barbara's affairs with Dan and Bert were common knowledge. Now, Beth was courting John. It caused much concern amongst the neighbours. Seeing the van, they hunched against their doors, voicing their opinions.

'It's not right. Them bairns should be told.' Grace Stuart stood, arms akimbo, gazing with great intensity at Mary Marshall, her neighbour.

'Aye,' said Mary. 'It won't do them any good. How can men not be content with what they've got?'

'Well, if my man went astray, I'd castrate the bugger.' Grace sucked in her lips as if picturing the mutilation. Savouring it.

'I'm glad my Alf is goin' out with your Elsie,' said Janet Tait. 'At least they know who their fathers are.'

'Aye, it's just pot luck with John. It's a bloody shame.' Mary stubbed her cigarette on the step and skimmed indoors. Grace and Janet followed suit.

At the big house, Dan reversed his van in the drive, ready for a quick getaway.

In a black polo necked jumper, flared, tweed skirt, black stockings and black shoes, Barbara reclined on the chaise longue. A smile of pleasure lightened her face as he stepped to her side.

Unable to contain himself, Dan was already casting his clothes onto the carpet. He couldn't wait to go upstairs. He had to have her – now.

'Oh, Barbara, how I've missed you.' His arms crushed her to him and pulled her downwards. The soft white rug welcomed them. Fingers crept lacy knickers over shapely legs and feet. As his body covered hers, Barbara felt her own desire sharpen and her lips sought his.

Not having seen Dan's van, Bert walked with silent steps into the house. At the door of the sitting room, he stopped dead; for there on the rug, writhing in ecstasy, lay Barbara and Bert. The rug where he and Barbara always made love. A great rage swelled in him, and with it, a black wall of despair. On blinded legs, he walked away.

Later in the day, the children filed from the school bus. They were happy and laughing. Ready for fun.

'Let's to the barn, the night. Play on the straw and the swing,' said Harry.

On the rafters, they had a long rope. The end was knotted, so that with legs crossed, they were able to swing to and fro.

Changed into older clothes, they congregated in the yard. Harry, being first, slid open the door of the barn. What he saw made him gasp and recoil with shock.

'Get back,' he shouted. 'Don't let Cathy in, for God's sake.' But the momentum of their surging feet catapulted them forwards and inwards. Seven pairs of eyes stared.

'Dad, oh dad,' wailed Cathy. Then she screamed. Scream after scream after scream. Stunned, the others stood, unable to do anything to stop the flow.

'Get Dave,' the subdued voice of John issued the order. Awakened by the words, they raced across the yard, coming to an abrupt halt at the lambing shed.

Dave raised his head; sensing alarm. Seeing the panic written on parchment faces, immediately he came forward.

'What's the matter? Has something happened to John? Or Cathy?'

'It's Bert.'

Harry – loud, fearless, devil-may-care Harry, burst into a flood of tears. Words tumbled out in a confused heap.

'Dear bloody God!' Dave's utterance was a piece of pain torn from his heart. Poor Alice. Poor Cathy.

'Look, I'm going to phone Tom Garrick. You kids rush on home. Thank you for telling me.' The phone shook in his hand as he dialled Tom's number.

A devastated silence sobbed over the line. Like Dave, Tom's thoughts were for Alice and Cathy – and Bert, who had been his best friend. What had tipped the scales? What torment had run amok in his head as he made that fatal jump?

Tom's head drooped. He felt sick, but he must be strong. For Alice and Cathy's sake.

Back at the barn, John tried to stop the stream of Cathy's hysteria.

'Stop it, Cathy. Stop it,' he cried. 'Please.'

A throbbing pulse beat a tattoo within him He hoped this was only a dream, but knew it wasn't. Seizing her by the shoulders, he firmly shook her. His fingers dug into her flesh. Bert's limp form dangled from the rope that was their swing; head askew; eyes bulging, as if he'd shocked himself with what he'd done. The sight nauseated John. He turned away.

Cathy's screaming continued. Suddenly John remembered a storyline in a play, where a disturbance of this sort was cured by a slap. Raising his hand, he smacked her solidly on the cheek. The screaming mouth quietened, then sprang shut. Not another sound did she utter.

Weeks dragged by and still Cathy remained silent; locked in a world of her own. A world of bewilderment.

Alice was worried and consulted a doctor.

'Be patient,' he advised. 'Shock is a funny thing. Even time cannot best it. Treat her normally. Often another shock can do the trick.' Kindly eyes held her grey ones. Smooth hands reached to clasp hers. 'Come in any time you wish. Don't bottle it up.' His long frame rose from behind a mahogany desk. He held open the door. She thanked him and hurried out.

April was almost finished. The year thudding its way through life. Daffodils again heaped their glow along the countryside. As they faded, primroses, pale and delicate, sprinkled themselves in little dells and woodlands. Buds seemed to open overnight, so gradual their awakening.

Winter wheat grew lush and green. May came, covering hedges and fruit trees with raiments of pink and white. Forget-me-nots, blue and beautiful, hazed grassy road edges.

Turnips were singled, sheep clipped and haymaking in progress. A baler swallowed huge swathes of the silvery green grass and churned out bale after bale. Lambs were separated from their mothers. Their bleating rang from field to field. Within days, the crying ceased.

All this happened and still Cathy had not spoken. She joined Elsie and the lads in the usual games but laughter never touched her face. Sometimes Elsie thought she saw a flicker of interest in her big blue eyes.

Mostly they were dead.

John and Beth were still an item, but they took things quietly, refraining from doing anything hasty.

Another hot day had the gang sitting around doing nothing; tired without moving. Adulthood had come to them prematurely the instant they saw Bert hanging in the barn.

For Barbara Fairbairn, the episode had cut her to the quick. Cathy's outward scream, had become her inward scream. She knew that had Dan and she gone upstairs as they usually did, the awful tragedy would never have happened. She withdrew into herself.

Dan couldn't understand her sudden remoteness. 'Was there something going on between you two?' he asked.

'Why, who have you been talking to?'

Her eyebrows arched upwards, folding her brow into her hairline.

'So there was something?'

Her silence thereafter, was answer enough.

Pains stabbed him in the region of his abdomen. Sharp pricking pains that sucked all the colour from his good looking face. How long had she strung him along? Baby faced Bert and himself? He felt as though she'd amputated him down below. It felt numb.

Would it ever work again? Gosh, he was a fool. He had cared for her. Even loved her in his own way.

Now, she'd gone all holy. He knew her well, though. Being a bible punching bitch wouldn't quench the flame in that secret part of her.

Secret, be buggered. God knows how many men she'd wiled into her bed? What a stupid dolt he was for falling under her spell. A long look into the deep brown tint of her eyes, stretched what lay before him. Miles and miles of bleakness. An arid desert.

Deflated, he spun on his heel and walked away.

Barbara's resolve almost weakened as she saw him go; but guilt rose like a phoenix and squashed it dead. She had a new life now. Every hour consumed. Culpability driving her on.

Later, she went shopping. Her new Jaguar swept into the yard and halted at the door. The sound of laughter and squeals assailed her ears as she opened it.

She cursed.

John and Beth tussled on the chaise longue. Beth's cheeks were rosy. Her green eyes shining. John's were like bright chestnuts peeping from their cases. Animation burned in them, stroked by the intensity of his feelings. Barbara was angry, her new found piety forgotten.

'John – it's time you took Beth home.' Her red nailed hands shooed them up from the sofa.

'OK, mum.' Thoughtfully, John helped Beth on with her coat and, arms round each other, they departed.

Beth shuddered and straightened her posture. Proud, she looked, and defiant. Not for a million pounds would she show defeatism in front of that shrew.

John was unhappy. Would Beth be another Cathy in his mother's eyes. Would she be like this with every girl he liked?

Instead of going straight back after seeing Beth home, his steps led him to the stables. Maybe Tony would still be there. A whistling from within, told him he was.

A douser detects water with a forked stick. One didn't need a divining rod to seek out Tony. Just follow his whistle. Everybody knew which tune was number one in the top twenty. The melody flew from his lips every Monday morning as he sped to work. His rendition of the latest, stopped when John entered. Tony's keen eyes studied him. Something was wrong.

'Are you all right, John? You look a bit down in the dumps.'

Tears nearly found an outlet at Tony's burst of sympathy. Manfully, John blinked them back, but not before Tony saw the telltale glistenings on his lashes. Grasping the lad's shoulders, he guided him to the tack room. 'Now, tell me what's the matter. I'm in no hurry. Just take your time'

'It's mum. She treats Beth like scum. It's as if she doesn't want me to have a girl.' The words spouted from John like water from a fountain; spilling out his misery. 'I like Beth, Tony. I liked Cathy too. The same thing happened with her. Am I jinxed or something?'

John bowed his head.

'Cathy gave me up because Harry implied that Bert was having an affair with mum and that he might be my father. I don't think he was. I'd have felt it – in here' John patted his chest where his heart thumped like a trapped rabbit.

Tony had heard the stories about Bert and Dan and Barbara and grieved for the lad. Shedding the leaves of boyhood. Sprouting the buds of an adult. Sometimes a difficult time in a boy's life. A rocky road God had chosen for this one.

'I've found a girl I like,' said Tony, tactfully changing the subject.

'Have you? I'm pleased for you, Tony. Who is she?'

'She's called Rachel. She works in Baird's shop. Mum had flu last week and I had to get the shopping. I met her then. Her hair is black and her eyes are dark as the night sky. She is Irish. She's like a ray of sunshine. I've never met anyone like her. She's great.'

'Gosh, Tony. You sound like a poet.' John smiled. Already, he felt better.

Dinner was a dried up heap under the grill and inedible when he arrived home. His mother railed like a banshee. He let her rant on with deaf ears. Her behaviour of late was fast distancing him from her. Her so-called goody-goody actions didn't pull the wool over his eyes.

Corn, wheat and barley ripened. Fields and fields of swaying gold, not harsh in colour, but subdued mellow tints, were harvested. Hips and haws and rowans donned their autumn faces. Apples hung from heavy trees.

Sunday was harvest festival in the kirk. Fruit, jams, vegetables, chutneys and all sorts of fine produce, lay at the front of the kirk. A bunch of straw leaned against the pulpit; its straggly heads bent as if in prayer.

Barbara did the reading.

'Look at her,' whispered Mary Marshall to Jenny, the blacksmith's wife. 'She's like a cat that's had the cream. All prim and proper she is nowadays.' Mary gave Jenny a nudge.

'Aye, they say that sins are forgiven if you repent; but wait until another man takes her fancy. Whether he's married or not, she'll have him flat on his back in no time.'

A head turned round, eyes admonishing. Others stared straight ahead, ears straining for more.

The minister stood, his words flowing over the heads of his congregation. In the pulpit, his eyes roamed the sea of faces, not letting them linger too often or too long on any one female, lest his intentions be misconstrued.

'Bless this bountiful harvest. Bless the little mice left homeless in the bare, stubble fields. Bless the righteous. Bless the sinners. Bless –' but what he was about to bless next, failed to reach Mary and Jenny's ears. Too busy sifting out the sinners' bit, rolling it about in their heads – their minds fixed it like a badge – on Barbara.

'Bless the sinners indeed. Do you think he has a fancy for her?' Mary rolled her eyes at Alice.

'Don't be silly, Mary.' Alice, quick to defend Gordon, glared daggers at her.

'Well, he's been a long time without a woman. What's he been thinkin' about all them years? A man's a man for a' that, Robbie Burns wrote, and look at the women he had.' Mary Marshall pulled on her gloves. Forcefully, she stabbed the fabric between each finger to the hilt, dragged her tweedy effect coat sleeves down to cover her wrists and marched starchily onwards, leaving a trail of speculation in her wake.

Back home, Barbara and John ate their lunch in silence. With a mumbled, 'Please may I leave the table?' John disappeared. Piling greasy dishes into the sink, Barbara retired to read. Her hand scrabbled along the sofa for her bag. She needed a smoke. 'Bugger,' she swore. No bag. She must have left it in church.

Dave will be going later to help distribute some of the goods to the elderly and housebound, she thought. I'll ask him to fetch it. The smooth tone of his voice on the phone, gave her a shiver of pleasure. Her own husked over in response.

'Just bring it on your way back, Dave. It should be on third pew. Thank you very much.' Reluctantly, she ended the conversation. A rush of adrenaline coursed through her body. She hurried to change. Something seductive, she mused. 'Dave Hart, you come here at your peril.' The walls, the ceiling, and the sofa caught her words, but it was the soft white rug in front of the fire, where she aimed to bring them to fruition.

The wind of the morning had abated. A mist hung, and was beginning to merge with darkness, when Dave's black Austin pulled up beside the porch.

'Hello, here it is.' His tanned hands held out the missing bag. His eyes regarded her warily.

'Thank you. Come in a minute, Dave.' Her voice was a purr. 'I'm very grateful.' Slender fingers grasped the bag, red leather, with a flap that snap fastened at the front. It was an expensive bag. Everything Barbara bought was of the best quality.

With swaying hips, she walked towards the fire. Dave followed.

Half turning, she beckoned him to a chair. 'Have a seat. I'll get you a drink' Her eyebrows rose. 'Whisky, is it?'

Dave nodded. He felt uncomfortable; like a stag sensing danger. The crystal decanter gurgled a rare blend of malt whisky into a large glass. Her fingers brushed his as he clasped its stem. He downed the contents in one gulp and stood up. 'I must be going. I've still got work to do.'

'Oh, don't go yet, Dave.' She stepped closer. Her perfume stung his nostrils. She was almost touching him. He lurched backwards.

'No,' he cried. 'I love Maggie. I'm here as your employee, not this. If you want both, then you'll have to get someone else.'

'Damn it, Dave, you know you're roused. Why fight it? Who would know, anyway?'

'I would, Barbara. This is just a normal hot-blooded males' reaction. It will keep – for Maggie.'

'You'd be willing to put your job on line?' she taunted.

'Aye, I would. So what's it to be?'

Barbara's mind raced. He was excellent at his job. She needed him. The farm needed him. Envy covered her like a cloud. What had that mousy wife of his got that was so special? She stepped away from him with a sigh. 'So be it, Dave.' Pride hurt at his rejection, she turned away. When she swung back, he was gone.

With thoughts dark as night, she tackled the dishes. A cigarette dangled from her lips like a hooker on a street corner. It was not a habit of hers. She thought it common, but what was elegance, when she wanted comfort? Hell, she missed a man. She inhaled deeply.

Back home, Dave stepped to the kitchen door and stood watching Maggie who was methodically cutting circles of dough and placing them on a tray. She looked round as his arms wound round her middle.

'Hello, Maggie.' His voice was hoarse.

'Mighty me,' she cried, feeling his hardness against her buttocks. 'It's you that should be out there amongst the yowes, my man, not the tups – and look at my hands, they're covered in flour. Let me get them washed.'

'Never mind your hands.' Divesting himself of his coat, Dave turned her round and pulled her close. On the flour covered kitchen table, nearly white with Maggie's zealous scrubbing, they made love.

'I'm away to finish my chores, now.' Dave placed a brief kiss on Maggie's button nose and shut his fly.

Maggie smiled, her face animated. The hungry aroma of baking filled the kitchen. Well risen and golden, the scones emerged from the oven. 'Aye,' she said, speaking to the scones. 'You're just like my Dave. Well – maybe not the golden bit.'

She giggled like girl.

Dave was her man. Whatever life threw at them, she'd always be there waiting in the wings.

With a grin, Dave went about his duties. What did he want Barbara for, when he had Maggie?

Chapter Seven

Over two years passed. Harry was a trainee in a bank, Raymond with Fleming the builder. Alf, in one of the local tweed mills. Elsie, was an apprentice in the village hairdressing salon. Cathy, still living in a world of silence, had managed to procure a position in major Townsend's big house at Manor farm.

Dusting, cleaning, making beds, serving at table, and helping in the kitchen were her main duties. She liked best working in the kitchen beside Mrs Clark, the cook. Rounded and motherly, Mrs Clark sweated her hours away there. Chopping vegetables. Pummelling mounds of dough. Stirring sauces. Vigorous activities that made her plump arms shake and quiver.

Cathy liked her.

Tonight, the kitchen was a hive of activity. The reason being, the return of Donald, the major's eldest son, from the navy.

Mrs Clark turned anxious eyes towards Cathy. She watched over her like a mother hen. Worried sick she was about Donald coming home. He was bad news. Lots of maids had left with big bellies. The result of Donald waylaying them in the many dark corridors and isolated bedrooms where work duties took them. How could the major and his spouse Catherine, have spawned such trash?

The major had a dark side to him too, though. Churlish, mean and dour, he could be at times. Maybe Donald had inherited his genes, the bad ones, magnified a hundred times over. Mrs Clark's mind raced on. It was their break time. They sat on high backed chairs, knees tucked under the long kitchen table of matching pine, hands curled round steaming cups of tea.

She looked at the bonny face of Cathy. Her grey hair peeped from under a white cap. Her broad face was stern.

'Watch out for that Donald, Cathy,' she implored. 'He's not to be trusted. Don't be alone with him if you can help it.' She sucked in her lips then took another sip of tea. 'Keep a hat pin in your peenie pocket. Stab him where it hurts if he tries anything on. They should have drowned him at birth. He's rotten to the core.' The old head shook vigorously, her double chins trembling with the force of it. 'God, if he harms a hair on your head, lassie, I'll swing for him,' she raged.

Cathy's blue eyes stared at her, comprehension widening them. Fear lurked in their depths. To be caught unawares by an evil stranger, was a terrifying thought. She'd best be on her guard.

Graham, the youngest of the major's brood, was a complete contrast to his older sibling. A wide welcome forever framed his mouth. His eyes, tawny in colour, reflected the message from his full but firm lips. Farming was his love. It burned like fire in his veins. Another term at university and he would be finished. He could hardly wait. He studied history to please his father. He had not yet divulged to him that he was not making a career out of his education. His father would be livid.

'He's a lovely lad,' said Mrs Clark to Cathy. As different from his brother as chalk and cheese. His sister Hannah's not too bad either. A bit flighty at times, but her heart is in the right place.' Her eyes filmed over with an angry glaze. 'It's yon Donald. He's not a bit interested in the farm. Wanted to see the world, so joined the navy. Lords it around when he's here. Booze, fags and women. He's worse when the drink's in him – and cruel. He once dropped Hannah's wee kitten from the bedroom window. Broke its leg. Worst of it was – he just laughed. I can't stand the man.' A huge sigh, like the hiss of air from a bicycle tube, escaped her. She strained to her feet and resumed preparing the dinner, her anxiety expressing itself in the clanking of lids on pans. Steam blew them up again, the strength of it matching her gathering wrath. Her eyes, black as treacle, swung upwards as a noisy screeching of brakes brought the person in question, to their door.

'Listen to that, months of purgatory we'll have. He's a maniac.' Cook's body twisted towards the window. 'If God ever made a mistake, then it was letting him be born.'

Her words, uttered with unaccustomed venom, made Cathy look at her in amazement. She reached to touch the plump arm, comforting her. Rolls of flesh enfolded Cathy's small frame. Tears dampened her fair hair. 'Oh, lassie, keep close to me when he's here. You're like my own daughter, but nicer. She scarpered years ago. I've no idea where she is. She could be on the moon, or at the bottom o' the sea.' Her eyes closed, seeing a blank page that would never be written on.

Cathy wished fervently that she could answer. Words filled her brain, torrents of them; like rivers seeking the sea, but they had no outlet. She could only let cook's motherly figure hug her.

This was the scene that met Donald's steely eyes as he opened the kitchen door.

'How touching!'

The two sarcastic words shot cook and Cathy apart. Infused with a sudden trembling, Cathy gaped at the stocky fellow standing in the doorway.

Legs splayed, as if still on board a ship, he stood. Square jawed, full lipped, haughty. Bronzed with being in sunny climes. Hair close cropped.

His presence stopped time.

An exultant look crossed the rugged contours of his face as he observed their discomfort. Angrily, he flung his bag of possessions onto the linoleumed floor.

'Take this upstairs, girl,' he ordered. 'And be quick about it.' Turning, he strode arrogantly away.

'I'll do it, Cathy; you stir the sauce.' Moon cheeks puffed out with the effort, Mrs Clark ascended the steep stairs. Breathless and weak kneed, she returned, and flopped onto the nearest chair. 'Help! them stairs are far steeper than I thought. I'm fair fagged out. This arthuritis in my knees doesn't help.' She scowled, then peered at Cathy. 'Make another cup of tea lassie, please. I've got an awful thirst. Then get back to stirring the sauce in case his nibs comes back.'

Cathy smiled inwardly at Mrs Cook's use of the word 'arthuritis.' It sounded like she had an uncle called Arthur with an infection. As she was bid, she handed cook a nice warm cup of tea, lifted a wooden spoon, and set to work on the sauce. Unable to resist, she dipped her finger into the smooth whiteness of it.

'Well, what have we here? I thought I told you to take my bag up to my room.'

The voice whirled her round. The sauce never reached her lips. She froze.

'Are you dumb or what, girl?' His gaze cut through her. He noted her beauty. The barely budding breasts. The long legs. The fair hair – and lust blasted through him.

'Leave the lassie alone. She can't speak. So get out of my kitchen, Donald Townsend.' Cook sprang between them.

'Just remember who I am,' Donald reprimanded, and astonishingly left without further ado, but had cook seen the rabid look in his eyes, she would have shuddered.

The dark cloud was already descending.

Chortling to himself, Donald took the stairs at a gallop. 'A dumb wench,' he breathed. 'Lovely – and soon to be mine.'

At dinner that evening, he was courteous and on his best behaviour. If his gaze lingered on Cathy and followed her round the room, no one noticed. Not even Cathy. Perhaps cook worried too much. She was only trying to protect her. Maybe Donald wasn't as bad as she inferred. Cathy crossed her fingers just in case.

Roast beef, roast potatoes, Yorkshire pudding, cauliflower and white sauce, followed cock-a-leekie soup. The sweet, done especially for Donald, was bread and butter pudding; his favourite.

Hurriedly, Donald devoured it, then excused himself from the table. 'I must congratulate cook. She excelled herself with that meal.' His gaze flicked backwards. 'See you later for a port, father.'

'What? Huh! Right.' The major barely looked up. Turning his huge bulk, he reached for the racing paper. A practiced eye perused the entries at Market Rasen.

The surprise of Donald's statement touched only his mother. What was he up to now, this unpredictable son of hers? she wondered.

She looked perturbed. Her husband's gambling upset her. His losses at Perth had been massive. Between the dogs and the horses, serious amounts of money shifted from bank to bookie. Thank God for Graham. The estate would be in safe hands under his care. Hannah too, was a balm to her dispirited heart. Trevor, her husband, she'd long banished from the marital bed. His womanizing ceased to bother her.

Fancy women, whore houses. He could have them all. And those quirky traits of his. All anathema to her. How had she countenanced such behaviour in the earlier years of marriage?

Across the table, she viewed him. A man's man, one might surmise. A shooting, fishing, racing, hunting and curling fanatic. Where did the rogue cells come from, she wondered. Should the folk outside see in – what would they think of their tweedy, strutting squire?

Dinner finished, she rose. She felt hot. A walk in the garden seemed a nice idea. On the top step, she stood; enjoying the coolness of the night. The figure of Cathy disappeared down the poplar lined path. The bottom gate creaked open, then shut. Catherine made a mental note to have it oiled. She would ask Hamish, the gardener, to see to it tomorrow.

Smoke whisked the air above a rhododendron bush. The shape of Donald unwound itself from a seat behind it. His fingers stubbed the end of a cigarette. Angrily, he threw it down and ground it viciously with the toe of his shoe. He was getting impatient. Being a good boy had lost its glamour.

His mother cupped her hands to her mouth. Her mind skimmed the past, like turning the pages of a book. There was Lilly, bonny and blue eyed, who had left in a hurry. Then Ruth. Then poor Jean; so distressed with her condition, she'd thrown herself into a slimy, stagnant pond a few miles away. Now, her dastardly son had designs on Cathy. She could sense it – but how could she prevent it?

Resolutely, she strode towards him. 'Don't even think it, Donald.' Her quiet voice brought him round to face her.

'What do you mean. mother? And why the po-face?'

'You know what I mean. Defile Cathy and you will be disinherited.'

'Huh! you haven't a say here. Dad is boss. Why would I want a dumb little commoner like her anyway?' He aimed a spit at the trunk of an aged apple tree and sidled off.

Rain and sleet vented their anger on the last day of March. Lambs stood hunched. Ewes fed with their backs to the wind. Virgin buds closed against the onslaught. They wanted heat. Warm, sunny heat to caress them open. It came next day. Earth sucked it up like a hoover.

Before noon, a green haze touched hedges, trees and woods, giving them an alluring kiss of colour. Cathy saw it as, light of step, she made her way homewards. It was Wednesday, her half day. She enjoyed the two miles walk to and from the estate. Enjoyed hearing the many different kinds of birds. The mooing cows. The ewes bleating to their lambs, and their answering calls.

Caught up in such joys, she didn't hear the stealthy steps behind her until a strong arm grasped her round the neck. Then a voice. Donald's voice; malicious and overbearing.

'Got you, dumbo,' it said. 'Did you think I'd let such a beauty like you escape my clutches?'

The arm tightened, pulling her over the grass and into a thicket. She was choking. Her foot struck at his leg, catching his shin bone. He swore. Next thing she was on her back. He was doing things to her. Her throat tensed. She heard a scream and realized it was coming from her. It was like the continuation of the one she'd given that awful day they found her dad hanging in the barn.

'Shut up, you bitch.' He slapped her face. The scream went on and on.

Tom Garrick, tending sheep in the pens, heard it. Stopping what he was doing, he ran. At the source of the scream, he beheld Cathy on the ground. She had been violated. Gently, he cradled her in his arms. She became hysterical.

'Hush, Cathy. It's me, Tom. Hush lassie, hush.' His rhythmic rocking soothed her. She hiccupped and lifted her eyes to Tom. They were blue pools; water logged. At Cathy's home, he phoned the police.

At the manor, the loud clanging of the bell, resounded through the hall. Major Townsend, snoozing by the fire, woke with a start. 'Who the dickens is that? See to it, will you, Catherine.'

Resignedly, Catherine pushed aside the mosaic topped table on which she was playing patience and stood up. Long ago, she'd learned that the line of least resistance kept a happier ship.

The sight of two policemen on the step startled her. 'Good afternoon, how can I help you?' she asked with a quaking voice.

'I'm detective inspector Hargreaves. This is chief constable Baker. Is your son Donald, at home?'

'Yes.' Inwardly, she shivered. What had he done?

Thoughts clawed her mind, like raking leaves into a heap. Seeing only a bare surface underneath; waiting to see what fate would print on it.

'Can we have a word with him please, madam?'

'Certainly, come in.' She noted their serious faces and a coldness stole over her. From a range of bell cords on the wall, she selected the one to his room and pulled.

Thus summoned, Donald donned his shoes. Shined up without a trace of having been out, he reckoned they'd ensure anyone into thinking otherwise. A grey pallor won through his tan when he saw the officers.

They had no evidence though – and the girl was dumb. Or was she? Had her scream signified the return of her speech? Jesus, he hoped not. She could write though, he thought with rising panic – and, with trepidation, he saw the detective, eyes hard as granite, cross to where he stood.

'Donald Henry Townsend, I am arresting you for the assault and rape of Cathy Wilson. Anything you say will be taken down as evidence.'

Blah, blah, blah, thought Donald, as the detective intoned the indictment.

'I've been here all day. Look at my clothes. My shoes. Clean as a whistle. You're barking up the wrong tree, lads.' Donald tried to sound jocular.

'We have a signed statement here. That's good enough for us. Handcuff him, constable Baker.'

A whole spectrum of emotions engulfed Donald. He could go inside for this. What would it be like in jail? Cooped up. No women. No drink. Badgered because of the seriousness of his crime.

Months on the raging seas seemed like heaven to him now. He hadn't a conscience, so it didn't smite him. Self-pity did. As he was taken away, his thoughts were black. And vengeful. The snake in him lay coiled. It could wait to make its spring.

'Jail's too good for that monster,' said Jenny Taylor.

'Aye, the birch is what he needs. I'd do it myself if I got the chance. I'm fair vexed for the poor wee soul.' Mrs Clark glowered and tightened the belt of her camel coat. Her hand itched to twine it round the blighter's neck.

'He'll get the punishment he deserves one day,' said Elma, Bobby's mother. 'What's God thinking of anyway, letting such an awful thing happen?'

'Well, here's the minister. Ask HIM' Nettie Shaw pointed to Gordon McKenzie as he swung open the door of the shop. It was crowded. Folk muttered and shook their heads. Sad faced, Gordon stood. An irate Jenny poked his arm. 'Well, minister, how do you expect us to worship that being above, now? How could he let that happen to Cathy?'

Eyes darted like bees, focussing on him accusingly. Gordon looked down. He couldn't give them an answer; even if there was one. He felt like Cassim, in the story of Ali Baba. The right words wouldn't come. Not that he'd forgotten them.

They just had not yet been formulated.

Alice was crushed. Her dreams for Cathy shattered. And Cathy – how did she feel? Questioned by police. Examined by a doctor. The trauma of the attack. The whole episode. She watched as with infinite care, Tom laid her on the couch. Curled with knees up, still innocent despite her ordeal, she slept.

'She's been sedated. She'll be the better of a long sleep, Alice. Tom's gaze held hers, caressing her as of old, but it was a shared thing now, with a lass who worked in a bar. She knew the instant he walked in from the pub the night of the dance. The agony in his eyes as he sought her out. The holding back because of his friendship with Bert had screwed him up. It had screwed her up too.

At first she'd liked Bert. Then hated him. Seeing him coupling with Barbara Fairbairn on the rug like an old ram, had opened her eyes, but it had closed her heart. Or whatever bit of it Bert had claimed. Now, she was free, and Tom had Daisy. They were engaged. The Fates must be laughing their heads off.

She looked at her slumbering daughter. Sleep was a good healer. She'd let her lie.

'Thank you, Tom. For everything.' Once more their eyes locked. Mesmerized, she moved towards him.

Shoving all restraint aside, Tom opened his arms. 'Oh, Alice,' he groaned. 'You don't know how much I've wanted to do this.'

'I do, Tom, because I've wanted it too.'

'Let's not waste time then, Alice.' Hands lovingly clasped, they climbed the stairs.

'That was wonderful, Tom.' Through half-closed eyes, she observed his handsome features. A radiance showed there – yet a sadness. 'What's the matter, Tom?' she asked. 'Do you regret it?'

'No, that was the most beautiful experience. It's Daisy I'm worried about. How am I going to tell her it's over?'

Don't tell her. Just come and see me sometimes when Cathy is out. Wantonly, she kissed him. From now on, she would enjoy things as they arose. Life was too short. She was thinking of her pain. What if it was serious?

'Is that what you want, Alice?'

'Yes'

Suddenly, Tom grinned. Who would have thought it. The so pure Alice, flaunting the rules. Himself also. He, who had veered away from indulgencies of this sort. Would his father notice a change in his demeanour? He was a shrewd man. Little passed his knowing eyes. I'd better tread with care, thought Tom as, light of heart, he made for home.

A whole new life lay before him. Stopping, he gulped the tangy, fresh air, appreciating it as never before.

Chapter Eight

After tea, Elsie went to see Cathy. 'Are you comin' for a walk, Cathy? It's a grand night. We'll have a blether and meet the lads!'

'Yes.' The word was hardly audible.

'Oh, Cathy, how nice it is to hear you speak again. Get your coat. We've a lot o' catchin' up to do.'

Along by the paddock they went. All the jumbled up horrors in Cathy's head found release and tumbled out like a river in spate.

'It was awful, Elsie. At first he was bossy. Then he was quite nice. Not a bit like the wastrel Mrs Clark spoke of. She was right though. He IS evil.'

Cathy looked for Carma. It nickered as they neared the fence. As Cathy stroked her soft nose, bits of her stress crumbled away. It was therapeutic. 'No sugar lumps today,' she whispered. 'Sorry.' Carma nodded her head and snorted, inflating her nostrils, showing the pinkish, almost transparent fineness of them.

At that moment, John appeared. On his shoulders, he carried a bale of hay. 'Hello,' he cried. 'Come to help, have you?' His mouth broke into a mischievous grin.

Much against his mother's wishes, he had insisted on being a farmer; learning crop management and animal husbandry from Dave. A few evening classes had taught him the rudiments of bookkeeping. His mother, still a paragon of virtue since Bert's death, hadn't yet accepted Beth. It saddened John. Angry, he continued to defy her.

Self-righteous do-gooder, he thought. Hugging the kirk with empty arms. Charities, committees; everything. All to assuage her own guilt. What plagued him most though, was the way her silly intrigues had separated him from Cathy. Looking at Cathy now, his tongue dried up, his stomach churned and his heart stood still.

Time skipped to August. Cathy was worried. Four months had passed and her periods hadn't shown. Her breasts tingled. Changes of all sorts were invading her body. She was pregnant, she knew – to that beast Donald. She went to see Elsie. Frantically, she knocked on her door.

'I'm comin', I'm comin' Don't knock the door off its hinges.' Elsie peered into the night. The hall light wasn't on and everything was steeped in darkness. From its depths, swam the ghost-like figure of Cathy. Her eyes, black and haunted, stared up at her.

'I've got to talk to you, Elsie. It's urgent.'

'Come in. We'll go to the kitchen.' Elsie gave her a long discerning look. 'Is it what I think it is?'

A nod confirmed it was.

'My God. Have you told your mother?'

'No.'

'You'll have to.'

'I know. Will you come with me?'

'Of course.' Elsie laid a hand on Cathy's arm. 'I'll get my coat.'

Alice paled at Cathy's outpouring. She thought her heart was impermeable, but not so. The news stabbed the soft case like a wasp stinging an unsuspecting object.

Involuntarily, she opened her arms.

Feeling like a child again with a scraped knee, Cathy rushed towards them.

During interminable, sleepless hours as she tossed and turned neath sweating sheets, Alice made a decision. Unbeknown to anyone, she had parents in the Highlands. Factor on a large estate, her father was a strict, unbending man. Bert, his then gardener, had taken a fancy to her and they'd started going out together.

Her father – and mother, had not countenanced their relationship. 'You're not marrying a gardener and that's final,' he'd stated. 'You'll be no lassie of mine if you do.' His lips clamped in a tight line, he'd turned away from her, shoulders tense, eyes, pebble hard.

They had married anyway. Quietly, with Phil and Joe as witnesses. Now was maybe the time to rekindle the fire. Build new bridges.

'I'm going to send you away,' she told Cathy next morning. 'You may be surprised to know this, but you have a granny and grandad up north. The welcome you receive could be stormy. Be strong in your attitude to your grandfather, Cathy. He cannot stand simpering fools.'

Astounded, Cathy stared at her mother. She had a granny and grandad in the Highlands, and she never even knew. With shining face, she took in the news her mum had just imparted. Stifling the desire to run and tell Elsie, she listened as her mother continued.

'My marriage to your father angered my parents.' Alice looked downcast. 'Perhaps you and the baby will help soften them.' Alice hoped so. A great chasm cut her heart in two. Her money was on this baby to help her mum and dad glue it together.

The day of Cathy's leaving arrived. Those who could not see her off, phoned. Those who could, hugged her as if they'd never see her again.

Even Harry.

'Hurry back, Cathy. If I get a cuddle like that every time, I might even fancy you. It's fair set my pulses on fire,' he cried.

Laughingly, Cathy responded by landing him a huge smacker on his warm cheeks.

'Right, if she's dishing out kisses, let's get our share, lads,' shouted Raymond.

A lot of kisses later, a rather dishevelled Cathy boarded the bus. The door banged shut. Her arm ached with waving. Her heart ached with leaving. Her last look was to Elsie.

'I'll write,' she mouthed.

Damp eyed, Elsie nodded. She'd miss her friend.

Journeying to Edinburgh by bus was agonizingly tedious. Little stops here and there. Folk trooping in. Folk trooping out. Studying them became a pastime. Time began to pass more enjoyably.

Up and down the aisle, the conductress swayed, issuing tickets. Each turning of the handle on her machine, emitted a ripping sound. It reminded Cathy of her mother tearing up old sheets to make dusters. Tears skimmed her eyes. She squeezed tight her lids lest anyone should see.

Outside a pub, in a sleepy village, the bus crunched to a standstill. At the stop was a middle-aged couple. Fat, red-faced and straggly haired, the wife stood, feet apart, motionless, as if cemented to the pavement. Small, thin and wiry, her husband looked henpecked and hassled. A large moustache, dark, threaded with grey, threatened to engulf his narrow face. He held two suitcases, so full, the locks strained to keep the contents from escaping.

On entering the bus, he set about lifting them onto the rack above. Heaving and puffing and almost there, the locks gave way. Bras, knickers, toiletries, night attire – everything – spilled onto the hapless pair.

'You careless twit,' shouted his wife. 'You can't do anything right. You mustn't have locked them. Look at my things. What an affront.'

Unfitting teeth clicked up and down. Podgy fingers shoved them in place, terminating her tirade. She gave him a baleful look.

Cathy sniggered to herself. Had Elsie been here, they would have screeched with laughter. Poor man, tied to a battleaxe like her.

Put in the pending box her own predicament lay, and neither lid nor lock would conceal it for much longer. What would her grandfather say?

An explanatory note from her mum to him, burned a hole in her pocket. She'd like to peek, but daren't. The constant motion lulled her to sleep. When she awoke, the couple had gone. In the back seat, the conductress puffed happily on a cigarette. The driver's jaws went up and down as impassively he chewed chewing gum. Cathy had biscuits in her bag. Taking one, she quietly nibbled.

Dousing her cigarette, the conductress tottered her way down the bus, holding on to seats as it swayed and rattled round dizzy corners.

'Next stop's yours, lassie. Do you know where to get your train?' She smiled at Cathy from a scarlet lip-sticked mouth.

'Yes, thank you.' Heart pitter-pattering, Cathy reached for her case.

At the station. she hadn't long to wait. The steady motion of the train soothed away her fears. Fields with cows, sheep and horses, sped by. Quite unconcerned the animals grazed, used to the clanking, caterpillar-like machine winding its way along the skyline. Wedged in the window corner next to a portly, business looking gentleman reading a paper, and a fat-faced lady, she let drowsiness once more overtake her.

When she opened her eyes, the train was sliding to a halt. An illusion of motion deceived the mind into thinking that the platform was moving, or the train was going backwards. A momentary giddiness swam her head. The man beside her lurched sideways. He puffed as he struggled with his case. Cathy looked at his face. It was the colour of ripe tomatoes. He had hairs in his nostrils; long grey ones. It repulsed her.

Cross looking, the lady stretched to retrieve her belongings. 'Ignorant man,' she growled to Cathy.

'Can I help?' asked Cathy.

'No thank you, lass. It's him that should be helping. That's men for you. Fancy suits and no manners. I'm glad I never got married.'

With her own worldly goods held firmly in her hand, Cathy stood up and followed her out.

Still as a heron, she waited. Her grandparents were coming for her. She didn't know what to expect. Didn't know what they looked like. For ages, she waited. So long, she feared they had forgotten. A timid touch on her arm. An equally timid voice, saying, 'Are you Cathy Wilson?' broke into her thoughts. Cathy found herself staring into the same grey eyes as her mother.

She was overwhelmed.

'Granny,' she cried. 'May I call you that, please?' Gently, she kissed the wrinkled cheek.

'I'm so pleased to see you, Cathy. How are you? And how is Alice?' Sadness tinged her face. Regret filled her quiet gaze.

'She's well, thank you, granny.'

Before another word could be exchanged, a gruff 'Come on, we haven't got all day,' frightened the life out of her. 'Well, don't stand there like a scared rabbit. And you, Ivy, get back in the car.' He inclined his head. 'You go with her.' Angry eyes glared at Cathy.

'Yes.' She was about to add sir, but remembered her mother's advice. 'Stand up to him Cathy,' she had said. Compressing her lips, she stepped into the car, a silent mutiny raging in her head.

In the front seat, her granny was silent too. Old misery guts, she thought. Imagine intimidating a lovely lady like granny? Already, she liked her. They would have to join forces. Show him they were human beings, not slaves. A firm decision to tackle him head on, bit into Cathy. Maybe she'd inherited some of his genes!

Darkness was on them now as round endless corners, the car twisted. To the right, she could see faint fingers of light from a half hidden moon, stroking the surface of a large expanse of water. Everything seemed to be huge here. High peaks, winding roads, and what appeared to be a dark, deep loch.

What seemed to be miles later, they swished through wide, fancy looking gates. From the beam of the car lights, she saw eagles carved on the outer posts. Light from one window, like a pinprick in the dark, was the only indication of habitation.

'Right, Cathy. We've arrived, dearie.' Granny clasped Cathy's hand and gave it a quick squeeze. 'Never mind your grandad. He'll come to his senses, you'll see,'

'Stop whispering, Ivy. It's inordinately rude. I'll garage the car. You two get inside.' Her grandad's voice was scornful.

'I've got a letter for grandad from mum, granny,' said Cathy in low tones as they made their way towards the house.

'Have you? Well, you'd better keep it for a while before producing it. Get to know him a bit first. He's awful bitter.'

'But why, granny? Dad was a lovely person. He didn't deserve to die the way he did.'

'Bert's dead?'

'Yes, he committed suicide.'

'Oh dear. My poor child. How did Alice take it?'

'Not too bad. You see – he was having an affair. I think mum knew.'

'Gracious me. That's one thing about him.' She thumbed towards her husband. 'He's never ogled other women. Can't stand the giggling creatures. Now horses, that's different. Gentle as a kitten he is with them.'

Aah, thought Cathy. Something nice must beat inside his hardened heart.

Near to, the house looked imposing. Swinging back the brass studded door, granny shoved Cathy inside. The hall was dank and chilly. It was like entering an unheated kirk. A welcome stream of light beckoned from a doorway along a passage. Also the enticing aroma of food.

The kitchen was big. A Raeburn cooker was the centre-piece of one wall. Over it, bent a little lady who turned as they entered. She had a rosy, cheery face. Granny steered Cathy towards her.

'This is Jane. She's the mainstay of our abode. Jane – this is my lovely granddaughter. She's come to stay with us for a while.'

Jane's face creased into a welcoming smile. 'Hello,' she said shyly. 'Welcome to Rathburnie.'

Cathy took to her immediately. She seemed to have an affinity with cooks. Old Mrs Clark at the manor. Now, Jane.

From the dim passage, a girl emerged. Long brown hair curved round an oval face. A fringe met arched eyebrows. Her eyes, a greeny-yellow, were warm and friendly.

'This is Paula. She does household duties. Her parents live in a tied cottage on the grounds. Her father works on the estate.' Granny brought Paula forward.

'Paula, will you take Cathy to her room, please. Show her the necessary amenities.' She smiled at the two girls. She hoped they'd become friends.

Guided along the wall by touch, they reached the end of the passage. Paula switched on a light, showing the stairs. They were carpeted and nice. The banisters, shiny and curving.

'He's awful stingy with electricity, Mr Geddes. It's run by a generator. He watches over the stock of bulbs like a broody hen sitting on eggs. No lights after ten o'clock. If there's a function on and at Christmas, he allows them. He's really mean.'

'Does he shout at you?'

'Yes, sometimes I feel like shouting back, but I might get the sack – and I need the money. Mum helps at an occasional dinner party and at harvest time. She does the stooking. It's time he bought a baler, but he won't.'

'My mother helps in the manse in our village. She makes soup and prepares vegetables and cooks the main meal. The minister adopted a boy called Bobby. You would like him. You'd like all my friends. Especially Harry.' Cathy laughed. 'He's the ringleader of any escapades.'

'I'll go down with you for a holiday sometime, if I may.'

'Will grandad let you?'

'Yes, we're entitled to holidays.'

On that companionable note, they separated. Paula to resume working. Cathy, to her bedroom.

At what she thought might be dinner time, Cathy shut the

bedroom door and slowly descended the stairs. On the last step, her foot halted, as a resonant dong, dong, dong, juddered the air. The arm of her grandfather was about to fall again, when he saw her.

'You're late. Dinner is at seven. The dining room is this way.' Abruptly, he turned, a mere shape in the darkness.

How could he even see the gong? she wondered. Far less hit it. This was carrying stinginess to excess. He's probably worth a fortune too, Cathy surmised. Golly, what will he say to her revelation about the baby? He'll have another mouth to feed.

Seated demurely at a long, oak table, Cathy looked at the granite bearing of her grandfather. She studied his face. Lips firm and topped with a silver moustache. Eyes pouched. Brow lined as if he frowned a lot. Not a bad face. A certain discomfort lay there, but it was deceiving. He had a sting in his tail, her grandad. His treatment of granny and herself proved it.

The meal passed in near silence. An occasional 'Thank you.' Or 'May I have the salt please,' or a sniff or a cough, broke the spell.

Afterwards, granny and Cathy retired to the sitting room. Logs spluttered and sparked in the huge fire. From an iron, cauldron-like pot, granny tonged a few lumps of coal and flung them on the flames.

'He doesn't skimp on coal,' whispered granny 'And there are plenty sticks on the estate.' She raised a finger. 'Here he comes. You'll be reeked out. He smokes a pipe.'

Muffled steps could be heard. The door closed. The chair creaked as he sat down. From a shelf on his left, he took down his pipe and tobacco pouch. A few sucks on the stem, an upside-down thump on the palm of his hand, then he set about refilling the neat bowl.

From a cardboard packet, he broke off a safety match and struck it down the rough sandpaper and held it above his pipe. A few puffs pulled the flame inwards and ignited the tobacco.

Then he spoke.

'You'll muck out the byre, tomorrow.' His gaze directed itself to Cathy. 'There are two cows. Learn to milk them. While you're here, you will earn your keep.'

'Yes, but who will teach me? I've never milked a cow before.' Cathy plucked up courage to stare at her grumbly grandfather on whose hospitality she'd been thrust.

'Hell, lassie, are you useless or what? Brought up in the country and cannot milk a cow. Get Jim McDonald to show you. Learn it first time. He needs all God's hours to tend to the cattle. Being bothered by a chit of a girl like you, is not on.'

With that long speech, he concentrated on reading the paper. Downcast eyelashes hid his thoughts.

Cathy wondered what else he was cooking up for her to do.

At dawn, the hateful gong awakened the whole house. With a start, Cathy flung back the covers and peered at the clock. Six o'clock. What an awful time to be getting up. Oh, of course – it was milking time. What should she wear? She'd brought two skirts and a pair of slacks. It'll have to be the trousers, she thought. Old misery guts might say her legs would turn the milk sour with a skirt on. Then she reckoned, just to spite him, she'd wear her skirt.

Eyes, dark blue, with a faint white line merging with the iris, focussed on her apparel. Bushy eyebrows rose in a frown.

'What the hell kind of get-up is that?' he roared. 'You are going to be working, not skiving off to a dance. Get something more suitable on.' He flung his eyes back to the paper. Cathy heard him rustling the pages to death as blindly he turned them. He was riled.

Up the stairs, she flounced. What right had he to treat her in such a way? She'd give in this time. Tomorrow was another day. Today was just beginning, though. Surely it would pass in a more amenable fashion.

In the pantry, she found two white milking pails. She looked around, wondering what else she'd need. Seeking out granny, she asked her advice.

'You'll need a cloth, dearie. To wipe their udders. And some lard. You'll require it when doing the stripping at the finish.'

'Stripping?'

'Yes, that's the motion of finger and thumb pulling down the teat to extract the last drops.'

'Oh.' Cathy nodded. Understanding.

In the byre, Dolly and Petal stood awaiting their morning feed. Jim McDonald, dressed in navy overalls, appeared bearing scoops of bruised oats.

'Hello,' he said, holding out his hand. 'You'll be Cathy?'

'Yes. How do you do. You'll be Jim?'

'Aye, now let's get started. They'll not move when they're eating. Sometimes Dolly gets a bit restless, but she doesn't kick or anything.'

'Are you from the Borders, Jim?' said Cathy, surprised.

'I am that. Been here nine years. The Borders are still home to me, though. Kelso, bonny Kelso, that's where I was born. Living here has knocked some of the Border dialect away, but it's still there inside me.'

'I live near Hawick. On a farm near Torwell village. You remind me of my friends. The dialect. It's the same.'

'I'll find out more about them later, but we've got to get the milking done first.' He kneeled down. 'Here, let me show you. Start with the teats nearest her belly. Pull and squeeze, pull and squeeze. It's easy when you get the hang of it.'

Pail in hand, he stood up. Cathy hunkered onto the stool and placed the pail under the cow.

'Look, Jim. I've got some.' Excitedly, Cathy watched the spray trickle into the pail.

'You're a natural. The pail will be full in no time. I'll do Petal. Don't tell his nibs. He can't abide folk going against him. I don't understand the man. There's something grieving him, but he needn't take it out on us, or his other workers. Acts like he's pissed on a nettle half the time.'

Cathy laughed. Jim reminded her of Harry. A joke or funny saying always on the tip of his tongue.

'I don't think I'll get paid while I'm here,' Cathy said to Jim. 'Earn my keep, he said. Paula says he's really mean.'

'Aye, he's as tight as a duck's arse.'

Jim made to rush off, then turned. 'Keep your pecker up, lass. Things might change.'

Cathy saw the froth rising on the milk as the pail filled. Knees stiff from sitting on the low stool, she struggled to her feet. The pail was heavy. The wiry handle dug into her hand.

'Oh – Cathy.' Jim blocked the doorway again. 'There's the cat's dish, put some milk in when you're finished.'

As if by telepathy, an influx of cats streamed through a hole in an adjoining door.

'They keep the mice down – and rats. Make messes in the hay, though. It's awful. What a stink!'

'Talking about stink, grandad said I was to muck out the byre.' Cathy eyed the volume of greeny gunge in the trough behind where the cows stood.

The rugged features of Jim spread into a smile, and from a corner, he produced a course haired brush and a shovel. 'Here, use these. There's a barrow outside. Take the muck to the midden. Get a pair of wellington boots. His - bloody - nibs - should see that you're properly equipped. Hells, bells, he can't see further than his nose most o' the time.'

His eyes scanned the pail nearly overflowing with milk. 'The workers get a pitcher full each. Oh – and the pig gets some. Now, I'd best be away, else he'll have my guts on the end of a pitchfork.'

In the cold pantry, Cathy measured everything out and put what remained in two basins, then washed the pails.

For her next task, as Jim had stressed, she'd need wellies. Maybe granny had a pair. She found her in the sitting room. A book lay on her lap. Skittles, her black cat, played with a ball of wool at her feet.

'Good morning, granny. You're up early.' Cathy gazed at her care-worn face. 'Have you a pair of wellies I could borrow, please? I've to muck out the byre.'

'In the cupboard under the stairs, Cathy love. How did you get on with the milking?'

'Fine thank you. Jim said I was a natural. He's a good laugh.'

'Yes, he's a very responsible lad. His son Greg is about your age. Works on the farm. Helps the men and does extra chores when needed.'

'Are there any girls in the cottages?'

'Just Gertie. She's the gamekeeper's girl. Paula of course you have met.' Granny screwed up her eyes and gestured towards the door. 'You'd better get back to the byre. His lordship will be in soon. No use asking for trouble.'

Two sizes too big, the wellies felt like boats. Hard and unyielding, the insides chafed her legs. They felt damp. She should have brought thicker socks.

Tiptoeing on the cold floor, she returned to the sitting room. She heard the rhythmic creaking of a rocking chair. It was granny. Silver curls graced her noble head. Grey eyes squinted sideways at Cathy. Though guileless, they seemed all seeing. Like a clairvoyant's.

Self-consciously, Cathy pulled her fisherman's knit jumper over her hips. She imagined her granny noticing the swell of her tummy a tight girdle did its best to hide. Very wise her mother had been. Every item of clothing bought for her stay here, was large enough to alleviate any signs of the bulge of her baby, but not for long.

Whoosh, whoosh, in stops and starts, the wiry brush pushed the cows' excrement along the channel until it reached the wall. Phew! it was hard work. She looked at her hands. They had the beginnings of blisters on them. She leaned on the smooth handle of the brush for a brief rest. Steps approaching, did not cause her undue concern. It would be Jim, she thought.

A roar and a swipe, sent the brush and nearly Cathy, clattering to the floor.

'You lazy, good-for-nothing, girl. I'll give you ten minutes to finish the job. Now pick up that brush.' Grandad's hostility shocked Cathy. Something broke inside her. He'd gone too far this time.

'No.' The refusal shot from her like a bullet.

Her grandad's face leaped into a frown. His lips opened and shut in astonishment. 'What did you say?' he mouthed.

'I said no.'

'You will do it, you little madam. Well – perhaps half an hour should be time enough,' he conceded. His eyes, darkened with some inner conflict, burned into Cathy with a fury directed as much at himself as at her.

With rigid spine, he made his exit.

God, she had spunk, he mused. Not even Phil, with a temperament like a firework, spoke back to him. Marching into the kitchen, face stuck in its usual ill-tempered groove, he thoughtfully sat down. 'I'll have a cup of tea, Jane, please, and one of your scones, if I may?' His fingers tapped the pine table with a faraway unseeing look.

'Yes sir.' The request was as normal, but the voice? Something different there, thought Jane. His expression too. Surely there was a smile turning the corners of his usually dour mouth – but it was quickly doused.

Huh! glasses were what she needed. A leopard never changes its spots. Not in her book anyway.

Chapter Nine

Seen in daylight, the Highland scenery embraced Cathy's heart. High, rugged mountains held captive the land, the loch and the many wooded areas that studded them. Silver birch, slender and pale as ghosts, reflected on the glistening water.

It was now August, and fields were alive with the sounds of harvesting. Grandad forever studied the sky. If he saw a cloud, he urged his workers on, allowing them to cease only when darkness fell.

A new day began. It was bright and sunny.

'You do the stooking,' he told Cathy. 'Try to keep up with the reaper. Tomorrow, you will fork to the stacker. Get some muscles in those puny arms.'

Tomorrow came. All morning, Cathy forked the jaggy sheaves to the chap building the stacks. By mid-afternoon, she was exhausted. As her strength ebbed, so did the speed in which she was able to work. Sighing, she let her arms dangle a minute to ease her shoulders. Perceiving this, her grandfather was incensed. 'Buck up, girl,' he shouted. 'Or I'll send you back on the next train.'

'Never mind Cathy,' whispered Winnie, Paula's mother, when he'd gone. 'I'll take a turn when he goes to town. He takes the missus shopping on a Wednesday. You can have a rest then. It's a hard job forking to the stacker.' Crinkling her eyes into slits against the glare of the sun, she stared at the youth standing midst the sheaves on a loaded trailer. 'Your grandad's brains must be in his backside,' she added. 'Half a day would have been enough to start with.'

Cathy tried to laugh, but her back was hurting. More and more difficult it was getting to hide her condition. She felt suffocated. Her girdle was too tight. A sudden pain gripped her tummy. 'Oh,' she cried, nearly doubled up with the severity of it. A cold sweat soaked her body. Once again, the pain took hold. Not so bad, but enough to make her gasp.

'Goodness me, what ails you lassie?' Worriedly, Winnie observed the contorted face and bent body of the girl. Alarm bells rang. Heaven's sake, the lass was pregnant.

'Here, Phil,' she shouted. 'Get somebody from the big house. Tell them to phone a doctor.'

'No – please, don't say anything. Promise me,' sobbed Cathy.

'Mmm – if you're sure, but I'm not happy about it.' Winnie looked troubled – and angry. Angry at the lassie's grandad. All he needed was a whip. What had turned him into such an embittered and obnoxious beggar? Did he not realize the girl needed him.

'It's all right, it's only a stitch.' Cathy glossed the incident over. She took a deep breath and let it out slowly. Now, she decided, was the time to give him the letter.

Dinner as usual, was silent. The first course was soup. During this, Cathy handed him the envelope. 'This is from mum. It explains the reason for my being here.'

Between courses, his fingers hovered, itching to touch it. Meal over, he disappeared upstairs, taking the missive with him. When he returned, the same ritual with his pipe took place. Smoke billowed upwards. The fire caught his attention – and held.

Still not a word. Pale, he looked, as if the contents of the letter had shocked him. Head back, resting on his chair, he inhaled deeply. From under his lashes, he shot Cathy a look. To her surprise, it held no malice. The opposite. It was almost tender.

'So, lass,' he said. 'You're breeding. Sorry about your dad. Maybe I wronged Alice cutting her off the way I did. Could you tell her that when you write.'

Shed was the caustic tongue. The brow of thunder. His visage was now benign and twinkly. Such a change from the grumpy grandad she'd got to know.

In happy bewilderment, granny and Cathy gazed at each other. 'Oh, grandad,' with a shy smile, Cathy rose. Her kiss on his cheek startled him – and melted him. His hands, gentle on a horse's mouth, were now round her shoulders and drawing her close. The texture of his woollen cardigan was soft on her cheek. As she languished in this safe haven, the tears she'd withheld for so long, stolen by a scream, at last found their way to the surface.

'Cry, my lassie,' he murmured. 'Let it come. You'll feel better if you let it all out.' Fine boned fingers summoned Ivy. 'Come, share this moment, Ivy. Let us bury the past and start afresh.'

Clasped in his loving arms, Ivy sent up a prayer of thanks. Sending Alice away had left him an embittered man. She'd seen him pick at his food. Knew the nausea he'd felt. The emptiness, not of hunger, but of loss. Her own heart had seconded those feelings. Presented with a second chance, they must grasp it with both hands.

'This calls for a toast,' he cried. 'Jane – Paula, come and join us. The dishes can wait.'

Two curious faces peered round the kitchen door. 'You called, sir?'

'Yes. Come and join us for a drink We are celebrating.'

'More like he's already had a few,' whispered Paula to Jane. 'Or gone off his rocker.'

On the sideboard, glasses were generously filled. Sherry for the ladies. Whisky for him.

'Here's to us, ladies. Ivy and I have good news to impart. Cathy is with child. My daughter Alice, we hope to be reconciled with before long. That is splendid news, isn't it?'

So he hadn't drunk too much. Or flipped his lid. Jane and Paula stared in amazement.

'Don't stand there like ninnies, then. In you come. I'm not an ogre, you know.' Heartily, he laughed. 'Well – not any more.'

'He actually laughed,' said Paula later to her mum and dad.

'I'll believe it when I see it. Or hear it,' said Roddy, her father. Lashes of tongue fell on him every day at work. One never became inured to them. Giving the old tyrant a straight left to the jaw, was more consistent with his thoughts.

In early February, Cathy's baby had been born. Now, time having rocketed on, he was a happy, lovable toddler. His hair was fair. The colour of ripe corn. The eyes that gazed up at Cathy every day, were big and blue.

Bert's eyes.

Today, the sun shone. On a little side gate in the garden, Cathy leaned; listening; enjoying a break from the needs of little Ben. In the quietude of a late summer's day, every sound seemed magnified. Her mood was pensive. She had written to Elsie and was awaiting a reply.

Back home, the weather was scorching. After tea, the gang went swimming. The deep part into which the lads dived, was covered with a white scum. Flies hovered under trees. Testing the water, Harry jumped in.

'Hey, lads, it's as warm as water from the tap. It's great.'

One by one, tentatively, the others followed. Elsie, Beth and John, remained on the banking, sunning their legs and watching.

A splashing contest caused much hilarity, until they tired of it. They needed a diversion.

Harry found it.

'Look at John,' he called scornfully. 'Sitting there like a big sissy. Let's sort him out, lads.'

Dripping and shivering, despite the heat, they scrambled onto the grassy bank. Grabbing John, and on the verge of throwing him in, their eyes plunged towards his shoes. Always a mystery to them why he never showed his bare feet; now was the time to unveil them.

'His shoes. Off with them, boys. Whoopee.' Midst roars of glee, first one, then the other, plus his socks, hit the water. Suddenly, there was a hush, as all eyes gazed at John's webbed toes.

Beth gasped. Her dad had the very same defect on his feet. That meant – oh, no – It meant that her dad was John's father, not Cathy's dad.

The hesitancy about everything they did. How glad she was now they hadn't gone that far. Abhorrent that would have been. She felt sick. The urge to vomit took control. Damn her dad. Damn Barbara Fairbairn. Damn this God awful place. Tomorrow, she'd pack her bags and leave.

'I'm away home,' she cried. Apple cheeks tinged with grey, mouth solemn, she went.

The strangeness of her voice perturbed John. Why was she so upset? Stricken, he watched the resolute shape of her disappear.

His bloody webbed toes. That's what it was. But they didn't look so horrid. Only different. He picked up his clothes. His shoes were in the river. Stuff them, he thought. Stuff everything.

Slowly, the gang dispersed. 'See you the morn, John. Bring that old catapult o' yours. We'll smash a few cans.' Harry patted his back. He was the perfect foil for his awkwardness. A born diplomat, he was turning. John warmed to him. Always a bit of friction between them as children. Quite often the butt of his sarcasm. Now, the psychology of the lad rubbed salve on his wound. John knew that had his mother not insisted on keeping his feet hidden, nursing her vanity, her snobbishness, everyone would have accepted his webbed toes.

Children accept everything at face value Like in the scriptures. If Jesus walked on water – then to a child's mind – he did.

John groaned. He'd have to reassert himself. Girls were taboo from now on.

'Harry, wait.' Naked except for his pants, he ran to catch up.

'You comin' back like that?' The others stopped in amazement.

'Yes, I've nothing to hide any more. My mother will have a fit. Worried about what people will think. Hell, I can't wait to see how she reacts when she sees me.' He smiled. 'Why don't you come with me?'

As the chortling group filed into Barbara's sitting room, she stared – aghast. John – almost naked – and without shoes and socks.

'John, what on earth is this? Why are you in such a state of undress?'

'Hello, mother. This is me – John. The son with webbed toes. Quack, quack, quack, I'm a duck. Well – a drake.' Spreading his arms like wings, John waddled round the room. Quack, quack, quack. 'See lads, your pal is a drake.'

Softly, Elsie laid a hand on his arm. 'Sssh, John. She was only trying to protect you. Not that it was necessary. I have a relation with only one hand. So what! She's as happy as a lark.'

'Protect herself more like,' cried John vehemently, ridding himself of bilious thoughts. He'd lost Cathy. Lost Beth. All for what?

Ah – the reality hit him.

Paternity reasons.

'Right mother, who IS my father, then? Did Bert have toes like mine?'

'I don't know. That's the truth, son.' Barbara was flustered, and sorrowful. This was a different John. A John lost to her. Soured by life. She looked at the floor.

'Listen to that, lads. That means he did it with his socks on. Let's pay Dan Sykes a visit. One of your lovers too, wasn't he mother?'

John's tirade ended. His head dropped. Beth's expression when Harry and Colin tore off his socks. The white cheeks. The Stygian black of her eyes. His question was already answered.

Chapter Ten

'I'm sick of this place,' Beth told her mother. 'I'm going south. To London.'

'Why, Beth?' Twisting round from her stance at the sink, her mother gazed at her daughter. 'What about John?'

'I've finished with John. Not his fault. Things got too much for me, that's all.'

Beth quietened her heart. Gradually, she would build a covering round it. Hard, like a tortoise's shell, so that no one could penetrate it. In London, she'd start anew. Doing her dad's books had given her clerical experience. An office job would do. Or shop work. For some reason her dream came back to her. In a way, it HAD been an omen. By leaving – she was liberating John.

She travelled light. Her dad took her to the station at Edinburgh. The Sleeper train left at eleven o'clock. Her savings were meagre. She had no idea of the cost of things in London. Accommodation would be first on the list.

Then a job.

The jostling of people bustling for their bags and cases at King's Cross station, woke her up. Retrieving her own, she stepped down onto the platform and gazed around.

It was early, but folk were already scurrying about. A porter rushed by with a trolley, lips parted, eyes channelled. Light from a cafe drew her. As she entered, the smell of coffee made her thirsty. The lady behind the counter smiled.

'What would you like, luv?' She spoke loudly, as if she had to shout above a continual din and it was now a habit.

'Can I have a coffee, please.' Beth looked at the neatly wrapped sandwiches. 'And a cheese and pickle sandwich.' Mentally, she counted her money. Of her savings, she had six pounds and a few pence. Her dad had slipped her a five pound note at the station. 'It'll help you get settled,' he said. How right he was. She'd need every penny. She seated herself near a window. The coffee radiated within her a welcome warmth.

She relaxed.

An elderly man with a stick, shuffled up to the counter. 'I'll have me usual, Fran luv.' His voice was gravelly; his hands, blue veined and cold looking.

Beth smiled and moved along a bit to let him sit down. He aimed a spit at an imaginary spot on the floor, then wiped his mouth with his hand.

'You're a dirty old devil, Hugh. I'll bet your wife doesn't let you do that.' Fran was cross.

'No, but you do, luv.' He gave a gummy laugh.

'Well, no more, I can tell you. Enough's enough.' Fran passed him a withering look. 'Do you want one sandwich, or two?'

'Two, please Fran. Yer a dear.'

Beth listened to their chat with amusement. When their sandwiches came, he moved his attention to her. A fount of information, he turned out to be; knowing the time of every train; right up to the furthest station in Scotland.

London began to stir. She said goodbye to them and picked up her case. Once on the street, she stopped a minute to get her bearings. She'd never seen so many people. Seeing a row of taxis, she made for the nearest.

'Where to, luv?' the driver asked.

'I don't know. Do you know any boarding houses or youth hostels?' Her voice quivered. She felt like a cork bobbing in a big ocean.

'You have any friends here, luv?'

Taxi drivers have minds like maps. Blind folded, they can find their way through the busy streets, where buses, cars, lorries and bikes, whizz by in indefinable numbers.

Fascinated, Beth watched. Excitement clutched her tummy. This was the big city; breathtaking, secretive and beautiful.

'Ever done kitchen work?' Head never turning, the driver spoke. Hands on wheel. Eyes everywhere. Traffic, mirrors, signals.

'No.'

'Mmm. Would you like to try?'

'Yes, I'd try anything.'

'You're luck's in, then.' His car veered this way and that through the now heaving streets. After a while, he came to a halt and cut off the engine. 'This is Nottinghall Gate. Plenty boarding houses here. I know a special one, though.'

At a red door, he rang a bell.

'Ooo is it?' From an above window popped a dishevelled head. Grey, it looked. Like the wall.

'It's me, Mrs Fraser. Bernie.'

'Gor blimey! Wot you doin' 'ere, Bernie? Thought you'd gone to the knacker's yard.' Lusty laughter shook her balloon breasts leaning on the sill.

'Large as life, Mrs Fraser. I've brought a girl for you. I saw your sign. Will I bring her up?'

'Yer come this far, yer may as well.'

He held the door open for Beth. 'Out you get, lass. You'll do all right here.'

'Thank you. How much do I owe you, Bernie?'

'Oh, have this one on me. Your first venture into London.' His hand reached for her luggage.

'Well, take sixpence out of this for a tip. You deserve it. I'm very grateful.'

Bernie whistled. 'Wow! a Scottish five pound note. Thank

you, lass.' Fishing in his pouch, he counted out the correct change and shoved the sixpence tip in his pocket.

'Yer not in the family way, are yer?' Mrs Fraser addressed Beth with a calculating eye.

Beth was shocked. 'No,' she shouted. 'And if I was, I'd not be spreading it around.'

'Huh! keep your knickers on. Yer's got spunk, or is it cheek. Whatever, bring 'er up, Bernie.'

Mrs Fraser's entrance was amazingly clean. The smell of paint invaded the air. Long after Beth was in her room, it still clung to her nostrils.

The door opened to Bernie's knock. 'Come in. Don't stand there like a dog wi' the pox. Bring the lass with yer.' With a podgy hand, she ushered them in. Round her broad hips a floral skirt hung. Brown, with yellow and orange. A yellow, low-necked top, showed her ample cleavage. Black lashed eyes narrowed as she weighed up Beth. 'Yer Scottish, aint yer?'

'Yes.'

'Yer run away?'

'Not really. Just left home. I'll write when I get settled.'

'Can yer cook?'

'No, but I can learn.'

'Ye'll 'ave ter learn if yer want a position in this 'ouse. Yer must be able ter cook, make the beds, do the ironin' and lots o' other little jobs. Anythin' that 'ands can do, they does it. 'Ow's that suit yer?'

'Fine thank you.' Beth grinned. This plain speaking lady, was alright.

'Bye,' Bernie said, looking at Beth. He quirked a craggy eyebrow at the landlady. 'Bye, Mrs F. Good to see you again.'

Across the space dividing them, Mrs Fraser rushed and flung herself at Bernie. 'Come 'ere yer old renegade. And don't be so long in comin' back. I still like a bit company, yer know.' Her bosoms flattened against Bernie's chest.

Beth almost listened for a bang.

Mrs Fraser's attention rebounded to Beth.

'This is a boarding 'ouse,' she expounded. 'I've got five guests. All men. No hanky panky wi' them, else yer out. Along 'ere is yer bedroom – next ter mine. The bathroom is two doors ter yer right. Theirs is up a floor. It'll be hard work. Are yer sure yer able for it?'

Her face was a question mark.

'I'm much stronger than I look,' Beth assured her, flexing her arm.

'Huh! I've seen a bigger knot in a thread. Bacon and eggs every morning. That's what builds the brawn. Come on through. We'll 'ave a cup of tea. Then I'll show yer the ropes. Dinner is at six. They likes their food on the table quick as a fart.'

Beth giggled.

'Yer may well laugh, but they're a rum lot. Sour cream with a look, Gerald would. 'E's a judge. Paul – 'E's young and flirty and works in a clothing shop. Clem's an insurance man. Dave, a teacher. Last but not least, is Jonny Cairns. Thirtyish, plumpish. Jogs miles when everybody else is asleep. 'E's a doctor.'

'Gosh, what a mixture.'

'No girls allowed in bedrooms. Music not too loud. Rules is rules. Got ter think of others.'

At dinner, Beth scrutinized the folk she'd be dealing with. Paul, brown haired and slim, flashed twinkling glances at her every time she brought food or collected dishes.

Dave, thin as a telegraph pole, had the hint of a beard round his jawline. It was neat and he suited it. An aquiline nose and high cheek bones, gave him a gaunt appearance. From beneath bushy eyebrows, he cast her cursory looks.

Then there was Gerald. Creepy looking; long lanky hair; bulbous nose, receding chin. Thin red veins criss-crossed his cheeks. He was from Yorkshire. He didn't converse with the others. He slurped his soup, but mostly ate slowly, taking in his food and digesting it as thoroughly as he did the stocks and shares and news items he avidly read in the daily paper, which he propped in front of him at every meal.

Clem was kindly. Very mannerly. Fussily dressed. Gold cufflinks. Pristine white shirts. Snazzy ties. Of the older men, Beth liked him best.

Jonny, round-faced and pleasant, endeared himself to everyone. His preference for tweedy outfits made him look more like a vet than a doctor.

Her first morning in her first job, Beth walked in with their breakfast.

'Good morning, Beth,' said Clem. 'How are you?'

'I'm fine, thank you, Clem. Are you well?' She looked round at the others. 'All of you?'

As if waking from a trance, Gerald blinked. 'He's guilty,' he shouted, his mind back on a case. 'Most definitely guilty.'

'Silence in court.' Paul banged his knife on the table. 'You at the front. Another word from you and you'll be held in contempt of court.'

Boisterous laughter followed.

'What's all the racket?' Mrs Fraser interrupted. 'Leave the bleedin' man alone. Yer know 'e lives on a different planet 'alf the time. Shame on yer, Paul. The rest of yer too, for laughin' at 'im.'

'Sorry Mrs Fraser.' Paul gave her a cheeky grin.

'I'll clip yer ears, yer saucy scoundrel.'

Feigning fear, Paul shrank into his chair. 'Never mind, Mrs Fraser, we all love you. Don't we lads?' he said.

'Ger on, yer daft ha'pence worth. Yer not 'ere ter love me. Yer 'ere ter make me rich.' Giving him a smile, she straightened her shoulders, forcing her massive breasts outwards. A hint of pink tinted her lacklustre skin, pushed into pouches with the force of her smile. Head up, she all but marched into the kitchen. Ah, she thought, 'tis worth the graft just ter get a compliment like that. Even if it were spoken in jest.

London was full of action; the shops full of colourful and elegant dresses. The river Thames rushed by, bits of wood and other objects getting carried along on its heaving back. Boats of all kinds, stirred the brooding water. Seagulls flapped above them, wings whipping the air. Beth was enthralled.

To a small cafe, she ventured one day. There, she met a nippy called Shirley. They became firm friends. Seeing a crowd at Marble Arch, one day, curiosity drew them to it.

'Enjoying it, are you?' A voice at Beth's side made her turn. She gazed into the nicest eyes she'd ever seen. Blue, magnetic, and admiring, they made something inside her do a flip.

'I'm Mathew Lovejoy.' He held out his hand.

'I'm Beth Sykes. This is my friend, Shirley.'

'Hello, Shirley.' His eyes appraised her then fell upon Beth once more. 'Do you come to Speaker's Corner often?'

'No, this is our first time. We were drawn by the crowd.' Beth looked at Shirley then at him. 'We haven't much time. We must go. See you again, perhaps.'

'Oh, you will. There's nothing more certain, I'll meet you at Lyon's corner house tomorrow. Come on your own.'

'I'm off out, Mrs Fraser,' cried Beth next day. 'I'll be back to help with dinner.'

'Yer better, lass. By the look on yer face there's a feller involved. Be careful.' She threw Beth a discerning look. 'Yer be too innocent ter be gallivantin' on yer own. Especially in London.'

Beth halted in her stride. Innocent, hmm – she supposed she was. She'd never indulged in sex. Was that innocence? She didn't know. Cathy, even though she'd been raped, was still innocent, mused Beth. She'd have to get her address to tell her about John. She should be told.

In the cafe, she and Mathew held hands. 'Come to my flat,' he urged. 'Tomorrow.'

But when the time came, a shyness washed over her and tugged her feet back the way she'd come.

From the window, Mathew watched. He was angry. Then he grinned. He'd get her yet.

He played a waiting game.

'Why did I not go?' Beth chided herself that night. 'Twas like vibes, stronger than thought, defying her wishes. 'Oh, Mathew, the beats of my heart blow in the wind towards you,' she whispered. 'Can you not feel them?'

Mathew, his wants guided by lust – and the need to get it satisfied, was not receptive. His feelings were for himself. Every day Beth haunted the cafe, but he kept his distance.

Shirley went with Beth when she could. She was worried about her. A feeling of deja vu, swamped her. She was a little girl again; spying between the banisters on the landing. Men, mysteriously coming and going. One at a time. Mostly at night, but in daytime also. Her mother's throaty laugh.

The sitting room door closing. The furtive looks as the men made their exit. Mathew didn't have that look – yet she felt uneasy. Shrugging off her dark thoughts, Shirley went to serve another customer.

Feeling down in the dumps about Mathew, Beth immersed herself in the onerous task of letter writing. First to Elsie, then her parents. Although she'd not quite forgiven her dad for being the cause of her break-up with John, she realized that life was too short to bear grudges.

I've met this lovely bloke, she wrote in her letter to Elsie. He has the most gorgeous eyes. His name is Mathew. How are you? And Harry and the rest of the gang? City life is different. So busy. I met Shirley in a cafe. She is a waitress. We go out whenever we can. Please write soon.

Elsie's reply came by return.

Alf and I are still going out, she wrote. Harry has a new girl every week. Colin works for Tom at week-ends and sometimes after school. Bobby is clever. He wants to be a vet, but can't make up his mind. I'm enjoying work. I wash and rinse and fetch things and tidy up. I have not yet been taught how to cut or put rollers in.

John hasn't got a girl. He is more one of the lads now. His mother is still without a man. Some say she is after the minister, but he's not interested. Mum says if a woman lay naked before him, he wouldn't have a flicker. Anywhere!

Beth laughed and cried when reading Elsie's letter. Wistful feelings she thought she'd quenched, rose to disturb her, but she had a new interest, now. Mathew!

Dinner at the boarding house was pea and ham soup and stew with potatoes and dough balls. They all loved it. Even Gerald leaned back in his chair and patted his tummy when he'd finished.

'Mother made dough balls when I was a child,' said Dave with a faraway look. 'Usually with mince.'

'Where do you live?' asked Beth with curiosity.

'In Kent. Amongst the hops.'

''Ave yer room for steam puddin?' Mrs Fraser stood in the doorway, her face red from the heat in the kitchen.

'Ooh, Mrs Fraser, you're a dear. I'm sure I could manage some.' Paul loosened his belt.

'Blimey! yer like a pail with 'oles in it. Else yer have a tape worm,' she joked.

Surprisingly, Gerald expressed his wish to have a portion of pudding. As Beth placed the plate before him, she jolted with shock. Surely she was dreaming, but no – there it came again. The nip on her left buttock.

Scarlet faced, she rushed to the kitchen.

'Yer awful agitated, lass. Are yer still hankerin' for that bleedin' feller?'

'No.'

'It'll be that Paul then, likely. Flirt with a tabby cat 'e would.'

Beth didn't gainsay her supposition. She daren't tell her about Gerald in case she flung him out. What had instigated this sudden coming to life? she wondered.

Next morning, he peered short-sightedly at his paper as usual, but was he tidier? He'd had a hair cut and he sported a brand new waistcoat in Black Watch tartan. Goodness! Where had he unearthed that? In her chest, a laugh was born and took flight.

The old codger fancied her.

'God sakes, Beth; get a grip on yourself,' cried Mrs Fraser. 'An' whatever 'appens – the customer is always right. An' jobs is jobs.' Her warning glare suffocated Beth's mirth. A finger wagged in front of her nose, admonishing her.

Meal times became an ordeal for Beth. Then one day, when she was leaning over with his soup, his hand, stealthy as a snake, slipped over her thigh. This was the last straw. With great deliberation, she tipped the contents onto his lap.

'Careless girl,' he berated. 'Can't you watch what you're doing?' Bandy legged, he left the table, clutching the wet fabric of his trousers, pulling it away from his precious private bits.

Loud guffaws filled the room.

'Poor Gerald.' Paul wiped away tears of glee. 'That's him finished as a super stud for a while.'

'Gerald – a super stud? Cripes, what woman would want HIM?' Jonny slapped his chest with gusto. 'Me Tarzan, you Jane. Can you imagine him saying that to a woman? Or swinging from trees?' Jonny collapsed along the table in merry abandon.

'Now, now. 'E's no different from any other man.' Mrs Fraser viewed her ebullient lodgers with twinkling eyes. 'They've all got the same apparatus.'

'When are you buying that telly, Mrs Fraser?' asked Paul next morning. 'Think of the pleasure it would give on the dark nights.'

'It'll come when I thinks fit. I'm not made of money, yer know. Anyhow, what's wrong with the radio? Yer never satisfied you lot.' Mumbling to herself, she swished back to the kitchen.

September ended. Trees put on their autumn coats. Beth's relationship with Mathew turned her life into autumn too, her heart shedding leaves of despair as he twisted it to his will.

'Look,' he said. 'If you don't want me, there are other girls around.'

Next day, he came to the cafe and flirted outrageously with an attractive lass at the nearest table. Not verbally, but with his eyes. She knew he was trying to spur her on to go to his flat; to give him her body; but emotional blackmail and trying to make her jealous had the opposite effect. She withdrew into herself. Her heart ached with wanting to go, but the war bombing her from within, kept her from yielding.

Shirley was angry with Mathew for hurting Beth, and decided to pay him a visit. 'Look,' she said to Beth on their day out. 'I've got an errand to run. You go on home. I'll see on Saturday.'

'Saturday?' Beth's face looked blank.

'Pictures, remember. Be early. I must rush. Bye.' Along the street, she hastened. He lived nearby, Beth had said. Oh, well. she'd try this block. In the dim alley, she knocked on a green door.

'What you want, luv?' The words came from a cupid mouth on a white face. An apron with a floral design, nipped in an already tiny waist. From its pocket, stuck a packet of fags and a hanky.

'I'm searching for Mathew Lovejoy. Does he live here?'

Kindly eyes regarded her a moment, then she nodded. 'Number four. Up that flight of stairs.'

'Thank you.' Shirley smiled. 'You're very helpful.'

'A pleasure, dear.' Gently, the lady closed the door.

What a nice person, Shirley reflected.

Puffing her way up the stairs, Shirley paused at a red door, then pressed the bell. The door opened.

'Oh, it's you.' His look of eagerness turned to dismay. 'I thought it might be Beth.'

'No, she doesn't know I'm here. Can I have a word with you, please?'

'Come in.' His eyes looked into hers. 'Nothing wrong with Beth is there?'

'Well – not exactly. It's you I'm anxious to see.' Shirley's gaze wandered round the room. It was sparsely furnished. Two chairs and a table. A rug. One picture on the far wall. An electric fire in the centre of another. It was out.

Shirley shivered. 'Are you not cold?'

'No, I'm a hardy species.' His face was expansive. Shirley saw everything Beth saw in him.

'Would you like a cup of tea?' His voice was mellow. 'Then you can tell me what this is all about.'

'That would be lovely, thank you.'

He waved her to a chair. It was leather and comfy. With a sigh, she sank into its deep softness. From the kitchen, sounds of cupboards opening and closing could be heard. Cups and saucers rattled. She stood up and went to help. Shirley liked him. How could she question him when all her antennae were saying he was genuine. She had to though – for peace of mind.

'So, get on with it, then.' His eyes were serious.

'It's just, well – are you being above board with your intentions concerning Beth?'

A long silence held the room and Shirley's heart sank.

Nervously, Mathew cleared his throat. 'I like her a lot, but I'm afraid I'm not free. You see – I have a wife and three daughters in Edinburgh. My wife won't move to London. I see them as often as I can. Meeting Beth has turned my life upside down. I don't know what exactly my feelings are for her.' Frustrated, he rose and paced the room; his face gloomy; his distress evident.

'You'll have to tell Beth you're married.'

'I know.'

'Tomorrow.'

'Yes, the sooner the better, I suppose.' He cupped his head in his hands. 'Christ, I hope she'll still want me on those terms.'

Shirley stood up to go. She laid a hand on his arm. 'Don't worry, Mathew. What will be, will be.' Knowing Beth and how stubborn she could be, she had an inkling their relationship would blossom.

On a whim, she knocked on the friendly lady's door on way out.

'You back again, dear? Was he not in?' She opened the door wider. 'Have you time for a cup of tea?'

'I've just had one, thank you, but I'd still like to come in.'

The flat was warm, like the lady. A heater was on. It drew Shirley's eyes towards its glow. On a fluffy rug, a cat curled; black as ebony. At her approach, it sat up. Its eyes, round and golden, stared.

'That's Lucky. He was run over. We took him in and nursed him and he's been here ever since. He loves my son. Up on his knee as soon as he gets back from work.'

'Where does he work?'

'In a butcher's shop. He's been there seven years.'

'I work in a cafe. That's where I met Beth, my friend. She was a customer and we got talking.' The lady was a good listener, sort of mumsy and nice, and before Shirley could stop herself, she was recounting Beth's encounter with Mathew.

'Goodness me, what a saga. He's a very nice chap. Works in a bank. He's on holiday at the moment, but he hasn't gone to Edinburgh.'

'He's hardly any furniture.'

'Most of his wages will go towards his daughters' keep. Two of them are at school.'

'Did he tell you?'

'Yes, I ask him in for a meal sometimes. My son and he play darts. See that door. It's got more holes in it than the dartboard.'

Shirley laughed. She liked this woman. 'I'm Shirley by the way.' She reached to clasp the lady's hand.

'I'm Margaret Sanderson. I have a son called Alan.' Her eyes shifted to the door. 'Here he comes now.'

Shirley looked at the broad, round-faced lad hurtling through the door, his merry, brown eyes dancing with fire – and blushed.

Confused, she chased her eyes away from him and fixed them on the cat. It stood, stretched, yawned, and followed Alan to the kitchen.

'See,' said his mother. 'Where he goes, it goes.' She went to the table. 'Stay and have dinner with us. It's bangers and mash. It'll stretch to three.'

'If you're sure.'

'Of course I'm sure. Fetch another plate, Alan please.' She turned to Shirley. 'Where do you live, dear?'

'I live in a bedsit not far from here. It's a bit cramped, but it suits me fine. The only real friend I've got, is Beth.'

'You've got us now, Shirley. Come as often as you like. Have you a mum and dad? Or any kin?' Her kindly face brought forth a flood of tears from Shirley, and, try as she might, the river would not be dammed.

Alan's mother eyed her with concern.

'Might me, child, whatever is the matter?' From her capacious pocket, she withdrew a frilly hanky. 'Here, take this.' She sat down. 'If you don't mind, I'll have a smoke. A bad habit, I know, but I enjoy them.' As the tip of her cigarette blazed to life, she regarded the appealing, young face before her.

Coming from the kitchen, Alan gaped in surprise at the weeping girl who, only a minute ago, had been laughing. Once the flood gates were opened, Shirley couldn't stop the flow.

'My mother was a loose woman. Dad left her when I was six. One day, he went home and found her with another man. I was at school. At break time he came to the playground and stood – waiting. I ran down, and he hugged me so tight it hurt, but it was a nice hurt – loving. Then he was gone.' Shirley's sobbing ceased. She had never even told Beth about her parents. In this happy household, something had generated a trust.

Suddenly, two arms engulfed her. 'You little cherub. You are safe with us. Isn't she Alan?' Mrs Sanderson released her and stood back.

'Thank you. I can't wait to tell Beth.' On an impulse, Shirley stepped forward and hugged the slim figure of Mrs Sanderson.

'What about me, then?' Alan teased. 'Do I not get a cuddle?'

Shirley flashed him a smile, her heart hammering like a woodpecker in her chest. She'd like very much to give him a cuddle.

Back at the boarding house, dinner was about to be served, and Gerald was absent. 'Never known 'im ter be late before. I 'ope nothin's 'appened ter him.' Mrs Fraser turned to Beth with a worried look.

'I hope it's not my fault.' It was Beth's turn to look anxious.

'He's maybe away to the doctor – with burnt balls,' laughed Paul.

'Less o' yer lip. There's no cause ter be rude, yer silly goof. 'E's a long standin' guest o' mine.'

The humour in Mrs Fraser's eyes belied her stern words. It found her mouth and gave vent to a hearty laugh.

Just then, a taxi drew up at the door.

Pushing against each other, heads jammed close to the window, they watched as the driver and Gerald retrieved from the boot, a large box.

'Now what's he bought? We'd better give them a hand,' Dave rushed to open the door.

'Where do you want it, then?' the driver puffed.

'In the corner. Take that vase off the table, Jonny, if you please.' Sweat covered Gerald's top lip and ran down his chin. He was unused to physical work.

'Hell Gerald, you'll have a coronary.' Quickly, Jonny jumped to his aid. His arms slumped as they took the weight of the box. 'Whooo blimey, it's heavy. Is there a body in it?'

'Trust you to you to think of coronaries and bodies. It's easy seen you're a doctor,' Paul quipped.

When the box was safely deposited on the floor, Gerald shook hands exuberantly with the driver. 'Thank you, my good man, You've been very helpful.' From his wallet, he withdrew a note.

'My money bag is in the cab. Wait a minute.'

'No, you keep the change, it's been worth every penny.'

'Many thanks. Hope they enjoy their surprise.' The driver's toothy grin spread, easy as butter across his face. 'Bye, then.' Raising his hand in a wave, he departed. So the lodgers got their telly. From Gerald.

From then on, he was one of them.

Beth got to know and like them all. Mrs Fraser was a gem. The only conflict that arose between them was her continued association with Mathew.

'Yer wastin' yer life, Beth,' she warned. 'Nothin' will ever come of it. 'E's only interested in one thing. God love a duck, lassie, yer should 'ave more sense.'

'I know, Mrs Fraser, but I love him. I've never felt like this before. I know he has faults. He's only human, but we've got to accept folk for what they are.'

'Mmm, well, I'm always here if yer need advice.' Mrs Fraser turned away. She went to the cooker and switched it on. 'If yer know what I mean, luv.'

In a grey-blue sky, a watery sun hung. Pigeons pecked on pavements and streets; quite tame; heeding not the traffic and jostling people.

Beth still hankering after Mathew; brooded as she went about her duties. Mrs Fraser was annoyed.

'Yer only young, girl. Life will 'ave many turnings. Don't be too serious,' she muttered. She leaned over the sink, her hands frothed with soap suds. Dishes emerged spotless and shiny. She laid them on the draining board and looked at Beth. 'In any case,' she added. 'Men's thoughts are all in their trousers. A bit o' skirt and they're rarin' for it.' She nodded like a sage.

Had she had bad dealings with men? Beth wondered. But no – her next words refuted this thought.

'My hubby were a real gentleman,' she said, a distant look curtaining her eyes. 'Liked his rumpy pumpy, mind you. Every night when we was first wed. He had a weak chest and got pneumonia and died. Only thirty five.' She let out a long sigh. The clattering of dishes silenced, as time winged her back.

'I'm sorry, Mrs Fraser.' Beth bit her lip, not knowing what else to say.

'I've had a few men since, but none that gripped my innards like my Sam.' Mrs Fraser smiled at Beth. 'So I knows a bit about what yer feelin' pet. Yer'll just 'ave ter ride the storm when it comes, as surely it will.'

Beth thought of her father and Cathy's dad and their affairs with Barbara Fairbairn, and silently agreed.

Could she cope with the emotional trials and possible hurts that lay ahead?

In the cafe, she talked to Shirley.

'You've got to either go, or not go, Beth. It's your decision. Your conscience should guide you.' After a bit of cogitating, she went. Mathew's eyes lit up when he saw her. Her heartbeats raced as he took her hands and drew her in. They made love on his hard, creaky bed. It was lumpy and smelt musty. They met again – often.

Then he began backing off, being evasive, not answering the door. Like a prat, she'd stand, for what seemed an interminable time, hoping he'd open it. He knew she was there. That part hurt and made her cry, but her fervour never diminished.

One afternoon he was in the cafe, obviously waiting for her. With mixed feelings, she approached his table. So capricious he'd been lately, that she dreaded even speaking to him, far less sitting beside him.

'Sit down,' he said. His eyes spoke to her body, not daring to dwell on her face. Elbows on the table, hands knuckled against his cheeks, he sat. 'Look,' he said. 'I'm having to go to Edinburgh for a while.'

Instantly, Beth was wary. Was this the big brush-off then?

'Yes,' he continued. 'Patricia, my youngest daughter is poorly.'

'What's wrong with her?' Bleak eyes watched his face.

'Measles. A bad dose.'

'Well, I won't hold you back.' Beth shoved herself up from her chair.

'Wait!' Leaning over the table, he softly kissed her cheek. It was like the kiss of Judas. She wiped it away. He wouldn't be back, she knew. All of a sudden, home beckoned.

Next morning, she told Mrs Fraser.

'I won't say I told yer so, dear,' she said. 'But it's for the best.'

That afternoon, she said goodbye to Shirley. 'Keep in touch,' she cried. From her pocket, she took out a piece of paper. 'Here's my address. Come for a holiday sometime. Bring Alan.'

At the door on Friday morning, she gazed around for the last time and said farewell to the lodgers. Mrs Fraser saw her off. They embraced. The same taxi driver who brought her, took her to the station.

'Cheerio, Bernie, and thank you,' she cried. 'Go and see Mrs Fraser sometime. I think she likes you.'

He grinned. 'I think the missus would have something to say about that.'

Beth laughed. 'I suppose she would.' Damp-eyed, she watched the cab disappear and mingle with the traffic. People flecked the streets. Hurrying, hurrying. Always hurrying, she thought. She locked the pictures in her mind. Like photos, she'd bring them out now and again.

In the compartment, a man coughed and picked his nails. They were black underneath. Perhaps he was a coalman. Or a factory worker.

A lady was engrossed in a magazine. Another slept. A little boy by her side, fished inside his nose with a grubby finger. Beth looked away. She gazed out of the window. White clouds floated by, changing shape as they went along.

Like her life, she mused. How would IT shape from now on?

Chapter Eleven

Feeling tired and crumpled, Beth alighted from the bus at the stance nearest her house. The door was ajar. Stepping over the threshold, she surveyed the familiar hall.

The circular stick stand. The hat stand on which her dad's favourite deerstalker limply hung; oily at the peak with so much handling.

Her mother's aspidistra on the table at the foot of the stairs. A photo of the royal family gazing down from the landing wall. She was a great royalist, her mum.

This was home.

Her heart jumped as the grey form of Lucy, the cat, leaped at her feet. Beth leant to stroke her. She purred and wound herself round her legs.

Just then, her mother appeared at the living room door. 'Beth!' she shouted. 'You're back!' With outstretched arms, she ran towards her.

'It's grand to be home, mum. I didn't realize how much I missed everybody and everything. Even that stupid aspidistra.'

'Your dad would agree wholeheartedly with that.' Her mother pulled a face.

'Where is he?'

'Watching telly. At last, he opened his wallet and bought one.'

'That reminds me of where I stayed and worked in London. It's a long story, though.'

Arm in arm, they went to the sitting room. Beth stopped to stare at the familiar head resting on the back of the chair.

She had finally forgiven him for being the cause of her splitting up with John. The reason unbeknown to him. What a shame. What must he have thought when she left? Did he know the truth? she wondered. But how could he? He didn't even know of John's webbed toes.

'Hello, dad.' The words skipped from her in a dance of joy.

Telly forgotten, Dan's head spun round. 'Beth! is it really you? Hell, lassie, we've been worried sick about you. That letter you wrote told us nothing.'

'No, I'm sorry. It was just to let you know I was fine.' Beth looked around. 'Is my old job still available?' She crossed her fingers.

'Available! You'd get double the wage if I was boss.' Her mother raised her eyebrows and rolled her eyes towards Dan. 'He expected ME to do it. Right in at the deep end, I was. Still am.'

'You're not blonde and busty with long legs and sexy lips. Hell, woman, you've no qualifications whatever.' Dan winked at Beth.

Swiftly, he detached himself from the chair and took hold of Emma round her plump waist. 'You have other assets, my dear,' he said. His grip tightened. 'You make a good hot water bottle in bed.'

'Oh, and who is it cooks your meals every day, Mr know all? And does the housework?' She struggled in his arms. 'Get away, you big oaf, we've a lassie to see to.' A strong shove sent him reeling back into his chair.

Beth was surprised at the rapport between them. A new vitality that hadn't been there for years. Maybe he had given up Barbara Fairbairn?

Next evening, Beth visited Elsie. The gang was there. Harry swaggered around in dark trousers and a white shirt. He looked smart. Spiky hair gone, it now hugged his collar in the longer style and had a side parting. His eyes bored into hers. They were the colour of bluebells, and nice. Surprised by this revelation, she dropped her gaze.

Raymond gave Harry a nudge. Feeling at odds with himself, Harry stamped firmly on his foot.

'Ouch! that was sore. You've got feet like bloomin' spades, Harry Marshall.'

'And you've got an overactive mind, Raymond Stuart. Don't let it form words.'

'Truce, truce, please. What a welcome back for Beth.' Elsie held up a supplicating hand.

'OK, sorry.' Harry glanced at the others. 'We might as well go to John's place. He'll be happy to see Beth.'

'Aye, let's go.' They made for the door.

A look sparked between the girls.

Harry, always perceptive, saw the look and fobbed the lads off. 'Wait till I get changed. Have a seat. I think they –' he nodded at Beth and Elsie – 'want girlie talk.'

'Gabble, gabble, gabble. It's a' lassie's do. It'll be about lads likely.' Raymond screwed up his nose. 'At least John can talk about rugby.'

Over a cup of tea in the kitchen, Beth told Elsie of her romance with Mathew.

'Help! you did it on your first date. I've gone for ages with Alf and we still haven't done it.' Elsie gave Beth a quick look. 'Did he take precautions?'

'Yes.'

'Phew! that's a good job. At least he was sensible.'

'He was lovely, but I've got to get on with my life, not dwell on him too much. Wherever he is, he'll always have somebody on the side. He's that way inclined.'

'Have you told your mother about him?'

'No, you're my agony aunt. To be so young, you seem to know an awful lot about relationships In an another life, perhaps you were married with ten kids. Maybe that's why you refrain from doing it now?'

'You're as bad as Cathy with your big words. I wonder how

she is. She'll have had the bairn by now. I hope it doesn't take after Donald.'

'No, he's like a rotten apple. He taints everything he touches.'

'Aye, he's a right sleeze bag.'

'Do you think she'll worry about that?'

'Aye, she probably does. She likes livin' with her granny and her grandad. At first, her grandfather treated her very shabbily, but when he knew about the bairn, he changed. The workers can't believe it's the same man.'

'That's good. Do you think she remembers the better times here?'

'Of course she will. Everybody has a fondness for their childhood. It's the happiest time of our lives.'

'You're right. Being grown-up causes nothing but tears and heartache.'

Elsie laughed. 'You'd think we were old women talkin' like this. Get your coat on. We'll go and see John. I suppose Alf will have gone with the others.'

'You still like Alf?'

'Aye.'

'Harry's improved a lot, hasn't he? More a suave, man about the town sort of person.'

'Harry! Suave! Gracious me, Beth, are you feelin' all right? He's the same irritating brother he's always been.'

'Has John a girlfriend?'

'John never looked at another lassie after you left. He got a scunner, I think. Cathy was his real love. You were second best – but he liked you.'

'Does he know he could have Cathy now that the paternity situation is sorted out?'

'He knows, but Cathy will have to make the first move. Most likely she still thinks he's her dad's progeny.'

'You should tell her.'

'I'll wait till I see her.'

'Let's stop hashing and be on our way.' Beth was already fastening her coat.

Elsie did likewise, talking animatedly as she did so, trying to keep Beth abreast of the local tittle-tattle. 'Do you know Alice, Cathy's mother?'

'Yes.'

'Well, she and Tom Garrick are an item. They have clandestine meetings a few times a week. They think the neighbours don't see, but they do. He's engaged to a lassie called Daisy. She's nice. They sit in the back row o' the balcony on a Saturday night.'

'Why does he want Alice, then?'

'Och, men like to eat the grass on both sides o' the fence. Mind you, some women are as bad.'

'Do you think I fit that category?' Beth looked at her solemnly.

'No, that would be a one-off. You'll have learned your lesson.' Elsie turned to face her. 'Have you?'

'I hope so.'

'There's shoals o' men out there waiting to be caught. When you find somebody special, just reel out the bait. My Alf's still got the hook under his skin.'

Roaring with laughter, they stepped outside.

Another October was nearly over. On its last day, it spoke with a vengeance. Branches swirled. Windows rattled. Loose slates lost their fight and hurtled to the ground.

It was in to this, that Elsie and Beth ventured. The wind roared the last rites on an aged tree. On top of the dyke, it fell, gouging a huge hollow, ruining hours of time spent labour.

Shocked, Elsie and Beth stared.

'Good job we didn't go that way. We'd be mincemeat by now,' cried Beth.

'Too right, we would.' Elsie patted her chest. 'My heart nearly stopped then.'

'At least it would have been a tree that stopped it, not a laddie. Or does Alf have that effect on it?'

'Aye, he does. There's a fluttering there every time I see him.' Elsie giggled. 'Or maybe it's just wind.'

'Poor Alf. What would he say if he heard?'

'He'd just laugh. He's got a grand sense o' humour.'

'He'd have to, with you for a girlfriend.'

The wind tore through their hair, blowing it away from faces robbed of colour by the cold.

At the porch of John's house, they hurriedly drew a comb through their tangled tresses. It was a futile task. As the door opened, their coiffure had already been reshaped by the teeth of nature's strength.

'Blimey! look what the wind's blown in, lads,' said Harry as John ushered them in. 'A pair o' scarecrows.'

From the onset, he was captivated by Beth; his eyes finding her wherever she sat or stood. Demurely, Beth smiled, then looked down. Uncertain. Thinking of Mathew. How she'd been hurt. Young, naive – and him a city slicker with years of experience.

'Hey, stop daydreaming, Beth. You were miles away there.' Elsie gave her a shove. A few wiggles and she fitted her bottom between Beth and Raymond on the sofa. 'My, how posh,' her eyes scaled the furniture in the room. 'This is the chaise longue, you know,' she voiced, mimicking Barbara. 'Trust her to find a fancy name for it.'

Beth felt awkward. For Elsie and herself. Forcibly, she jabbed her in the ribs.

'Ouch! what was that for?' The shout reached every corner. Eyes turned towards her. Elsie shrunk inside. What would Alf think? She'd die if he gave her up. Unsure of his reactions, she avoided him the rest of the evening.

'What's up?' he cried when finally he bumped into her in the hall. 'You've been giving me the slip all night.'

'Nothin's up,' she replied.

Nonchalantly, he shrugged and walked away. Maybe she needed a bit space. Oh, well – he'd give it to her. 'Thanks for the coffee, John,' he said, snatching his jacket from the back of a chair. 'I'm away.' The door banged shut.

Elsie's mouth opened in astonishment. Full of concern, she scrambled for her coat and rushed after him.

Alone midst the gang, Beth felt awkward. John smiled across, chestnut eyes forgiving. She smiled back, pleased that he understood.

The one who didn't know, and should, was her father. She'd have to enlighten him. A drink was placed in her hand. It was frothy, made from granules and mixed with water. Foam lined her top lip. Harry watched her lick it away. Sensual feelings flooded him. He turned from her, acutely aware of the tightness at his crotch.

One by one, they began to leave. Along the road, they walked, strangely subdued, each with different emotions dusting their thoughts. Lights from shadowed windows, studded the countryside. Words, buffeted by angry gusts, searched around in a void, but were lost, sucked into timelessness.

Beth was staying the night at Elsie's house. Harry held the door open as she stepped in.

Next morning, she rose early. She had to get home to speak to her dad before he left for work.

The pop of the toaster as she entered, signified that her mother was in the kitchen. No voices. Her father must be in the bathroom.

Quietly, she tiptoed upstairs. At the bathroom door, she and her dad collided. 'Ooops, sorry dad.' Laughing, they both jumped back. He made to pass, but she stopped him. 'Dad,' she whispered. 'Can I talk to you?'

Years of being a father crowded in on Dan. 'You're not pregnant, are you, Beth?' The question hurt him to ask.

'No, silly It's about John. He's your son. He's got webbed toes the same as you. I saw them when they threw him in the river. That's why I left. It means he's my half brother.'

Her father's face blanched. His hand found the door handle and held it tight. A knot twisted in his gut. 'How many know?'

'Just John and his mother and myself – I think'

'For hell's sake don't tell your mother. She'd kill me. Or leave.' His other hand spanned his eyes. In the darkness thereof, the words were written.

John's your son.

That bloody Barbara knew and never let peep. Well, he'd go and see her. What benefit it would bring, God knows, but he needed to do something.

As his van screeched to a standstill outside her porch, Barbara smelled trouble. What brought Dan here at this early hour? What brought Dan at all? Their fling was over. Ad infinitum.

The door burst open. No knock. Nothing. He took the bull by the horns, did Dan. A few strides and there he stood, tall and commanding beside her.

'Why didn't you tell me?' he barked.

'Tell you what, Dan?' Instinctively, she reached for her cigarettes. She viewed his face with glinting eyes. It was white as chalk.

'You knew John was my son.' His gaze accused her like a judge in court. 'I had a right to know.' Sadness compressed his lips. The thought of what might have been, was a drumbeat in his head.

'I've not long known myself. What could you have done, anyway? He was my responsibility, but not now. He's distanced himself from me since finding out. Very unforgiving he is, and judging by your behaviour, he must take it after you.'

'You're a callous bitch, Barbara. I could have watched him grow. All the different stages. I'd have taken a special interest. You've cut seventeen years from my life.'

'Hell, Dan, I didn't know. I thought he could have been Bert's son.'

'Huh! if you hadn't been such a nymphomaniac, it would have been self-evident.'

'Let's not quarrel about it, Dan. Sssh – ' she raised a finger to her mouth. 'Here's John for his breakfast. Sit down and don't make a scene.'

John stood in the doorway, shoulders blocking the space. He looked strained. This vendetta with his mother was getting him down.

'Hello, Dan,' he said.

His nod included his mother.

The hiatus that followed his greeting was like a loaded gun, but filled with promise, not bullets. Dan savoured seeing John for the first time – not just as a lad – but as his son.

On Saturday night, Beth and Elsie went to the cinema. In the balcony, the usherette, showed them to their seats. Already seated viewers had to stand, half bent, to let them pass. Smoke from the stalls, rose upwards. Light from the screen beamed through it, making a grey haze.

At intermission, a lady with a tray suspended by a halter strap, sold tubs of ice cream. Beth and Elsie joined the queue.

'This is great,' said Elsie as she delved into it with the small wooden spoon provided. 'It tastes better in the pictures, somehow.'

'Yes, it's the atmosphere.' Beth pulled back the top on her tub and held a spoonful to her mouth.

Everything dimmed. The big film started. In the stalls, boys whistled and shouted. Beth and Elsie settled to watch the film. As they filed out at the end, their minds were still caught up in the screen. They wanted it to go on and on, but it was like trying to catch a dream.

Elsie nudged Beth as their feet struck the street. 'There's Tom and Daisy. He'll set her home, then be off to see Alice. They say he's always had a notion for her.' Sensing their stares, Tom's head swung in their direction.

'Hello,' he said and smiled; the full chemistry of it warming them like an oven.

'You see, that's how he gets them. He could charm a snail out o' its shell.' Elsie slid her eyes to Beth. 'Well – what's your verdict?'

'He's all right, I suppose. Not a patch on Mathew though.'

'Forget him, Beth. He's like the pot o' gold at the end o' a rainbow. Unobtainable.'

'I know.' Beth spoke in a dull tone. She was all mixed up. How could her life not be simple and untrammelled like Elsie's?

At the bus stop, the lads were scoffing fish and chips with gusto. The aroma wafted to the girls' nostrils in appetizing whiffs.

'Have a chip, girls.' A gallant Harry held out what was left of his.

'Thank you, kind sir.' Chirpily, Beth played up to his gallantry.

Along the street, came the bus, tyres squelching and spraying in the wet. Jostling and capering, showing off in front of Beth, the lads fought to gain entry first.

'See,' said Elsie, turning to Beth. 'They're like a lot o' kids.'

Beth alighted first, a dark shape blending with buildings, lampposts, and pavement. Elsie waved. The window was mottled with raindrops and mud. Everything was clouded.

Returning Elsie's wave, Beth turned on her heel and made for home. Harry's lingering look as he boarded the bus, filled her with expectation.

She smiled.

Chapter Twelve

At the manse, the minister pondered over his Sunday sermon. Wrinkling his brow, he stared into space. What topic would he introduce to his motley flock this week, he wondered.

Bobby had just come in from seeing his pals. They played pool in the back room of the Red Lion pub some nights. From six to eight. They drank juice and ate crisps and chatted to the lassies. He fancied a drink of milk and went to the fridge. As he bent to open the door, the bell rang. Long and imperious, it shattered the still night.

'Crikey! Have patience whoever you are,' he mumbled. Straightening, he went to answer it, and stared goggle-eyed at the vision on the doorstep.

'Is this where Reverend McKenzie resides?' The girl's voice was as overbearing as the bell.

'Yes, he does. He's in his study though. Can I help?' Bobby put on the best tongue he could muster. Why, he didn't know. She was only a lassie after all. A horrid nature of a one, too. Why should he genuflect to her?

The male instincts in his young body surfaced and he knew why. Hell, she was stunning.

With a baleful look, she thrust past him and flung her bag on the floor. 'If you are a servant, then kindly take my belongings upstairs and find me a suitable bedroom.'

'Look, you can't just barge in here orderin' folk about.' Bobby straightened his back and fixed her with a stiff glare. 'Anyway, he doesn't want to be disturbed.'

Haughtily, she pushed her hair back from a perfect face. Her eyes, the colour of grass, glared balefully at Bobby.

'You uncouth, country bumpkin, do as I say. I am his daughter. Get used to it – and kindly fetch him.'

Bobby's Adam's apple jumped up and down as he swallowed. The minister's daughter. Cripes! He never knew he had one.

On shaky legs, he scurried to the minister's study. Gordon looked up, his face registering alarm at Bobby's agitated expression.

'Bobby, whatever is the matter?'

'You'd better see for yourself, minister.'

Before he had time to get his mind round things and rise, the apparition, who'd followed Bobby, crashed into his office. Gordon stared as if he'd seen a ghost. In a way, he had. She was the incarnation of Maureen.

'You must be my father? I'm Caroline.'

'Caroline! But where is Maureen? Isn't she with you?'

'She's dead. I've come to live here.' Her words were clipped.

Gordon sat back, appalled. This girl. This unfeeling, hard creature – was his daughter. His thoughts roamed for miles, trying to find a suitable way to solve this solution. He was at a loss.

'I've travelled far. I'm hungry.' She broke the silence for him.

An awful rage filled her father. He stood up, thrusting his chair with such force, it skittered along the carpet and fell against the bureau. A storm pounded inside his head like waves lashing against rocks. Its only means of escape was verbal.

'Yes, I am your father,' he shouted. And if you wish to stay here, then you must treat us with a morsel of respect.' Gordon drew his hands through his sandy hair. 'Bobby,' his voice gentled. 'Take Caroline's belongings to the spare bedroom, please. Caroline, this is Bobby, my adopted son. I'm sure you'll get on together – when you learn some manners.' He turned away, dismissing her. Too quick to see the bleakness veil her fine eyes, but Bobby saw it.

She's just scared, he thought as he led her up the stairs. Between the minister and him, they'd soon get her thawed. Wait till the lads see her. Bobby's thoughts zoomed ahead. She was out of bounds to him, though. He accepted that.

Mince, left from dinner, boiled tatties and cabbage, were put before Caroline who had taken her place at the table in a huffy silence. Gordon and Bobby munched ham sandwiches. Across the table, they gazed at each other, each wondering how they were going to cross this river. Her hostility seemed in no way lessening. A string of tension, thin as a spider's web, bound them together. One word could break it, so none were said.

At last, Bobby took the initiative.

'I'm going to John's place tomorrow. You can come if you like. My mates stay in the cottages there. They're a queer lot, but you'll like them. John's got a horse called Carma.' On he chattered, trying to find a crack in that hard exterior of hers.

The word horse, lighted her eyes. In London, elegant ladies rode in the park. In the meagre flat where she and her mother had lived, she'd watched, and imagined herself one of them.

Hastily, she averted her gaze, not wanting them to notice her eagerness. 'I'll go,' she muttered, directing her attention to her mince as she forked it to her mouth.

'You will! Great!' Bobby was exultant. His fanned lashes winked at the minister. 'That's round one to us,' he whispered.

Abruptly, Caroline rose and left the table and made her way up the stairs.

Bobby opened his mouth to protest, bewildered, and angry. Well, he thought. If it's a heavyweight bout she wanted – then so be it.

Gordon observed the play of emotions flitting over Bobby's face. Vulnerable, he was, but by God, this young protégé of his would go far. He couldn't envisage life without the rapscallion.

The events of the night took their toll. Nightly ablutions done, they too made for bed. Dressing gown on, and barefooted, the minister padded along the landing to his room. Sounds of muffled crying coming from Caroline's room, caught his ears. Baffled, he stopped. What should he do?

Her unfriendly attitude, too extraordinary for words, had cut him up. No knife. Just words, sharper than a razor blade, had done the damage. He would leave her alone, he decided. Not out of pique, but some inbuilt intuition telling him so.

Sniffing into a hanky, Caroline heard his steps hesitate, then pass by. Part of her wanted him to come. Wanted the comfort of his arms. Wanted the bedclothes tucked round her like her mother had done when she had come to turn out the light.

Why was she being so nasty? He was nice, her father. So was Bobby. She tossed and turned. It was late when at last she succumbed to the pull of sleep.

In the morning, she was washed and dressed before the others. She hadn't much in the way of clothes, but they were clean. 'Cleanliness is next to Godliness,' her mother used to say. She'd had lots of sayings, her mother. Maybe she learned them from dad. Caroline pondered on what to make, then plumped for a fry-up.

The smell of bacon frying filtered its way through the house. Bobby, in his room, and the minister in his, sat up in astonishment. In ten minutes they were up and ready. 'That's round two to us, minister,' cried Bobby, giving him the thumbs up sign at the top of the stairs. Let's get down and demolish it before it ends up in the waste bucket. You never know with her moods.'

Covertly, they studied her as she ate. Such a mixture of anger and hate for one so young. Still – things seemed to be going in the right direction.

Harry, Raymond and Colin were kicking a ball about along the front of the cottages, when Bobby and Caroline appeared. Eyes riveted on Caroline, they froze. First to gain his speech was

Harry. 'Wow!' he cried. 'Take a look at that, lads. Where did he find such a beauty? See that hair – and them tits?'

Colin was mesmerized. He'd never fancied a girl before, but now – one look and he was hooked.

'Hi, lads,' said Bobby on nearing them. 'This is my sister, Caroline. She's come to stay with us.'

'Your sister? We never knew you had a sister.' Possibilities flared.

'Neither did I. She's the minister's daughter.' He brought her forward. 'Caroline, this is Harry, Raymond and Colin. Harry has a sister called Elsie. She's a hairdresser.'

Caroline had not spoken, but inside she had come alive. Though not possessed with a worldly woman's experience, the reactions of the lads as she walked towards them was obvious.

'Come in.' Harry, quick to recover, showed her into the house. Like lambs, the others followed.

Elsie raised her eyes from reading a magazine, and at once stiffened, jealousy rising before her Alf had even seen the girl.

Just then, John sauntered in, hands stuck in pockets, head down. He'd finished work for the moment and needed a retreat. One other than his home. He looked up into a sea of green. Least he thought it was the sea the way his head swam.

'Hello, John. You're just in time to meet my sister.' Proudly, Bobby introduced her.

'How do you do, John?' As she held out a slender hand, her voice rippled over him. All other girls paled against this one's vivacity. They were like small blips on the screen of his mind.

Of the many boys who vied for her affection, it was John she chose.

While her behaviour was still a matter of concern in the manse, her outward persona was much more friendly. Then the devil seemed to enter her soul. She bulldozed her way through people's minds and feelings, dropping bombs of destruction wherever she thought fit. If she meant to shock – then she certainly did.

Openly, she flirted; causing arguments with John and disturbing the good nature of the lad.

'You go over the top,' he chided. 'You give fellows the wrong ideas.'

'Pooh! you are too serious, John. You should live a little. Enjoy life.'

Even her father castigated her, but she laughed away his words like chaff blown by the wind.

Once more it was autumn, and acres of stubble fields showed that harvesting was completed. It was Friday, and a harvest dance was being held in the village hall. Young and old, went to this every year.

The lure of the pub drew the young ones. Huddled at the bar, the lads sipped appreciatively at the cool, soft drinks. Caroline, the only one old enough to drink alcohol, had Vodka and orange. She drank quickly; downing two before Elsie had finished her first pineapple drink. Smoke clouded the air. Caroline moved closer to Alf, rubbing her knee against his leg. Alf felt this going on and tried to ignore it. A troubled look passed over his face. What if Elsie saw her? Alarmed, he made for the door.

Taking this as an invitation, Caroline followed.

Once outside, in the alley beside the pub, Alf gave a sigh of relief. The sound of steps on the paved surface, made him turn. Before he could utter a word, a mouth clamped on his, and a hand proceeded to explore what was inside his trousers.

'Wow! you're a big boy, Alf, aren't you?' It was Caroline's voice.

It acted like a cold shower.

'Get off, you stupid cow,' he shouted, angrily pushing her away.

In the pub, Elsie peered round with anxious eyes. Where was Alf? Opening the door, she called his name. A to-do outside drew her like a magnet. 'ALF!' she screeched. 'What are you doin?' His trousers were open at the front. Caroline lay writhing on the ground. Misconstruing the situation, she flew at him in a hazed fury. 'You rotten sod, Alf Tait. It's over between us. You can have her. She's trash. You're well suited.' With a wail, she fled. A light pouring from the hall, pulled her in that direction. Tom Garrick was at the door. She had no money, but seeing her distress, he let her in. She made a beeline for the cloakroom, and there, amongst a pile of coats, she cried her heart out.

Alf was upset. Putting his clothes to rights, he set off home. Grief numbed him.

He had lost Elsie.

It had turned frosty. Stars crowded an inky sky. Dots of light peeped from windows. On reaching his home, Alf let himself in. His mum and dad looked at him in surprise. It was still early.

'You all right, son?' His mum's voice, worried, and gentle, touched raw nerves. Tears sprang unbidden. His mother hastened to his side. In the warmth of her embrace, he spilled out his woes.

'Give her time, son. She knows you're not like that. Caroline's just tryin' to cause friction between you and Elsie.' She patted his shoulder. 'She's born from Satan's spawn, that one, not from the minister's loins.'

Alf's dad sat, head behind a paper, listening. A film of smoke curled to the ceiling from his pipe. He coughed and nodded in silent agreement.

Caroline was furious. At Alf, at herself, at the world in general. The pub door shut with a bang behind her. She found John in a corner talking to a farmer friend. His gaze rested on her like a benediction. So predictable.

So nice. She'd have to mend her ways. For a while. If he found out about Alf, it would be curtains for her, and he was too good a catch to lose.

Tom's eyes roamed the hall. Folk were streaming out, buttoning up coats and jackets, but there was no sign of Elsie.

In the cloakroom, Elsie sat. She had nowhere to hide any more. A lady she didn't know, with a chest as big as a cow's udder, removed from a peg, the last coat. The one under which she was concealed.

'You waiting for somebody, dear?'

'Yes.' Elsie's voice was a whisper. Inwardly, she was quaking. What if they locked up the hall and she was stuck here all night?

The band gathered up their gear and exited. The building felt hollow. Elsie was scared.

Tom was sure that the last lady to leave had spoken to someone. The boards creaked as his weighty steps crossed the floor. Elsie peered from beneath puffy eyelids.

'Well, young lady, are you going to stay here all night, or are you coming with me?' Not waiting for an answer, he held out his hand. 'Come on, I'll take you home.'

In bed, Elsie tortured herself with thoughts of the night's events. She cursed Caroline. Had Alf really done it with her? Or had he fended her off? The open breeks though, how could he explain that?

She must see him. It was essential she see him before he left for work. She wished her dad had a phone. Alice had one. She'd ask her.

Snug in her new tweed coat, she knocked softly on her door. Would she answer? Elsie wondered. So much abuse had been hurled at her over the years, she'd understand if she didn't. Mainly her own mother's caustic jibes, Elsie realised with shame.

The door opened an inch and Elsie had to communicate through this space. 'Can I use your phone please, Alice? I've got to speak to Alf without anyone else knowing.'

Aware of her urgency, Alice let her in.

'Here it is. Do you have his number?'

'Aye.'

'I'll leave you to it, then.' Her voice sounded strange, causing Elsie to reverse her gaze. She noted the pallor of her skin. One didn't have to be a prophet to see that something was amiss. 'Are you well enough, Alice? You look awful white.' Alice nodded, but clutched at her side as if pained. Elsie had doubts. Should she write to Cathy? Best not, she decided. Maybe she was an alarmist. Surely Tom would have noticed if anything was wrong.

Heart beating to the dozen, she phoned Alf, concentrating on what he was saying; hearing his side of the story; feeling guilty at having doubted him. They held hands in Harry's car on the way to work.

More besotted with Caroline than ever, John saw her at every opportunity possible. He took her home to meet his mother.

The large, imposing house enthralled her. This will be mine some day, she decided. The avaricious gleam in her eye, still lingered as she held out her hand to clasp Barbara's perfectly manicured one.

In that split second Barbara weighed her up, and her sympathies went out to John – but this time – she wouldn't interfere. He was man enough to make his own decisions.

That very same week he proposed. His mother was out. Caroline reclined on the sofa. The green material picked up the colour of her eyes, accentuating her feline look. John drowned in their depths.

'Will you marry me, Caroline?' he blurted. His throat felt constricted, and he stood mute – gazing down at her.

She watched his eyes. They had the look of a dog waiting to be taken for a walk. The fire sparked in the silence that ensued. She decided to play it down.

'If you like,' she said, and turned her head away as if bored.

'You could be more enthusiastic, then.' John was angry.

She was a frustrating bitch at times, but he loved her. At least he thought he did. Not in the same way he'd loved Cathy, but she had a wild, untamed quality that he couldn't resist.

'When?' She ran her fingers through her hair.

'When what?'

'When will we get married?'

'Christmas. What do you think?'

'All right.' She spoke in a monotone.

A niggle of doubt clicked in, then out, of John's head. Was he doing the right thing?

That night he lay staring at the ceiling in the darkness, unable to sleep. As dawn pointed silver fingers of light into the sky, and birds began their morning chorus, he was still awake. His mind was in a quandary.

What should he do?

Chapter Thirteen

In the White Swan, Daisy slid pint after pint along the bar. The act was done automatically. She hadn't slept all night. She was anxious. Her relationship with Tom wasn't quite what it should be. Perhaps she was being paranoid; but no, there was definitely a cooling off in his attitude lately. Insidious fears stormed her eyes. Dark circles hung under them.

'You all right, love?' Doreen, her boss, looked at her worriedly.

Daisy watched her lips move. Slashes of red, mouthing words of concern. It disconcerted her. Abandoning the pump, she ran outside. In astonishment, the customers stared.

Aimlessly, she walked. Tears coursed down her cheeks. She brushed them away with her gloved hand. Had Tom found someone else? she wondered. Or was he just fed up with her? The thoughts were knocked out of her in a gasp, as she collided with the chest of a fast walking man. Hard as a wall, it flung her backwards.

'Hello, what's the hurry?' The voice, vaguely familiar, was deep and cheery.

'I'm sorry. I wasn't concentrating on where I was going.' Ruefully, she rubbed her front. 'Are you made of bricks or something?'

'No, lady. Just flesh, bones and blood. You can bump into me any time you want.' His forefinger touched his lips. 'Hey, I know you. You're the lass who works in the White Swan.'

'Yes.' Recognition dawned for Daisy too.

'Is this your night off?'

'No, I was upset for some reason and left.'

'Hell, we can't have that. Come with me. I'll treat you to some fish and chips.'

'I'm sorry. It's very kind of you, but I have a boyfriend. He wouldn't be pleased, I don't think.'

'Hmm! If he makes you as unhappy as you are tonight, he doesn't deserve you.' Searching in his pocket, he produced a white card. 'Here, take this. It's my address and phone number. If you ever want me, I'll be there.'

Thoughtfully, she watched him go. Slipping the card in her cardigan pocket, she about turned. A feeling told her she would be seeing more of him. Back in the pub, she shoved her way between the many people standing in groups or hugging the bar.

'Hooray, she's back.' A roar of applause hit the rafters crossing the ceiling.

Daisy smiled. If Tom didn't appreciate her, then her customers surely did.

At that moment, Tom and Alice were breaking free from a lingering kiss. 'I love you, Alice,' he whispered. 'This double life is doing my head in. Why don't you marry me? Then I can do the honourable thing and tell Daisy. She's too nice to be treated in this manner.' His stocky frame slumped against the wall. The euphoria of lovemaking was still within him, but the palm of his conscience slapped it away. He cupped Alice's chin and probed her eyes. 'What about it, then? I'm game if you are, Alice.'

'You must tell Daisy, but not yet.' Alice paused. 'Stay friends. There are miles of space out there waiting to suck us up. I'll be there first probably.' Alice was thinking of her pain. What if it was serious?

'You're talking rubbish, Alice. I want you for always.' Fiercely, he gripped her arms. 'Say you'll marry me. Please. There are no obstacles in our way now, so what's stopping you?'

'Nothing.' She leaned against his body, waiting for another spasm to pass.

'What's wrong, Alice?' Concern filled him as he saw the whiteness of her face.

'I'm fine. You worry too much, Tom.'

'Only because I care about you. Goodnight, my dear. See you tomorrow.' His mouth lifted in a smile. The door clicked shut.

Mary Marshall, peeping from an opening in her curtains, saw him go.

'There he is,' she cried. 'They've been at it again. That poor lass he's engaged to hasn't got any sorrows to seek. Somebody should tell her.'

'It's none o' our business, Mary. Don't meddle in other folk's affairs.' Fred raised his eyebrows. Like hedges in full leaf, they stuck out from above hooded eyes, giving him an intimidating appearance.

'It is our business.' Undaunted, Mary carped on. 'If it was happenin' to Elsie you'd be the first to whinge.'

'Well it's not happenin' to Elsie. So shut up, woman.'

Fred resumed gazing into the fire. Sparks fluttered up the chimney. Some settled on the soot already sticking on the side of the pot. He watched them flicker and die.

Women were contrary buggers, he thought. Only good for food and bed. Even bed had lost its magic. He let his head fall on his chest and dozed. Dreams of Audrey Hepburn woke him up. He felt randy. Mary saw his obvious arousal and smiled, thinking she'd caused it. In bed, he slaked his thirst on her thoughts. God, women were easily gulled.

Gradually, little bits of tittle-tattle concerning Tom, reached Daisy's ears. Snippets heard during the course of her work. Tale ends of sentences – cut off as she approached.

Monday nights were quiet. Daisy took Doreen aside. 'Can I have the night off, please. I have something to discuss with Tom.'

'Yes, love, of course.' Doreen looked solicitously at Daisy's face. It was the colour of chalk. Quiet of late she was too. Poor lassie. Men were callous bastards. Although Tom seemed a decent enough chap. Still – one never knew.

'Thank you, Doreen.' Quickly, Daisy wiped tables, rearranged beer mats, took away empty glasses, then collected her coat, bag and gloves, and hurried out.

Arriving at her flat, she picked up the telephone and looked up Tom's number. Garrick, Garrick, her finger slid down the names. Well, there was only one farm called The Spinney. His dad's name must be Norman. Some time elapsed before her call was answered. The voice was breathless.

'Is Tom available, Mr Garrick? I'm his girlfriend.'

'Oh, so you're the one giving him a glint in his eye and a spring in his step?' said his father with a laugh. 'He's in the steading right now, but I'll get him to give you a call when he comes in.'

'Thank you, Mr Garrick. Nice to speak to you. Bye.'

'Bye, lass. You can call me Norman. Any lassie who can make my son happy gets my vote.'

The rattling of pails preceded Tom's entry into the kitchen. Two thuds indicated the removal of his wellies. Water slashing into the sink, told he was washing his hands. His father knew every sound.

'Your girlfriend phoned,' he shouted.

'What did she want?'

'Don't know. You've to call back. She sounds nice. Why don't you bring her home with you?'

'I've only gone with her a few months.' Tom's voice was brusque.

His dad sensed an evasiveness.

'Hell, your mother and I got married within six weeks.'

'I'm different, dad. I don't leap headlong into things. That's a recipe for disaster.'

He stepped into the room.

'I thought you were happier lately. If it's not Daisy – then who?'

Tom's cheeks flamed. Slinging his jacket over a chair, he sat down. He hated being deceitful, but Alice had pleaded with him not to tell.

'Get on that phone to Daisy, then.' Eyes widened with displeasure, Norman glared at his son.

'Alright, dad I will.' Leaning over, he picked the dratted thing up. His dad would burst a blood vessel if he didn't. Guilt jangled his nerves when Daisy's clear voice vibrated along the line.

'Tom, can I see you later? We could go for a meal in town. I'd like to talk to you.'

Tom grumbled inaudibly under his breath. He hoped she wasn't getting all matrimonial on him. Not now, when he and Alice had reached an understanding.

'OK, I'll pick you up around seven. I've got a job to do first.'

One guess what that was, thought Daisy.

He arrived in good time. In the flash of lights from the oncoming traffic, Daisy studied his features as he drove. Grimness dragged a veil over them. His face was a closed book.

In the restaurant, they found a corner table. A light on the wall beside them glinted like gold on their hair and glanced over their faces. She's lovely, thought Tom. What a bloody fool I am. But it was Alice he craved. Nothing would ever change that.

The ambience of the restaurant relaxed them. After perusing the menu, they ordered. Both choosing a mixed grill. Taking a deep breath, Daisy decided to take the bull by the horns. 'Are you seeing someone else, Tom? You're acting as if you're not interested any more.'

Startled, he sat back in his chair, the unvarnished truth depriving him of words. His mouth opened then clamped shut, like a trout gasping its last breath. Daisy nearly laughed, but it was too serious to scoff at.

'Well – are you?'

Torn between his pact with Alice and his allegiance to Daisy, Tom's mind hammered for a solution. Then he sighed. Why put off the inevitable?

'Yes.'

The word was a dagger. It dug into her heart, rowelling her happiness into splinters.

'Who?' Eyes dull with the revelation, held his.

'Alice.'

'Alice Wilson?'

'Yes.' Pride oozed from him as he said it.

'But she's —' Daisy stopped, embarrassed.

'Old, you were going to say. She's not. We are of similar ages. Early forties. Still in our prime.'

Ah, that explained a lot. Daisy felt defeated; but never would she reveal the true extent of her hurt. From beneath the table, she unwound her black stockinged legs.

Tom saw the half turn of her body as she said a quiet 'goodbye' and, straight backed, head high, she took her leave.

Once outside, her indifference evaporated, and every part of her plummeted. On the cool stone wall of a pub she leant, taking stock.

'Where to now?' she wondered.

A familiar figure stepped from the building, his arm round the waist of a sniggering girl. It was Tony and Rachel.

Giving herself a mental shake, she moved towards them.

'Hello, you two, have you been for a drink?' She put on a cheerier demeanour.

'Aye, we come here often. They make good bar meals.' Tony's eyes sparkled down into Rachel's merry ones. Her left arm wound round his body and there, in the busy street, they hugged. Lifting his head, Tony grinned at Daisy. 'She's a man-eater, this. You know how Saturn devoured his children at birth? Well – she devours grown men.'

'Sure and if I tried to eat you, you'd be as tough as Jimmy Baird's old shoes – and the horse muck you work with – just as stinky.'

Daisy laughed.

Rachel had that effect.

'Do you want a lift?' Tony motioned to an old Ford hugging the kerb. 'This is mine. It's better for taking Rachel places. The bike has its uses, but it's hopeless for courting in.'

'Thank you, Tony, I would. I'm at a loose end. Tom and I have parted company.'

'Oh, I'm sorry.' Tony was flustered.

Rachel clasped her in a silent embrace. Ever hearing bits of chat in the shop, she knew of Tom's duplicity. Decibels louder than anyone else, Mary Marshall's voice trumpeted the news of his trysts to everybody.

'You get in here.' Rachel pointed to the front seat. 'I'll sit in the back.' A wicked smile spread across her face. 'Sure and we spend more time there anyway, don't we, Tony?' The lilt of her Irish brogue was like music.

Thanking Tony profusely for the lift, Daisy crossed the street and let herself into her flat. In a zombie-like state, she switched on the lights, the kettle and a hob on the cooker. In the cupboard, she found a tin of soup. The meal in the restaurant had been wasted and, despite being down in the dumps, she still felt hungry. Going to the fire, she stared at the dead ashes. Vigorously, she poked them, choking on the powdery particles that had a will of their own and flew upwards onto her face and hair. Screwing up pages of the daily paper, she laid them on the grate. Topped with kindling and coal, soon she had a blazing fire sparking up the chimney.

She switched on the radio for some music or voices, but the only voice she could hear, was Tom's – telling her he was seeing Alice.

Meanwhile, up in the Highlands, Cathy's grandad had disappeared for the afternoon. When he returned, he was driving a huge, black Bentley. He had been a frugal man over the years and his money had grown considerably. Now, he had a desire to spend some of his fortune.

'Bloomin' heck! Look at that machine,' breathed Jim. His eyes swept from the car to Cathy. 'Do you think he's going to be travelling?'

'I don't know. He's never said anything.'

He soon did.

'We're taking you home, Cathy. It's time we made physical contact with Alice. Phone calls are fine, but we want to see her in the flesh. Get your things packed. We'll be setting off in the morning.'

Cathy was knocked for a six. 'We're going home, Ben,' she whispered. 'To see your granny.' She reached for his hand. 'Come on, let's tell Paula.' She turned shining eyes to her grandad. 'Can we go to see the loch before we leave? One more look. Please, grandad?'

The loch looked dark and depthless as they all piled out of the car to say a silent goodbye next morning. The wee kirk hugged the edge, its reflection disappearing into the murky depths. With jumbled feelings, Cathy took in the scenery. October was on its way out. Trees were losing their rich tints. Pine forests drank from the many different gradients of the high hill whose rugged contours etched the sky. The loud roar of a stag resounded over the hill top. The rutting season would soon be over, but, as yet, the hinds were still receptive to his overtures. Eyes glazed with lust, he made his move.

Cathy breathed deeply of the wild air.

She'd miss all this.

It was a long journey home, but soon, in the fading light, Cathy could see the outlines of familiar buildings and woods and the snaking grey glitter of the river.

'Grandad, look! We're nearly there.' Excitedly, Cathy waved her arms. On her knee, she jiggled her son, Ben. 'You're almost home, Ben,' she murmured. Her lips nuzzled his hair, soft as down, combed across his head. His eyes looked trustingly into hers. In his hands, he held a much loved, one-eared teddy. He took it everywhere.

Cathy couldn't wait to see her mother's face when she opened the door. Her grandad, dressed in his Sunday best, looked every inch a prosperous squire.

Granny, a picture of elegance in a plum coloured suit, sat in the front seat staring straight ahead.

From the back seat, Cathy watched them as they sat; adrift in an ocean of thoughts. Ben's head nodded. Soon, it lolled to the side and settled in the crook of her arm; his body relaxed and hot against hers. Protectively, she held him. He was her life. Paula, beside her, smiled and touched his soft cheek.

At last they were there. Shivering with excitement, Cathy got out. Ben woken from a deep sleep, began to cry. 'Sssh, my baby. This is your granny's house. Try and smile for granny.' Cathy held him tighter. His thumb found his mouth, and his eyes swung expectantly to the door.

Dozing by the fire, the sound of knocking roused Alice. Goodness me, who could that be? she mused. Tom had left not so long ago. Had he forgotten something? Hand clutching her side, she switched on the hall light and opened the door.

'Cathy.'

'Mum.'

A look of disbelief circled Alice's face. On their own volition, her arms opened. Two figures waited in the shadow, unseen until a cough pulled Alice's eyes over Cathy's shoulder. Quickly, Alice stepped forward. Her welcome was for yesterday, today and the future.

'Oh, and this is Paula.' Cathy pointed to a waif-like shape outlined against the gleam of the car. Unravelling herself from her parents' embrace, Alice waited. She wondered who Paula was, and where she fitted in.

Paula blushed and held out her hand. 'I'm pleased to meet

you, Mrs Wilson.' Her voice was musical. The voice of the Highlands. Alice took to her at once.

Lying awake later, Alice tried to assimilate her good fortune. Was this really true? Or was it only a wonderful dream? The moon beamed through a chink in the curtains. It shone on Cathy's hair, still fair, the colour of ripe barley, and skidded off Ben's arm as he turned in his sleep.

Oh yes, it was true all right.

'Jesus, look at that!' Bruce and the other workers expressed the same awe as Jim McDonald had as the shiny, black Bentley caught their eyes next morning as they left for work. 'Some o' Alice's rich friends come out o' the woodwork.' Fred Marshall squinted at Bruce. Tom and her might be gettin' spliced and not tellin' us.'

'What a chassis.' Bruce Tait ran his hand reverently over the glossy bumper, his eyes assessing the sleek bodywork like a farmer valuing a prize ram.

'Never heard it come in last night.' Fred moved to touch it too. 'It's engine must run as smooth as a ballet dancer.'

'No wonder you didn't hear it. The racket them bairns were makin' would have wakened the deid and drooned a thunderclap.' Walter grimaced. 'Mind you, I've no room to complain. My lads were responsible too.' He looked at his feet. 'That pop music is just a noise – and they play it that loud. What's wrong with the good old Scottish dance music?'

Falling into step, the trio set off. Dave Hart hurried to catch up, Spot and Bess at his heels. He and Maggie lived in a house further back than the row. It was bigger, and nicely sheltered on either side by trees. Head down, he strode on, lost in thoughts of the day's work. A tap on Alice's bedroom window, made him pause. Looking up, he stared. It was Cathy. In her arms she held a child. His steps quickened. Maggie would be pleased, but would John?

Dave knew that he and Caroline had fixed a date for the

wedding. Yet the lad was unhappy. He didn't want to pry or interfere. There were no boundaries and no closed doors in their relationship. Ever since he was a nipper, John had tagged on to him. Dave loved him like a son. If he wanted to unburden himself, he would do it in his own time.

In silence, they worked. 'Did you know that Cathy's home?' he asked, breaking the spell of quietness.

'No.' John's head shot up. 'When?'

'Last night. She has a bairn with her. There's a big Bentley outside the house. It'll be her grandparents likely. I've heard they're monied.'

'Could be.' John's knife quickened as he pared bits from a ewe's foot. 'Anyway, it's none of my business.' His outward calm didn't fool Dave.

'Then you should make it so. A ring on the wrong finger could spoil your life forever.' Dave spoke sternly.

'I don't know what you mean.' John looked at Dave with blank eyes.

'Ah, son; don't throw your life away.' Dave stood with hands clenched, his face racked with worry. He looked at the ewe struggling in John's grasp. 'Hell, if you slice any more off her feet, she'll need clogs.'

It broke the tension, and they laughed.

Word of Cathy's return spread like a flood. From house to house, from shops to pubs and finally – to the manse.

'Who's this Cathy everyone is talking about?' Caroline buttered her toast, pretending not to be interested, but she was; very.

'Oh, she and John were an item once. They split up. I don't know why. Pity, they made a nice couple.' The minister's eyes stared unseeingly over the table. 'I must go and see her. She's been through a lot.'

Caroline seethed. She thought fast 'Take me with you.' Like danger signals, her words whipped the air. Gordon was alarmed.

'No, you'll meet her soon enough. It's time you found employment, Caroline. You spend far too much time thinking idle thoughts. Evil ones, he wanted to say, but bit his tongue. All sorts of rumours were circulating in the village concerning her behaviour.

Bobby kept him enlightened. 'She nearly had Alf's breeks down, minister. Outside the pub. Raring for it, she was.'

Dear God, he thought, what next? Now, she'd joined the young farmer's club. His sympathies went to the lads. She'd go through them like a piranha fish.

In his study, he covered his face with his hands. Her presence had become a drain on his energy. If John gets to know, there'll be hell to pay. Bobby had the measure of her, but John – the minister sucked in his breath – poor John.

The frosty sky of the previous evening had changed, and by mid-morning, a layer of tattered nimbus clouds darkened the wide firmament as Gordon set out to see Cathy.

It's going to rain, he thought. Blast! that means that Caroline will hang around the house all day moaning. The phrase, God why hast thou forsaken me? entered his mind. He let it go. He was hardly going to be nailed to a cross.

Along the road, Cathy walked, little Ben clutching her hand. Gordon pulled his car to the edge and stepped out. 'Good morning, Cathy.' He crossed to her side and held out his hand.

'Mr McKenzie, it's nice to see you.' She looked down. 'Meet Ben. He's a little rascal.' Lovingly, she lifted him up. 'Look, Ben, this is my very good friend the Reverend Gordon McKenzie. He's our minister.'

Ben's eyes studied Gordon. Then he smiled. Bert's smile, Gordon recalled, and Bert's eyes. He shifted his gaze, not wanting to mention Bert's name in case Cathy was still raw inside.

'I'm on my way to see Dave and John. Would you like come? I'd like you to –' Cathy hesitated. 'A bit of moral support won't go amiss.'

'Certainly, Cathy. Wait, I'll lock the car.' Pocketing the keys, he matched her steps, slow and sometimes stopped, depending on the whims of Ben.

'Umm – Cathy. Do you know that my daughter and John are betrothed?'

'No, I didn't know you had a daughter.' Cathy stooped to pick up Ben and fiddled with his shoes and mitts, head bent, avoiding the minister's gaze.

But he had seen the shock, no – he had felt it, stealing the light from her lovely face. So her quondam feelings for John still existed. He pondered on this, wondering how he could bring about a happy conclusion. Caroline was the bugbear he had to contend with, though.

From the big, five-barred gate, Dave and John watched their snail-like progress. 'That bairn will be everything to Cathy.' Dave passed his gaze to John. 'If she ever marries, her husband will have to accept him like his own son, else the relationship won't last long.'

'Yes, I can see that.' John spoke automatically, trying to stifle the urge to run to her. To lay her on the soft grass. To love her. But he was getting married at Christmas. He felt the stuffing ooze out of him, like sand in an egg-timer.

His eyes were dull as he greeted her. 'How are you, John?' she said. 'It's good to see you again.'

He nodded – speechless. Kneeling down beside Ben, he gazed into his eyes.

With a child's intense stare, Ben surveyed John. In his grasp he held a dinky toy. 'Car,' he said, giving it to John.

'Is it for me?' John's hand reached out. The small head nodded, then shook. 'Mine,' he whispered. With a brrring sound like an engine, he ran the wheels over John's knee, and an irrevocable bond was founded.

'How is Maggie, Dave?' Cathy addressed him for the first time.

'She's fine. Come in and have tea and scones when you have time. You too, John.' Like the minister, Dave was determined to bring them together. 'Your daughter won't mind, Gordon, will she?' He winked at the minister.

'Hmmm – well – I hope not, Dave, but she hasn't been blessed with good nature unfortunately. If I live to be as old as Methuselah, I will never understand the girl.' The wind ruffled his hair. Face angry, mouth downward tilted, he spoke to John. 'You've still got time to change your mind, John. Take heed.'

His gaze rested on Cathy once more. 'It was very nice seeing you again, Cathy. Bye, for now.' Patting Ben on the head, he walked away.

Dave, with his quietism and good sense, strode quickly after him Like an extension of himself, his dogs rose too. Left to themselves, John and Cathy stood in an awkward silence. With a husky voice, John spoke first. Did you know that your dad was not my father?' His brows gathered together as if fighting the rays of a strong sun.

'No, I didn't.' Cathy's hopes rose, then were dashed in the same second. He was about to be wed. He was somebody else's property now. With a sob, she twisted away from him and ran.

'Cathy, come back.' Shocked into action, he raced after her. Grabbing her arm, he held her and whirled her round. 'Oh, Cathy, don't run away from me.' His lips, having hungered for hers for years, fell upon them in a long, passionate kiss. Slowly, they drew apart, then, each holding one of Ben's hands, they made for home.

'What about Caroline?' Cathy was reluctant to bring her into the conversation, but knew she couldn't just brush her under the carpet as though she didn't exist.

'I'll tell her tonight, but watch her, Cathy; she can be dangerous.'

'Surely she cannot be that bad?'

'She is.'

'What could she do?'

John pursed his lips. He didn't know how spiteful she could be, but he did know that if she were thwarted in any way, it bode ill for those responsible.

'You two took your time.' Dave stepped from the byre doorway and stood, clothes soaking up the rain that had begun to fall. His quick eyes, used to counting scores of sheep as they streamed from the pens, noted the new togetherness and rapt faces and he rejoiced.

'When's the big day, then?' he shouted.

'You'll be the first to know, Dave. I'm taking Cathy to see my mother.' John screwed up his nose. 'Send up a prayer for us, will you?'

Dave chuckled. 'It'll be Gordon needing a few words of prayer; living with that siren of a daughter once she finds out about you two. She'll be wanting to scratch your eyes out, Cathy.'

Cathy shivered and clung to John's arm.

'Well good luck anyway, John.' Dave's look was quizzical. 'On both counts.'

Barbara was setting the table when John arrived with Cathy in tow.

'Hello, mum, see who's back.' John beamed a smile to Cathy at his side.

Between the table and the unit, Barbara stopped, her hand suspended. The plate which she'd been holding fell to the floor with a crash.

'Cathy!' The word was an arrow, pulled by the strings of her mouth. Like Dave, she noticed the cosiness between them and swore under her breath.

'This is my future wife.' John brought Cathy forward.

Barbara was astounded. This put a different complexion on things. Then she laughed. That upstart Caroline would not give up so easily.

Like Rembrandt, seeing people from within the light and dark,

John saw his mother preen the feathers of her mind. He knew what she was thinking. That Caroline would be a better choice – that she would oust Cathy – but she was raking cold ashes.

'Set another place for Cathy, mum please.' John spoke with a new authority.

Meekly, she complied with his wishes. She wasn't beaten yet, though. Caroline she had accepted to keep the peace, but her antipathy towards Cathy, ran as deep as a well. Action was needed – and quickly.

As soon as they'd gone after their meal, she picked up the phone. 'Caroline.' Barbara didn't beat about the bush. 'John is about to renege on your wedding plans. He's met up with Cathy again. You must do something.'

'Do what?'

'I don't know. You'll think of something. Anything to put a spoke in their wheels. Use your womanly wiles.'

'Oh, I can do that all right.'

Taken aback by the virulence of her tone, Barbara felt a tinge of regret. 'Nothing too drastic,' she said, by way of atonement.

A rabid laugh sizzled along the wires.

Barbara trembled. What had she done?

All day at work, John's mind was full of Cathy. He had only one hurdle to jump. Telling Caroline.

Rain had fallen intermittently all day. It pattered on roofs and plopped on the fallen leaves skirting buildings and trees; tattered piles of them, caught there, awaiting another buffet to toss them elsewhere.

It was now November and darkness cloaked the land early. With unwavering steps, John walked to the manse door. Caroline answered the bell.

'Hello,' she said, beckoning him in with a flourish.

'I'm not staying.' John passed a clammy hand over his brow. 'I've come to tell you the wedding is off. I can't go through with it. I love Cathy.'

In silence Caroline heard him out. Then she dropped her bombshell.

'You'll have to marry me. I'm pregnant.'

Her voice mocked him.

'What!' John was stunned. 'I thought you said you used some form of contraception?'

Dark clouds were gathering in his brain.

'More fool you, then.' She gave a derisive laugh. John staggered back. She certainly knew how to twist the knife. How had he let himself get embroiled with such a nasty lassie?

'You'll rue the day you did this to me.' His words fell on her like a witch's spell.

She blanched, but quickly recovered her composure.

'Such melodrama, John. You'll toe the line, like it or not.' With a flick of her hair, she swept into the house.

As if the world had fallen on him, John turned away. How was he going to tell Cathy? Hell! The Fates really had it in for him. Or God. Or whoever pulled the strings dictating their lives. He'd have to marry the bitch now. Why had he not used condoms? He swore again. Loudly. Then, crashing his fists against the bark of a tree, he laid his cheek against the cool, smoothness of it and cried.

Alice answered his knock. 'John, you look like a corpse. What's wrong?'

'I might as well be a corpse,' he cried. 'Oh, Alice, how can things be fine one minute, then up the spout the next?' John's face collapsed in a heap of misery.

'Come in. Cathy's in the kitchen.'

Hope drained from Cathy as she saw John's downcast countenance. 'You didn't tell her, did you?'

'I did, but she says she's pregnant. I'll have to marry her.' Hopelessly, he shrugged. 'What else can I do?'

In the kitchen, they embraced, clinging to each other like ivy to a wall. 'See me later,' Cathy whispered. 'Somewhere secluded.

I want you to make love to me.' She looked at his face. 'I know you are an honourable person, but do you have to marry her?' He saw the resurgence of hope run over her features and dropped his arms.

'Yes, Cathy, I must. I'm sorry, but I'll never touch her in that way again.'

Cathy gazed at him with sad eyes. He was really whacked. Her indefatigable John – beaten by a scheming woman. She touched his cheek. 'See you in the tack room at nine.'

As Barbara saw his broad figure fill the doorway, her gaze alighted more on his expression than his bulk. She watched as, with apathetic steps, he walked to his chair and sat down. So engrossed was she trying to fathom his mood, she failed to observe how close was his examination of her.

She knows, he thought. He detected a conspiracy here, and didn't like it. In fact, he didn't have to put up with it. When he and Caroline were wed, he'd move in with Dave and Maggie. If they'd have him. Caroline and his mother can be happy living in their own cooked-up bliss.

Full of enthusiasm, he went to meet Cathy. The door was ajar. Stepping into her arms, he sighed. They had waited a long time for this.

'We'd better go. They'll be wondering where we are.'

Cathy patted the creases of her skirt and gazed at John's face. 'I love you, John.'

'I love you, too. I always have. It's a blessing Beth found out about my webbed toes. You'd still be thinking we were related.'

'I know.'

What they didn't know, was that the hereditary webbed toes characteristic had not gone to sleep. Nor its consequences.

But tonight, they bathed in the nectar of their love.

'Mum's got Tom in tonight, we'll have to be discreet and knock loudly. I'm worried about her, though. She keeps holding her side as if she's pained.'

'You should tell her to see a doctor.'

'She does work at the manse. I'll maybe get the minister to speak to her. She'll listen to him.'

'Yes, he's a very caring man. I think he's quite shocked by Caroline's behaviour.'

'Sssh, don't spoil things by mentioning her. Let this be our time.' Cathy pressed her cheek to his. 'And our place.'

'You're right. Come on, I'll take you home.'

A surprised Dave stared at John's face, now on a level with his own, as he stood on the threshold. Light from the hall, revealed the grave countenance of the lad.

'Why hello, John. What brings you here at this time of night? Anything wrong?'

'Where do I start, Dave. Could you by any chance put up with a lodger? I know it's a big decision, but I'm desperate.'

Nonplussed, Dave scratched his head. He noted the set jaw, the trembling mouth, the eyes, still with the glow of lovemaking on them, and wondered how such contradictory expressions could invade anyone's face at one time.

He made an inward gesture with his hand.

Mutely, John stepped in.

'Maggie, get the kettle on; we've got a visitor. A very hungry one too, I bet. So butter a couple of your scones.'

Ten minutes later, seated by a blazing fire, with a cup of tea in one hand and one of Maggie's scones in the other, John's icy thoughts thawed.

To have found her and lost her in the same day has cut me to the quick, Dave. We are going to meet whenever we can. It may not by honest in your eyes, or Maggie's, but we have consummated our relationship and made a pact. I can tell you both because you're my best friends.'

'Aw lad, we are sorely grieved for you, but are you doing the right thing in leaving your home?'

'Yes, I couldn't thole living close to that hard, selfish creature.

She has canker in her soul. I hope God makes her suffer – that is if there is a god.' John leaned forward. 'I have doubts sometimes, but we've got to believe in something, don't we, Dave?' Letting his head slump on the back of the chair, John closed his eyes.

'You can stay here as long as you like, son. Maggie will be like a hen with a chicken, won't you, dear?'

'I've already got a chicken.' She gave John a mischievous grin. 'Well – more like an old cockerel.'

'Not so much of the old, wife of mine. There's plenty life left in this cockerel yet.' A smile played on his lips. An amused smile, with sexual overtones.

John enjoyed their banter. The warm way they treated each other. Cathy and he would've had that same rapport had they been married, but it was not to be. Unless some being from another planet whisked Caroline away. To the Antarctic, or any such climes as cold and biting as she was, hopefully.

He rose to go. He had conceived a plan. Now to carry it out.

Each with a drink in their hands, his mother and Caroline sat chatting. On his entry, all talk ceased. By the shrewish look in their eyes, it was clear he was the pivotal part of their discussion.

He decided to be blunt.

'I'm bringing the wedding forward, and it's going to be in a register office. That's final.' Feet apart, hands in pockets, he glared at the heartless pair, his whole demeanour defiant. He was a man on a mission.

Their eyes zipped towards each other. He hoped the catches of their thoughts would fuse and turn them into statues; or pillars of salt, like Lot's wife, when she dared to look back. But no, they swung their beady way to him. He jerked away, breaking the link.

On the day of his wedding, he woke at dawn. Wind beat branches against the wall next to his window. It was the end of November and the bare, twigged boughs scratched and scraped the rough surface. It was colder now and John was loath to get up. Especially on this day.

The register office was austere. Everything was brown, even the light shades. As he pressed the ring on her finger, he felt as though he was putting a noose round his own neck. He refused to wear one.

'You're mine now,' he heard her say as they stepped on to the street.

Little did she know, he thought. What a shock she was going to get.

The Land Rover was parked across the street. In a proprietorial fashion, she linked his arm. Shrugging her hand away, he fished in his pocket for the keys. In the back of the Land Rover were his clothes, boots, shoes, books and radio. Almost everything he owned. He drove fast, drawing up at the farmhouse with a screech of tyres.

'Right,' he said. 'Get out.'

With alacrity, she did so, thinking he would follow. He didn't. In a whirl, he turned and was gone. With furious feet, she stamped inside.

Barbara looked up in surprise. Where's John? Her eyebrows rose into double arches. 'Surely you haven't fallen out already?'

'Ask your precious son. He's done a bunk. I saw his clothes on the back seat when he ordered me out.' Her lip curled with displeasure. 'He may have left – but I'm still his wife. If he's away to Cathy, he'll regret it.'

Exasperated, Barbara let her rant. She was becoming thoroughly sick of her. Since hearing about Cathy's grandparents. How nice they were. How distinguished. How polite, but most of all – how rich – owning a big Bentley for God's sake, she'd had a change of heart regarding Cathy as a partner for John. Her mercenary mind ticked over, kicking a ball of 'what might have been,' thud, thud, thud, against the wall of her brain. At last, she spoke, preceding her words with a long, quivering sigh. 'You'll just have to make the most of a bad situation, Caroline. You brought a lot of this on yourself, you know.'

'Well, you've changed your mind all of a sudden. Of course I don't have wealthy relations, but my father is well enough off. Being a minister is a very prestigious job.' With a tilt of her chin, she defied Barbara to refute her. Had she been a nice person, Barbara would have been proud of her stance. How did her father fare with her moods? she wondered.

Even as she thought this, Gordon sat cogitating in his study. Cogitating and worrying. With certainty, she must be a changeling this daughter of his. Or had his wife had an affair and Caroline was the result? Maybe she'd inherited bad genes from him. He didn't know much about chromosomes, but sure as hell they'd got mixed up along the line.

He stared at the blank sheet of paper on his desk. No words would come. Frustrated, he grabbed his jacket from the back of his chair, yanked open the door, and blazed down to the kitchen.

For a minute, he observed Alice as she worked. She worked quietly. Everything was quiet about Alice, he mused. Even Caroline never had cross words with her.

'I'm going for a walk, Alice. I'll have a pot of tea when I return, if you please.'

He was gone before she could answer and Alice stared at his retreating back. Dressed in a smart, tweed suit, he cut a fine figure of a man striding down the path.

From the oven, she removed a small roast. She had partially boiled potatoes for roasting, cut vegetables and made gravy. Turning to switch off the cooker, suddenly she bent double. 'Oooh,' she gasped. Her face whitened. Sweat blistered her brow. Her eyes swung upwards, and she fell in a dead faint on the kitchen floor.

That's where the minister found her.

'I'm back for that pot of tea, Alice.' His gaze swept the kitchen, then the floor. 'Oh, God, Alice.' Hunkering beside her, he felt for a pulse, then stumbled to the phone. 'An ambulance, please. Quick,' he roared.

'Where to? And what's the problem?' The voice at the other end asked.

'It's the manse, Torwell village. It's Mrs Wilson; she's just lying there.'

A groan, followed by the sound of retching, had Gordon once more kneeling at her side. She tried to straighten, but collapsed in a heap, yelling in agony.

At the hospital, they wheeled her to the operating theatre. 'Acute appendicitis. We'll have to operate, I'm afraid, Mrs Wilson.' The doctor, round faced and large eared, gazed down at her with kindly eyes. He reminded Alice of a donkey. The big ears. The honest look. Had she not been in such pain, she might have smiled. Instead, she cried out and gripped his hand.

Back in the ward after the operation, she lay in a state of torpor. The anaesthetic was still in her system when Tom visited.

'You gave us a fright, darling,' he whispered. 'They all send their love.' He held out a parcel. 'Paula made this especially for you. It's a chocolate cake. Gordon will be in later. I'm sending Paula to work at the manse in your absence. She'll keep Bobby out of mischief.'

A slow movement of the head and a flicker of her fair lashes, were his reward. He went away satisfied.

At the manse, Paula set to work like a whirlwind. When Bobby rushed home from school, he was met with a host of appetizing smells. Furniture gleamed; the mirror sparkled – but best of all was the fire. Darts of flames flickered and danced their way up the chimney. He sat down. The front of his chair was hot to touch. Happily, he let it seep through his trousers.

'Hello, Bobby.' The voice whirled him round. It was Paula.

'What are you doing here?' He looked at her in surprise.

'Alice is in hospital, so I'm standing in for her.'

'Does the minister know?'

'He doesn't know I'm here. Tom drove me over.'

A light step in the hallway, then the squeak of the study door, heralded the minister's arrival. Like an arrow shot from a bow, Bobby ran in behind him.

'Minister, don't sit down, your dinner's ready.' Bobby's face was alight with excitement.

Already seated, the minister smiled.

'I think it's roast meat and roasted tatties. Then pudding,' Bobby added with a grin.

'Now, you're having me on. Although it sounds very nice.' Gordon heaved himself up from his chair. He was tired. He had a board meeting tonight too. Just when he'd like to stretch his legs in front of the fire and have forty winks.

'You've to come into the dining room, minister.'

'We always eat in the kitchen, Bobby.'

'Not tonight. See —' Bobby held open the door and waved him in.

'I know I'm tired, but do I really see the table set with a white cloth and steaming plates of food? Aaah,' he sniffed the air.

Then he saw Paula.

'Hello, Mr McKenzie.' Her soft Highland tongue was enchanting. She had cat's eyes. Yellow, like when the sun shines on them, making them all iris.

He had only seen her about twice in church and had not really noticed her. He did now. Feeling like he'd walked miles in a desert and was in the sway of a mirage, he held out his hand. 'Paula, how nice to see you. I didn't expect all this. Will you join us?' Her hesitation, he took for a yes. 'Bobby, set another place for Paula, please.'

'Thank you, but I should be getting back.' Paula's feelings were all jumbled up, as though they'd been tossed and turned in a cement mixer. Bobby gave her a cheeky grin. She relaxed. It was nice here. She'd like fine to be working on a permanent basis.

Gordon's eyes appraised her as she sat down. A heat crept under her skin; rising to her cheeks. They shone like two rosy apples.

'Would you care to come with me to visit Alice?' I could drop you off on the way home.

'Yes, I'd like to. She's been very kind to me.'

'Good.' He turned his gaze to Bobby. 'What have you planned for tonight, Bobby?'

'Me – oh –' Bobby screwed up his face. 'I might see the lads for a while. Have a game of pool.'

'Just the lads?'

'No, the lassies will be there as well. Some of them are better players than the laddies.'

'Oh, well, if you can't be good, be careful,' Gordon quipped.

In amazement, Bobby looked at him.

The minister – making a joke?

'Is that you on about condoms again, minister?' he chirped.

'Now, now, Bobby. There's a lady present.' Gordon's gaze lingered on Paula.

She smiled. He flushed.

Bobby's observant eyes perceived all of this.

'You might be needing them yourself one of these days, minister. I'll lend you some.'

Bobby waited for him to cough and splutter, like he always did when he was embarrassed, but instead, he hooted with laughter.

Paula linked Gordon's arm, feeding Bobby's conception of things. 'Let him think what he likes, Mr McKenzie,' she whispered. 'But don't think I'm a walkover. I've old values. I believe in waiting.'

The door banged behind them. Hardly daring to breathe, the minister stood. 'You mean —?' He started to speak, but was unable to go on. She nodded.

They embraced, there on the step, oblivious of any people peering with prying eyes from behind curtains.

'We'll make it soon.'

'Yes.'

'When?'

'We'll wait until Alice is better. She can be matron of honour.' Paula's eyes sparkled. She needed someone to pinch her to tell her she was awake and not dreaming.

Alice was still lethargic when they stood by her bed, but aware enough to notice their state of happiness.

'Well – tell me then.' She spoke in a whisper.

'We're getting married. Seeing you were the one who brought us together, inadvertently, we would like you to be in attendance at our wedding.'

'My you're a quick worker, Gordon McKenzie. After all those years of abstinence, you're taking the plunge. How did you manage to break the hard shell protecting that elusive heart of his, Paula?'

'Oh,' Paula laughed. 'I smashed it first shot. Like Julius Caesar's defeat of the Pharnous' army. Veni, vidi, vici.'

'I came, I saw, I conquered. Mind you —' she peeked coyly at the minister. 'I think we conquered each other.'

A reflective look made solemn her face for a moment. 'From now on,' she added, 'I'll let him be the conductor in this band. Then again, I might have enough force to make up the whole brass section on my own.'

Alice smiled. Gordon had met his match in this young lass. She was happy for them.

In the White Swan, Daisy smiled as she pulled pints, measured drams and chatted to customers. It was her public smile. Tom had stolen her real one. Sometimes she thought she was over it – but her trust in men had plummeted.

She looked at the clock. It was nearly closing time. 'Right, folks,' she cried. 'Last orders now, please.'

From the chorus of orders, she managed to satisfy each individual's needs. Letting her shoulders slump, she breathed a sigh of relief. She could go home now. Collecting her things, she left the bar. 'Cheerio, then, Doreen. I'm off now. See you tomorrow.'

'Sure, duckie. I'll see this lot off the premises. There's a bobby in the vicinity, so they won't take much shifting tonight.'

The night was calm after the day's rain. Daisy's feet plip-plopped through mini puddles as she wended her way homewards. The fire's face still wore a glow. She discarded her shoes and wriggled her toes to relieve the strain of standing all night. Switching on the radio, she sat back and relaxed. Suddenly, she shot upright, shocked into listening to what the newsreader was saying.

'Donald Townsend,' he relayed. 'Jailed for the rape of a young girl, has escaped. On no account approach him. He could be dangerous.'

Prickles shivered down her spine. Some inner sense, or portent, told her to be on guard – and Cathy.

Pride forgotten, she rang Tom.

'Is that you, Tom? Did you hear the news?'

'Yes, it's hellish, isn't it?' Cathy will have to be very careful. Little Ben must be guarded at all times in case of abduction. People with Donald's evil intent most often make for home.' Tom paused. 'Anyway, thank you for calling. I'll tell Cathy.' He hesitated. 'I'm sorry it didn't work out between us, Daisy, but I do love Alice.'

'I know. Good luck with her, Tom.'

'Thank you – and take care, Daisy.'

Daisy rang off, feeling more at ease with herself than she'd been for ages Thinking about other folk instead of dwelling on her own woes, was a good antidote.

Chapter Fourteen

News of the minister and Paula's forthcoming marriage, shook the village like a storm.

'He's never looked at another woman for years. Just shows you. There's no fool, like an old fool. Not that he's old, really. What will he be? About fifty-four?' Mary Marshall looked at the faces of her audience in the shop.

'She's a nice lassie, though, and he deserves a bit of luck. He's had a hard time over the years. Well, good luck to them, I say,' said Janet with a grin.

In the shops, pubs and on the streets, the same words could be heard. 'Have you heard about the minister? He's got himself a woman. A young bit stuff she is, too.'

It spread like the measles.

Hard on its heels, indeed, almost simultaneously, was the report on radio and television of Donald Townsend's escape.

Living in perpetual fear, Cathy never dared to venture far from the farm. Ben, she kept at her side at all times.

Donald didn't know about him, but if he happened to find out – Cathy's mind cringed – there's no telling what he might do.

Weeks slipped by. A fatigued Donald slumped neath what little shelter a bare hedge could afford. He needed a change of clothing. It was night. The moon hung like a golden ball, illuminating everything in its path. He turned away from its knowing gaze. Finally, he did sleep. A fitful one, full of the horrors of prison and the abuse meted out to him by inmates. Even hardened criminals abhorred a crime such as his.

At dawn, he awoke. Groaning, he tried to sit up. He seemed stuck in the foetal position in which he'd slept. Back on route, his limbs loosened a fraction. In a field curtained by woods, a shepherd was tending his flock. Donald's eyes lit up. This was providential.

Seizing a large stone, he stole across the soft grass. His hand rose, then fell. Thud! Like a log, the shepherd fell. Quickly, Donald disrobed the fellow and struggled into his clothes. They smelled of body odour, grease and sheep. Screwing his rejected clothing into a ball, he stuffed them into one of the many rabbit warrens that dotted a banking by the hedge.

Down the field, the shepherd's dog, was gathering sheep, running in fits and starts, eyes fixed on them, unaware of his master's plight. Raising its head when an expected call failed to come, it flattened its ears and sped up the field. Fearful of it, Donald sprinted to the safety of the wood.

Torn between two loyalties. To chase – or stay. The love the dog had for the shepherd, won.

Whimpering, it lay down beside him. He was unconscious. It's panting breath fanned his face.

Feeling more at ease in his new garb, Donald continued his journey. His quest. Time inside had altered him. Stolen his tan, thinned his face and made his bid for revenge even greater. Though he was the culprit, he blamed Cathy, everybody, the whole system.

He now sported a beard. It half hid his face and made him older looking. His shaved head had begun to show a grey-black stubble. Only a very careful examination would reveal his identity. He was on home ground now. Legs apart he stood, confident, sensing victory.

Christmas was only two weeks away. John took Cathy shopping. Along the street they went, each holding one of Ben's hands. In and out of shops, buying presents, crackers, tinsel, nuts, and other little things that help give Christmas its magic.

A few flakes of snow flecked the air. Ben laughed as they plopped on his nose and cheeks and lips.

'Snow,' he cried excitedly. 'Look Mummy. Look John.'

'Yes, isn't it lovely, Ben. If it snows all night, we'll make you a snowman in the morning.'

'What's a snowman, mummy?' Ben blinked as the snow got thicker on his lashes. 'Am I a snowman, mummy?'

'You soon will be if this keeps up,' said Cathy with a laugh. 'Come on, let's go for some juice or tea.'

As the happy trio entered the cafe and the door clanged shut behind them, a gaunt figure on the other of the street, stood watching. He made a quick calculation. 'That's my kid,' he muttered, and in his head, a scheme was already forming.

He'd been existing on turnips taken from a nearby field, and apple cores lying in the school playground where he went by stealth in the night. Sometimes he slept in the shed where the children played on rainy days.

He took to studying people's movements in the street and around the farm where Cathy stayed. He watched Daisy. Where she lived. When she started work. The time she finished. He was her shadow.

By ten o'clock, the snow had melted. A babble of voices came and went, as the door opened and closed behind Daisy. Head down, she hurried along the damp pavement. She'd turned the lock and was almost in her door, when Donald pounced. The strength of his push sent her sprawling into the passage. His fingers dug into her neck, and the scream in her throat was never born. An embryo of sound – aborted. Her eyes were black, like a cornered doe accepting defeat.

Roughly, he pulled her to her feet, twisted her arms behind her back and marched her to the kitchen. 'Food,' he rasped. 'I need food.'

Daisy did some fast thinking. Better go along with his wishes. Maybe he'd go away if she fed him, but he had other ideas. Once in the kitchen, he grabbed a knife, banged shut the door and leaned his body against it.

'Right, little bar lady.' He brandished the blade in a threatening manner. 'Get cooking.'

'I've only got corned beef. You'll have to wait for the cabbage and potatoes.' Daisy struggled to get away.

'Be still, bitch!' His hold on her tightened. 'I can't wait for them to cook. Make me a sandwich with corned beef, then put them on. We'll have them together, just you and me.' He prodded the blade in her side. 'Nice and cosy,' he sneered. 'With no one knowing – and that's the way I want it. Understand?'

Without moving her head, Daisy slid her gaze to his eyes, then recoiled with fear. Black and venomous, they spat at her like a snake. She felt the blood drain from her face. When she handed him the sandwich, her hand trembled.

Inwardly, Donald gloated.

'Where's the bathroom? I need a bath. You can wash the clothes I take off. They stink.' His eyes roamed the room, ascertaining her wealth by her possessions. The furniture was good quality. The table with the twirly legs was antique. She had taste. Perhaps she had money stashed away somewhere? He'd need it when his task here was done. Then he'd go to Ireland or Wales and get a job. He'd take Ben with him. Not because he wanted to, but to spite Cathy.

'Come with me.' Once more, he grabbed her arm. 'What! I can't go in there with you when you're having a bath. It would be unseemly.' Daisy was shocked.

'You can, and you will. You'll have seen a naked man before.' His lips curled in a sneer. 'Well, you might more than see one if you don't comply.'

The implication was clear and, rather than endure being molested by this fiend, Daisy capitulated.

'What about work tomorrow,' she asked.

'You've got a phone, haven't you? Tell her you're sick, but do not try to give signals, either verbal or physical.' His voice was cold as a mortuary.

'What about groceries and meat?'

'Christ, shut up and stop snivelling.' Snatching her wrist, he drew the blade across the back of it. 'Beware,' he said. 'That's just the beginning.'

After a sleepless night, Daisy was shattered. She felt she'd been swimming in endless circles in the muddy water of the Styx.

At nine o'clock, she phoned Doreen. Telling lies was very much against the grain, but she had no option. If Doreen felt anything was wrong, she didn't say.

Three days passed. The larder shelves were bare of essential things like milk and butter and bread. She must go to the shop. Today. That Donald was getting on her wick. She'd blow up if she didn't get out.

'I'm going for provisions,' she said next day, casting him a malignant stare, daring him to protest. He had a voracious appetite, so no way would he disallow this outing. His first interest was in himself. Maybe this was her chance. She had to let somebody know she was a prisoner in her own home.

In black, pencil skirt, belted camel coat and high heeled shoes, she strode purposefully along the street. In her right hand, she carried a wicker basket. Her left was tightly clenched. The sound of footsteps behind her, made her turn. It was him. He was like a bad smell, she couldn't get rid of him.

'Did you think I'd let you out on your own? I'm sorry, lady, I wasn't born on Mars. Now get into that shop and behave as you normally would. This knife is eager to be used.'

The bell jangled as she entered. 'Hello, Daisy.' Rachel looked up with a smile. 'Sure and I thought you'd eloped with some bloke.' Daisy laughed for the first time in three days. The sight of Donald standing in the doorway like a guard dog, wiped it away.

Rachel observed the transition. She thought of school. The teacher erasing writing from the blackboard with a duster. Something had erased Daisy's laugh like that. It worried Rachel. 'Are you well enough, Daisy?' she enquired. 'I'm not prying. Just concerned.'

'Oh, just a touch of flu. Thank you for asking, Rachel.'

Daisy threw a furtive look behind her. She opened her mouth to speak, then briskly shut it again. One couldn't outdo one as cunning as Donald Townsend.

The door was panelled. Through it, Rachel could see a man. A stranger. His apparel was that of a country, working chap. His face was pale. There was something fishy about him.

Giving a jaded sigh, Daisy laid the items she wanted on the counter. 'Phew!' she gasped. 'That should last me a while. You'd better not tell Doreen I've been in. I'm supposed to be in bed. I don't want the sack.'

Rachel totted up the prices. 'That will be ten pounds, Daisy please.' She nodded at the extra food Daisy was packing into her basket. 'Expecting visitors, are you?'

'What? No, just in case I'm off work a bit longer.' Daisy gave a half-hearted cough and patted her chest. In the silent space, their eyes locked.

Daisy's looked stricken.

'There is something wrong, isn't there, Daisy?' Rachel leaned her elbows on the counter expectantly.

'Sorry, Rachel, I've got to get back.' As the bell tinkled and the door opened, a huge gust flicked the newspapers onto the floor.

Begorra, 'tis a hurricane you are, Daisy Davies. If Jim Baird sees them papers lying there it will be me that'll be getting the sack.' Giving a merry chuckle, she knelt to pick them up.

Closing the door, Daisy hunkered beside her.

The door crashed open. Surprised by the velocity of the act, Rachel looked up. It was the stranger. Daisy looked up too.

Donald's eyes challenged her. His gaze wandered round the shop. Hell, he could do with a smoke, but he had no money. He'd have to side-track the assistant.

'Umm – do you have brewer's yeast?' His evil eyes snapped to Daisy then back to Rachel. 'I make wine,' he explained.

'We did have some.' Rachel searched the shelf, then shook her head. 'If you wait a minute, I'll look through the back.'

Donald chortled to himself. This ruse worked every time. He prodded Daisy with the knife hidden in his pocket. 'Get me a packet of cigarettes.'

'I can't just take them.' Daisy was shocked.

'Buy some then.'

'What kind?'

'Players, Capstan. Any kind.'

In the stock room, Rachel listened. The words were inaudible, but a conversation of some kind was taking place. She tried to tread carefully, but they heard her and became silent.

'You two know each other, then?' Her midnight eyes appraised them. The sleuth in her told her that two and two were not making four, here.

'No, I'm new to this locality, I was asking the lady directions.'

The glibness of his tongue made Daisy want to puke. He was clever. Far too clever for his own good. He'd come a cropper yet. As she asked for the cigarettes, she hoped that day would come soon.

'You've never started smoking, have you, Daisy? Not with your bad chest?' Rachel flopped onto a stool behind the counter.

The seconds stretched – but Daisy did not answer. Without a backward glance, she left.

So did the stranger.

The atmosphere at dinner was strained. 'I can't stand this,' cried Daisy. 'You've got to remove yourself from my house. My friends and work mates don't have their heads buried in the sand, you know. They're bound to realize something is the matter.'

'I'll go when my business here is finished. It could be tonight.' His words were snarled and cryptic. A fear began to build inside her. Fear for Cathy; fear for Ben. Her thoughts careered this way and that, like a bike out of control. How could she get word to them?

Donald was gearing himself up, getting prepared for the carrying out, the fulmination of his plan. He'd gleaned all the facts he could. What he needed now, was money.

At dinner next day, the silence was like mud. Donald's thoughts waded through it. Daisy's were stuck – caught in the mire of his mind.

Scraping back his chair, he made as if to go to the sink, then turned and seized her by the shoulders. 'Now,' he said. 'I want money. Whatever you have in the house, give it to me.'

'I just keep what's in my purse and handbag. I don't keep a lot of cash in the house.'

'Liar.'

'I'm not lying.' Daisy winced as his nails dug into her shoulders.

'I'll take what you have, then.'

Shakily, Daisy pushed herself up from the chair and crossed to the drawer. Two notes and some coins, were all she had. 'That's the lot,' she said, grudgingly handing him the meagre amount.

'Have you any scissors?' His black eyes dived into hers.

'In there.' She nodded towards the cupboard.

The table cloth became his next victim. Viciously, he cut it into strips and with them, bound together Daisy's wrists.

'That's too tight,' she yelled. 'Loosen it.'

'Shut up, or you'll get what Cathy Wilson got.' Cruelly, he yanked her hair, then proceeded to bind her mouth. She could hardly breathe. Twisting her head from side to side, she tried to slacken the gag, but was awarded with a punch so severe, it knocked her unconscious.

When she came to, she was tied firmly to the chair. Her eyes, feet and hands were bound. She was totally helpless. The only active part of her was her mind. Her intuition had been correct. He WAS Donald Townsend. His admission about Cathy proved it. Ooh, her head ached. She felt as though she had three of them, like Pluto's three-headed dog Cerberus, that guarded the gates of hell. Only she wasn't guarding the gates of hell – she was in it.

Donald strode with raging steps along the perimeter of the wood. It was a rage aimed at himself Why had he mentioned Cathy's name? How could he have been so stupid? He'd have to act fast. Nearing the stables, he stopped. He knew Cathy brought Ben to see the horses in the afternoons. He'd have to intercept them before they reached the buildings. On the right of the road, was the stackyard. He would wait there.

In a happier frame of mind, Cathy walked with Ben. No sightings of Donald had made her feel more secure. Her progress was slow. Ben's ever curious nature, kept her stopping and starting.

'There's a bird, mummy,' he said, pointing to a lone crow perched on a naked branch.

'Yes, that's Mr Crow or Mrs Crow. It will be looking for food.'

Black wings fanned the air as suddenly it took flight. Two pairs of eyes peered upwards. The sky reflected them; blue upon blue.

'Don't scream, or I'll shoot.' The order came from behind. Cathy felt an inner dread. The owner of that voice haunted her dreams. Anxiously, she glanced at Ben. His eyes had a hurt look, as if he'd been scolded.

'Do as he says, Ben,' she whispered.

'That's sensible. Now start walking; normal like; as though we're friends.' Donald's tone was menacing.

Cathy reached for Ben's hand. The tightness of his grasp revealed the terror in him.

'Make for the stackyard.' Donald's gaze darted, still seeking new avenues. In the cart shed, stood a tractor and binder. Strewn on the ground, were tangled piles of twine. 'Ah,' he cried. 'Change of plan. We'll go here instead.' Roughly, he pushed Cathy towards the shed and, grappling around for a decent piece of string, proceeded to tie her to one of the iron pillars holding up the building. For Ben, this was too much. Opening his mouth, he gave vent to a loud shriek.

Angrily, Donald swung him round. 'Be quiet, you stupid little brat. Do you want to see your mother shot?'

Ben shook his head. Tears filled his eyes and streamed down his cheeks.

'I've no time for cry-babies, so stop your weeping, and come with me.' Donald's patience had reached saturation point.

'I don't want to go, mummy, Mummeeee.' Ben's yell echoed from the cobwebby walls.

Filled with panic, now, Donald yanked at Ben's arm and dragged him along the yard.

'Don't worry, Ben,' cried Cathy. 'John will be here shortly.' She forced a smile, hoping against hope that he would.

'Will he, mummy? Tell him bad man has taken me away. Tell him he hurted me.'

As his little face, still turned hopefully towards her, faded from view, Cathy broke down inside.

It was Fred Marshall who found her. 'For cryin' out loud, lassie,' he shouted. 'What's happened?'

'Get the police, Fred. Quick! Tell them that Donald Townsend has captured Ben. They went that way.' Her eyes jumped in the direction of the stackyard. 'Better untie me first, though. I must follow them.'

'You'll do no such thing. Come back with me. I'll rally round the men. It's a man's job this, no' a wee slip o' a lass like you.'

'I'm going with you, Fred. Ben's my son. He'll be scared stiff.' Her voice broke into a sob.

Fred's arm slid round her shoulders in a warm hug. 'We'll find him, lassie, don't you fret. That bastard Donald will be locked up for good when they get him.'

Cathy relaxed. Fred was nice. She'd never really talked much with him. Too busy with John and the gang to notice grown-ups. Sort of 'hello' and 'cheerio' to the parents, then out to play.

Meanwhile, having gained his objective, Donald stood awhile in one of Tom's fields trying to think what his next move should be. Ben, more a hindrance than an asset, started to howl. Instead of shouting, Donald decided to cajole him.

'Look Ben,' he said. 'I'll take you back to your mother, but not yet. Pretend this is an adventure. It will only be a few days. Do you understand?'

Ben's wailing ceased immediately. Eyes big as planets, peered up into Donald's dark fathomless ones, fear gone. In its place, beamed rays of trust. Donald felt a tightness in the region of his heart. The feeling, so alien to him, drew him up short. Immobilised, he stared at the small, upturned face. 'Come on,' he said gruffly. 'We'd best get going.'

In his range of vision, he espied Tom's Land Rover in the yard. Grabbing Ben's hand, he sidled surreptitiously up to it. His luck was in. Tom had left the keys.

'In you get, Ben; upsy-daisy.' Heaving him onto the high seat, he scrambled in the other side.

Nobody heard it go. Before the alarm was raised, they were miles away approaching the nearest town.

'Me hungry,' cried Ben, looking askew at Donald's bearded face.

'So am I. Do you like pies?' Donald kept his eyes firmly on the road, withholding the need to look at the child so small and innocent by his side.

'Mummy makes chips. Me want chips.' Resolutely, Ben set his chin, tears once more nearing the surface.

'Drat it.' Donald swore under his breath. His plan had been to buy some pies at a baker's shop, then away as fast as possible, but Ben would need milk and lemonade. He'd have to take a risk and go to a cafe.

At a small car park shooting to the right of a club, he stopped and got out. Going to the passenger side, he opened the door, lifted Ben and gently placed him on the ground. His son, he thought proudly. The feelings this lad wrought on him were amazing. He had never known such emotions. He, who was spoiled, arrogant, unprincipled, selfish and downright mean – tamed, by a kid.

In the cafe, he ordered chips and beans, a glass of milk for Ben and tea for himself. A couple sat by the window, talking and drinking tea or coffee. Donald chose the darkest corner. By his left, was a toilet. The desire to go arose just by seeing it.

'Do you need a pee, Ben?' he asked.

Ben nodded.

Will he be able to manage by himself, thought Donald, or would he have to help him? Taking prisoner of the lad was not such a bright idea. So many hurdles to overcome. So much at stake for himself.

'Christ!' he gasped as his eyes slewed to Ben's rear. He still wore a bloody nappy. It would be filled and stinking likely. Slumping against the wall, he felt a rising despair. Straightening, he grasped Ben's hand. 'Let's go, Ben. You can pee later.'

'Me need now.' Ben's face crumpled. He was on the verge of screaming again. Exasperated, Donald hauled him in and closed the door. It shut with a bang that echoed in the bare, coldness of the toilet.

Slightly abashed, he pulled down Ben's trousers. After a bit of fumbling, he found the safety pin, opened it, and removed the offending nappy. The smell filled his nostrils. Thinking he was going to be sick, he leaned over the wash basin and spat into it. A tap on his leg, made him look down. The solemn face of Ben peered up at him.

'You got sore tummy, mister man?'

The anxious voice snapped something inside him. Suddenly, he wanted Ben to know he was his father, but why give him hope when he'd already decided to leave him. Some place where he would easily be found.

Darkness was falling when they emerged from the cafe. He'd go back the way he'd come, abandon the vehicle and sleep in the hayshed at Hawthornside farm, thought Donald.

By now the hue and cry of the search party had abated. The stealing of Tom's land Rover had led them into the false belief that their quarry was further afield.

'It's no use carrying on in this light,' said the officer in charge. 'We'll continue first thing in the morning.'

'We'll do the bugger over if we get him first,' muttered Fred Marshall to one of the lads who'd joined the search party.

'Aye, he'll wish he'd never been born. If he hurts that wee mite o' a laddie, I'll string him to the nearest tree.' Eddie, the blacksmith, pinched one nostril with a finger and angrily blew. Slimy snots shot onto the grass. It was a habit of his, but in this instance, a way of showing his disdain.

Cathy, her grandparents, Alice and Tom, stressed and desolate, sat before a dying fire.

'How can a man like Donald care for a bairn Ben's age?' The ragged voice of Cathy, sawed through the wooden silence that pervaded the room.

'He won't harm him.' Alice tried to pacify Cathy, though her own fears were splitting her apart.

'He's evil though, mum. What if he takes Ben abroad and we never see him again? He must have guessed he's the father.'

'Possibly, but he won't have any money. We will have to put ourselves into his mind, his thoughts, his whole being. A fox hunts under the cover of darkness. Maybe we should be out there now.' Alice's arms drooped. She had said her piece. She felt drained.

'No,' said her father. 'We'll wait until morning. We must save our strength.'

His face was drawn; his eyes clouded with worry. 'You, Cathy and Ivy, stay at home. We need you to make up food and to be near the phone.'

'He's right.' Anxiously, Tom stared at the women.

Alice's mother sat, ready for bed, teeth out, mouth puckered like a wound unevenly stitched, eyes closed. Her mind a tightrope, she tried to reach backwards into her thoughts.

She was a child. There were visions. Thundering hoofs; screams; a trampled body. Her friend lying in the dust. Shapes here, then gone, quick, quick, in a hazy flash.

A few weeks later, she had watched from a distance, her friend's little coffin being lowered into a dark hole and she had cried. Partly for her loss. Partly – with the fear of knowing. It was a secret she'd kept all those years. Now, the fey Highland bit of her was trying to resurrect pictures of the whereabouts of Ben, but nothing would come.

Tom rose to go, breaking her train of thought.

'See you all in the morning,' he said. The deep timbre of his voice fed through the space of the closing door. It had a calming effect.

The others too, began preparing for bed. Cups, hastily washed, were left to dry on the draining board. Cathy's grandad gave his pipe a final tap and methodically put it away. Her granny traipsed to the bathroom to empty her bladder before retiring. Alice, put the fire guard on and half set the table for breakfast. Cathy, trundled coal and sticks into the kitchen in readiness to light the fire in the morning. Stairs creaked. Soft footfalls trod the carpet on the landing. Doors opened and closed.

Then silence.

In the stillness, thoughts of Ben tossed in the sea of their minds – and no one slept.

Chapter Fifteen

For Donald, settling down to sleep on the solid bales of hay in Barbara's hayshed, was difficult. Ben played up. Having just realized that his teddy was not available, there was no appeasing him.

'I want my teddy,' he sobbed. 'I want my teddy.'

'Your teddy is at home, Ben. You'll get it when you go back.' Donald was in a quandary. I know, he thought. I'll make him a teddy with hay.

At the bottom of the bales, lay lots of loose hay. An old sack hung over the side of the trailer in the shed. This he retrieved and filled with hay. With the aid of some twine, he created an image, not so much of a teddy, but more like a rabbit.

Swiftly, he climbed up the ladder. A moon peeped from between dark clouds. Its beam followed every step he took. He felt vulnerable, preferring the pitch black of a wet night.

Ben was still crying, his lashes clenched against the flow of tears. Gently, Donald laid his hand on his arm. 'Ben,' he whispered. 'Look what I've got.'

'No, I want my teddy.'

'Here's something quite like a teddy. See, it's got long ears and wobbly legs.'

The sniffing ceased. The tear-stained face lifted towards Donald. The semblance of a smile touched his features as he saw the makeshift animal. 'Rabbit,' he cried. 'Mine.' His hands reached out, and happily he clutched the toy to his body. A heaviness hung over his eyes. With thumb in mouth, he curled onto his side. Almost instantly, he was asleep.

Before dawn, Donald awoke. His first instinct was to find food. Milk was a food in itself, therefore he must get to the byre before the early bustle of milking started. Descending the ladder, he looked left, then right, his seafaring eyes taking note of the layout.

The buildings were near the house. He'd have to be cautious. Lifting the latch of the byre door, he gingerly pushed it a fraction. 'Bugger!' He sprang back as the hinges squeaked and groaned.

On the straw, two cows lay. He gave one a prod. 'Come on, up with you, old lass. It's milking time.' Flashing the white of her eyes, she looked sceptically at his urgent face. She knew to the exact minute when milking time was, and this was too early. She wouldn't budge.

He tried again, giving her a hard jab with his toe. Swishing her tail in protest, she clambered to her feet.

Heck, he'd need something in which to hold the milk. The cat's dish was there. That was no use. It would be full of germs. He remembered Barbara had a horse. There would be a pail in the loose-box, but how to locate it? The clock was turning fast; eating time he couldn't afford.

A voice from behind, made him nearly wet his pants. The slim figure of a lass stood there. She had long red hair that hugged a perfect face. She was like a movie star. Her eyes glowed, half with warmth, half with an undercurrent of sadness.

'I was looking for a pail,' he said. 'I need milk. I need food of any kind. Can you help?' He gave her his most beguiling smile.

'I could give you something better than food,' she hinted. Her tongue circled her lips provocatively; her body inclined towards his. Hell, she was sexy.

'Where are you hiding?'

'In the hayshed.'

'What better place. See you in ten minutes.'

Feeling cock-a-hoop, Donald waited.

Good as her word, she came, bringing with her the lovely aroma of fried bacon.

'That smells delicious.'

'Yes.' She opened the tea towel in which she'd carried her spoils. Bacon sandwiches and two pieces of apple tart. 'Is he up there too?' She nodded towards the bales.

'Yes, he's a fine laddie. Being with him has given me a new perspective in life – and meeting you.' His gaze stabbed into her. 'If I get settled somewhere, will you come and join me?' His brow screwed up with perplexity. 'Who are you, anyway? You don't sound from this part of the country.'

'I'm Gordon McKenzie's daughter and I'm married to John Fairbairn, but I've behaved like a right bitch. He left me and stays with Dave and Maggie Hart.'

'The minister's daughter. Wow!' For several seconds Donald watched her, taking in the flawless skin, the green eyes, the pointed breasts, the confident attitude.

She was his kind of woman.

'Oh, one more thing,' he asked, as she turned to go. 'Can you get me a bonnet?' His fingers traced his stubbly short hair. 'It would be good camouflage.'

Back up the ladder, he went with a lighter heart. 'Wake up, Ben. Breakfast is ready. A fairy waved her magic stick. Come and see what she's brought.'

As if electrified, Ben sat up. 'A fairy? Can I see the fairy? Please mister man.'

'Oh, she's gone. She had other little boys and girls to help.' Donald handed him a sandwich. 'She made this one especially for you.'

At midday, slow footsteps on the ladder made him duck low. With his right arm, he pulled Ben down beside him His heart beat frantically in his chest. Squeezing shut his eyes, he held his breath. If it was the police, he was done for.

'It's only me.' The voice preceded the face, but another few steps brought her in line with the top of the bales.

Letting go of his suspended breath, Donald jumped to his feet. 'Hell, what a fright you gave me.' His hand reached to help her. With a laugh, she collapsed at his feet. Picking her up, he held her close. For the first time in his life, he felt kindly towards a woman.

'Here's your hat.' Giggling, she thrust it on his head.

'I now christen you king of the hayshed.' Her expression changed from being frivolous to serious. 'When are you leaving?'

'Tomorrow. As early as possible.'

'Can I see you tonight? Alone? When the lad is asleep?'

'Yes. We'll need more provisions, though. Ben requires a lot of milk.'

'I'll slip by at lunch time.' She held a finger to her lips. 'Sssh, here's John and Dave. They'll be seeing to the stock before joining the hunt for you and Ben. The rest will be long gone.'

Clutching her skirt, she stepped from the ladder.

'What's she doing out at such an early hour?' John looked enquiringly at Dave.

Seeking not to interfere, Dave kept quiet.

John didn't.

'Where have you been?' he asked. 'It's not properly light yet.'

Caroline was flustered, but undaunted. 'Oh, there's a hen lays up there. No eggs today, though. Sometimes she misses a day.'

It seemed a plausible enough answer, but John was sceptical. 'She's up to something, Dave. She was civil. That in itself, is a bad sign for somebody. Do you think she's got another fellow?'

'Och, don't let it worry you, son. She's maybe seen the error of her ways.'

'Hmph! and pigs might fly. No, she definitely looked devious.' John scuffed his boots as he walked. A habit he had when deeply in thought.

Later, with the men out of the way, Caroline joined Donald

and Ben. The sight of another lass, conjured up in Ben thoughts of his mother. 'Can me go home, now?' he pleaded. In his arms, he grasped the rabbit Donald had so patiently fashioned out of hay.

A lump filled Donald's throat. He'd become fond of the boy. 'Tomorrow,' he said. 'You can go home tomorrow.'

A shock ran through him as two plump arms wound round his neck and a soft cheek pressed against his. His arms crept round Ben's sturdy body in a hug that encompassed both gladness and regret.

A quick squeeze on his shoulder, and Caroline left. He needed this moment to be alone. The joy of it would have to last a long time.

The night was drizzly and dark when she set out later for her assignation with Donald. She shivered as the dampness filtered through her coat and jumper. With open arms, he waited, and wordlessly they sank onto the ground beneath the bales. They had known each other only a matter of hours, yet it seemed to have been forever.

'I'll think of you always,' Donald whispered. 'I wouldn't be in this mess if I'd met you earlier in life.'

Pillowing his head on her chest, he felt like a child again and nearly wept.

'When you find a job, give me a ring.' Caroline spoke in a husky voice.

'What if I get caught?'

'I'll wait for you.'

'Will you?'

'Yes.'

'I'll need some money. Do you think I could borrow just enough to get me down south?'

Caroline fumbled in her pocket. 'Here, take this. There's forty pounds there.'

Donald turned over and sat up. 'Wow! thank you.' His lips covered hers. They made love again, then lay in silent contemplation in the dark. 'I'll maybe leave you with a little present,' he murmured. 'Would you mind?'

'No, it would be something of you I could treasure in the days you are away. Perhaps years.' Softly, she kissed him. 'I must go. Good luck, Donald.' Sighing, she scrambled to her feet, then like sylph, she was gone.

In the morning, he and Ben ate what was left of the food Caroline had brought, then prepared to leave. 'We're going now, Ben. You follow me down the ladder. I'll see you don't fall.' Donald's heart was filled with guilt at what he was about to do, but it was for the best. They'd soon find him. He hoped. How he wished things could be different.

Tom met John at Cathy's house. Chores finished, they thumped their boots against the front step to get rid of the worst of the mud, then made for the kitchen.

'We'll try the fields by the meadow again today.' Tom drew a chart from his pocket. 'He's a wily customer.' With eyes shadowed from lack of sleep, he peered at the places they'd previously checked. The wood sprang to his attention, but they'd scoured it yesterday. No – a gut feeling told him he was nearer at hand. His fists ached to smash Donald's jaw. His own jaws tense, he thrust back his chair and shoved himself to his feet. With one accord, he and John made for the door. Shoulders hunched, they plunged into the raw coldness of an early winter's morn. The drizzle had changed to a steady rain. Visibility was poor.

'He could be anywhere,' Tom said as he strained his eyes through the gloomy air.

'I'm going with them.' Resolutely, Cathy stood up. 'I'll go mad if I don't do something.'

'Wrap up well, then. Take an extra coat for Ben.' Alice lifted her gaze to Cathy. 'Poor wee soul, he'll be freezing out there.'

'Wait for me.' Cathy's voice smashed Tom and John's thoughts like nutcrackers squashing nuts. Grim-faced, they waited. Grim-faced, they stepped onwards.

From his hide-out, Donald saw them go. The elements were in his favour, but it would be cold for Ben. He needed him as a decoy, so couldn't leave him here. Experienced eyes saw them stalk the edge of the wood. Their reasoning clicked into place like a piece of jigsaw puzzle. The meadow would be next.

It was time to go.

At the bottom of the field, he stopped and laid Ben down. Stooping to his level, he gazed for endless moments at the angelic face; taking in the blue eyes, the winsome smile and the fine features, and a great sadness swamped him. Quickly, he straightened, stood to attention and saluted. 'Bye, Ben. Be a good boy for your mum. Now you salute too, and say, aye, aye, sir.'

'Aye, aye, sir.' With an impish grin, Ben saluted, his tiny hand copying Donald's gestures.

Donald felt very proud.

'Stay here, Ben,' he cautioned. 'Don't forget me.' He traced the soft cheek with a finger, then let his hand drop. 'I won't ever forget you.'

Face suddenly solemn, Ben shook his head.

Like a shadow, Donald skirted the bare Hawthorn hedge. The rain lessened, then ceased. Bits of blue pushed aside dark clouds and the morning became lighter. Donald swore. The rain had been in his favour. Now, he'd be more easily seen. He would have to take a risk and make his break down the field.

'Wait, mister man, me coming too.' Ben's cry slowed his steps.

'No, go back, Ben. For God's sake go back,' but Ben's sturdy legs drove him on. In desperation, Donald raced for the river. From the breast of the hill, a loud roar scattered the sheep and struck fear in Donald's heart. Ben's yells of 'man, man, wait for me,' changed to dismayed shrieks.

'There he goes.' The scent of victory giving them added momentum, Tom and John, tore down the field.

All the while, Ben was striving to reach Donald who by now had attained his goal and reached the brink of the river. A splash, and a scream further upstream, rooted him to the spot. Turning, he saw Ben's blue coat, white face and little body being swept along by the swift current.

'Oh God, BEN. His shout alerted Tom and John. He looked at them. He looked at freedom. He looked at Ben. His decision was already made.

Back on the bank he scrambled, then ran. 'I'm coming Ben. I'm coming.' Taking a huge gulp of air, he dived in. Tears mingled with water as it swirled in a ruthless race. Choking and gasping, he reached the limp form of Ben.

His pursuers, having gained the river, saw him struggling. 'Grab his coat,' they yelled. 'Grab his coat.'

There was a buzzing in his ears as they filled with water. Arms flailing like windmills, Donald strained to find a hold on Ben's coat. Frozen fingers parted the water, but he seemed to move only inches. Somehow, he managed to fix his grip on the sodden material. Lungs nearly bursting, he made for the edge and thrust Ben up to the hands stretching to receive him.

'Hell, he can't swim.' The fact hit John like a bullet. Laying down Ben, he jumped to Donald's aid. Even half-drowned, Donald tried to resist being rescued. He hated water, but life in jail was a worse prospect than drowning. What had he to lose?

'Be still, you stupid idiot,' John railed at him with sudden anger, but on he fought. With unerring aim, John shot him a stabbing right to the jaw. His head fell sideways and he was still. The dead weight of him was dragging John under. 'Tom,' he gasped. 'You'll have to help me. Quickly.'

Between the two of them, they managed to haul the inert Donald onto the grass. 'He'll need artificial respiration. Can you do it, Tom?'

'Yes, I learned years ago. Let me try.' A cough and a splutter, showed he was alive. Vacant eyes stared, then gradually began to focus. They rested on John. 'Why didn't you let me drown?' he croaked. 'They'll only send me back.'

'It might be curtailed, though,' John said quietly. 'That was a very brave thing you did.'

The feather touch of a child, skimmed Donald's brow. 'Hello, mister man.' Like gold dust, Ben's familiar voice greeted him.

'My name's Donald, Ben. Not mister man.' He tried to laugh, but it hurt.

'No, it's not Donald to you, Ben. It's dad. This is your dad.' John surprised himself by revealing this secret. Yet, in all fairness, the boy should know.

Especially now.

'Dad!' Ben gazed in wonder at the man lying like a corpse on the ground.

In the background, stood Cathy. She had just caught up with them.

'Mummy,' Ben tore his eyes away from Donald and ran towards her. She bent to pick him up, but he struggled to be free. 'My dad,' he said, pointing at Donald.

Transfixed, Cathy stared.

'I'm sorry, Cathy.' The words came from the figure lying shivering on the ground.

'Sorry?'

'Yes, for what I did to you. Ben is a credit to you. He's a grand lad.'

'Donald saved his life, Cathy.' John spoke over Tom's shoulder. 'And he can't swim. It was a very great feat.'

'Oh.' Cathy was nonplussed.

Seeing her confusion, John explained what had happened.

'Did he?' Fixing her gaze on Donald, she gave him a tremulous smile. 'Thank you.'

As they jolted along the bumpy fields to Manor farm and Donald saw his home, it was like seeing it for the first time. Still wobbly legged, he alighted from Tom's Land Rover.

'Let me knock,' he volunteered, and, long and loudly, he clanged the brass knocker.

'God sakes, I'm coming. Can you not have patience?' It was cook's voice.

Donald grinned. 'Just the same old cook. Wait till you meet her. Her bread and butter pudding is divine.' He was about to knock again, when the door creaked open and cook's plump face peered out at the sodden group. Her dark eyes widened as they took in the dishevelled appearance of the fellow before her. It was his stance that hit the nail on the head.

'Mercy me, it's Donald, isn't it?' Expressions of all sorts ran over her kindly face. They seemed all at variance with each other, fighting to get a foothold on her feelings. 'You'd better come in, then. Don't stand there and get pneumonia. And don't think I've forgotten all your cheek,' she admonished. She smiled and looked at her watch and bustled them in.

'Oh, Mrs Clark, you're a sight for sore eyes.' Grabbing a roll of fat that was her waist, he twirled her round in joyful circles.

'Hoots man, what's got into you? My head's like it's been in the washing machine.'

'Get the oven heated, cook. I want this lot to taste your delicious bread and butter pudding.' He splayed his hands towards the fatigued figures standing behind him. 'They'll be back for more once they've feasted on its delights.'

'Bread and butter pudding? At this time o' the day? Man, you're worse than a bairn.' She looked angry and pleased at the same time, but they were never to find out which won because, at that moment, the major shuffled through on slippered feet towards the untimely commotion.

'What the devil's going on, cook?' His eyes took in the foremost fellow on the step, and his pink-cheeked countenance sagged with shock. For him, recognition came from the eyes. Black as coal, they were Donald's eyes. Yet different somehow, but the complexities of folk and their feelings were not in his field of interest. With a sigh, he turned away. 'Better tell his mother, cook,' he muttered.

Once inside, Donald stood savouring the scent of polish filling the high ceilinged hall. Who would have thought he'd relish such a simple thing?

'Well, don't stand there like a wet week-end, bring them through to the kitchen.' Cook was in charge. The kitchen was her domain. Then her eyes fell on Ben. 'Och, my wee lamb, you're like a drooked rat. Get them clothes off him, Cathy. There's some o' Graham's things from when he was a bairn in a kist in the spare bedroom. They might just fit.' Muttering to herself, she bustled along the passage and up the stairs, returning with an armful of clothes that smelt of mothballs, but were amazingly dry.

'A bit iron and they'll be fine, but shove this lot on him now, or it'll be the death o' him.' Cook's eyes swivelled to Cathy. Her head inclined in the direction of the room. Understanding, Cathy guided Ben there. 'What happened Cathy?' Cook's voice was half a whisper and half a hiss. From pale lips, the saga unfolded. Cook's head nodded and shook in turn, living every part of it. 'Poor wee soul,' she said. 'Poor wee soul.'

'You pour some drinks, Cathy and give them a shout. I'll inform Catherine. The change in her wayward son just might be the tonic she needs. She's pined away to nothing with the worry of it.' With a sniff, she waddled back up the stairs. On the way up, she met Graham coming down.

'Your brother's back,' she informed him. 'Don't be too hard on him. He's a reformed character. After all them years o' whorin' and skulduggery, he's seen the light.'

Graham halted in mid-stride, surprise writing reams on his honest face. Stepping aside to let her pass, he bounded the rest of the way down.

For an hour, Donald basked in the warmth and caring of his family home. He telephoned Caroline and held Ben in a last embrace. 'I'm going away for a while, Ben,' he said. 'A long, long time. I'll think of you, I promise.'

Like an adult, Ben stood, absorbing Donald's words. Then,

clutching Cathy's skirt, he hung back, half hidden behind her leg. That was the picture stamped on Donald's mind as he took his leave. It would sustain him in the dark days and nights when back in prison.

In Daisy's house, a traumatised Daisy, in her efforts to wriggle free from her bonds, had capsized the chair and lay in a heap on the floor. The tightness of the gag hurt her mouth and jaws. She lay in a curved position, shaped to the contours of the chair. Her limbs ached. She moaned. The thought of choking, filled her with panic. 'God, her mind pleaded, if you're up there, please help me.'

In Baird's shop, Jenny Taylor was in the throes of a paroxysm of coughing. Bent double, her face nearly puce with the effort, she looked awful. Alarmed, Rachel rushed for a glass of water. 'For the love of God, Jenny, have a drink of this – and have a seat. Here —' She pushed her onto the stool which she used if trade lessened or when her feet throbbed nearing the end of her day's work.

'Thank you, Rachel. You're an angel. Mind you, a good drink in the pub would probably cure it.' Another spasm racked her body. She took a gulp of water. 'Eeeh!' she rolled her eyes as the cool liquid slid down her throat. 'That was grand, Rachel.' She rubbed her hand across her mouth and continued to drink.

'You're welcome, Jenny. Talking about the pub. Have you seen Daisy?'

'No, but her curtains were still open last night. I remarked to Eddie about it, but he just stuck his head behind the paper and wheezed like them bellows he works. A right pain in the behind he is sometimes.'

'Have you heard anything, Bill?' Rachel fixed her midnight eyes on the young rep studying her stock of biscuits.

'No, is there something wrong, do you think?' His kindly face was covered with concern.

Aha, thought Rachel. There's a bit interest there. I wonder if Daisy knows? Her anxiety crushed those lighter thoughts as the image of the surly stranger flashed before her eyes. Instantly, she made up her mind. 'I'm going to see if she's all right. Coming, Bill?'

With alacrity, he agreed and, shooing Jenny out, they put up the closed sign on the door and hurried to Daisy's house.

Her door opened to the touch. That in itself, set off alarm bells. 'I'll go in first. I know the police are after that chap Townsend. If he's the one you saw with her, then she could be in danger.' Purposefully, Bill strode along the passage. He stopped, then ran, as he beheld Daisy tied to a chair, her face almost blue. He was distraught. 'You phone the police, Rachel. I'll see to Daisy.' His voice was hoarse.

'Holy mother of Jesus,' cried Rachel. She took in the scene with a horrified glance, then fled to find a phone. It was neath a chair. The wires had been cut. It was useless. In a tizzy, she flew next door.

A little girl of about seven years old, answered her frantic knocking. Her hair, dark as a raven's feathers, gleamed with health. Her eyes, inky blue, fanned with long curving lashes, stared up at Rachel. 'Me mum's in the toilet,' she said. 'She won't be long.' Her accent was like from over the border.

'I can't wait. Can I use your phone, little lass? Please —' Rachel squatted down beside her. 'It's urgent.'

The small head nodded. The door opened wider and Rachel followed the neat figure into the cluttered interior of a house obviously in the middle of a family moving in. Cardboard boxes, some with lids open, others bound with thick string, were everywhere. On the window sill, stood the phone. Snatching it, Rachel dialled. 'Police,' she gasped. 'Five main street. Three doors from the pub.' Not bothering to answer the brusque questions from the other end, she crashed it down, redialled, and called a doctor.

Mesmerized, the girl stared and listened, her eyes widening at the mention of police and doctors. Her heart skipped a beat with excitement. Her friend back home in Yorkshire would never believe it. But this was her home now, she mused. Her first week here and see what's happened. Smiling, she tittupped along the passage after Rachel.

Within minutes, a police car slithered to a stop outside Daisy's house. 'This way,' Rachel showed them in and pointed to where Daisy sat white and shaken by the fire. Keen as mustard, one officer held ready his notebook and pen. His hands were square as shovels. His voice, as sharp as their blades.

'You say he left after lunch? Was he carrying anything? What was he wearing?' The questions were fired at Daisy like arrows. She felt giddy trying to recall the events. Her memory was hazy with the blow she'd received.

Rachel, seeing her pain, was angry. 'Hey you –' she glared at the macho policeman. 'Can you not see she's not well enough for questioning yet?'

'Sorry ma'am, I'm only doing my job.' He glared back. 'Now, Miss –' he raised his eyebrows and stood, pencil poised, notebook held high.

'Davies,' whispered Daisy.

'Right, Miss Davies, tell me all you can. From the very beginning.' His tone softened, bringing a flood of tears from a vulnerable Daisy.

A white hanky was thrust into her hand. She threw a grateful glance at Bill, whose hanky it was. The naked look in his eyes, shook her. She blushed.

Observant, the officer noticed her rising colour. 'See,' he said. 'She's looking better already. Now, let's get down to the nitty-gritty, Miss Davies.'

Doctor Scott knocked and entered. His gaze landed on Daisy seated by the fire.

'Well, young lady, what can I do for you?' His experienced

eyes assessed her for a moment. He noted the bruised cheek, the enlarged pupils and the pallor beneath a receding flush.

'We'll go somewhere private, shall we?'

'Yes, please.'

In the privacy of the bedroom, he examined her. Pulling up her lids, he gazed into the depths of her eyes. 'Mmm, you've been concussed. We'll get you to hospital and keep you under observation for a night.' He twisted round to see Rachel. 'You call an ambulance, Rachel, and you, Daisy, lie straight and still on the bed. I'll get rid of the men in blue.' With one finger, he pushed up his glasses, which seemed to have slipped down his nose. They were dark rimmed, with big round frames, giving him an owlish look. With a nod and a smile, he departed. The smile was warm and humorous. It conflicted with his studious demeanour.

'Thank you ,doctor,' Daisy said in a faint voice. 'You too Rachel. Say thank you to Bill for me, will you?' She had a feeling, like once before, that she'd be seeing more of him. At that time, she'd been wrapped up in longings for Tom.

Now, she was free.

Unaware of the recent drama with Ben, a whole group of police officers gathered beside a rustic gate. They were later in setting off than the previous day; and miles further up river. 'Spread out everybody, he must be somewhere in the vicinity.' Joe Fraser, chief of police from the nearest town, flung his arms wide, showing the expanse of land he wished to be combed.

It was at this precise moment that Donald, having said farewell to his family, was alighting from a bus in town. With mixed feelings, he watched it shrink and disappear from view. The whiff of fumes stuck in his nose as he proceeded along the street. His steps were heavy and slow. At the door of the police station, he halted. The stark solidness of it seemed to taunt him as he stood there with churning stomach. He hoped he wasn't going to disgrace himself and soil his trousers. Cook would get a good laugh at that, he thought, and, in spite of his fear, he found he was smiling.

As he entered, he collided with a policeman on his way out. 'Ooops, sorry,' the chap said. 'I'm in a hurry. I've got to go and help catch a man.'

Donald stayed him with his hand. 'You need look no further, sir. I think I'm your man.'

Statued, the policeman stood, hardly daring to believe what he'd just heard.

'Wh - wh - wh - what did you say?' he stuttered.

'I think you heard what I said.' Donald held out his wrists. 'Slap them on then, and get it over with. Donald Townsend at your service.'

Chapter Sixteen

The officer was jubilant. Out there in the woods and surrounding countryside, nearly the entire police force was looking for this man, and here he was, holding out his hands in supplication – to him.

'You'd better come in, then.' Ignoring the outstretched hands, he waved him in. Once inside, he telephoned the chief inspector. No answer. Oh, well, this was his baby. He must deal with it as he saw fit.

Stretching his legs, he stuck them nonchalantly on the desk, crossed them, and sat back in his chair. Curiously, he observed the fellow before him. In his many years in the police force, he'd scrutinized the faces of numerous people. This man seemed harmless. His demons exorcised. Regret etched his rugged features. Only time would iron out the creases.

'Have a seat,' he said. 'Then let's get started.' Unwinding his legs, he put them on the floor and sat up straight. From a drawer in his desk, he brought out a notebook and pen. Staring at Donald, he tapped his pen on the desk. 'You'd better get on with it then,' he urged. Excitement grew in him. He couldn't wait to see the others faces when they returned from yet another fruitless day.

Hearing the story to its conclusion, he cleared his throat. 'Well, lad, that was very heroic of you, but I'm afraid it won't affect your prison sentence. You will have to remain there for the duration. Then there's the incident with the shepherd. Assault won't help your case.'

'How is he? Did he survive?'

'Yes, he did, but long exposure in such harsh conditions, gave him pneumonia. If the barking of his dog hadn't raised the alarm, he'd have been a goner.'

'Thank God for that.' Donald had never thanked God in his life, before. It shocked him to realize this. A sudden desire to see the minister, enveloped him. 'Would it be possible to have a word with Gordon McKenzie?' he asked.

'Who's Gordon McKenzie?'

'The minister in our village.'

'Fair enough. I'll get through to him for you.' He thumbed through the directory, then dialled. On the third ring, the receiver was lifted. 'Good morning. Gordon McKenzie here.'

'Ah, good morning to you too. I'm police officer Hunter. I've a Donald Townsend here. He would like to see you. His stay here will be brief. As soon as chief inspector Hargreaves gets back, wheels will turn. It'll be back inside for this fellow.'

'Have you got Ben too?'

Apparently the minister had not been informed of the episode concerning Ben.

'No.' He looked at Donald. 'Do you know where Ben is?'

'At Cathy's house. Hawthornside farm.'

'He's at Hawthornside.'

'That's good. They'll be very relieved.' Gordon paused. 'Tell Donald I'll be right over.'

'OK.' The officer swung his eyes back to Donald. 'He's on his way.'

'Thank you.'

'Mmm, just for the record, did you have anything to do with the terrorizing of that bird Daisy Davies?'

Dumbly, Donald nodded.

'You don't do things in half measures, do you?' The officer shook his head. 'It looks bad for you I'm afraid. Three of our men are at her place now, questioning her.'

Donald let out a groan. He hung his head between his knees. He'd forgotten about Daisy. If anyone was in the soup, he was.

This was how Gordon found him as he arrived at the station. As the whole sorry saga was reiterated, Gordon was suffused with compassion for the chap. He stared at him long and hard. It was obvious that some inner struggle had been fought – and possibly overcome. 'You know,' he said. 'You should learn something worthwhile when you're back behind bars. Why not try theology? You could train to be a prison chaplain.'

'Me – a prison chaplain?' Donald was amazed at Gordon's suggestion. However, as the minutes ticked by, the idea took root, and grew. 'If I do that, will you allow me to marry your daughter? She said she'd wait for me. Oh, and another thing; will you go and see her?'

'Hmm, she has turned a lot of people against her with her wanton ways. How do I know she is any different?' The minister looked pensive.

'You'll know when you visit her. If I can change, then so can she. I found her charming. Think of it as a game of chess. Somebody has to make the first move. Why not you?'

'Very well. I'll take Paula with me. She has a way with folk. Maybe even Bobby. He tried hard to make her welcome, but was rebuffed. It takes a lot to put Bobby off. He never gives up.' A smile smoothed the contours of Gordon's face. Adopting Bobby was the best thing he'd ever done.

As he rose to go, so too did Donald. At the door, they shook hands and locked eyes. Each trying to reassure the other of the desire to fulfil any promises.

'Thank you for coming, minister. You've given me hope. Give my love to Caroline.'

With the minister gone, Donald's mask fell, his confidence evaporating like water in a desert.

'I'll take you to a cell now,' the police officer said quietly. He'd seen the change crossing Donald's face when the minister left the desk and went out. The hope reverting to despair. As he turned the key of the cell door, he knew it was like twisting a knife in the chap's guts. Where he was going, there would be a great many wanting to do just that.

At Hawthornside, Caroline was in the act of peeling potatoes at the sink when she heard a car drawing up in the yard. The newly fitted bell, gave one long, imperious ring. In the kitchen it seemed louder, and jangled in her ears. Drying her hands on a roller towel behind the door, she went to answer its call.

'Dad!' She gaped in astonishment. 'What brings you here?' Then she noticed his uneasiness and was full of contrition. 'Oh, dad – come here.' Her arms found their way round his neck. She felt the past touch her. The pent up longings. The wanting to be tucked up in bed by a father as well as a mother. The wanting to jiggled on his knee and carried piggyback up the stairs. Now, at last, he was really hers.

Wordlessly, her father held her, emotions tying his tongue in knots. Releasing him, Caroline saw Bobby and Paula in the background. 'Hello,' she said. It seemed all that was needed.

Bobby nudged Paula and gave her the thumbs up sign.

'Come in.' Caroline waved them inside. Holding open the door, she watched them fondly as they trooped in.

Barbara, seated on the sofa, was varnishing her nails. She looked up. 'Gordon,' she exclaimed. 'It's nice to see you.' Her eyes pored over his fine figure. Blast! she thought. Why couldn't he have fancied her.

Her gaze came to rest on Paula. She was nice, she admitted grudgingly. More suited to him than ever she'd have been. Except in bed, she mused. With her expertise in that field, he'd have been crawling into the pulpit on a Sunday morning; exhausted. Else frisking up the steps like a five-year-old. The creation of such images cheered her immensely. She gave him the full blast of her suddenly sex-filled eyes – but he was still oblivious. He must be made of wood, the bastard.

In the kitchen making a pot of tea, Caroline was joined by Paula. 'I'm pleased you are friends with your dad again,' she said. 'If you're not happy here, there is always a spare bedroom at the manse. I know about Donald. He told Gordon.' Paula's eyes searched the lovely face. It was suffused with a radiance at the mention of Donald's name and the thought of going home.

'Could I really come home?' she queried. She couldn't believe her luck, but wanted it said twice to let it sink in.

'Of course, go pack your things.' Paula smiled to herself. Gordon would be surprised.

'I'll take the dishes in first. You pour the tea. There's a lemon sponge in the cupboard.' Caroline rubbed her hands together. 'I'll be ready in fifteen minutes.'

When she re-entered the room, Paula drew Barbara aside. 'I've asked Caroline to come and stay with us. Do you mind?'

Barbara's lips parted, showing even white teeth. Today, the lipstick she wore was purple. The shade of mulberries. The colour of her cashmere jumper matched it perfectly. She certainly had style, Paula admitted.

Paula had noticed her inviting Gordon with a sensual look in her eyes, but she trusted him. It was a non-event as far as Gordon was concerned.

Before Barbara had time to reply, a loud rap on the door thundered through the hall. A quick preen in the mirror, a quick pull on the rib of her jumper, purple lips placed in a pout only she could produce, Barbara glided across the carpet to see who the impatient caller was.

A well-built chap with a thoughtful, expressive face, filled the doorway. 'Hello, I'm Dick Gardner, the new vet. I'm looking for Dave Hart. He phoned earlier. There's a cow with an injured teat.'

Stepping back, he waited to be given directions to Dave's whereabouts. His eyes scanned her from head to toe, like a potential buyer looking over a horse. They were blue-grey, the colour of a dove.

A shiver of anticipation ran through Barbara as she met his gaze. She studied him further. Brown hair, broad brow, lips well defined, face round but strong. Stocky, powerful, mysterious – and dead sexy. She wished she was the cow. He could examine her teats any time he wanted.

'Wait a minute and I'll take you.' The spontaneous offer flew from her lips.

'Thank you.'

Her mind galloping like a greyhound, she raced upstairs.

From her large, built-in wardrobe, she chose a thick woollen jacket. Pulling it on, she walked sedately, even demurely, down the stairs.

With smiling lips and eyes, the vet watched her.

'I'm Barbara Fairbairn,' she said, holding out a slender hand. 'I own this farm.'

'How d'you do?' His clasp was firm, his gaze steady. His face unreadable now, as if he'd pulled a cover over it. He would take things at his own pace, she decided. Though lust ran rampant in her veins, he'd be the one doing the chasing. The thought excited her.

They found Dave and John in a shed next to the stables. Dave, this is Dick Gardner, the new vet. Dick – this is my manager and John, my son.' Hazel, chestnut and blue-grey eyes, sprung towards each other, then to the cow.

'Must have been something sharp amongst the straw,' said Dave. 'Yet it's jagged.' He looked thoughtful.

Bending down, the vet examined the wound.

'Mmm, it looks like a bite. Are you plagued by rats here?'

Funnily enough, there are more of them around. Maybe they've done a flit from a dumping area or another farm. We've poisoned some, but the place is still rife with them.'

'Aaah.' The vet nodded and stood up. 'Easy lass,' he murmured, patting the Friesian cow on the rump. 'I'll get my bag of tricks. We'll soon have you better.'

Barbara watched as he tended the cow. Sleeves rolled up, face serious, engrossed in the job at hand. God what a hunk, she thought. She turned to John. Hesitantly, she touched his arm. 'Caroline is going back to the manse. Do you want to come home?'

His answer was long in coming, and so subliminal, that had her senses not been so acute, she'd have missed it.

'Good.' Her shoulders slumped with relief. 'You can bring Cathy and Ben whenever you like.' She saw a light dazzle his handsome features and felt a peace settle over her. For once, she'd made the right decision. She turned for a last look at Dick still kneeling beside the cow. 'Bye,' she cried. 'It's been nice meeting you.'

Back at the house, Caroline was trauchling her battered suitcase down the stairs and into the room. Gordon's face lit up with pleasure as he became aware of the full portent of her movements.

'That's the bout finished, minister,' said Bobby, giving him a nudge. 'It was Donald that provided the knockout punch, though.'

'Yes, we owe him a lot. Strange how things work out, isn't it?'

'Aye, who would have thought you'd be getting spliced after all those years, and to someone so young. You'll have to eat up your greens, or take vitamin pills.'

Laughing, the minister cuffed the air. Bobby grinned and ducked.

'Let's go, then.' Gordon shepherded them towards the door. 'Thank you for the tea, Barbara. You must come to us sometime.' Looking preoccupied, she darted her eyes beyond him to where the vet was now getting into his car.

So that's the way the wind is blowing. Gordon smiled wryly to himself. Poor chap.

'Is the vet married?' Barbara asked John, sotto voce.

'No, he was engaged, but it fell through. She went off with his best mate. Some bloody mate. Anyway, I must get on. I'll have tea with Maggie and Dave. I shall miss Maggie's scones – and them.' He smiled warmly. 'See you later, mum.'

John didn't know how to tell them he was returning home. Leaving their wonderful hospitality. Dave was like a father to him. And Maggie meant more to him than his own mother. Although she seemed to be more amenable of late, she'd never be Maggie.

From across the table, Dave observed John's face. He saw the emotions battling there and his heart sank. 'So you're leaving us, son?' Dave spoke first, rescuing John from his inner torment.

'Yes.' John gulped. 'Caroline's going back home. Mum is willing to accept Cathy and Ben. Oh, but I'll miss you both. It's been great staying here.'

Dave reached to clasp John's hands, 'Maggie and I feel the same. You're like a son to us, John. You know that, don't you?'

'Yes.'

'Right, then let's have another look at that cow. Seems a nice bloke, the vet, I think your mother was quite struck with him.'

'Was she?' John was surprised.

'Yes, a sort of love-struck look.'

'Mum – love-struck? That'll be a new thing for her. It's always been sex and more sex. Not that I knew then, but I'm old enough now to understand what's what. I thought she wouldn't reign long on a goody-goody diet. The poor fellow won't have a leg to stand on.'

Dave doubled up with laughter. Barbara had lost a boy when John left home.

She was gaining a man on his return.

Chapter Seventeen

That evening, John and Cathy popped in to see Elsie and the lads. Earlier in the day, Cathy had watched her granny and grandad zoom up the road, homeward bound. Funnily, her mum and Tom had gone away too.

'We're going to Berwick for the day,' her grandad had said. 'We'll stay the night there, then tomorrow, make our way to Edinburgh.'

Quick looks had licked the air between the grown-ups. Conspiratorial looks that Cathy saw, but didn't interpret.

'Where do you think mum and Tom are going?' She peeked with curiosity at John as they made their way to Elsie's house.

'Oh, ummm, I don't know.' John was at a loss as to what to say. His promise to Tom rolled to the tip of his tongue. It wanted to be freed and teetered on the brink, but he held it back. A promise was a promise.

Early afternoon next day, Tom brought his car to a standstill outside his house and cut the engine. 'We're here, Mrs Garrick.' His voice was gentle. 'Come and meet your in-laws.'

Involuntarily, she clutched his arm. 'What will they think?' she whispered.

'Don't worry, dad will be overjoyed. He's always on at me about getting a girlfriend.'

Tom guided her to the door. His eyes swept the yard. 'Mum must be out. She can't be far. She'll be back for dinner.' Picking

Alice up, he shoved aside the door with a strong knee and set her down in the hall.

Her skirt had worked its way up her thighs. The wild beats of her heart thumped against her ribs. Over the threshold for a second time, but this time, it would be different. Although they'd still be living in the cottage, one day she and Tom would reside here. This was his way of substantiating that.

When the grinning pair went in, Norman Garrick was viewing racing on the telly. A good judge of horseflesh, his avid eyes watched the graceful beasts as they flowed over the last jump. 'Yesss, yesss,' he roared as the horse of his choice romped home with lengths to spare.

'Hit the jackpot, have you, dad?' Tom's voice climbed through the haze of Norman's euphoria.

'Oh, hello, son. Had a good trip? Did Cathy's family get away safely?' Still concentrating on the winner being led in by a delighted stable lad, he didn't look round.

'Yes, we had a run to Edinburgh. Stayed in a very nice hotel.' Tom paused. 'By the way, dad, meet Alice, my wife.'

Had he dropped a bomb, the effect would have been less startling. Norman's head jerked round with shock. 'You're what?' he shouted.

'My wife. Alice, come and meet dad.'

'Well I'll be damned. You've gone and done it at last.' His capable hands twisted his wheelchair round to face them. 'Alice Wilson, begorra. So you're the one. Come here lass and let me give you a hug.'

As the woollen-sleeved arms enfolded her, Alice knew she was going to love this man. Norman's eyes, the colour of a grey sea, but with wavelets of warmth dancing in them, met Alice's quiet ones, and something applauded inside him.

Going to the sideboard, Tom poured three drinks.

'Here, let me help.' Alice stepped to his side in a slow, flowing movement.

Norman noted her figure, seeing her as a breeder sees a brood mare, his mind jumping in leaps and bounds. Legless he may be, but he could nevertheless offer a lot to a grandchild, and a grandchild to him.

The land and buildings were folded in darkness when Jean arrived home. She noticed Tom was back and was pleased. To the sound of laughter, she walked in, coming to a puzzled standstill as she beheld Tom with his arm wound round Alice. The implication did not at first reach her. Then she saw the ring. Alice hadn't worn a ring since Bert's death. That meant – good heavens – that meant that they were married.

Tom turned at the sound of her gasp. 'Mum, sorry to spring this surprise on you. I see you've guessed our little secret. Our BIG secret.' He pulled Alice close, placing a kiss on the crown of her silken head.

Her mind recovering faster than her legs, Jean yawed across the carpet. 'Welcome to the family, Alice, and congratulations, Tom. It IS a pleasant surprise.' Though outwardly calm, inwardly she was in a flurry. Only one kitchen. How will it work? Two women bumping around getting in each other's way. Hell, she needed a drink. 'Pour me a gin and tonic please, Tom.' Sinking like lead onto the armchair, she looked at Norman. His face was alight; animated. But he didn't see the pitfalls as she did. Men never did.

'We're going to stay in the cottage,' said Alice, sensing the turmoil fermenting inside Jean's head.

Jean breathed a sigh of relief.

'You'll do no such thing. You'll stay here with us.'

'No dad, we've discussed it.' Tom was just as resolute. On a silver tray, he placed his empty glass. 'Drink up, Alice, we must get going.' Shyly she stepped to Norman's side, kissed him goodbye, said 'cheerio' to Jean, and she and Tom sailed gaily out.

'We'll have to rectify that situation, Jean. We are in our seventies. How about us buying a cottage in the village? There's one for sale next to the manse. We could put in an offer.'

'Really!' Jean perked up instantly. That was near to where Frank, the new librarian lived. She'd gone off Gordon a bit. He went around now in a besotted world of bliss, his mind full of Paula – but Frank – wow! He was a dish. Just to receive one of his smiles. Smiles that stormed her veins like tornadoes. She thought of the lines in Shakespeare's Love's Labour's Lost, 'The mind shall banquet, though the body pine.' Well – her body wouldn't pine exactly, but she would certainly feast on his smiles.

Alert now, she gave her husband a long look. 'That seems a sound idea, Norman. It is time Tom held the reins, in every sense of the word, here on the farm.'

'Right, we'll see about it tomorrow.'

Cathy was making dinner when her mum and Tom came in. She looked up. 'Hello, you two. I'm afraid there's only enough for one, but if you wait, I'll make some scrambled eggs for you.'

'Never mind making dinner. We are taking you out to dine. We are celebrating.' Tom glanced at Alice. 'Well, show her, Alice.'

'Show me what?' Cathy was bewildered.

'This.' Alice raised her hand.

'Gosh, congratulations.' Cathy took the proffered hand and peered closely at the ring. 'It's lovely. Wait till I tell Elsie.' She paused. 'Can she come with us? She'll be back from work soon.'

'Of course she can.' Alice smiled bashfully.

'You'll get some ribbing from the men when they find out, Tom.' Cathy giggled, knowing the lewd remarks that would follow.

A grin spread over Tom's face. He knew fine what the workers would say.

The minute Elsie came home, an eager Cathy skipped along to see her.

Mary listened with greedy ears. 'The fly buggers,' she cried, forgetting she was eavesdropping. 'No wonder he didn't say anything.' From surprise to agitation, her face changed, her mind willing Cathy and Elsie to be gone so that she could tell the Taits and the Stuarts.

Chapter Eighteen

At last, it was the night of the dance. Barbara wore a dress of the same brilliant red as holly berries. In frilled layers, it clung to her shapely figure. She looked fantastic.

Dick Gardner, the vet, bestowed on her a long, steady stare, then looked away, pretending indifference. To her chagrin, he crossed to where Daisy stood, and led her onto the dance floor for a quickstep.

Barbara was perturbed. For the first time, she felt the sting of jealousy. Bitter barbs, like cat's claws, raking raw incisions inside her every time she cast her eyes in their direction. Yet deep down, she felt he liked her. She was sure of it. Well, two can play at his game, she fumed.

Dan Sykes stood by the door talking to Tom. In a dark brown shirt, fawn tweed suit and fawn tie, and his skin still holding traces of a tan from a recent holiday, he looked very handsome. Plucking up confidence, she made a beeline for him. 'Hello, Dan. Would you care to dance with me? No strings, I promise.'

Gazing into her eyes, his peaty ones, even now, were aware of her allure, but he was immune to it. He and Emma had reached a new understanding. He was strictly a one woman man now. His eyes were discerning as he looked at Barbara. There was an anxiety, a vulnerability about her now. Bloody hell, he must be going senile. Barbara – vulnerable?

'Please Dan,' she implored.

Looking into the chestnut depths of her lovely eyes a moment longer, he raised his eyebrows at Tom and guided her into the crush of the dancing couples. 'Right,' his gaze was intense. 'What's this all about?'

'You'll think I'm being foolish, Dan, but the thing is, I think I'm in love.'

'You – in love? Are you on drink or drugs or something Barbara?' Dan roared with laughter, his white, even teeth glinting in the subdued light.

'No, it's him.' She nodded to where the vet circled next to them with Daisy in his arms. 'I'm really trying to make him jealous, because that's what he's trying to do to me. I feel it.'

'Mmm —' He studied her with incredulous eyes. 'We'll better make it convincing then, won't we?' Winding his arms round her, he moulded her body to his. He felt the familiar stirrings in his nether regions and inwardly swore.

'You're like The Sirens, Barbara, only you entice men with your body, not your voice. Men are but ships on a turbulent sea, cast on the rocks of your desire.'

Lost in her scheming, Dan's eulogy skimmed over her thoughts. Her gaze scrambled between the jostling dancers. There was Daisy talking to Rachel and Tony. Surely Dick Gardner had not been so ill-mannered as to have dumped her in the middle of a dance.

As the final notes drew the dance to a close, Barbara stood, her hand still in Dan's clasp. 'Thank you, Dan, but it seems my quarry has made a quick exit.' Her despair was so real, that for once, Dan felt sorry for her. Like a gentleman, he led her back to a seat. Stirred as he was by the proximity of her body when dancing, he knew the temptation to do anything about it, had gone.

He felt free.

'Thank you for trying, Dan.' A smile broke through the depths of her despondency, softening her face. 'I'm not finished yet, though,' she said firmly. 'You know how relentless I can be when in pursuit of something I really want, don't you, Dan?'

Dan exchanged glances with Tom as Barbara walked unsteadily on pencil thin heels along the hall. He wiped his brow, relieved it was over. He saw Beth dancing round the hall in Harry's arms, laughing up into his face. She seemed to have laid a few ghosts as well.

Thoughtfully, he made for the door, then turned to Tom. 'If I tell you something, will you keep it under your hat for a while, Tom?' Dan's sensuous lips were squeezed tight. He seemed troubled.

'Yes, of course.' Tom gazed at Dan. They weren't bosom buddies. Just friends of a sort who met in the pub or when any plumbing needed done on the farm, but if he wanted a confidential talk, Tom was ready to listen – and help if necessary.

'It's – well –' Dan stopped, as if embarrassed. 'It's Emma. She's pregnant.'

Eyes big and round as buttons, Tom heard Dan's stilted confession. Hands in pockets, he bent double, laughing uproariously as the humour of the situation took hold.

'She thought she was on the change,' continued Dan. 'Then she became sick in the mornings and knew straight away. We'll be the laughing stock of the village, Tom. Hell, look at the age of Beth.'

Releasing a hand from his pocket, Tom laid it on Dan's shoulder, feeling a sudden kinship with the man. 'Och, Dan, it'll be a nine days wonder, then folk will accept it. As long as they are both all right when the time comes, that's the main thing.'

'I suppose so,' Dan shrugged. 'I'm off then. I said I wouldn't be late.' He half turned. 'You know Tom, I just don't understand how it happened. I'm usually that careful.'

Tom grinned. 'Accidents do happen, Dan. Just think – getting wakened in the middle of the night to give it a feed. Dirty nappies to change. Clean ones hanging wherever there's a space. You've let yourself in for a lot of work there,' he jested.

From some inner source, Dan managed a rueful smile, then turned the tables on Tom.

'You wait until Alice springs the same surprise on you. At least I've had experience on such events. Aye, I can see you staggering about with half closed eyes when it howls in the night. Well – see you, Tom.' Chuckling heartily, Dan stepped outside. Frost glittered the tarmac. The air was brisk, trees, ghost-like, branches and twigs white, as if dusted with icing sugar.

An owl huddled on a high bough, feathers fluffed, scouring the undergrowth. A mouse peeped from behind a projecting root, scavenging for food. In stops and starts, it flitted back and forth amongst the dead leaves, eye darting, whiskers twitching, heart thumping. On the crispy grass, its movements fed the night, and on the silvery branch the owl swivelled its head then fell in a downward swoop.

Some animal instinct terrorized the mouse into fleeing. Sharp talons clawed the earth where it had been. Thwarted, the owl flew off. It did not dwell on its loss. The night was long. It would be back.

As along the road, he crunched, Dan saw its light shape fly out before him and fade into the darkness.

The frost was severe. Little puddles were already iced over and the road glittered like glass. Dan rejoiced. It meant frozen taps and pipes. It meant work for himself and the lads.

His final remark to Tom had left Tom's thoughts reeling. Having children had never entered his mind. The idea was a pleasant one. How would Alice react to such a suggestion? he wondered.

Chapter Nineteen

It took a long time and a lot of conniving and months of heartache, before Barbara cut the ice with Dick Gardner. A puncture, on a narrow road to a farm she was going to visit, and where she knew he was going, started it off.

It was a dull day in early autumn. Her well manicured fingers drummed to the beat of a song playing on her car radio as she bumped along the rough road. The bumping became more evident and she fought to control the steering, but her speed was too fast and, with a shudder, the car veered to the edge and into the ditch.

'Blast!' she shouted, growing alarmed at the plight she'd got herself into. What if he didn't come? What if darkness falls and no one appears? She sank her head onto the steering wheel in despair.

How long she sat like this, she didn't know. It was cold. She huddled into the chunky polo neck of her jumper, and drew the neck up over her chin. All she could do now was wait.

'Are you all right?' The voice seemed to come from a distance. Startled, she looked up, gave a quick intake of breath and burst into tears.

'You're safe now. Here,' he pressed a crumpled hanky against her wet cheeks. Anxious eyes held hers. 'Can I have the key for the boot? You do have a spare tyre, don't you?' His look was expectant, yet unsure, as if he thought women drivers weren't capable of thinking in such technical terms.

Smiling triumphantly, she nodded and handed him the key, thinking – up yours too, son. Women are not so useless.

Shaky legged, she emerged from the car and knelt at his side as he worked. After a while, the last nut was screwed tight. Still hunkered, their heads turned towards each other and their eyes clung. Tied in a timeless vacuum, they rose. With a clatter, the wrench fell to the ground and his arms reached out. With a sigh, Barbara went to them.

He released her and stood back. 'We'd better go. I've a horse to see to at the next farm.'

'Alright – and thank you.' Barbara felt the ache of his leaving even before he'd gone.

'I'll see you later.'

His reply was so soft, she barely heard, but the simple words mapped her future.

Many futures were simmering in the planning pot of life. Tom's mum and dad purchased the cottage next to the manse. They moved in the week-end Tom and Alice were away to Aintree to see the Grand National.

On returning from Liverpool, there was no sign of Tom's parents. 'Funny,' he said to Alice. 'It's unusual for dad to be out. Mum – yes, but not him.' Cautiously, he opened the door of the room that was their office. No, he's not here either.' Tom was beginning to feel uneasy. 'DAD, we're back,' he shouted. 'DAD.' Curbing his instinct to pick up the phone, he wandered with dogged steps from room to room.

'Tom.' Alice's cry penetrated his fuzzy thoughts. Holding a brown, Manila envelope, she rushed to where he stood. 'This was leaning on the clock.' Fearfully, she eyed him.

With shaking fingers, he tore it open. From inside, he took a single sheet of paper on which sprawled his dad's large, sloping writing.

'Alice, you'll never guess what they've done?' Flopping onto the nearest chair, he handed her the letter.

'Are you going to change anything?' he asked later as they sipped mugs of coffee in the kitchen. Outside the window, golden daffodils swayed. Birds twittered, gearing up for the non-stop activity of nest making and the rearing of young. Lambs frisked and raced along the fields. Yellow curtains stirred in the draught of a slight opening in the window. Alice saw and heard it all. Turning to Tom, she smiled. 'No,' she answered with tongue in cheek. 'Just the bedroom.'

Huskily, Tom laughed. 'What about a nursery?' he queried, testing the water on the subject.

'You never know,' she said softly. She patted her tummy. She wouldn't tell him yet; not until she was sure.

Gordon McKenzie and Paula tied the knot on a blustery, cool day in July. Bobby, smart, in his first dark suit, was an usher. At the open door stood a girl. Her gaze darted past Bobby, taking in the lovely floral display on the table in the vestibule.

'Mum did that,' she said proudly. 'She's got the new florist's shop up near the forge.'

The tone of her voice interested Bobby, but it was her eyes that arrested him most. Dark as an evening sky, they were; yet how they sparkled; as though all the winter stars and constellations fought for supremacy in their inky depths.

'Are you wanting to come in?' he asked. His voice, now stopped skipping from bass to alto, was deep and manly. 'Are you a guest?'

'No, I'm by meself.' Smiling broadly, she went in; blue skirt, black sweater, black boots, black hair, disappearing up into the balcony of the church. She was a stunner.

Colin on the opposite side of the door, an usher as well, sniggered. 'You fancy her, don't you?' he said loudly.

'Sssh – she'll hear you,' Bobby hissed. All at once he was self-conscious.

'You're blushing, Bobby Telfer. Wait till I tell Harry.'

'Don't you dare.'

'I will so.'

Faces red as cherries, they glared at each other across the space. Then Bobby grinned. He did fancy that lassie. She was young, though. He'd have to wait a few years.

About to drive past in an old Ford, was a newly married couple from London.

'Look, Alan. It's a wedding. Let's stop and watch. You know —' Shirley paused. 'I think this is the village where Beth lives.' Her hair flew from her face as she wound down the window.

'I'm getting out, Alan. Are you?'

'Whatever you say, Mrs Sanderson.' A quick pat on her knee and he was round to her side and opening the door. 'See,' he laughed. 'Once a gentleman, always a gentleman. Come on, we'll have a shufti at the poor soul getting hung today.'

At the front of the church, smart in their wedding attire, stood Gordon and Tom. Doing the service was a minister from a nearby church. Plump, jovial, with bird-like eyes, he smiled at Gordon. He knew full well the confusion seducing his mind and heart.

From a black limousine, stepped Paula and Dave, who was giving her away. From another, came the matron of honour, Alice.

'He's not half doin' it in style,' Mary Marshall whispered to Grace Stuart. 'They must be well paid in that job. They used to call it a 'calling' but nowadays it's just a bloody occupation. They're all human beings like us. With the same wants and needs.'

'Be quiet, Mary. 'Tis an awful tongue you've got on you sometimes.' Grace turned up her collar. 'Ooh, it's cold. Mind you, that pair'll not feel it the night, will they?'

Cackling like hens, they continued watching.

At the door afterwards, the happy group posed for the usual photographs. The photographer, grey-haired, slightly stooped, with a pale, pleasant face, snapped away with patience and skill.

'Now,' he said. 'Stand this way. Just the four of you. Good. Now the bride. You stand by that tree, my dear.'

Shirley, at the front of the circle of bystanders, stood

transfixed. That voice — As the photographer gently issued instructions, the years fell away. The feeling of his arms as he held her in the school playground. Knowing within her it was the last time, yet understanding. The loneliness afterwards. With a cry, she ran to him. 'Daddy!' The involuntary use of her childish name for him escaped like a splash in the now hushed atmosphere.

'Oh, daddy.' Shirley nestled her head against the curve of his chest. He didn't smell of grease and oil any more, but had the fresh tang of aftershave and talc.

Shakily, he shoved her from him. His eyes, melting with emotion, asked the hundreds and thousands of questions that tumbled around in his brain.

'Later,' Shirley whispered, knowing what his thoughts were. 'You've still got some photos to take.'

From the back of the crowd, Beth espied her London friend and wriggled to her side. 'Shirley, how nice to see you. What brings you to the Borders?'

'We're on our honeymoon. It was a quiet wedding.' Turning sideways, Beth studied the rosy countenance of Shirley's brand new husband. He looked nice.

'And this is my dad.' Shyly, she pulled forward Stanley Raeburn.

'Stanley – is your dad?'

'Yes. Funny coming all the way to Scotland and finding him here.'

'How did you know?'

'By his voice.' Shirley loosened the hold she had on her dad's arm and peered up at him with warm eyes. 'We'll finish those photos now, dad.'

In a happy daze, her father retrieved his camera from the ground and stood, poised.

'No, I want you in the picture too.' Disengaging the camera from her father's grasp, she handed it to Mary Marshall, who was standing near.

With anguish, her dad observed Mary as she twirled his hundreds of pounds worth camera upside and round and round.

'Here, let me do it.' Daisy had seen the horror running across the kindly features of Shirley's dad. Happily, she watched it evaporate as she clicked film after film with the expertise of a professional.

'How come you're such an expert?' Bill Jenks eyed her curiously.

'It's my hobby' She gave him a coy glance. 'There's a lot of things you'll have to learn about me, Bill Jenks,' she joked. 'If you want to, that is.'

The mystique of her remark hung in the air. It draped over Bill like a blanket. Fondly, he stroked her cheek with the back of his hand, harvesting the feel of it.

At the end of July, Emma Sykes gave birth to a baby girl. She was small and dimply, with straight dark hair that crossed her head in black streaks. As she grew older, her eyes, violet as amethysts, swamped her face like two circular windows.

She was a cuckoo in the nest, resembling neither Dan, Emma or Beth. They called her Linda. Every time Dan peeped into her cot or pram, he was awarded with a gurgling smile.

He loved her dearly.

In September, Alice produced a sturdy, blonde haired son. Beguiling from the start, he won the hearts of anyone who gazed upon his contented face. As soon as he could toddle, he teetered to his grandpa sitting in his wheelchair by the fire. His first word was 'ganpa.' Sometimes he'd gently touch the empty trouser legs dangling from his grandpa's knees and stare at the face that was dearer to him than even his mum and dad, then off he'd scamper. Norman Garrick was gratified. He had a grandson, little Adam. The Garrick name was assured for yet another generation.

As if time was dictating to her, on a balmy morning a year later, Alice lay tired and sweating, in the throes of labour. At dawn, while birds sang and cows lowed at the gate and Spot and

Bess lay waiting for human sounds – she brought Samuel into the world. He was as dark as Adam was fair, his nature both sunny and stormy. All in one package.

That same month, Elsie and Alf were married. Cathy was bridesmaid. Harry best man.

After the photo session, Elsie turned her back, blindly throwing her bouquet into the crowd. Caroline and Beth jumped together, both catching it at the same time. 'Hey, when's Donald coming home?' cried Beth.

'Next year,' said Caroline.

'You can have this then.' Beth relinquished her grip on the flowers.

Harry bestowed Beth with a cheeky grin. 'You never know,' he said. 'You caught it together – and a lot can happen in a year.'

Something twisted inside Beth, but she shoved it away. She wasn't yet ready to embark on a new relationship.

Caroline and John's divorce had not yet been finalised.

There was a lot of waiting to be done.

The next year, Alf and Elsie became the proud parents of a little girl. She had brown hair and chocolate eyes, like her granny, Mary Marshall.

A week later, Cathy gave birth to a bouncing baby boy. He was named Todd. Lovingly, she unwrapped the thick woollen blanket from around his chubby legs. Relieved of the unwieldy fabric, he wriggled with delight. 'Look, John,' she whispered. 'His toes – they're webbed – like yours.'

'Are they?' John's eyes shone with pride as he gazed down at his child. Well – we'll show them to the world, not keep them hidden like mum did mine.' Impishly, he grinned. 'She won't be a bit pleased, will she?'

'She'll come round. Dick has a good influence on her.' The tiny bundle in her arms stiffened. His howl strangled the stillness of the ward. 'He's hungry.' Cathy opened the front of her nightdress and placed the grizzling mouth on her swollen teat. Like a limpet, it latched on.

Like a lion guarding its young, his dad watched. Picking him up when he'd had his fill, he held him close and patted his back. He burped – and farted. 'I bet you feel better now, little man,' John chuckled.

News of the baby's webbed toes travelled faster than who he resembled. 'Has Dan Sykes's bairn got webbed feet?' enquired Mary Marshall.

'No, I've seen her. She's no' like any o' them. You mark my words, that Emma Sykes's had a visitor – and he's left his trademark too.' Throwing back her head, Grace roared with laughter, appeased that for once, she'd outwitted Mary and got the last word.

Dan was thirsty. God, he could sink a pint. It was five thirty and traffic toed and froed in endless streams. People like himself, finished work for the day. Pulling his van up beside the White Swan, he locked the door and entered the near empty pub. 'A pint please, Daisy. This heat's given me a mighty thirst.' His elbow found the surface of the bar. He looked around.

Pete, the butcher, sat alone at a corner table. A cheroot blazed as he drew in, then died as he blew out. A brownish grey smoke rose to the ceiling. Dan clasped his glass, took a long drink and strode over to join him.

Pete had two drams in quick succession, making his florid face even ruddier. His moustache curled up at the sides like a smile. His eyebrows peaked in the middle in tiny wisps. He was like a dog at Crufts.

'Hello, Pete. Grand day, isn't it?'

'Aye,' A rough hand tugged at his tie; two fingers eased his collar, loosening it. 'Aah, that's a bloody relief. It's hot in here after being in the shop.'

Silence ensued. Dan gazed at the well-dressed fellow talking to Daisy. A briefcase lay at his feet. It was brown, with worn bits on it.

'Is this you finished then?' Daisy enquired of the chap. 'No,

I've one more call. I usually go to her earlier in the day, but I was held up.'

For some unknown reason. Dan found himself studying the man. Crinkly black hair, quite long, but not untidy. Decent profile. Strong. Eyes – he was yet to see them, but with his colouring, they'd probably be brown.

As if aware of his scrutiny, the chap turned. Dan was stricken. Rooted to the spot with shock. Looking down at him, huge, violet and unusual – were Linda's eyes. Dan couldn't think any more. It was too painful. His fists clenched. He wanted to knock that well-groomed figure into the middle of next week, but knew that he wouldn't. It would only draw attention to himself, and he didn't want that. In his mind – Linda was his.

Abruptly, he stood up, nearly knocking over the table in his haste. 'I'm away home, Pete. I feel a bit groggy.'

'Aye, you do look a mite anaemic, Dan. Get some red meat into you, lad.' Pete guffawed heartily, his piggy eyes disappearing into folds of fat. 'You know where my shop is. Send the wife in for some prime steak.'

'Who was that fellow?' asked the stranger as Dan went out. Something seemed to ring alarm bells.

'He's Dan Sykes, the local plumber. His wife's just had a bairn. A slip-up there, I'd say.' Pete harrumphed into his fourth nip. 'Still, it's none of my business.' A muffled thump propelled his head in the direction of the bar. Stretched out cold, his face ashen, was the stranger.

'Daisy, bring a glass of cold water. Chuck it on that lad's face.' He pointed to the floor. 'Must be the heat, Dan was poorly as well.'

'I'm sleeping in the spare bedroom tonight, Emma.' Dan dropped the bombshell at dinner. He'd never felt so het up. People prepared themselves for downward slides in life, but this'd knocked the stuffing out of him.

Green eyes squinted up at him. 'Why, things are all right between us, are they not?'

'No, they're not – and you know why.' Drawn with hurt, Dan's face flung febrile accusations at her.

All night, he tossed and turned, his mind a whirling mass sucking in his thoughts. He was no angel himself. If Emma had found out about Barbara, what would her reaction have been? It wasn't as if he was saddled with a brat he didn't want. He loved Linda. With the thought of her tiny hand gripping his pinky so tight, he wondered where the strength came from, he smiled. She would be the ribbon that bound them.

At breakfast, while Emma methodically buttered toast, he tucked in to a bacon roll. The smell of frying lingered in the air. Dan focussed his attention on Emma. 'I'll be back in my own bed tonight,' he said quietly. 'I missed you last night.' He made the pretence of brushing crumbs from his knees. His heart fluttered with the fear of what he was about to divulge, but he knew it had to be done. Everything must be above board from now on. Rising, he pushed his chair under the table and stood with his hands gripping the back of it. 'We're quits now, Emma,' he said softly.

Her eyes clouded over with disbelief. The enormity of what he was inferring sinking into her like stakes being hammered into the ground.

'Who?' she whispered.

'Barbara Fairbairn.' He looked at his hands. 'That's not all – John is my son.'

'So that's why Beth went to London?'

'Yes.'

'How did she find out?'

'He inherited my feet.' Dan shrugged. 'It's not a very common characteristic, is it?'

'No, I suppose not.'

'You've got to change insurance companies.'

Mutely, she nodded.

'Good, then let's get on with our lives.'

Up in the Highlands, Ivy Geddes was restless. In bed, she twisted and turned. She didn't know if she was dreaming or awake, but something sinister was dragging her down into a gurgling mass of water. There was a body. She couldn't make out the face. Then it turned towards her. She screamed. It was Todd – and he was in danger. His hands tried to reach out to her – then he was gone.

She thumped Ralph in the ribs.

'Wake up, wake up,' she shouted. Her breathing felt restricted and she tugged loose the neck of her nightdress. The pain was excruciating. She fell back on her pillow, her face waxen.

'What the blazes are you roaring at, Ivy?' Ralph turned on his back and looked at the ceiling.

Ivy came to life again and pulled at his arm. 'We've got to go to Hawthornside,' she gasped. 'Now! It's – it's – it's Todd.' Her voice trailed away. She clutched her chest and sat up. 'It's Todd,' she said again. 'He needs help.'

Alarmed, Ralph leaped from the bed and switched on the light.

'Ivy, my dear, what are you havering about? If there was anything wrong with Todd, Alice or Cathy would have let us know.'

'No,' she grabbed his arm. 'We've got to go.'

'Look, I'll ring Alice and see if he's all right.' He went to the door and turned. 'I won't be a minute.'

Alice picked up the phone. It was her dad.

'Is Todd alright, Alice. Ivy is anxious about him. I think she's had a nightmare. She's acting a bit strange, though.'

'Yes, he's fine, dad. Tell her not to fret.' With a worried frown, Alice laid the phone back on its cradle.

Ralph needed a smoke. Going to the room, he took down his pipe and filled it. Having puffed his fill, he bent over and tapped it on the grating on the fire, emptying it. Feeling less tired, he repaired to the kitchen and switched on the kettle. A cup of tea might benefit Ivy, he thought. Shoving the door open with his shoulder, he entered the bedroom, then stopped – aghast. Lying on the floor was Ivy. A pen lay within reach of her right hand. In her left, she clutched a piece of paper.

She was as still as a statue.

The shrill ring of the phone had Alice once more on her feet. This time, she knew what it was, but prepared as she was, a shiver of dread shot through her. Sensitive to her feelings, Tom sprang to her side. He was there to catch her when she fainted.

In his Highland home, her dad replenished his glass with another whisky. He was not a bibulous man, but Ivy's death had knocked the feet from under him. The doctor had been, the undertakers and the minister. The funeral was on Thursday. He went to the bureau and picked up the piece of paper he'd wrestled from Ivy's hand.

Todd, it said. Two sides to a story. The words were etched on his mind, but what did they mean? Putting on his glasses, he peered at it again. The writing was not shaky, but bold, as if Ivy had put all her strength into the act.

Did it mean Todd wasn't in danger, but one of the others? Or had her imagination played tricks on her? She was a Highlander through and through. He knew Highlanders could sometimes be born with second sight, spilling from blood ties centuries old, but he'd never detected any fanciful fey trends in Ivy. On the contrary, she'd been logical and down to earth.

Ralph sighed.

Back in the Borders, it was another hot day. With happy hearts, the youngsters trooped to the river. Ben was now fifteen and away playing with his older mates. Samuel was nine. Adam and Linda eight. Todd, Susan, and Katie, were seven. Jane, born to Caroline the year Donald was released from prison, was seven too.

Samuel had taken a frisbee, which they threw to each other midst screams and shouts from the girls. On the bank, stood Todd.

He didn't like water, not because of his webbed toes, but because it frightened him.

Also on the bank stood Charlie Irvine, whose family had moved to one of the new council houses in the village. With him were his sisters, Rose and Libby and Jane Townsend, who followed him around like a pet dog. Somehow, he'd managed to befriend her and gain her trust.

'Why do you not like water, Todd?' piped up Libby, Charlie's smaller sister.

'I don't know, Libby. I'm just scared.'

'Cowardly guts, cowardly guts,' jeered Charlie, who was a bit of a trouble maker. 'You should still be in nappies.'

'I'm not a coward.' Todd turned towards Charlie. 'Nearly everybody has a fear of some kind. Even you, I bet.'

'I'm frightened in the dark.' Libby's bright eyes gazed at Todd. 'Charlie frightens me sometimes and I wet my breeks.'

Todd laughed. 'He should try frightening somebody his own size. He wouldn't frighten me. I'm bigger than he is.'

An argument ensued. 'I could so frighten you. You're just a posh wanker.' Charlie's face was scarlet. 'Oh well, nancy boy, you've got feet like a duck, now see if you can swim like a duck.' Charlie's hand shot out – and like a stone, Todd fell into the shocked water.

So intent on their game, and making so much noise, the others didn't hear the splash. Susan noticed first that Todd wasn't there.

'Where's Todd,' she shouted.

'Maybe he's gone home. That Charlie picks on him all the time,' said Katie.

Adam stopped splashing and made for the bank. Charlie stood, white as a sheet. Rose and Libby were crying and pointing.

Samuel's eyes followed their fingers. He stared in horror 'He's in the river,' he screamed. 'Adam, everybody, come and help.' By now, all eyes were on the still form of Todd. Galvanized into action, they went to Samuel's aid. Between them, they managed to drag him out and onto the bank. Samuel grabbed his friend and held him in a tight embrace.

He was dead.

Dumbstruck, they all stood. Shakily, Susan knelt beside him 'He's smiling, Samuel, look. Why do you think he's smiling?' Tears streamed down her face and dropped onto his hand. Gently, she wiped them away.

'Get John!' Samuel's anguished eyes trembled over them.

'Where will he be?'

'I don't know. Try the house.'

Adam and Linda ran as if the devil was after them. They were speechless, Todd's body printed on their minds. John was at the stables talking to Dave. When he saw the wet figures and white faces, his conversation stopped.

'Oh, no —' he cried as he heard them out. He turned away from their intense stares and laid a hand on Dave's shoulder. 'Wait here, Dave, we'll have to bring Todd home. First, I must tell Cathy.'

'What happened?' John looked at the circle of frightened children shivering on the river bank.

'He slipped, didn't he?' Charlie glanced at his sisters, willing them to say yes, but silent as ghosts, they stood. He shifted his gaze to Jane. She loved him, he knew, in her childish way, but right and wrong had been dinned into her from an early age. A fierce battle was going on inside her. Eyes filling with tears, feeling a traitor to Charlie, slowly she shook her head.

'What will happen to him?' asked Cathy.

'He'll probably be put in a place for young offenders.' John wiped his eyes.

It was the biggest funeral ever witnessed in the village. Alice and Tom, just back from Ivy's interment, tried to put a brave face on, but it was difficult.

'Will Todd be in heaven, mum?' Samuel asked as they walked to the hotel after the service.

'Yes, he was too good to die so young.'

'Susan said he was smiling – and he was, mum. It must be somewhere nice where he is. Do you think we'll meet up there when we're dead?'

'I'm sure we will, son.' Samuel's words tugged at Alice's heart. She didn't know anything any more. A young life gone whoosh – just like that. What was it all about?

That night, sleep came slowly to John and Cathy. It had been a sad day. As the moon sent beams of light between the trees and over roof tops and through a chink in their curtains, at last they slept.

A light touch on Cathy's brow, opened her eyes. She blinked, wondering if she might be seeing things. Surely she must be, but no, there sitting on the bed – was Todd.

'Mum.'

Cathy sat up.

'Todd, is that you?'

'I've seen granny Ivy, mum. She came to me in the river. She says to say hello. Tell Samuel, thank you, and Susan and the others. I think I'd have married Susan if this hadn't happened. I love you mum – and dad. Tell him mum.

'Susan knew I was smiling, mum. It was an inside smile, but she saw it. I think I'm an angel, but I don't know. I think I see granny Ivy again. Maybe she's an angel as well. Tell grandpa Ralph, he'll want to know. I must go now. Oh – and mum. I don't have webbed toes any more, and I'm not afraid of water.'

A feather-light kiss fanned Cathy's cheek. She smiled, and turned towards John.

Drawing Under Fire

Drawing Under Fire

War diary of a young Vietnamese artist

by Pham Thanh Tam

Edited by Sherry Buchanan

Asia Ink, London

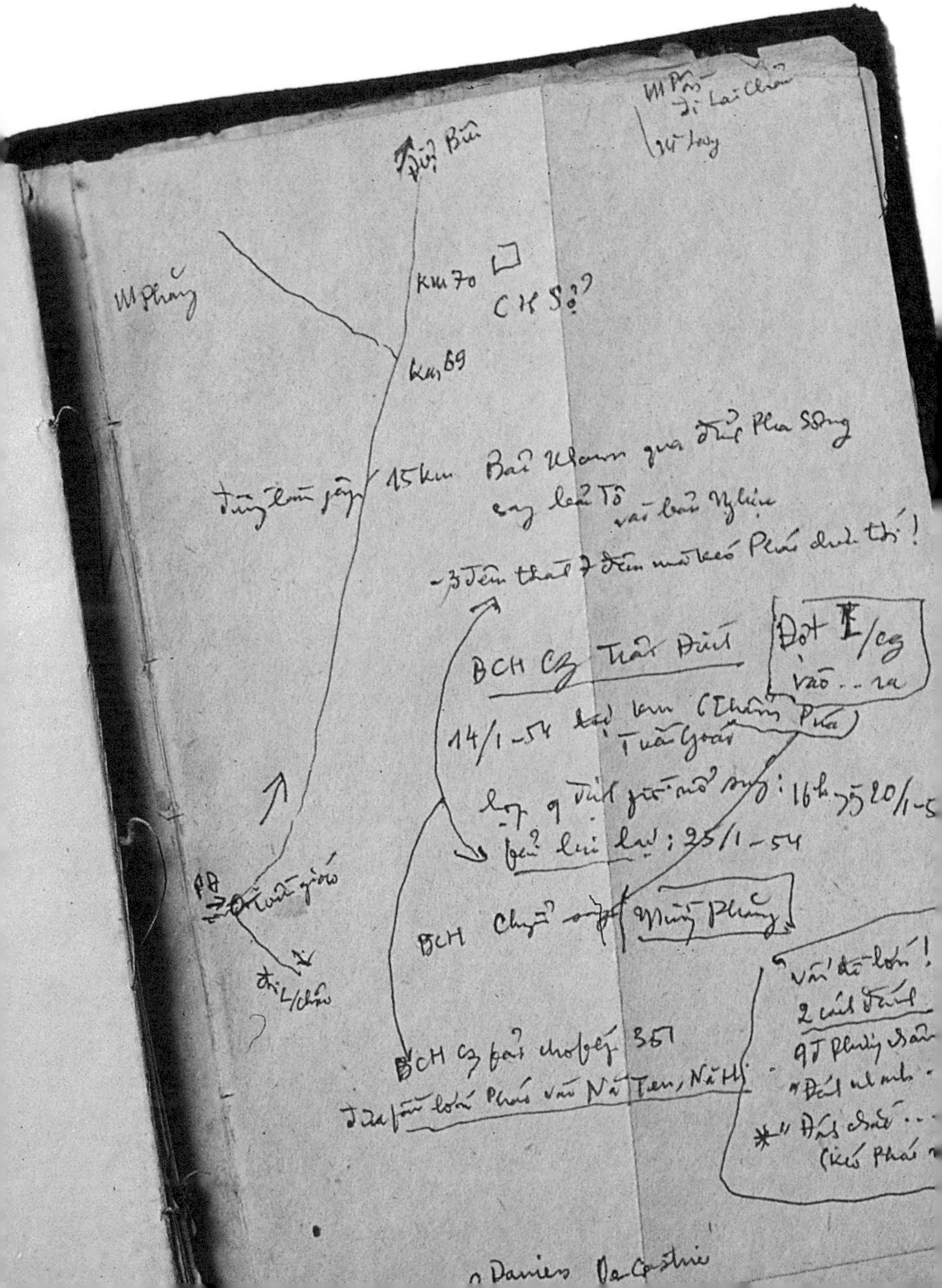

Điện Biên
km 70
km 69
Mường Phăng
15 km
BCH Cz Thân Đức
Đợt I/cg
vào...ra
14/1-54
Tuần Giáo
25/1-54
BCH
Mường Phăng
Vấn đề lớn!
Đi L/châu
Nà Tấu
Danies De Castrie

Published by Asia Ink
1 Alma Terrace, London W8 6QY
email: info@asiainkbooks.com

Translation from Vietnamese by
Nguyen Van Ha
Photographs by Hans Kemp
Copy editing by Yvonne Worth and
Clémence Jacquinet
Design by Misha Anikst, Anikst Design

Distributed by Thames & Hudson Ltd.
worldwide except for the USA, Canada
and Vietnam.

British Library Cataloguing-in-
Publication Data
Library of Congress
ISBN 0-9537839-3-6
Printed in Italy by Artegraphica

Title page: Facsimile of a map of the last 53 miles Tam walked from Tuan Giao to the battle of Dien Bien Phu. At the bottom of the page, are the names of John W ("Iron Mike") O'Daniel, head of the Saigon-based US military advisory group that supplied the French forces at Dien Bien Phu and of (Christian) de la Croix de Castries, the Commanding Officer of the French forces during the battle of Dien Bien Phu.

Contents

Preface

Pham Thanh Tam is a war reporter, artist and veteran of both the French and the American wars in Vietnam. This diary takes place at the battle of Dien Bien Phu, 1954, one of the most decisive battles of the 20th century. His war diaries and sketches are being published to commemorate the 50th anniversary of the battle and to mark the 30 years of peace in Vietnam that have followed the 30 years of war. His drawings form part of the two most important permanent collections of Vietnamese war drawings: those of the British Museum and of the Ho Chi Minh City Fine Arts Museum.

This book is the first publication in both English and French of an eyewitness account written under enemy fire during the battle of Dien Bien Phu. It is illustrated throughout with images of the pages of the author's diary along with some of his sketches drawn on the battlefield. As far as is known, few original sketches done at the battlefield during the 55 days of the battle still survive and even fewer have been catalogued and published, aside from a couple by the artist Mai Van Hien (ten years Tam's senior), which appear in the *Paris-Hanoi-Saigon* catalogue for the 1996 exhibition of Vietnamese painting at Les Halles in Paris. The British Museum catalogue, *Vietnam Behind The Lines,* has some images of the battle that were produced a few years later.

Facsimile from the diary: order of the battle of Him Lam, the first French stronghold to be overrun by the Viet Minh, on March 14, 1954; the ink bottle and the Waterman pen were used by the author to write the diary.

The diary

Tam's diary is a 24cm x 14cm (9.5in x 5.5in) notebook – the size of which is reproduced here – and consists of 44 handwritten pages written in Chinese ink and illustrated with occasional miniature sketches of soldiers, Molotova trucks, maps and one tiny self portrait of the author writing, sitting on the ground, head bowed in the position he had to adopt in the cramped underground shelters and trenches on the battlefield.

This important historical document provides a unique insight into the little-known aspects of the battle from the Vietnamese side and, in particular, into the courage, endurance and suffering of the Viet Minh soldiers. Hundreds of books by French, American and English authors have been published chronicling the French side of the war: from official accounts and autobiographies of French generals and politicians, through remarkable journalistic accounts by Lucien Bodard, Jules Roy and Bernard B. Fall, to individual testimonies and memoirs by French paratroopers, artillerymen, machine gunners, pilots and doctors, and, in commemoration of the 50th anniversary, a flurry of new publications including a collection of French soldiers' letters from the front and an exhaustive and balanced account of the battle by the British author Martin Windrow. There have also been a number of publications and narratives by Vietnamese authors who fought alongside the French against the Viet Minh.

In contrast, little has been published (in either French or English) from the Viet Minh perspective, except for the official memoirs by the military mastermind of the battle plan, General Vo Nguyen Giap(see bibliography). In his diary, Tam tells the extraordinary odyssey of the artillerymen and foot soldiers who dragged the two-ton cannons on foot, across the rugged mountain terrain of north Vietnam. He describes how, under bombing raids, they dug shelters to camouflage the cannons and besieged the supposedly impregnable French fortress of Dien Bien Phu. Tam benefited from the unique access he had to sources – from the rank and file, to the political commissars and military officers – since he was attached to the heavy artillery division of the Vietnamese People's Army, F351, the artillery unit crucial to Vo Nguyen Giap's strategy to win against the superior French military forces. Tam's battlefield notes, soldiers' accounts and personal observations have a rawness and poignancy that come from the universal camaraderie of

*"I wrote and sketched in the style of the time,
a socialist-realist style,
and I wrote with all my heart."*

Pham Thanh Tam

soldiers in war. Although officially attached to the division as a reporter and not a combatant himself, he was still one of them. He was 22 and close in age to the 18-year-old soldiers. He was unarmed and therefore trusted his armed comrades with his life. In the tradition of war reporters covering the First World War and the Spanish Civil War, Tam moved around the battlefield, through the muddy, bloodied trenches, seeking out artillery positions that were dangerously close to the enemy in order to collect first-hand accounts of the battles. He slept next to the cannons in shelters, he joined digging teams and marched with the troops hauling the cannons. He composed revolutionary songs and poems, reading them aloud before the attacks to encourage his friends into battle. He sketched portraits of the soldiers and organised recreational activities – even the simple act of sharing a cigarette rated as a social event, to "keep up morale and calm the mind."

The sketches

Dien Bien Phu, situated in a remote corner of northwest Vietnam, is remembered as one of the most horrific battles of the 20th century, where men confronted each other in hand-to-hand combat in trenches and on bare hilltops ravaged by bombings. There is something surreal and inspiring in the fact that in this hell hole Tam found the peace of mind to sketch, whenever he had time, both in the trenches themselves and behind the lines. To my knowledge, there were no sketches or drawings done on the French side.

At 22, Tam was too young to be an official war artist, having only completed the first part of his art training on one of the courses organised in the resistance zone. This, however, left him freedom to draw as he pleased, guided only by his own inspiration. The quiet poetry of the drawings and sketches from this time express the loneliness of a young artist in war seeking to share his dreams of love and beauty with his fellow soldiers. Tam never chooses to focus on bloody combat but instead creates a series of lyrical portraits of wistful women and pensive combatants, along with poetic landscapes and an evocation of the type of universal camaraderie brought on by war. There are also illustrations of various activities in the underground shelters and trenches: soldiers writing letters home, playing cards and song-and-dance groups entertaining the men. One unusual drawing even shows a soldier smoking an opium pipe. (Note: Dien Bien Phu is in the poppy-growing region of northwest Vietnam and Muong Thanh. The Thai town where the

French built their military base was an opium trading centre during the French colonial period. Opium, when available, was used by the Viet Minh for easing pain and soothing wounds.) Tam's graphite technical drawings and sketches of cannons and ammunitions depict these war machines as menacing and foreboding, not only for the adversary but also for the young Viet Minh recruits who had to learn to use them. The cannon carriage is seen as an instrument of death that crushed so many young soldiers as they tried to prevent the two-ton cannons from falling into the steep ravines; the 155mm French cannon and the French B26 and the Hellcats are symbols of French military superiority, the Viet Minh having no air power. There are even depictions of various means of communications and transportation: the Molotova truck used to haul the two-ton cannons across North Vietnam to the battlefield appears several times in both the diary and other sketches. This type of truck was crucial to the war effort, and relieved the men from having to haul the cannons themselves.

Tam's work shows a clear French influence. His professors in the resistance zone were from the Ecole des beaux-arts d'Indochine, the Vietnam art school created in 1925 by the French and modelled after the Paris school. Tam's portraits, for instance, reflect private moments of observation of the individual subject. This is in complete contrast to the traditional Vietnamese style of figure painting and portraiture that was influenced by Chinese artistic conventions, with figures generally shown in formal, rather than naturalistic, poses. Throughout the diary, Tam's illustrations are in pen and ink, pencil, black crayon and chalk. Some are finished drawings, others clearly sketches that the young artist later used as inspiration for painting the larger watercolours that were exhibited at the National Fine Arts Exhibition of 1954 in Hanoi, at which Tam was awarded third prize. The drawings and sketches survived war conditions and the hard economic times that followed, although, sadly, many were destroyed by Vietnam's ravenous termites. Sentimental combat art may have become less fashionable in recent years than it used to be, but, by showing war through the eyes of such a young soldier, these documents are a universal tribute to all young men and women and innocent civilians who perish in war.

Jessica Harrison-Hall
Curator of Chinese Ceramics and Vietnamese Art
Department of Asia
The British Museum

The artist under fire

by Sherry Buchanan

"War is always terrible."

Down one of Ho Chi Minh City's narrow alleys, in a white house protected from the blistering sun and the monsoon rain, the war artist and journalist Pham Thanh Tam lives with his wife Lanh and his youngest daughter Ly. We first met to photograph Tam's war drawings for the archive of Vietnamese war drawings being prepared with the assistance of the Ho Chi Minh City Fine Arts Museum and the Blue Space Contemporary Art Gallery. That evening, after a sumptuous meal cooked by his wife, Lanh, of fried spring rolls, giant snails and northern sweets, washed down with beer and a herbal alcoholic concoction of Tam's own making, Tam brought out his war memorabilia: his medals; his iron helmet, full of holes – "not bullet holes, I used it as a watering can," he explained; his People's Army uniform; his Waterman pen; his paints; his palette knife; his ink bottle and the 12mm bullet he kept it in. "I have been trying to get him to get rid of all these old things for years," said Lanh. She laughed, knowing full well she never stood a chance. Tam then dragged a heavy iron chest out from under a bed in the living room. The chest was his treasure trove and contained hundreds of the illustrations he created of the Vietnam War: pencil sketches, Chinese ink drawings, watercolours on paper and a few small oil paintings on board. "These are my true memories. They are my soul," he said. That first evening

Canteen used by the author during the battle of Dien Bien Phu, collection of the Ho Chi Minh City Fine Arts Museum.

with Ong Tam and Ba Lanh led to many more. The house offered warmth, hospitality and friendship, a place to talk and exchange ideas, to look at drawings and remember the past: one of those places we are grateful for, where friendship is all the more precious because it bridges wars. Night after night, Tam went through the drawings he had done over the ten years of the Vietnam War, following the troops fighting the Americans. A remarkable visual chronicle of the ten-year conflict emerged, starting with the American bombings of Hanoi streets in 1965, down the Ho Chi Minh Trail, to the battle of Khe San, the Tet Offensive and the end of the war in 1975.

One monsoon night, the streets in the district were flooded after heavy rain and I stayed longer than usual. Even the intrepid moped driver from next door couldn't drive through the flood waters. We were looking at a new batch of war drawings when one of the pencil sketches caught my eye. The yellow paper showed greater age, the sketch itself seemed more classical and rigorous than his later drawings: the soldier was wielding a bayonet, a model not used in the American Vietnam War. The drawing was dated 1954. "This one is from the war against the French," said Tam as he continued leafing through the drawings. During my research, I had not come across any drawings from the Franco-Vietnam War (1946–1954), let alone the epic battle of Dien Bien Phu in which the Viet Minh fighting for independence defeated the French in 1954. When I had asked several artists whether they had any of their works from that period, they all replied they had been lost or sold. Until then, it had never occurred to me that Tam could possibly be old enough to have served in the war against the French.

This chain-smoking combatant who had covered over 600 miles during the American War, mostly on foot, had the energy and the gait of a man much younger than his 70 years, with his military allure, straight back and strong handshake. An open smile and the twinkle in his eyes expressed a love of life that had sustained him during the best and the worst times of those terrible years.

"I was 15 when I joined the resistance against the French," Tam volunteered.

"Were you at the battle of Dien Bien Phu?"

"Yes, I sketched a lot during the battle."

"Do you have any sketches left?"

"Of course," he answered.

I decided to investigate further, since it was clear that Tam had been able to preserve more documents than most other artists I had visited. I had seen a few sketchbooks from the war and was interested in discovering any written diaries. "Did you keep a diary at the battle?" I ventured. Instead of answering, he stuck his cigarette between his lips, thought for a moment and disappeared upstairs. Lanh served up more spring rolls while I waited. I wasn't sure what to expect next. Tam returned carrying an old cardboard box. It had been forgotten under a wardrobe or a bed for so long that two inches of moist black dust had had time to accumulate and clung to the surface of the box. Inside were a whole series of diaries, wrapped in plastic to protect them from the termites that eat away at Vietnam's artistic paper heritage. He removed one notebook, covered in a piece of blue cloth, once brilliant, but now faded. "That was part of my shirt," he declared. "I had totally forgotten about the diary, until now." My heart raced with excitement. Fifty years on and here it was – the diary. And Tam was ready to share his notes and sketches of the historic battle of Dien Bien Phu.

"My sketches are my soul."

Tam started sketching in the resistance out of loneliness. His adolescent's quest for romantic love was channelled into a love for his country and a feeling of camaraderie for his fellow soldiers. For Tam, the act of continuing to be creative in time of war was as important as the drawings themselves. "There is an aesthetic in war," he says. "Because the events you are witnessing are too dreadful, it is up to the artist to use his art to reaffirm life itself and to communicate his belief in a better future. The French and the Americans burned houses and entire villages. War is so hard, I wanted to make the soldiers feel better by showing them something beautiful. They liked to have me around and to watch me draw. It seemed to calm them and made them feel special, rather like telling a beautiful girl how lovely she is. In his drawings the artist must express his love for country and for his fellow soldiers. I never showed hatred in my drawings, which is the inevitable and negative part of war. I wanted to convey uplifting, spiritual feelings and fragile emotions."

Tam's pensive portraits of young combatants and women militants, the delicate beauty of the Thai women and children in the northwest of Vietnam, victims of the war, and the unchanging and beautiful natural

Facsimile of pages from Tam's diary with photographs. From left to right: the author with his friends at the entrance to an underground shelter; a painfully thin Tam right after the battle of Dien Bien Phu and a healthier looking Tam a few months later; posing in front of a French tank captured at Dien Bien Phu with Thai villagers.

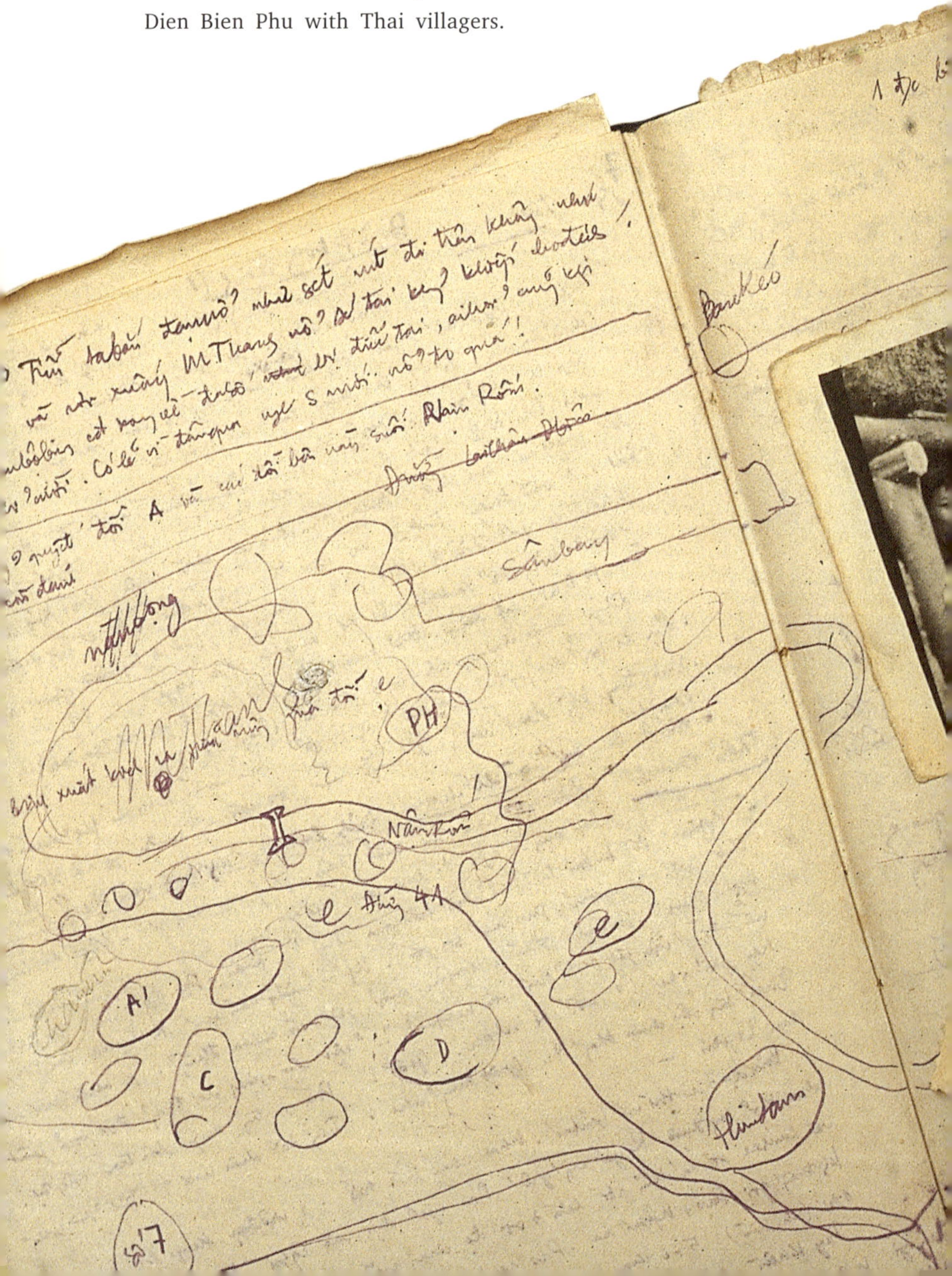

landscapes, have the effect of highlighting the murderous reality of the destruction of man by man in all its absurdity. Showing a repugnance for depicting the macabre, he explored instead, in a variety of different ways, the sharp contrast between the cruelty of war on one's own soil and lyrical artistic statement, achieving pathos and poignancy, a style that was close to that of the French war artists of the First World War who had witnessed trench warfare on their home soil.

"I wrote with all my heart."

Tam started writing a diary when he was an art student in the resistance. The young man's passionate desire to bear witness to a historic battle led him to record not only his own thoughts and experiences but also those of his fellow soldiers. An admirer of the Russian war correspondent Ilya Erhenbourg, he consciously wrote in the style of the time, a socialist-realist style that emphasises the positive aspects in war found in the courage and endurance of soldiers. He does not dwell on the inevitable acts of cowardice and brutality present in war. If this was his diary's sole intent, however, his youthful candour and innocence led him to portray much more. His detailed portraits and descriptions of young soldiers express the suffering and, although this was not his intent at the time, ultimately the pointlessness of war. As he says, "In war there is love and there is hatred. That is what war is. But hatred is not enough to win a war. We had great love, love for our country and love for each other. Those feelings of love are what I expressed in the diary and that I carry with me throughout my life."

The emotions and beliefs expressed in his diary and sketches come from a childhood and adolescence marked by the traumatic events that befell Vietnam at the end of the Second World War (1939–1945): the Japanese occupation (1940–1945), the great famine and the French determination to claim back their colony that led to the Franco-Vietnam War. As the rest of the world was finally at peace after two world wars, Vietnam was itself on the brink of being engulfed in three decades of war.

Childhood memories from Haiphong, 1933–1945

Born in the northern port city of Haiphong in 1933, Tam grew up in French colonial Vietnam. His parents worked for La Cimenterie, the French-owned cement factory and the town's major employer. The gifted youngster was admitted to Jean Dupuis, the French lycée. His parents belonged to the urban working class and supported independence from French rule. In 1941, they joined the Viet Minh, Ho Chi Minh's League for the Liberation of Vietnam (*Nam Doc Lap Dong Minh Hoi*). Initially the Viet Minh was an umbrella for nationalist pro-independence elements in Vietnamese society: the intellectual elites, the students, the urban working classes, the rural population and even part of the feudal classes. The Vietnamese opposition to the Viet Minh, who fought with the French during the war, was led by the emperor Bao Dai and included the Catholic community and feudal and commercial elites in the north and south of the country. Less well organised than the Viet Minh, the opposition suffered from internal factional disputes and was less successful in getting the people's support.

The adolescent Tam was swept up by the nationalist enthusiasm that gripped the country. Dissatisfaction with French rule and the struggle for independence had grown out of decades of colonial power. As a child, Tam was particularly affected by the injustice of the great famine of 1944 and 1945, a momentous, if little documented, historical event. Throughout his diary, Tam refers to this tragedy to explain the rural population's animosity towards the French. During the Dien Bien Phu campaign, most of the young recruits were farmers, as were the thousands of workers who transported rice and other supplies to the front. These farmers and their families had suffered greatly during the famine years. An estimated two million Vietnamese died of hunger when their rice was confiscated to feed the Japanese troops who were occupying Vietnam at the time. The French who administered the seizure were held equally responsible. As starvation gripped the surrounding countryside, young Tam witnessed the thousands of farmers streaming into Haiphong where they died in the streets. They were buried in mass graves. He remembers "their skeletal bodies and their open sores crawling with maggots. A terrible way to die."

The beginning of the Franco-Vietnam war, 1945–1946

When the war broke out, Tam and his family, along with thousands of others, became refugees. After the Japanese surrender in 1945, there was a faint glimmer of hope that Vietnam might gain independence without bloodshed. Ho Chi Minh proclaimed Vietnamese independence in Hanoi's Ba Dinh square, reading from the American Declaration of Independence. It was

September 2, 1945 and Tam had the day off school. He joined the children of Haiphong to celebrate, marching with wooden rifles, beating drums and waving the red flag with its single yellow star. Vietnamese independence, however, was shortlived. The Allies sent the Chinese Guomingdang troops to disarm the Japanese in the north of Vietnam. Caught between the Chinese (Vietnam's powerful northern neighbour and traditional enemy) and the French, Ho Chi Minh granted France a further five years in power on condition that they recognise Vietnam. Young Tam watched as the French navy moved into Haiphong harbour. Not long after the ships arrived, an incident shattered the fragile modus vivendi. The French shelled Haiphong. Their naval artillery opened fire on the city with a violent barrage, tanks moved in and fighter bombers fire-bombed the city, causing massive destruction. Tam's house was burnt to the ground. Along with thousands of others made homeless in the destruction, Tam and his family fled the city in flames to take refuge in the resistance zone. The shelling of Haiphong marked the beginning of the Franco-Vietnam War. When the French occupied Hanoi, Ho Chi Minh and his government left the capital city for the Viet Bac, a region northeast of Hanoi that became the heart of the resistance.

Art in the resistance zone, 1946–1948: "Down with war."

Tam was separated from his family and joined the resistance, working as a messenger and living clandestinely in villages. Away from family, friends and everything else that had been familiar to him, as a means of consolation, the city boy started sketching the simple beauty of the countryside that was now his home. With the encouragement of the artist Mai Van Nam, he was accepted onto one of the first art courses to be set up in the resistance zone. The course was entitled *Down with War*. Here young resistance fighters learned how to sketch and paint and, on a more practical level, to design revolutionary posters, banners and theatre sets. His director and professor was the artist Luong Xuan Nhi (1913–) one of many artists who had left Hanoi to follow Ho Chi Minh into the Viet Bac. Tam was influenced by the political themes that were popular with the resistance artists. In the jungles of north Vietnam, the exiled Hanoi arts community lent its creative energy to give visual expression to Ho Chi Minh's ideals, by designing revolutionary banners and posters (such as *Vietnam for the Vietnamese* by Tran Van Can) and painting the popular rallies gathered in streets covered in red silk Viet Minh flags, or the rice fields being replanted after the great famine and the

Demonstrators hold a rally in Hanoi in 1946 in support of Ho Chi Minh, leader of the Viet Minh movement for independence.
The demonstrators hold banners similar to those Tam would have designed in the resistance. One of the inscriptions reads: *We support our leader Ho, (Ung Ho chu lich)*.

heroic acts of resistance fighters. Luong's most famous work, *The Human Torch*, commemorated the sacrificial death of a young insurgent who set himself alight to blow up a French munitions depot. In their artistic style, however, the resistance artists remained faithful to their French masters. Both of Tam's professors, Luong and Bui Xuan Phai, had studied at the Ecole des beaux-arts d'Indochine created in 1925 and based on the Ecole des beaux-arts in Paris. "Phai used to tell us to keep the composition simple, that one detail is enough to express meaning," Tam recalls. " A painting should be elegant but meaningful. I never forgot his advice."

Apart from the French artistic influence, the poetic lyricism of the Dien Bien Phu sketches also has its roots in the six months he spent in the small village of Phu Lien Chanh. With little fighting going on during this time, in this oasis of tranquillity in Ha Dong district, near Hanoi, resistance and art became his focus and he devoted himself enthusiastically to both. "It was a wonderful time because I loved painting," said Tam. " I was so young, only 17, and I lived in harmony with nature and art. I missed my family, but it was the same for all of us, after all, the youngest in our group was only 10, it was natural at the time."

When Tam finished his course in 1948, he was assigned to a dangerous mission in the French occupied zone. Against the militarily stronger French, the Viet Minh waged a guerrilla war (*Du Kich*) and relied on help from the villages to feed and hide the resistance fighters. Tam's job was to draw revolutionary slogans and images on village walls. Operating completely alone, living undercover, moving from place to place every couple of nights, in order to stay one step ahead of French patrols, the wartime graffiti artist had little time to sketch. "I would find a wall, draw quickly, usually at night and then run for my life," he says. "I had no gun to defend myself with and I was not a soldier. If you were caught, you were killed. I lost a lot of friends that way. They were captured by the French and I never saw them again. I was afraid but, given the situation, I had to do it. I was too young to know what death really meant."

Portrait of a Thai child, Dien Bien Phu
1954, graphite on paper, 18cm x 12cm.

Covering the Franco Vietnam war, 1950–1954: "Sure to win."
The war escalated with the onset of the Cold War. The Americans entered the conflict to back the French against the spread of communism, while the communist Chinese backed the Viet Minh. Prior to 1949, the United States unofficially supported Ho Chi Minh and the Viet Minh insurgents against France's unpopular colonial war. After the 1949 communist victory in China and North Korea's invasion of South Korea, the United States changed its policy and embarked on a "crusade", the term used by the French military commander Jean de Lattre de Tassigny who had once been a benedictine monk, to defend the free world and to liberate the Vietnamese people from communism. Against the French, backed by American military might, the Viet Minh received Chinese training and weapons to transform a guerrilla force into a disciplined army. As the war magnified, the French tightened their security measures against the insurgents and intensified their bombing raids of villages suspected of supporting them. Life for the young resistance artist became even more precarious as French patrols were sent out to eradicate the insurgents. "The French arrested any young male, even if they had not been caught doing anything that was considered to be subversive," he remembers. "If you were caught, you were killed; the French did not release anyone or keep prisoners. They would divide villages into two groups. The young men were all shot. Of the women, children and older folk, only the suspects were shot."

In May 1950, Tam was given the opportunity to join the People's Army as a war reporter and illustrator. Operating as a lone street artist with no armed protection was becoming so dangerous that he jumped at the chance to enlist. In the army, Tam found friendship . The People's Army provided little material support and the young recruits relied on each other for survival. "We slept on the ground and wrapped ourselves in straw to protect ourselves against the cold," he says. "One shirt, a pair of trousers, a bamboo hat and bare feet. I was too poor to buy sandals!" The young soldiers took care of each other when ill and even shared their rations. These strong bonds are a dominant theme throughout his diary. "I wasn't armed and the situation had become extremely dangerous," he says. "Becoming a soldier meant I would no longer be working alone in the villages. I could rely on my friends to protect me." And when he was ill with malaria for two months, he was cared for by two of his friends from the regiment. He remembers his illness with the dry sense of humour that characterises his mode of expression: "When I was on my own I was always sick; I was too young to know how to care for myself. When I became ill with malaria, two of my friends from the regiment cared for me and nursed me back to health. We had no doctor and the clinic was far away. They gave me lime to cure the malaria, then rice vinegar to cure the effects of the lime on the stomach. I was lucky, since other patients had to swallow a huge worm, live! Even though they were hungry, my friends made sure I had two bowls of rice instead of the one bowl they had to eat. They also gave me extra peanuts and vegetables. The peanuts were so gritty we used to call them gun powder and the vegetables so prickly, barbed wire!" His own experience might explain why in one of his diary entries, Tam expresses genuine surprise when a French prisoner selfishly eats a whole ball of rice instead of sharing it with a sick fellow prisoner.

In the army, Tam gained his first experience at professional writing. He worked as a war correspondent and illustrator for the *Tat Thang* newspaper, *Sure to Win*, a broadsheet for the infantry regiment E34. Joining a staff of one other reporter and six printers, he was in charge of covering the regiment's guerrilla activities against the occupying forces. When advancing French troops took the city of Nam Dinh, where his regiment was headquartered, Tam retreated with the soldiers to the surrounding villages, where he wrote stories about village life under French occupation. His resistance experience convinced him the war could not possibly be won without the support of the people, a belief that runs through the first part of the diary, written on his way to the Dien Bien Phu campaign when he encounters youth brigades repairing dangerous mountain roads and bicycle carriers carrying 220lb of rice each to the front.

"We could not have survived without the help of the people. Even though they did not have much themselves, they fed and housed us. It was very dangerous for the families we lived with. If they were caught they were killed. These were the stories I wrote about."

The battle of Dien Bien Phu, 1954: "Determined to Win."

As the war dragged on, the French sought to extricate themselves from an un-winnable war and hand over power to a Vietnamese government that would oppose Ho Chi Minh and the Viet Minh. Anti-Viet Minh forces in Vietnam, including the former Emperor Bao Dai, sided with the French.

They feared that the Viet Minh, who by now were being supported by the People's Republic of China, were communists, even though they represented themselves as nationalists. To hold onto the territory they controlled until such time as they could broker a peace agreement, the French built a military base in Dien Bien Phu to defend their territories against Viet Minh incursions coming from the north. The Viet Minh were in control of the north of the country all the way to the Chinese border while the French held Laos, the Red River Delta, Hanoi and the surrounding region to the south where Tam was stationed. In the autumn of 1953, the Viet Minh took a huge gamble and decided to attack Dien Bien Phu. By then Dien Bien Phu had been turned into a military "fortress" as it was described by French and American military experts, defended by air power and heavy artillery. The French and Americans alike thought it to be impregnable. Without air power, the Viet Minh relied on their heavy artillery division F351 for their attack and siege strategy. Tam,

promoted to war reporter with the heavy artillery division' s newspaper, *Determined to Win* or *Quyet Thang*, was excited to be attached to such an important division. In mid-1952, he was sent with his regiment to a military training camp near Kunming in Yunnan in southwest China. As odd as it may sound now and as hard as the training was, he was finally free from the constant danger he had faced in the occupied zone and found time to start sketching again. At the end of January 1954, a few months after the Viet Minh decision to attack Dien Bien Phu, he left the Chinese training camp for the front. From Lao Cai, a town on the Chinese-Vietnamese border, he trekked 100 miles, on foot, through dense jungle, until he reached Yen Bai, where he starts his diary.

The diary in its historical context

Tam's diary starts in February of 1954, when he is about to begin the 200-mile trek on foot from the town of Yen Bai in Viet Minh controlled territory to reach the front at Dien Bien Phu. The main body of the diary covers the 55 days and nights of the historic battle of Dien Bien Phu that took place between March 13 and May 7, 1954.

As an historical chronicler, his notes bear witness to the Viet Minh odyssey, which by all accounts was an extraordinary military achievement. Tam's frontline analysis of the battle is one of the few to be published that was actually written on the battlefield. Given that he was writing under duress, the diary is remarkably precise in its appraisal of the events. He also gives an insider's view of the little-known inner workings of the Vietnamese People's Army and of the beliefs and ideological mindset of the combatants.

The political views Tam expresses in his diary are those of a committed young marxist and patriot. The war is against the colonial invader, the French, as much as it is against the old feudal classes, the oppressors of the people. His views reflect the Viet Minh's political platform at the time. Soviet and Maoist influences are evident in the tone and content of the slogans, poems, revolutionary plays and songs that Tam quotes throughout the diary. This is in direct contrast to the lyrical and poetic quality of his

Opposite: Tam and friends at the entrance of an underground shelter at the battle of Dien Bien Phu, 1954.

sketches and drawings. His account is therefore of interest to the ongoing debate among historians as to whether Ho Chi Minh and the Viet Minh were communists or nationalists. In the diary, the two are inextricably linked.

Beyond the politics, when Tam expresses his personal feelings and those of his fellow soldiers, they are raw and unusually candid. It was, of course, forbidden to write down one's private thoughts during war. Tam says that "since my job was as a reporter for the newspaper, nobody had the inclination or the time to check up on whether what I was writing was personal or official as long as I did my job." We meet a young man with a love for life, stoic under hardship and unusually compassionate towards others, perhaps because he himself had no close family ties to cling to and greatly valued friendship. He is a romantic who, after trekking a few hundred miles with little food, is still uplifted by the laughter and smile of a pretty girl he passes on the road to the war. Above all, Tam, even after seven years of a hard and dangerous life in the resistance, was not prepared for the cruelty of the battlefield.

The artillerymen and the infantrymen of the Vietnamese People's Army

The heroes of the diary are the artillerymen of division 351. The artillery was General Vo Nguyen Giap's trump card in his offensive against the militarily superior French. A common stereotype of the Viet Minh soldier, or Viet Cong in the American Vietnam War, is of a fanatic robot-like killer. Nothing could be further from Tam's portrayal of the lost boys of war, innocent and so young. The young recruits miss their families and wait with anticipation for letters from home. They fear death and shed tears for their friends. They endure privations – many had no shoes, no rain gear and survived on a single bowl of rice a day – with stoicism and humour.

With carefully chosen and often amusing details, Tam characterises the nature of a war fought by poor young men with second hand equipment against a superior adversary: for instance, he describes the young soldiers "stinking of French perfume found in the pararachuted supplies," or not liking the French chocolates because they were too bitter for their taste or mistaking smoke bombs for "mouldy" shells.

Although he was not a combatant, Tam led the life of an artilleryman and shared their daily brush with death. This closeness gives his notes immediacy, veracity and poignancy. Under enemy fire, he moved around the

battlefield, slept at artillery command posts in positions dangerously close to the French and participated in operations from transporting munitions, to digging shelters and seizing enemy munition depots .

The civic workers

One of the main problems for the People's Army at Dien Bien Phu was how to get supplies to an estimated 20,000 troops. They did not have transport planes to airlift supplies to the battlefield. So they used Molotova trucks mainly to haul the cannons and transport munitions.

For rice and other supplies, tens of thousands of Vietnamese civilians supplied the front from rice growing provinces in the northeast. The main rice growing region, the Red river Delta was occupied by the French.

Many more thousands helped build the roads and bridges to the valley which was inaccessible to trucks and other vehicles. In his diary, Tam gives a realistic appraisal of all of this – nothing goes unnoticed. Today, he estimates that 20,000 civic workers and youth brigades joined in the war effort. He also points out that the bicycle carriers transporting the rice had to feed themselves during their long journeys from the rear to the front and often arrived at Dien Bien Phu with half of the rice load they had left with.

Tam at Dien Bien Phu, wearing the quilted jacket of the soldiers of the Vietnamese People's Army, 1954.

Women in war

The women Tam portrays in his diary and sketches are young and innocent. They are participants in the military campaign as actresses or singers or as young volunteers building roads and bridges over dangerous mountainous terrain. They are also frequently the main victims of war, as were the Thai women from the villages surrounding Dien Bien Phu Tam drew with such tenderness. His sketches of women reveal repressed longing and the unrequited love of an adolescent who has grown up in a war zone.

The Vietnamese leaders

The two main figures of the battle of Dien Bien Phu were Ho Chi Minh and General Vo Nguyen Giap, the military strategist who devised the attack and siege of the French fortress. In the diary, the Viet Minh leaders appear as father figures who are in communication with the troops through letters of encouragement and slogans and Tam alludes to them several times in the course of his diary. Ho Chi Minh is referred to by the affectionate and

respectful term of "Uncle Ho". A letter from Ho was read to the troops before the start of the first Viet Minh offensive, General Giap's stern directives and admonishments before the second offensive. Overall, as shown in the diary, Giap's strategy unfolded remarkably according to plan. The diary outlines the three phases of the Viet Minh offensive against the French camp with clarity and accuracy given the chaos of any battlefield. Very early on in the battle, only a few days after the first Viet Minh attack, Tam quotes a political commissar explaining to the rank and file the three phases of the battle and how they were going to be implemented.

The Vietnamese People's Army and the political commissars

The People's Army was organised along Maoist lines. The Vietnamese Workers' Party, referred to as "the Party" in the diary, had considerable power over the military. On the battlefield, the Party was represented by political commissars and instructors. Tam's commissars are kindly former teachers who led the way on dangerous missions. Self-censorship no doubt, although other sources, inevitably censored, report a positive relationship between the political commissars and the men. When some senior-ranking military officers expressed doubts over victory during the second phase of the battle, the Party's power increased. In the third and final offensive, on May 1, Tam reports that the order to fire and attack the French position on hill C was given by General Vo Nguyen Giap to the political instructor and not to a military officer. Group meetings were frequent and, according to the diary, allowed the men to express their views and disagreements. Discipline was enforced through group and self-criticism sessions, a technique introduced by the Chinese advisers, to enhance performance and punish those who disobeyed the rules. Files were kept on individuals.

The Chinese advisers to the People's Army

Although he says he was aware of the presence of Chinese advisers, he does not make any reference to it in his diary. He considered the information too sensitive should the diary ever fall into the wrong hands.

Opposite: Facsimile of a diary page and self-portrait of the author writing, 1954.

The French commanders and the French Expeditionary Corps

The two main figures of the French Expeditionary Corps during the battle of Dien Bien Phu were General Henri Navarre, commander in chief of the French troops in Indochina and Colonel Christian de la Croix de Castries, who was promoted to the rank of general during the battle. De Castries was in command of the 10,000-strong French garrison that was later reinforced. Navarre and de Castries were well known to Tam, who mentions their names in his diary. It was Navarre who selected the remote valley of Dien Bien Phu to set up a military air base to defend Laos and the Red River delta against Viet Minh incursions until such a time that the French forces could negotiate their withdrawal from Vietnam.

Tam's attitude towards the French is ambivalent. He refers to the men's hatred (*cam thu*) of the French and their desire to avenge the deaths of their friends. At the same time he respects the adversary's military knowledge and strength, as expressed when he writes with joy and some disbelief after the French capitulation: "These infantrymen, these small infantrymen are victorious!" According to the diary, the French capitulation came as something of a surprise to the men. This is a measure of how much the Viet Minh admired French military might and knowledge. After all, the French had ruled in Vietnam for close to 100 years and had sent their most respected generals to Vietnam. The educated Viet Minh soldiers had attended French schools and appreciated French literature and culture. When the Viet Minh were finally victorious, they found it hard to believe.

An interesting anecdote sheds some light on the white flag controversy. The French did not want the humiliation of raising a white flag. Sources differ as to what actually happened. Tam reports that he saw a white piece of parachute being raised on the French high command.

As for the treatment of French prisoners after the battle, which is also the source of great controversy, most sources concur that the rate of survival of French prisoners marched to jungle camps after their capitulation was very low by international standards. At the time, Tam did not know the fate of the prisoners since he was with the first wave of soldiers to leave the battlefield. He did, however, note the medical care given to the prisoners the day after

Opposite: A very thin Tam drawing after the battle of Dien Bien Phu, 1954.

the capitulation, while, in another incident, he describes how the army intervened to prevent civic workers from humiliating a group of French prisoners at Na San.

The Vietnamese fighting on the French side

Brothers fighting brothers was the most painful part of the war. Twenty per cent of the French garrison was made up of Vietnamese. If Tam feels pity and contempt for them, he does excuse their behaviour. He blames foreign powers for pitting Vietnamese against Vietnamese, and creating a civil war in Vietnam. Finding common ground in the racism of colonialism, he also expresses feelings of solidarity for the "Africans", the Moroccans , Algerians and Senegalese, fighting on the French side.

The American advisers to the French high command

By 1954, 80 per cent of the war was being financed by the Americans. The US Military Assistance Advisory Group (MAAG) based in Saigon had been administering the material assistance programme to the French since 1950.

This was well known to the Viet Minh. Tam reports the death of American pilots after a Viet Minh raid on Hanoi airport. He also mentions the use of "American" napalm - manufactured in the United States and supplied to the French forces by the Americans. There seemed to be no illusions amongst the Viet Minh that the Americans might enter the battle at any time. Tam says that, although he did not write it in his diary, he knew that the French and the Americans considered using nuclear arms at Dien Bien Phu and says today, "Either they didn't have time or they didn't know how to do it without killing French soldiers as well. The Americans came to Indochina to help the French. When the American war started, as far as we were concerned, the Americans were already here."

After Dien Bien Phu: The Hanoi Institute of Fine Arts, 1954–1964

Tam left Dien Bien Phu a few days after the French capitulation for some R&R at a military camp in Tuyen Quang. He was commissioned by the army to paint larger-scale watercolours based on the sketches he had done during

the battle. He spent the next two or three months there painting. He was supplied with powdered paints and white paper. He used the pencil-and-ink sketches, reproduced in this book, as guidance and inspiration. During that time, an agreement was reached in Geneva on July 20 calling for a cease-fire. Vietnam was provisionally divided between North and South at the 17th parallel, pending national elections in 1956. Shortly after news of the agreement, Tam was given a post with the arts committee of the General Political Office in charge of organising the national art exhibition in Hanoi to celebrate the Vietnamese victory. He left Tuyen Quang at the end of August. His diary ends here with a premonition that he will have to go to war again.

The national exhibition was held in Hanoi in October 1954 after the French troops had left. Tam won third prize and was offered a job with the Army newspaper, *Nhan Dan*. In 1963, Tam enrolled at the Hanoi Institute of Fine Arts to continue his education, which had been interrupted by war. His tuition was paid for by the army and he continued to work for the newspaper. The national elections were not held in 1956 and the country remained divided between the communist Democratic Republic of Vietnam in the North with Ho Chi Minh as President and the anti-communist Republic of Vietnam in the South under Diem. The Viet Minh insurgency against the Diem regime continued in the South. By 1959, with national elections dead, the Hanoi leadership created the National Liberation Front for South Vietnam, to give military support to the insurgency in the south. Men, women, supplies and weapons were ferried down the Ho Chi Minh Trail. Fearing the spread of communism, US policy supported South Vietnam and the Diem government against the DRV and the former Viet Minh who became known as the Viet Cong to US forces in Vietnam. In 1964, the Gulf of Tonkin incident gave President Lyndon B Johnson the pretext he needed to go to war. This marked the beginning of the second Vietnam War and, in 1965, official US bombing raids were launched over North Vietnam. Sadly, the premonition Tam had had after Dien Bien Phu that one day he would have to return to war had come true.

Opposite: Tam as an official war artist at the battle of Khe Sanh in 1968.
Khe Sanh was the Dien Bien Phu of the American Vietnam War (1964–1975).

Sketching the American Vietnam War, 1964–1975

During the American Vietnam War, Tam was an official war artist and drew the first American plane shot down over North Vietnam. In August 1967, he was sent to sketch the Tet Offensive, the first full-scale North Vietnamese offensive against US troops in the south. As he prepared to leave Hanoi for the battlefield, he packed his backpack with the same palette and knife he had used at Dien Bien Phu. To be able to carry more paints, he even cut the bristles of his toothbrush! As he had done ten years earlier, he set off on a 600-mile journey on foot down the Ho Chi Minh Trail for the battlefield. The North Vietnamese Army was massing troops against Khe Sanh, a US military base set in rolling hills close to the Laotian border. When President Johnson was briefed by his top military advisers about Khe Sanh, he is quoted as having said, "I don't want another goddamn Dien Bien Phu!"

For Tam it was not another Dien Bien Phu, it was far worse. He remembers the American war as being much more cruel than the French war. "I wasn't as young anymore," he says. "At Dien Bien Phu, we surrounded the French. In Khe Sanh, the strongest elements of our army and the strongest of the Americans confronted each other on either side of the front line. Of course, we were much weaker. The Americans had everything – bombers, tanks, ships and huge cannons. Many many of our soldiers died, more than 37,000." In spite of the ferocity of the battle, Tam created many pencil, charcoal and Chinese ink drawings, even watercolours. The subjects were all too familiar. Examples of the inscriptions point to the similarity of themes with the Dien Bien Phu campaign: *Keeping watch outside an A shelter,* Vinh Linh 1967; *Marching to Khe Sanh*, 1968; *Exchanging thoughts in a shelter*, Khe Sanh, 1968; *Carrying the mail down the Ho Chi Minh Trail,* 1968; *Artillerymen firing cannons*, Con Tien, 1968. Ever resourceful, Tam carried the precious Chinese ink he used for sketching in an empty penicillin vial and stored the vial inside a 12mm calibre Russian-made bullet.

At the end of the Tet Offensive, in 1968, Tam was sent back to Hanoi. Before leaving for the war, Tam had wrapped the Dien Bien Phu diary and his drawings in plastic and left them in his room in the army's makeshift barracks in the centre of Hanoi. The buildings belonged to a high school taken over by the army when the students were evacuated to the countryside to evade the bombings. When Tam arrived back in Hanoi, all the soldiers were gone and the school buildings were deserted. He was not surprised since "you never know what is going to happen next in war!" When he reached his room on the first floor, the lock had been broken and he feared the worse. He was pleased to find his belongings were still there,adding with his sense of humour, "You can't imagine how happy I was. The thief had no use for my old things!" The Dien Bien Phu diary and drawings survived for another 30 years.

The end of war

Today, Tam continues to paint and to write a daily diary. He retired from the military with the rank of colonel. He is proud that his works are in the permanent collections of the British Museum, the Ho Chi Minh City Fine Arts Museum and the Dien Bien Phu Museum. His wife Lanh continues to cook the best spring rolls in Ho Chi Minh City. Ly, their youngest, is a modern young lady with her father's love of life and a mischievous laugh. She moves effortlessly and elegantly between the traditional *ao dai* of her school uniform and the jeans she wears to go out with her friends at the weekend. When she graduates from high school, Ly hopes to be a fashion designer. His eldest daughter Hoa Pham is a teacher and his son Pham Quang, a business executive with one of Vietnam's new telecom companies.

After sketching two wars, Tam remains an optimist at heart. "I enjoy every day of my life to the full," he says. "I love life because I know so well what it is to lose it."

Editor's note to the reader

Sketches, drawings and photographs

Sketches and drawings represented in the book are from the collection of war drawings of the Ho Chi Minh City Fine Arts Museum. The remaining photographs, sketches and drawings are from the artist's collection. Because of the war, some images do not have a signature or are signed with the artist's *nom de guerre*, Huynh Biec. Using an alias was a common practice during the Vietnam wars to protect the identity of the artist in the event that the drawings were captured by the adversary.

We decided to reproduce some of the sketches as they appear before conservation work to higlight the magnitude of the task undertaken by the Ho Chi Minh City Fine Arts Museum to restore these historical documents.

The diary

The text in roman type constitutes the original diary translated from the Vietnamese as Pham Thanh Tam wrote it in 1954, except for paragraphing and other style elements that have been added here for clarity.

The passages in the text between "quotation marks" constitute Pham Thanh Tam's notes from his interviews with individual soldiers and other participants in the war effort. These people speak in the first person in their own voice in order to enhance the immediacy of the account for the reader.

For the most part, Tam recorded soldiers' (and others') accounts the same day, or a few days at most after the event. In a few instances where events are recounted a week or so after they happened, they still appear here chronologically, for the sake of the narrative. A few diary entries ran over two or three days which led to confusion in the narrative. Each diary entry was limited to one day only and the suitable dates were added.

The paragraphs in *italic* type constitute the editor's notes compiled from her conversations with Pham Thanh Tam recorded between January and March 2004. They have been added to clarify the sequence both of the battle of Dien Bien Phu and of Tam's itinerary around the battlefield.

Translation
At the start of this project, Tam spent a month transcribing (in longhand) the original diary which he had written in Vietnamese, as the script in the diary was too small to read. His text was then translated from the new manuscript into English. It was then edited over the course of several months, with the assistance of the author and of the translators to ensure the correct meaning and intent of the author was retained.

Some Vietnamese terms that were too difficult to translate have been added as footnotes.

Tam, like most Vietnamese authors and journalists, is fond of wordplays. These, sadly, are lost in translation, so had to be omitted.

Style
The author's short sentences without pronouns, typical of a reporter's notebook, were only used sparingly in the translation. There were also too many exclamation marks, dots and words underlined for emphasis to be reproduced in the English text!

Facsimile of a map of Dien Bien Phu (following pages)
The facsimile is from a diary page and shows the author's itinerary during the battle of Dien Bien Phu. As the troops of the People's Army closed in on the French, the author advanced with the artillerymen. The French military camp was positioned in the valley of Dien Bien Phu, to the west of the Nam Ron river. It was defended by several French defence positions on nearby hills, represented here by small circles. The French had christened their defence positions Anne-Marie, Béatrice, Dominique, Eliane, Gabrielle and Huguette. The People's Army named them with letters from the alphabet. A stronghold typically included several hills. Each hill was surrounded by a deep barrage of barbed wire and a mine field. The only access into the valley for the troops of the People's Army was from the northeast, via route 41. As they prepared to attack the French, the Viet Minh artillery and troops positioned themselves on forested mountain slopes to the east of the French camp, facing and overlooking the French HQ and strongholds. This gave them a tactical advantage over the French artillery which was positioned in open gun pits in the valley.

Ban Tau village: Thai village bombed by the French, featured in the April 13, 1954 diary entry.

Ben Tre: headquarters of the Ben Tre division, an infantry division of the Vietnamese People's Army.

Doc Lap: French stronghold Gabrielle, north of the French HQ and one of the first French defence positions to be overrun on March 15, 1954. It is from here that Tam reported on the activities of the anti-aircraft gun units.

Dong 41: route 41, a dirt track that was built into a road by the engineer corps of the People's Army to enable their trucks to haul the heavy artillery to Dien Bien Phu.

Hills D and *E*: French strongholds Dominique 2 and Dominique 1. Hill D is described in the diary as one of the most difficult posts to overrun. From these positions only a few hundred yards from the French HQ, Tam writes the unfolding of the last few days of the battle.

Hills C and *A1*: French strongholds Eliane 1 and Eliane 2. A1 is described in the diary as the toughest of all the French strongholds.

Him Lam: French stronghold Béatrice, overrun by the People's Army on March 14, 1954. Described in the diary as a key strategic French stronghold.

H Cum or *Hong Cum*: French stronghold Isabelle, five miles to the south of the French HQ. The position had an airstrip and was linked to Muong Thanh, the main French HQ, by road.

Milestone 76: turn off on route 41 taken by the convoy of trucks driving Tam to the HQ of the heavy artillery division where he spends his first night at Dien Bien Phu.

804: command post of artillery Company 804, 105 mm cannons. The C804 artillerymen were Tam's close friends and feature often in the diary. They had trained together in the military camp in southwest China.

806: command post of artillery Company 806, 105 mm cannons.

Muong Thanh: name of the French airbase, military camp and central HQ and the author's focal point during the 55 days and nights of the battle.

Nam Ron: main river that flows through the Dien Bien Phu valley.

Sanbay: French military camp's airstrip. The airstrip was the lifeline for the French troops in Dien Bien Phu. As the diary points out, one of the People's Army's objectives was to stop supplies being airlifted from Haiphong and Hanoi to the French troops in Dien Bien Phu.

Tối nghe Hoả Tiễn ta bắn đạn nổ như sét rít đi trên không như đàn chim lớn và rơi xuống MThanh nổ, sự tai hại không cho tả. Sáng nay nhìn thấy bình cột nấm về đó bị đổ nát, ai nấy cũng vui nhìn thấy vui, đỡ sướng. Có lẽ vì đã qua ngày S mới nổ to quá!

Đêm qua, quyết đánh A và cái đồi bỏ này suốt khai hỏa.
Sáng nay còn đánh

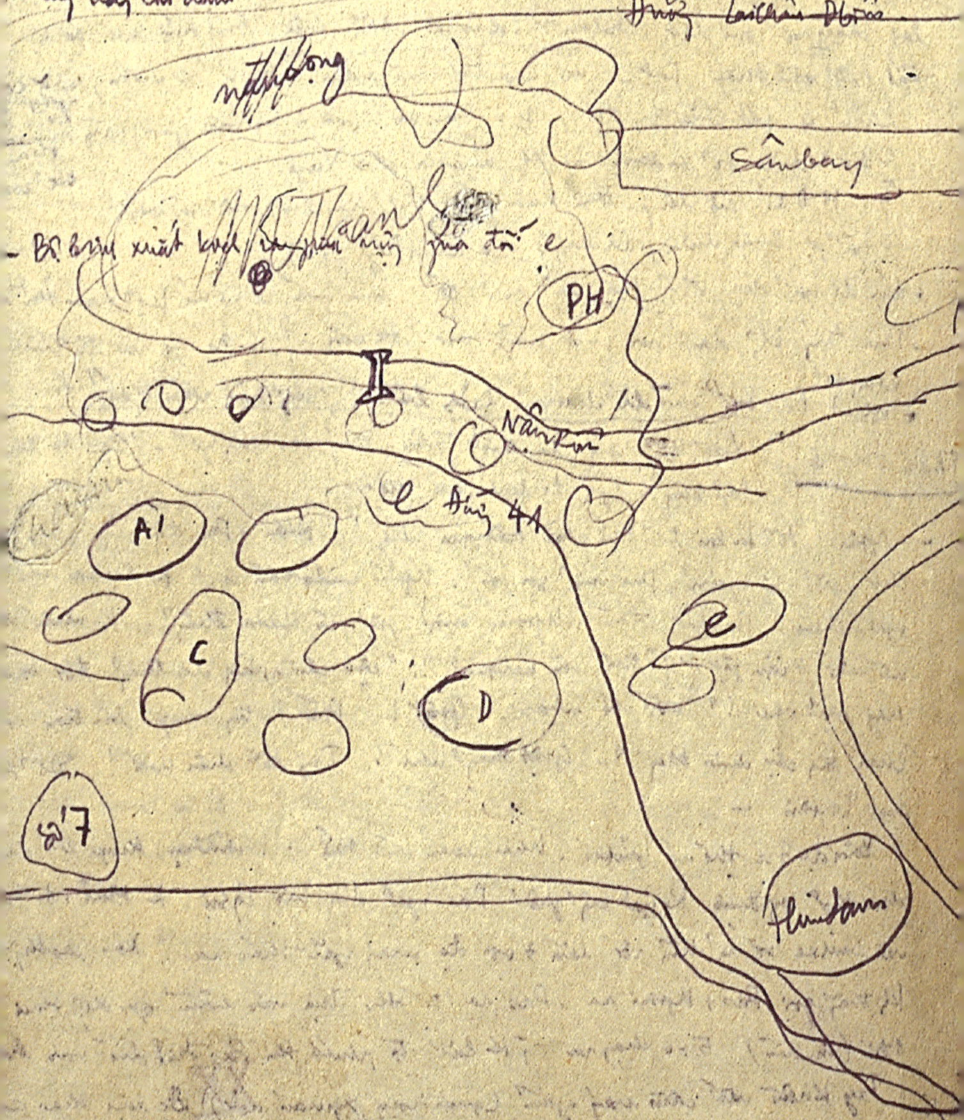

1 đại bộ binh mặt bao người xẻ ngồi [illegible] "ông Chỉ thắng rồi"!

° Bổ binh xuất kích nagáp thì [illegible] ở Mường Thanh [illegible] cả thây cát Tui!

+ Reo ran ran sôn sao [illegible] quân đất xa xa [illegible]. Nghe đại [illegible] tre + lu nhiều vậy trí thức Chỉ thắng! Vui quá!

Anh lời nhỏe thì [illegible] Mường Thanh ra ca lại ngay mấu quần áo Dù, Tây thấy [illegible] thấy cái tro sơ lịch. [illegible] sát [illegible] ra mắng.

— Hồi 5 giờ sau mấy loạt Hoa Tiễn vô đâng ở Mường Thanh + Hồng Cúm, tớ treo — cờ du trắng

— Dứt dưới lên gió xuân tan xoa vây hàng và lời nhỏe qua

• Chạy ra ngoài reo lên nhìn thoát nhục cái mào!

+ 1 đại đội [illegible] lên gò bắt mui chướng lối đưa chạy đi. 1 đại [illegible] mang [illegible] Chiến Thắng vào cầm lên và tung chỗ cao thuyết [illegible], đứng ngó đầu [illegible] lên nghe.

— Thấy Castries dùng đi xe dịp ra hàng [illegible]

Khi Cameron ra chiếu số Houlbay để lại chứa [illegible] lính, [illegible], vậy ra đi hàng 4..

(Trung đoàn 753 bắt [illegible] Tanh [illegible] đời d nhiều số chạy tay tung bởi cái sắt.

18 + Thủ tụng binh: "máy cái ông viên chỉ em, tự nay thôi" "cái ông binh sống mà Stalin chỉ [illegible]

— [illegible] khi ghét [illegible] nhìn [illegible] Thắng [illegible] quá vì bị [illegible] đau đớn!

— Trang [illegible] hàng [illegible] Dakota vào [illegible]

[illegible]

On the road

"We were young, but our faces were old."
Pham Thanh Tam begins his diary in the winter of 1954 when he joins the Dien Bien Phu campaign, the greatest Viet Minh offensive of the war. The young artist-reporter is travelling with an arts team sent to entertain the troops at the front. They are advancing in the footsteps of the 20,000 troops that have been crossing the Red River at night, marching on Dien Bien Phu. In the first entry of his diary, Tam writes that he is setting off in good spirits on the 200 mile trek that will bring him to the French military camp on the Laotian border (see the map on page 164). Considering that he has hiked across 100 miles of gruelling jungle paths to reach this point, his good humour is due to the fact that he has finally come to a road. The road is part of the 600-mile long network built by the engineers of the People's Army. Tam, however, continues on foot as the trucks are used to carry heavy artillery and munitions.

Through one of the toughest jungles in the world, he carries with him a backpack, a rice belt and his most precious possessions, his sketchbooks and his notebook. He has carefully covered the notebook with a piece of indigo-blue cloth, cut from his shirt, to protect it against the punishing humidity of the northwest region. In place of weapons, he carries his pencils, brushes, paints and crayons, a bottle of ink and, his pride and joy, his Waterman pen. He sketches soldiers on their way to the front, artillerymen pulling cannons,

Tam's diary, covered with a piece of indigo cloth cut from his shirt with his ink bottle and Waterman pen from Dien Bien Phu.

conscripted civilians carrying supplies to the front and young men and women who have left their villages to join the war effort to build roads and bridges. The bright colours he uses in his watercolours mirror the determined tone of his narrative. In contrast, in the dark charcoal sketch seen above, a soldier gives a last look to the forlorn figure of his beloved as he leaves for the front. The young combatant, wearing the helmet of the People's Army adorned with a star and carrying his backpack and his rice belt, cuts a solitary figure against a sombre and forbidding landscape. Tam, for all his youthful enthusiasm and his belief in the just cause of this historic campaign, like the soldier in his drawing, advances quite alone towards the valley of Dien Bien Phu.

February 21, 1954

As I start off for war, it does concern me that I am rather thin. I do feel healthy, however, and what I lack in size I will make up for in enthusiasm. I am travelling on foot with half of the arts team of the artillery division F351[1].

Shortly after beginning our journey, we neared the ferry landing at Ben Ngoc[2], on the river Chay[3], and as we continued walking on to the town of Ngoc, we were greeted by a grim sight. The town had recently been bombed by French fighter planes. The red earth was gouged with craters and the trees were stripped bare of foliage, their branches burnt to a cinder. Houses lay in ruin, the streets and market were deserted. All was quiet. A family of collaborators had been killed in the raid, which brought to my mind the thought that the enemy are even eliminating people who are on their side!

By afternoon, we reached a river that was at an unusually high level given that we are in the dry season. I stopped long enough to watch a flock of storks flying towards the north. As they flew over the still waters, the river turned white with their reflection. We continued our journey westwards and kept walking in the direction of the Red River[4]. Approached the town of Yen Bai[5], still at the rear of the campaign. Relaxed atmosphere, people are cheerful. The harvest has been good; rice production has increased; streets and markets are crowded with people buying and selling; children are dressed in colourful clothes, and mill about freely, unafraid of French war planes. In the reading room of the town library, young people were reading the novel *The Sharp Knife Brigade (Doi Dao Nhon),* a tale of soldiers fighting the invaders. At the market, we found plenty of fruit. We couldn't believe how fresh the papayas were! My friend Lanh and I had not eaten in so long that we ate four, all in one go!

We are spending the night in Yen Bai with our friend Thach and his family. He is newly married and his wife has just had a baby. The poor boy has aged since I last saw him and looks much older than his years! This must be the result of his new duties as a father and a husband! His father-in-law was so happy to have young soldiers as his guests that he went down to the garden to pick more fresh papaya and cut some sugar cane for us.

Opposite: *The soldier's farewell*, 1954, charcoal on paper, 20cm x 15cm.
Following spread: *After a bombing raid*, no date, watercolour on paper, 16cm x 24cm.

February 22, 1954

This morning, we said goodbye to Thach and his family and prepared to cross the Red River. As we reached its banks, it appeared as wide as the sea. During the ferry crossing, Thoa, who is only 17 and the youngest in the team, watched pensively as the river bank faded into the distance. He was missing his father and family who live in Phu Tho province in occupied territory on that side of the river. He has joined up as a medic, which is why we have nicknamed him "Baby Doc". We look after him as if he is our little brother, especially Vien who is 40 years old and the eldest amongst us. Thoa calls Vien "father", smiling sweetly at him, his round face lighting up and a dimple appearing on each cheek.

As we arrived onto route 13[6] a strong northwest wind was blowing towards the east. Every inch of this road winding its way through liberated territory has been built with the sweat and blood of our citizens and soldiers, determined to open the way to Dien Bien Phu[7]. They have been working on the new road over a period of several months. From what I have learned, the network of roads that has been newly built is one 600 miles long. Will it lead all the way to the campaign (Dien Bien Phu), I wonder? What I do know is that, from now on, we no longer have to fight our way through the jungle, up steep hills and down ravines and for that I am extremely grateful! I did see a poster by the roadside to reassure the troops that read: "The road is absolutely safe!"

We then started our ascent up the Lung Lo pass[8]. There was a forbidding wall of mountains ahead of me. Further up, a brigade of young volunteers[9] were building a field combat bridge across a deep gorge. This is incredibly dangerous work. The young men and women, wearing uniform blue padded jackets, shouted words of encouragement to each other and their laughter and hammering echoed through the mountains. (Once the convoys have passed over the bridge, it will be taken apart again[10].) I talked to one of the young men who said, "We don't mind the danger. We are building this road because we know the road belongs to the people!" We could never have organised volunteer youth teams to work so hard on such large public works without the Resistance movement under the leadership of Uncle Ho[11] and the Vietnamese Labour Party. These youngsters are here, on top of the mountain, because they believe that by helping the war effort, they are contributing to their own future. What they have accomplished using their bare hands and simple tools reminds me of a poem by Uncle Ho:

The only difficulty to fear is the lack of perseverance
There is nothing that is impossible to valiant hearts.

Tonight, after the climb, I feel completely exhausted, yet happy to have made it to the other side of the mountain. And, in the fading light, the scenery is spectacular!

February 25, 1954

Three days later, at a campsite on route 13. Over the last few days I have come across people from all walks of life who are joining the campaign. Yesterday, I met a dance team on their way to entertain the troops. They have come all the way from Vinh Phuc[12] in the occupied zone. I was surprised

On the road to Dien Bien Phu, 1954,
watercolour on paper, 35 cm x 25 cm.

Above: *Portrait of a young army woman*, 1954, watercolour on paper, 30cm x 23cm.
Opposite: *Woman carrying dried rice cakes*, 1954, ink and wash on paper, 25cm x 14cm.

at how many of the performers were young girls under the official age limit. The girls, nevertheless, begged their parents to let them join the military campaign, never imagining how hard the journey to the front would be. In Vinh Phuc, they had heard the journey would be easy, on roads large enough for trucks. Then, for most of the way they found themselves climbing steep jungle paths loaded down with 45lb packs. They cried from sheer exhaustion and because they were missing their families. Sister Bau, a beautiful, young and innocent girl from a very poor family, told me she joined up to get away from the restricted feudal ways of her village and family. She was encouraged to leave home after attending a political ideology course organised in her village that included singing and dancing.

Further along the road, I came across a group of porters and drivers[13] on their way to supply the front. In most of the provinces we have travelled through, civilians knew our theatre repertoire so well they would join in and sing along with us. But, coming from Vinh Phuc in the occupied zone, these men and women had not seen a revolutionary theatre before! Most of them have been on the road for at least a month, carrying supplies to the front. They have no news of the families they have left behind. The truck drivers work 18-hour shifts at a stretch. As for the porters, they carry exceptionally heavy loads on their shoulders over long distances. Some of them have been awarded medals and honour flags from Uncle Ho. Examples: A 47-year-old man was decorated for having carried a friend's sister who had been taken ill (as well as the 100lb load on his back) for more than six miles; and Mr Duy from the province of Phu Tho for having carried a 190lb load of supplies!

Throughout the day, French aircraft circled continuously overhead. They were mainly surveillance planes[14] going back and forth between the front and the rear to report on our movements. We had to remind each other not to cook rice in case the planes spotted the fire or the smoke. As for the trucks, they travel mostly at night. At one point, we stopped by the roadside near a unit of conscripted workers[15] who were enjoying a smoke. They each had their own bamboo water pipe. We asked if we could join them but they refused to share. I didn't get so much as a puff! I then heard a strange sound coming from the jungle. When I went to investigate, I found a 16-year-old boy drumming out his distress on an empty gas canister. He was on his way to the front accompanying his father who was one of the conscripted workers. He was hungry and desperate to go back home, but he knew he had no choice and had to keep going. He told me that beating the canister reminded him of his frog drum[16] back home and that he played to stop himself from breaking down in tears.

After consoling him as best I could, I left the boy behind and continued on. When night fell, we stopped at some shacks on the edge of the jungle since we had another day's walk ahead of us before reaching the Black River[17]. When a battalion of pack bicycles[18] arrived later in the evening, we put on a play from our repertoire to thank them for their contribution in supplying the front. Using bamboo mats, we improvised a set to represent the downed fuselage of an enemy plane, covering it with nylon and sweet and cake wrappers along with three pictures of Uncle Ho and a celebratory flag the battalion had received as a gift! Two bicycles provided enough power for the lighting.

After the play, we shared cake, honey and oranges, washed down with mineral water, while the pack bicycle porters entertained us with their stories: young Mr Tu had carried 400lb, double the normal load, and Thuyet from Bac Giang[19] province, an incredible 500lb, even though his bicycle only has one wooden brake. As the evening drew on, all of us, including some older delegates from Thai Nguyen[20] started dancing and singing and took bets as to who would be the first to win the enemy flag. We were in good spirits, although emotions were running high and there was tension in the air as we prepared for the battle to come.

February 26, 1954

Tonight, after walking without stopping for the whole day, we arrived at the Black River. In the distance, on the high peaks, wood fires lit up the villages of our compatriots, the Meo[21]. The mountains were reflected in the still waters of the river. As we prepared to cross the river, we had a bad scare. The battalion of pack bicycles were making their way down to the river bank, accompanied by the rattle of their wooden brakes – Kit... kit... kit – their tiny headlights joining together to create a single moving stream of light. I could hear the engines of the motorboat tugging the ferry in our direction. The ferry lights were shining on the water. Somebody laughed. Then, suddenly, two enemy reconnaissance planes appeared. The planes had been flying above us watching our every move throughout the day but I was surprised they were still there so late in the evening. If they had detected our lights, they would certainly alert their fighter bombers by morning, when the ferry crossing would have made us an easy target. We immediately put out all the

lights and the motorboat shut off its engine. We all waited in the darkness and silence, wondering whether we had been spotted. We stayed there for a while until we decided it was safe to make the crossing before dawn broke.

Where we set up camp for what was left of the night, a brigade of young volunteers who had arrived before us was settling down. They were all from poor rural families. Most of them were between 18 and 25, but a number of them were 16 or 17 and had clearly lied about their age in order to be allowed to join up. They possessed a childish innocence, dreaming only of wearing the uniform that would turn them into Uncle Ho's soldiers.

A soldier smoking a bamboo pipe at night,
charcoal on paper, 26cm x 36cm.

February 27, 1954
This morning we marched under the blistering sun that usually comes before the rain. Enemy planes harassed us continuously. The pack bicycles grew weary under their heavy loads. Young women from a theatre company[22] passed us, going in the opposite direction. They greeted us, laughing and smiling. It warmed my heart to see them and made me feel sweet inside. Along the way, we passed through a beautiful valley near Co Noi[23], flanked by steep hills covered in magnificent trees. Its natural beauty was spoilt by the old tin cans and barbed wire the French leave behind when they abandon camp. Late in the day, I accidentally knocked over one of the bicycles that was carrying a heavy load. As the bicycle fell over, the rice sack bent one of the wheels. I felt bad about it. I knew how fatigued the bicycle carriers must be. They had been pushing their bicycles all day long. I didn't know what to do to repair the wheel. "Keep going, don't worry about it, we'll manage," the driver reassured me. I thanked him and rushed to catch up the others. As I sit down to write tonight, I still find myself thinking about it and wondering whether he was able to repair the wheel before nightfall.

March 2, 1954
Today we walked as far as Hat Lot and then onto Na San[24], an old French airbase. The place has gone back to the wild.

March 5, 1954
Three days later, at a rest station near Son La[25]. The French camp on the hill is completely demolished except for one brick façade that is still standing. The flame trees have lost all their flowers. The ground was strewn with red petals mixed with the empty tin cans left by the French. We are staying the night in a deserted village.The villagers must have fled and taken refuge in the surrounding jungle. There are tamarind trees heavy with ripe fruit. Soldiers passing on their way to the front, stopped to pick some fruit and carefully packed them into their bamboo tubes as provisions for the days to come.

March 6, 1954
Tonight after an exhausting climb, we arrived at our campsite for the night, at the top of the Pha Din pass[26]. Pha Din in Thai[27] means "between heaven and earth". Before the 20-mile climb up the pass, I stopped to prepare myself

mentally for the long ascent. Even then I never expected the track to be so vertiginous and dangerous! On the way up, at the edge of the jungle, I did see some beautiful *ban*[28] trees still in flower! I had always heard how delicate these mountain flowers were, but it was the first time I had actually seen any. White with pink pistils and blue leaves, like the open wings of a butterfly, the flowers seemed to float along the slopes; the dark brown branches blending in so well with the surroundings that they were almost invisible. I was left with an impression of extraordinary whiteness.

The pass is a strategic point on the way to Dien Bien Phu and has been under heavy attack from enemy fighter bombers. I learned how dangerous it

was from Thuy, a company commander with the engineer corps[29]: "The road took longer to build than we had anticipated," Thuy explained, "because the slope was too steep to build straight up the mountain. My men have been here for three months and are working an average of 20 hours a day. Everything takes time. The jungle where we collect the wood and bamboo we need for the road construction is a long distance away; even our base camp is 22 miles from here. Then there are the bombing raids. Before they started in earnest, we knew from the enemy radio that they were planning systematic strategic bombings of our supply routes to Dien Bien Phu and that Pha Din was one of their targets. During the raids, we have counted up to 30 planes a day: B24s, B26s[30] and Hellcats[31].

The most punishing raids took place between the 6th and 16th of December of last year and the first few days of January of this year. During that period, in one night alone, bombers dropped 12 butterfly bombs[32] and time bombs on the pass, and released the same number of air-exploding bombs. As each butterfly bomb contains 70 mini bombs, it means that we were hit by close to 1,000 bombs on that one night alone. The butterfly and time bombs are particularly deadly. The night before the passage of General Giap[33], about ten bombs destroyed a mile of road that then had to be replaced. Where the bombs had fallen, the earth became floury in texture, which made the work of the teams sent to detonate the unexploded bombs even more dangerous. All my men worked to repair the road before the General's passage: one hundred men worked 50 hours non-stop to fill in the two-and-a-quarter tons of soil that had been displaced by the explosions. The General took one night to get through the pass, the regiment, three. (Nine workers filled 30 cubic yards in 45 minutes and one squad filled in two large bomb craters in three hours.)

After a bombing, the officers always set out first, each holding a six-foot-long stick out in front of them, not all that long, considering the potential danger they face. So far, they have been lucky. Two commanding officers (section and company) detonated a bomb that had fallen down a deep gorge. At first, the commanding officer of the regiment did not believe their

Fighter, ink and wash on paper, 16cm x 10.5cm,
bearing the inscription, *Chien si tri tu* (Fighter 4),
collection of the Ho Chi Minh City Fine Arts Museum.

report, thinking it impossible that they could have survived. One afternoon, the enemy planes changed strategy and bombed the same spot four times in a row. Nhu, one of the new recruits sent to detonate an unexploded bomb, was buried under the explosion. When we pulled him out alive, his first words once he regained consciousness were that he would report for duty the very next day! We keep telling our detonating teams to be careful. The enemy alternates the fuses on the time bombs making it impossible to predict when the bomb will explode. This makes it extremely dangerous. We have had several near misses. One comrade who hit a bomb by mistake, with his pickaxe, was lucky the bomb did not go off. A young recruit detonated 50 butterfly bombs in one night and survived. And a team was standing only ten feet away, when a 550lb bomb exploded. Miraculously, they too survived. Without the benefit of a calm mind[34], they would certainly have cracked! The men in the observatory towers are the ones who really have to be tough and stay calm. During the bombings, before they can take cover, they need to watch to see exactly where the bombs fall, so they can report their positions to the detonating teams. There is always a danger that a bomb that has fallen close to the watchtower will explode on impact while the men are still at their posts. The night before the General came through, a youth brigade, following the officers' example, volunteered to search for unexploded bombs. It was an exceptionally dangerous task but they wanted to make absolutely sure that the road was safe.

We work a great deal at night, even though it's pitch black. We frequently have to work without torches to avoid the risk of being detected. The flares sent up by enemy planes are a big problem for us. We flatten ourselves against the rock face in order not to be seen. Enemy planes try to intimidate the watchtowers by dropping bombs that explode in the air[35], as close to them as possible. One day they dropped six bombs that weighed half a ton each! It is equally terrifying for the men who have to go up there after the bombings to dig out men buried in the explosions. The squadron leader has had to keep encouraging them shouting, 'Get up there, now!' This gives you an idea why the Army newspaper refers to us as The Tigers of Pha Din!"

"We don't have enough medics either, so we have advised the lightly wounded to give immediate help, on site, to the seriously wounded," said Hoa.

"What makes you so determined? How do you keep your nerve?" I asked.

"I am afraid of death, we all are," Thuy answered. "But this pass is a strategic crossing point. All our troops and supplies have to cross here to get to Dien Bien Phu. It's our duty to our people and our nation to keep it open. And we are confident of our ultimate victory!"

March 7, 1954

Coming down the Pha Din pass, the road was teeming with troops on their way to the front: sappers, labourers, youth brigades and artillerymen. The surrounding mountains were deserted and eerily quiet. The landscape was hollowed out by bomb craters, on the road, in the jungle and on the hillsides. From where I am now, it is another 53 miles to Tuan Giao[36], a town located at the intersection of the roads from Lai Chau, Son La and Dien Bien Phu. And then from Tuan Giao to the front at Dien Bien Phu, it is a further 60 miles!

March 10, 1954

Three days later, at a campsite on route 41[37], six miles from the French military base of Dien Bien Phu. I was happy to meet up with friends from C804[38]. (We trained together in Yunnan in China). They have been here since the end of January. Trucks hauled their 105mm cannons[39] over hundreds of miles and then came to a halt. The road had stopped several miles before arriving at their battle positions. Over steep hills and deep gorges, the soldiers manhandled the two-ton cannons into position. Then, they received an order to withdraw without being told why [40]. After listening to their odyssey, I forgot about my own exhaustion!

A friend recounted how his battery came under heavy enemy fire during the operation. "We were on our way to the battlefront," he said. "We had left the road and were pulling the 105mm cannon through thick jungle. We progressed very slowly through the undergrowth. There was hardly any path: we bumped into tree stumps and sunk down into hidden streams. I don't think the officers knew how tough the terrain was going to be. We pulled the two-tons of steel to the top of a hill. It took us several hours. When the officers saw a near-vertical cliff on the other side, we were ordered to gather bamboo and make ropes to haul the cannon down. Each squad of foot soldiers, numbering 70 men, made two ropes, each one measuring 50 feet. We began our descent. The weight of the cannon was bearing down on the shaft, guided by artilleryman[41] number 4. Artillerymen numbers 5 and 6 were under so much strain they looked as if every bone in their bodies was about to snap. The following day, we wrapped the barrel of the cannon in straw to help it slide more easily down the hill. By the third day, we were all exhausted. And there were still two 65-degree slopes left to climb! So we installed the windlass at the top of the hill and attached the ropes to the wheels of the cannon. The foot soldiers inched up the slope, pulling on the rope. The battery commander was shouting: 'One, two, three, pull...' At one point, the cannon slipped back and the break hit artilleryman number 1 full in the face. With only six artillerymen instead of 12 and 70 foot soldiers (instead of 100), we covered only two and a half miles that night.

On the fourth day, disaster struck. The windlass let go. Xich and three artillerymen grabbed hold of the shaft as it thundered down the slope. They slowed the cannon down and manoeuvred it onto flat ground as it was about to fall into a stream. The foot soldiers were holding the ropes so tightly that their hands burned with pain.The same thing happened again on the fifth day as we were climbing the last hill, the windlass gave way, the foot soldiers clung onto the ropes. On the sixth day, we had made it to the top of the hill where we had orders to set up our position. We were about to take a well-deserved rest when a counter-order arrived.

'Order to withdraw immediately!'[42] shouted the company commander.

I had never felt so exhausted! We had also been told that the trucks would appear at some stage. Instead we dragged the cannons back again unaided. As we were hauling them, enemy artillery began bombarding us. Their shells landed 300 feet from our position. We kept going. All night long we pulled the cannon, without stopping to rest. The foot soldiers were furious. Our withdrawal was on a hillside in full view of the French artillery. The bamboo kept cracking. As we crept forward, our feet sank into the swampy terrain. Our advance was painfully slow. We tried not to panic. Then, enemy artillery blasted us again. This time, their shells landed 30 feet from our position!

Opposite: *Sketch of artillery men dragging a two-ton cannon uphill,* ink on rice paper, 14cm x 16cm.
Following pages: *Sketch of artillerymen pulling a 105mm cannon to Dien Bien Phu (Toi keo phao Dien Bien)*, ink on paper, 14cm x 16cm.

Did they know where we were? It certainly seemed like it. The hillside erupted around us under the explosions, the earth shook, the sound was deafening. We hung on, clinging to the ropes and to the shaft. Up, down, across hills blackened by napalm[43]. And then, a *bà già* (old lady), one of their surveillance planes, spotted us. It swooped down, to investigate what we were doing and quickly pulled up, to inform the fighter-bombers of our position.

'One, two, three… pull!' shouted the company commander, with greater urgency.

We kept dragging the two-tons of steel. We were exhausted, our bellies were empty, our eyes were blurry from tiredness. When daylight broke, the fighter planes, no doubt alerted by the *bà già*, roared out of the sky and

opened fire with their machine guns. All six of us in the battery were wounded. Tao's arm was blown apart and yet he kept driving the cannon shaft. Nhu had been hit in the stomach. His intestines were spilling out. Hien was wounded in the thigh. We quickly hauled Nhu and Hien over our shoulders. It was too dangerous to stop to bandage their wounds. By now it was dawn and we were advancing in broad daylight. We were fully exposed without any camouflage and there were no shelters in which to hide and look after our wounds. We had to keep moving. Then, the cannon went thundering 130 feet downwards, this time I thought it was going to break up at the bottom of the hill! Again, the foot soldiers stopped it in time. 'Good work, keep it up,' said the political commissar[44]. 'Remember how many times you had to fight without the artillery to back you up!' Several hours later, we delivered the cannon to the place where the truck was waiting to haul it back to the rear (while awaiting new orders)."

My friend Quy, an artilleryman with C804, described how French combat aircraft strafed and bombed batteries 2 and 4. His narrative : "To get to our fighting position, we hauled the cannon across six miles of ridges covered in scrub. We had arrived close to our fighting position. The men in battery 2 spent the last night pulling the two tons of steel uphill. By sunrise, at 6am, they had not reached the summit. It was too dangerous to keep climbing in broad daylight. They were within firing range of the enemy. They would have to wait it out in the open. The slope was so heavily bombed there was hardly any long grass left on it. They gathered as much of it as they could and tied it into bundles. It still wasn't enough to camouflage the cannon. They hurriedly built a shelter, but it was far too small for so many soldiers. They were spotted by a *bà già*, which must have radioed their position through. Soon after, enemy planes started bombing their position. Nghia, Ty and Loc[45] hit the ground beside the cannon. A one-ton bomb landed only 65 feet away. The company deputy commander rushed down from the top of the hill to see if there was any damage; even the division enquired whether men and guns were safe. A foot soldier who had been holding onto the lever of the windlass that secured the cannon on the slope was killed during the attack.

After the attack, batteries 2 and 4 manhandled the cannons to a temporary position near Tan village – the sappers and infantrymen were waiting to help dig the casemates[46] (shelters) for the cannons. The French were roughly two miles away. We needed to know the exact position of their artillery.

When night fell, we set off on a reconnaissance tour to find out. We crossed over to the other side of the Lai Chau road (route 41), down through a ravaged ricefield and passed through some villages. Not a soul. The whole area was deserted. The thatched roofs[47] were in tatters, the rice fields, which must have been abandoned for some time, were dry and hollowed with bomb craters. Water buffaloes wandered aimlessly, while one lay dead, its body in a state of advanced decomposition. Towards dawn, a few villagers appeared and then disappeared again. We set up our firing position away from the villages, in the middle of ricefields. The following day, we transported munitions to our new position and waited for the sappers.

That night I went into the jungle with a small unit, to cut down trees for the beams of the shelters. As we came back out into the open paddy field, carrying the wood on our shoulders, enemy artillery started shelling us. We all dropped to the ground. When there was a pause in the shooting, we tried to make it back to our encampment but the shelling started up again. Several of us were killed during the attack.

Battery 4 had a narrow escape. The rice paddy where they were digging their shelters was humid and, as they dug deeper, their shelter flooded. They moved to a new position and started shovelling again. The French surveillance planes were flying overhead continuously. To avoid detection, they built the gun fortifications at night. The officers stayed in constant radio contact – sleeping a couple of hours during the day – to warn of any pending air attack they might intercept over the radio. In spite of these precautions, they were spotted. It is difficult to know whether it was a plane which had spotted them or a spy from one of the villages who had informed the French of their whereabouts. Tinh and a team of scouts were scrambling out of their hole, when fighter bombers appeared. The gunners aimed their machine guns straight at our scouts and fired several rounds. Xuat, the topographer, hit the ground. The others took refuge in the jungle. Luckily, this time, nobody was injured.

Then, shortly after we finished digging our defences, we received order to abandon them – we were not told why[48]. Before we left our position, during the night, I went with Thang and a few men to within 300 feet of enemy lines to demolish and fill in their trenches. On our way back, we went through a village, it was deserted when we got there... a small camp fire was still burning...

In the dead of night, all the men, about one hundred of us, started our withdrawal. We drove the cannon donwhill, doing what we could to relieve the infantrymen of as much of the weight of the shaft as possible. The foot soldiers pulled the two-ton cannons up and downhill all through the night. They began chanting to keep up their spirits, once they were far enough away from the French positions.'Even dead, we will never let go of these ropes!'they repeated in rythm as they crossed the blackened hills. By dawn, we had manoeuvered the cannons safely onto the road. Trucks that had driven through the night were waiting to take them to the rear where they would be camouflaged (until new orders arrived).

We reviewed the operation and rewarded individual acts of bravery. We agreed that great care had to be taken to make ropes that are tough enough to bear the tremendous weight of the cannons. Cannon-pulling should be done at night to avoid detection and casualties. The day should be spent looking for the right kind of bamboo (*giang*) to make the ropes and the camouflage. Camouflage is essential, when dragging cannons over such a long distance.

After the meeting, I saw someone I thought I recognised lying down on the road, under a blanket. It was Phuc, the comrade who had been guiding one of the cannons during the withdrawal operation. His foot had got caught between the cannon wheel and a tree stump hidden by the long grass and had been crushed to a pulp when the cannon accidentally slid backwards. When I rushed to his side to offer to carry him on my back, he refused. 'Don't worry about me,' he said. 'I can still crawl!' He had found a small grotto in the limestone where he bandaged his wound and rested for a while. I was happy to see that he had made his way back to the road."

C804 was awarded a third-class medal for pulling the cannons over 12 miles in seven days.

Later:

Comrade Nguyen Dinh Uoc, commanding officer of regiment 675[49] talked about the operation in Upper Laos[50]. His troops crossed 50 hills to get into position; they built gun defences and six shelters in two days; they shot down three French planes (one Dakota[51] and two surveillance planes) and destroyed one enemy artillery position. Then their mission was aborted. This caused grumbling among the men who wanted to know why.

"The men were dissatisfied with the rations as well," said Nguyen Dinh Uoc. "When we returned to base camp, my men complained that they were healthy when they left and that when they returned, they were skin and bones. During the nine-day operation, rations were scarce and were made up of rice mixed with other cereals (two *lang*[52] of rice a day mixed with manioc and jungle spinach[53]). A few soldiers served themselves larger rice portions while others showed exemplary behaviour: they might have been hungry yet they politely refused to eat the sticky rice the villagers offered them (knowing they had very little for themselves); Nhung and Thung only ate half a portion of rice each[54].

Our evacuation plan for the wounded went according to plan. Company commanding officer Hung, political officer Chan and squad officers Ho, Bong, Nang, Kien and Thung carried the wounded back to base camp and tended to them throughout the journey. I can also report good cooperation between the infantry and the artillery.

The biggest cause of dissatisfaction among my men was that we were ordered to withdraw and not to pursue the French into Laos, and this just as we had finished building our entrenchments! The men wanted to know what the point of the operation was. They asked why they were not allowed to attack, why they had to withdraw and whether it was because our position had been detected by the French.

To calm their anxieties, I explained to them the meaning of our victory in Muong Sai[55]. I pointed out that even though we did not pursue the French into Laos, we had achieved our objectives. The operation demonstrated our support for an alliance between Vietnam and Laos and for the Laotian prime minister Souvanaphong[56].

The question of Laos does remain unanswered however and some comrades want to know why we don't liberate the people of Laos, who are our allies and friends, when we eat their rice.

On our return we were awarded a third-class medal and a pig from one of the allied Laotian units."

Following pages: Facsimile of the diary pages with sketches of soldiers and trucks, one of which is loaded up with cannon tubes.

PHÁO Trẻ tuổi

Dưới ngọn cờ Đảng, Bác chúng ta.
Bao chồi non
Trong mùa xuân khói lửa
Vẫn ra hoa
Là chúng ta
Con em của nhân dân trong bộ đội
Đầu xuân này trưởng thành tiến tới
Xiết chặt hàng ngũ mạnh vang lời ca.
Tương 1 gia đình.

Vinh dự thay, đơn vị "chúng mình"!
Cao Xạ và Trọng pháo
Lần đầu tiên xuất trận tuổi còn xanh
Cùng anh Công binh, bộ binh
Hiệp đồng chiến đấu thắm tình anh em
Sức mạnh chúng ta lên,
Quân thù tan gục xuống!
"Quyết đánh thắng Điện Biên!"
Ý chí chúng ta bền.
Vì yêu dân, yêu mình: theo Đảng, Bác
Chúng mình đi - Kiên quyết
- Tiến lên!

19/3-54

Trời mưa mưa xuống cho ướt
Tây khó tiếp tế là pháo ta
Hắn tây chật chội đi đồ
Lại thêm ẩm ướt kha kỗ c
nhau.
Nghe xa: cho mà gần gần
Nghe gần: thấy giặc thua
cần cau
Pháo ta dọt mạnh, bộ binh
tiến tra
Mưa xuống lại càng ngập
ngụa đồn t
Phen này bọn nó chúng
Sống như bọ dưới nước
nhảy nhóp n
Tương lai như khói hoả
Như phân 3 vàng, chuột
bị bi
Mưa nhiều: Tây
sẽ thành,
Điện Biên cũng giống
Him Lam đi đ
3/54

Đến Ninh Quan (thị điểm tập kết)

– Kéo máy nổ cùng vào xe xong, sinh hoạt C; Đại đội bố trí nhận nhiệm vụ.

. Sinh hoạt không vui như thường ; Đại nhắc: các đồng chí sau ... khung khoắt xung đột thắng lợi ; anh em tranh thủ ngủ trên xe, sương lạnh.

– 1 giờ dậy vào đèn rồi đi ; 1 người đi bộ để bảo đảm vì đường và lái xe nặng.

– Xe bị lầy, chờ lâu rét, tranh thủ "ngủ" : mấy đ/c ôm vào đầu máy xe hơi ấm áp đứng ngủ ; vẫn cả lên đầu máy ngủ – Cố Thắng đi lại lo lắng. 1 chiếc đỗ xa, 1 chiếc cứ bên bờ suối.. – gọi anh em dậy ngụy trang, đẩy kéo xe lên dốc ! (cố gắng.)

– Xe pháo qua ngầm chạy nhanh. trăng 19 ; trên trời máy bay địch vẫn bay, máy bay 646 vẫn nổ? (địch sợ bộ đội ta nên ngừng hoạt động đêm) – 5 cây số mới ra thị đường cái

. 1 số anh em bộ binh mấy năm ngày ven đường ngủ lại bãi, dậy để ở lô đi.

– 1 quãng dốc lầy lội, xe bị patinê rồi chèn rồi kéo ; tìm gỗ lát đường, xe rút. lên khỏi mấy bận mới qua được thì vừa sáng.

Đêm nay là thứ 2 đêm 1 ngày : anh em mệt vẫn vui. Sáng cơm vào đã phân tán, đào công sự súng, ngụy trang xe : ăn cơm rồi mới ngủ.

1 giờ. lệnh trên Kđịnh + số 1, 8 : tất cả đi 5 ngày (đào công sự).

Nhớ lời Đại Tướng : Chúng ta quyết mang sức lao động ra xây dựng trận địa của chúng ta cho vững chắc, bởi vì chúng ta biết rằng : chúng ta càng tốn sức lao động, đổ nhiều bồ hôi bao nhiêu thì càng khỏi đổ máu bấy nhiêu!

Later:
Just heard on the radio that our commandos blew up 18 enemy planes at Gia Lam, the Hanoi airport and 60 planes at Cat Bi, the Haiphong airport. There were some American pilots among the French pilots[57].

March 11, 1954
At the headquarters of the heavy artillery division. I have arrived at the command post of my division at Dien Bien Phu!

At 3am, we boarded the trucks for the two-mile drive to the division's headquarters. A thick fog rolled in. The headlights lit up the road. How happy I was to be in a truck for these last two miles, I didn't care how cramped we were! At the 50-mile point along route 41, stood a banyan tree. The truck turned left, up a steep road for a mile and a quarter and then stopped halfway up the slope. We had arrived at divisional headquarters.

Trucks transporting us towards Dien Bien Phu, 1954, wash on paper, 16cm x 24cm.

At HQ, there are soldiers everywhere digging shelters and defences to camouflage the heavy artillery pieces. Each unit has been given a code name: division 351 will be known as Long Chau, regiment 675 as Chau Giang and regiment 45[58], as Hai Lang. As for the Ben Tre [59] infantry division, they have a new motto which is: "Increase rice production without fail." We were also told the fighting mottos for our attack against "Tra Dinh" (the code name for Dien Bien Phu):

Steady attack, steady advance![60]
Fight for as long as we have to!
Be determined to win!

A French war plane roars in the sky above!
We open fire !

In the trenches

The first general offensive of General Giap's army against the formidable French fortress, referred to in the diary as Muong Thanh, is only hours away. The exact timing is unknown to the men. As he reaches his HQ, Tam reports in the diary that morale among the troops of the People's Army is high even after the months of arduous preparations, the long marches to reach the battlefront and the hardships and privations endured by the men. Young recruits have no protective clothing against the cold and the rain and have trekked barefoot for hundreds of miles to reach the battlefront. Tam is one of the lucky few who owns a pair of shoes and a thin green quilted jacket which is the uniform of the People's Army.

With extraordinary accuracy for a military reporter in the midst of combat, Tam early on and throughout the diary, gives a remarkable analysis of the overall attack and siege plan. General Giap's strategy is in three phases: to cut off French air supply routes and destroy the airfield in Muong Thanh; to secure the French strongholds on the surrounding hills that are defending Muong Thanh and to build a network of tunnels and trenches that will gradually besiege the French HQ from under the ground.

In anticipation of the first general offensive, an anxious and excited Tam, aware that he is about to witness an historic event, spends his first couple of nights at Dien Bien Phu a few feet underground, lying on the bare earth, in one of the hundreds of shelters built in preparation for the battle. Full of youthful confidence, Tam is not prepared for the cruelty he will witness on the battlefield of Dien Bien Phu.

Soldiers in the trenches on hill D, detail from a sketch, Dien Bien Phu, 1954, graphite on paper, 25cm x 20cm.

The evening of March 11, 1954

Tonight, at the command post of my division, F351. Artillerymen from C805[61] described the preparations that have been underway since they first arrived at headquarters, 25 days ago: "Our main concern has been to keep our position secret from the French. To get here, we took a shortcut through the jungle. The track was covered by a roof-like structure made of wood and bamboo covered with foliage, making it difficult for enemy planes to spot our vehicles and cannons. It was a very ingenious contraption built by our engineers. We had one nasty incident when a truck pulling a two-ton cannon slid backwards. The driver jumped from the vehicle to block the wheel with a wooden chock and stopped the cannon from crashing down the hill into the stream below. When we reached HQ with the cannons, the infantrymen were so pleased to see us that they cheered us on saying: 'Hey, it's been a month since we last saw you! Can we touch the cannon, just for a second?' We spent our first night unloading the ammo from the trucks with one torch light between us. Then at 3am,enemy shells exploded only 300 yards away from us. When we realised how close we were to the French, we continued digging shelters and building defences in complete silence!" [62]

March 12, 1954

At the division's command post. Morale is high. We are all certain of victory. The officers took time to explain to some of the more impatient recruits who were anxious to start fighting that we were not yet sufficiently prepared. We then debated the optimum size for our undergound shelters. Two thirds of the men are satisfied with the shelters as they are; the rest suggested making them wider so we would have more living space. In the end we decided to keep them narrow, it would be safer and better for defence. One field officer thought it there wouldn't be sufficient space to store the ammunition.

We must be nearing D day. This evening's front-page newspaper headline read: "General Vo Nguyen Giap calls for the destruction of the entire enemy army at Dien Bien Phu!" It also reported that C757[63] shot down one Dakota and 12 surveillance planes in Dien Bien Phu!

Tonight there is a crescent moon. I am having difficulty getting to sleep. Enemy artillery is shelling us from the French headquarters in Muong Thanh[64]. The sound of the explosions fills the night. Their flares light up the surrounding jungle and mountains. The dugout is narrow and cramped and I am lying directly under a ceiling made from a mixture of earth and dried rice stems. The wind keeps blowing clumps of dirt into my face and onto my uniform. See if I care! I am sharing the space with the printers. There are no printing machines so they are using stencils to print the division's newspaper. Earlier in the evening, I took a steep path up to the watchtower to orientate myself. I had a magnificent view of the whole of Dien Bien Phu. As the crow flies, we are only three miles away from the enemy camp. This made me feel confident since it is the perfect distance required for our attack plan to take control of the battlefield. The men posted at the watchtower have built a solid underground shelter that is surprisingly welcoming. It is made out of hard wood (*trac*) with enough space for them all to sleep lying down. Cloth and green bamboo mats (*nua*) cover the earthen walls and floor. Books on the Pathet Lao[65] along with the squadron's battlefield schedules are laid out on display. On a partition built out of the same cloth (*bat*) as the walls, timetables and maps have been posted. When I paid them a visit, Comrade Tich was on guard duty. He was sitting at his table, studying and taking note of the enemy's every move. "Mmm...," he said, "Their cannon has a rather cute range finder and compass."

We received more good news from C757 who shot down three surveillance planes! And Huan was awarded a third-class medal. The division command sent a messenger to examine the positioning of their automatic machine guns to report back on any procedures that might be used as an example for other batteries.

March 13, 1954

Today at divisional headquarters. A letter from Uncle Ho arrived, addressed to all the troops. Mau, the political commissar, read it out loud, sitting on top of a gun shelter to make sure everybody could hear him:

"As we prepare to go into battle, I look forward to hearing of your exploits. I will reward each one of you for your acts of courage. I wish you a great victory," and Uncle Ho signed the letter, "I embrace you all."

At 4pm exactly, Thuoc, deputy commander of the regiment, received the order to open fire. Comrade Tong Tu passed the order onto all the units: "Comrades, this is an historic battle. Fire, and be determined to win!" Then, a company fired on the eastern targets[66] before the official order went out

(it was a company from Trung Kien's battalion 954[67], and the attack was in time to surprise the enemy). Then the commander in chief of the regiment, Comrade Huu My, gave Ho De of C803 orders to open fire:
"Hello! Ho De, fire immediately! Tell both companies to open fire! And tell the 12.7mm machine guns[68] to co-ordinate their fire."

Ho De followed up immediately and ordered: "803, to your left, fire!" I had never seen such a big smile on Ho De's face, he was so proud to be the first to receive the order to start the historic battle. Then, Comrade Huu My again: "All regiments, fire!" Shortly after, the companies reported back:
803: Opened fire at 4.12pm.
801: Opened fire at 4pm.
802: Opened fire at 4.25pm.

Then this report from commanding officer Hong Linh came in by radio: "The airstrip is on fire in the southeast! A fighter bomber has been hit."
Soon after, the companies reported back.
801: "A shell from our first round hit its target; all the shells from the third round hit theirs. There has been no response from enemy artillery; one of their trucks[69] is stranded."
802: "After the first two rounds, enemy artillery fired back. They aimed at our wooden cannons[70]."
801: "We hit 80 per cent of our targets. Five of our shells hit the airstrip, close to where the helicopters[71] are standing."
And 802 again: "One shell out of three hit their targets. We are waiting to see if enemy artillery from the central zone will counter-attack."

Following the reports, a new order went out to companies 801, 802 and 803: "Continue to fire on the enemy wherever they manifest themselves."
803: "We have grounded the enemy planes, they are not taking off!"
This report from our battalion followed:
"There are still eight bombers and two surveillance planes on the runway."
Immediately the order went out to the companies:
"Shell the airfield until it is under our control, don't let the planes take off or land, aim continuously at the same position."

Portrait, 1954, signed Huynh Biec, the *nom de guerre* of the artist, graphite on paper, 16cm x 10cm, collection of the Ho Chi Minh City Fine Arts Museum.

Then enemy artillery from Muong Thanh started shelling our positions. We fired back.
803 reported: "We destroyed an enemy artillery post on position 203, a munitions depot is on fire (53 shells)!"
801 continued shelling.
802 started shelling enemy position 307.
Eight French batteries counter-attacked.
A surveillance plane took off, flying to the south!
On the runway, enemy vehicles were hauling fighter-bombers to safety!
At 5.25pm, a helicopter landed on enemy position 307 (near the central zone of Muong Thanh).

Later:
Four French cannons were bombarding our infantry from position 201[72], near one of the D[73] hills; our foot soldiers kept advancing, moving forwards under fire. Enemy guns kept shelling as they approached position 201.

Then an order went out: "Attack enemy artillery on 201 so our soldiers can keep advancing. Shell the entire hill from top to bottom! Our foot soldiers are moving up the trenches, they are within a quarter of a mile of the enemy defence barrier; 801, 802 go ahead, give it everything you've got!"

The voice of Pho, deputy political commissar of the regiment, came over the transmitter loud and clear: "I am talking to the unit firing on hill D, don't let the enemy artillery oppress our infantry!"
801 started shelling position 307, a surveillance plane burst into flames!
The company was rewarded.
803 destroyed 100 per cent of enemy artillery to the north of the airstrip.
Then, 801 fired on 307a, 802 on 307b, 803 fired two rounds of six shells.
Each battery fired ten shells!
A Dakota, at the south end of the airstrip, was hit and caught fire!
802 started shelling hill D.
Firing continued on the southeast of the airfield.
A surveillance plane and a Dakota were hit.

Mau, the political commissar of the division, shouted the following order to the artillery batteries: "You must fulfil your duty and responsibility towards the infantry, continue to shell Muong Thanh!"

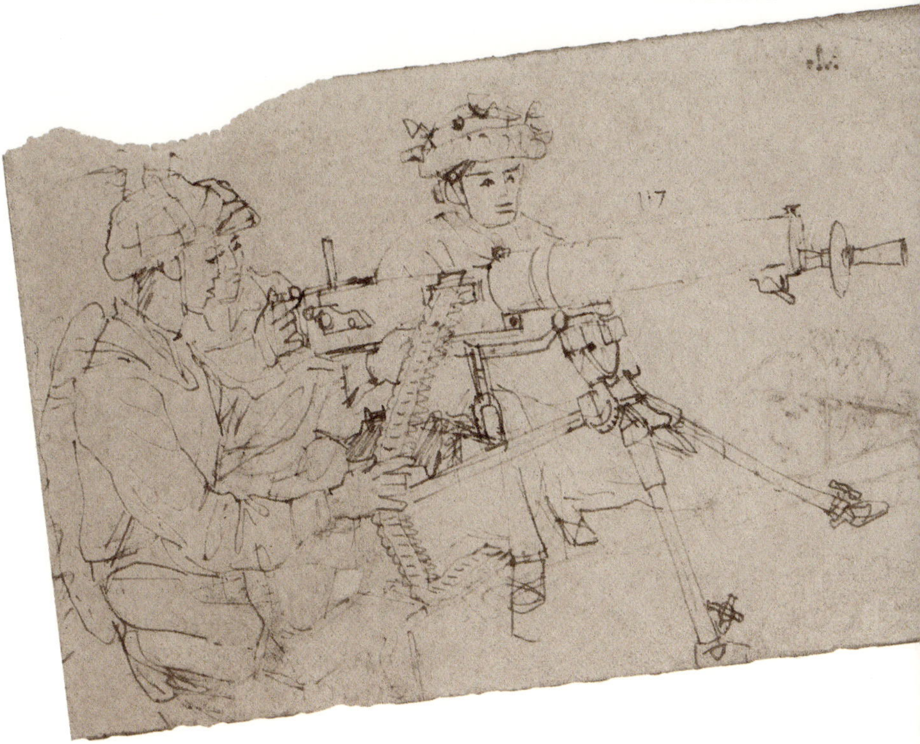

French cannons from Muong Thanh attacked our infantry, our regiment 209[74] was not able to blast through the barbed wire barrier... then regiment 141 blasted through!

Mau repeated: "I remind the infantry to be cautious on the battlefield. Do not overestimate or underestimate the enemy[75]! The situation is not clear! We are not in control of the enemy's eastern positions yet, nor of the area around!"

Our infantry had cut through one set of barbed wire; then quickly breached through five more! We were now in control of three enemy posts[76]! One of the enemy commanders had fled but was caught by our soldiers. They fought in hand-to-hand combat. The commander gave himself up. "If you give yourself up, so do I!" said a captain standing next to him.

Combattants, 1954, graphite on paper,
10.5cm x 16cm, collection of the
Ho Chi Minh City Fine Arts Museum.

Under cover of the artillery, in enemy positions 304, 306, 303, our soldiers slipped underneath the barbed wire, advanced closer and then attacked with hand grenades.

Later:
At 12.30am, we occupied the easternmost enemy stronghold[77] of Him Lam! We captured 300 prisoners[78] and destroyed 13 planes! Huong Thuy shot down one surveillance plane and one fighter plane.
As I write in the early morning hours, the cannon fire has started to die down. Soon, it falls totally silent. The soldiers have orders to sleep wherever they are, so that they are in position in the event of enemy counter-attacks. Before going to sleep, I hear a soldier close by crying out in his sleep : "Fire! Let's get them!"[79]

March 14, 1954
At C804's command post, a few hundred yards southeast of HQ. After very little sleep, this morning, we were ordered to penetrate an enemy camp and seize their munitions depot. The operation was code named "victory". I was one of the 80 men selected from C804 for the mission. Our commanding officer was comrade Quang, an officer with the battalion. The depot was situated at the top of hill 6. It was one of the French positions that protected the central zone of Muong Thanh. It was in a particularly dangerous position between two enemy strongholds. The depot was defended by machine guns with telescopic sights, which made the exercise even more hazardous. As our team approached Him Lam, enemy artillery started firing and shells exploded all around us. The shelling was so intense we were forced to a halt.

"We can't advance under this," one of us shouted over the noise of the explosions.

"They can shell us as much as they like, we must keep going!" replied Quang our commanding officer.

We started running again. I ran for two and a half miles. I was doubled over, head down, to avoid being hit by the shrapnel from the explosions.

Combatant, Dien Bien Phu, 1954,
ink on paper, 34cm x 23cm, collection of
the Ho Chi Minh City Fine Arts Museum.

I was out of breath by the time I reached the base of the French stronghold on hill D. The enemy post was only 200 yards across from the barbed-wire barrage that surrounded hill 6 where the depot was located. The foot soldiers, who were ahead of us, had not had time to use explosives to blow up the barrier. Behind the barbed wire was a minefield. That had not been cleared either. We somehow got through the barriers, across the minefield and positioned ourselves on the slope of the hill. There, we split up. Some stayed where they were, lying face down on the ground, in position to pass the ammunition on down the hill once we had taken the depot. I kept climbing the hill towards the depot with the others.

The foot soldiers had almost reached the top of the hill and were closing in on the depot. As we advanced, firing broke out followed by violent explosions. A deluge of rock and earth pounded our backs, we stayed where we were as if we were paralysed. I don't know how long we were there for. I lost track of time. At some point, two officers came up from behind us. They told us to stay calm and encouraged us to move forward.

"Lying here isn't going to get us anywhere! Let's follow the example of the infantrymen who led the way," shouted one of the officers.

We had started back up the slope when a second blast went off. A shell fragment dug into Quyet's back. Thinking he was badly injured, he reached back to patch up his wound, then realised it was luckily only minor.

Then, a third round of artillery fire broke out. Everybody froze, all eyes glued to the depot. We saw our soldiers emerge, carrying the ammunition: they had seized the depot! All 80 of us arranged ourselves in a human chain, to pass the 105mm shells down the hill as quickly as possible. Meanwhile, our engineers had come to open a path through the minefield when, suddenly, artillery fire exploded. Then, a fighter bomber roared out of the sky. It nose dived down over the minefield like a gigantic bird, flying very close to the ground and opened fire. Three sappers were hit and wounded. The bomber then swooped down over the depot. Most of us had climbed back down to the bottom of the hill to keep the shells moving down the line. Hoe was still up there. As he was climbing down the east side of hill 6 (facing hill E[80]), one of the gunners blasted him with machine gun fire. He cried out:

"Hey, Hanh, I've been wounded. We have lost two comrades, Hue and Tam. I think they have been killed. Can you go and look for them?"

"Where are they?" asked Hanh.

"They must still be in the depot," said Cheo.

"Let's go! We are one team, we are fond of each other and we trust one another. We cannot leave any of our comrades behind!" Quyet shouted.

Cheo took several comrades with him and went back to the depot. Artillery shelling was ferocious. Bent double, they ran up the hill through the smoke of exploding shells. When they came back out of the depot, Cheo signalled that they had found only one body. Quyet was determined not to leave anybody behind. He went back in there. Once inside, he noticed a place where the earth had caved in. He started digging with his bare hands. When he found Hue, he was dead. We wrapped Hue and Tam's bodies in parachute cloth to carry them back "home", to the command post.

Under the cover of darkness, we headed back across the minefield and through the barbed wire. Eight of us carried our two friends. The soldiers, loaded down with shells, shouted words of encouragement to one another to keep up their spirits. I didn't think it possible for men to carry such heavy shells over such a long distance through such rough and muddy terrain. When we reached the foot of Him Lam hill, Quyet stopped to count the number of shells seized so Hoe could report the count back to the division by radio. We had captured 200 shells!

We arrived "home" before sunrise: the operation had lasted all day and night. Before catching a few hours of rest, the artillerymen thanked the foot soldiers for seizing the depot and carrying the munitions. Here at Dien Bien Phu, the footsoldiers feel they are being given support by the artillery in a way not experienced in previous campaigns! Quoting from one of my military strategy books: "The artillery is like a military march that provides the infantry with the rhythm they need to attack."

With the amount of munition we captured, we will be less dependent on supplies coming from the rear. Our comrades who died during the operation did not give their lives in vain. They died for those of us who have to fight on, so that we will not have to pay with our own blood!

Following pages: *Artillery men manning a 105mm cannon in a casemate (underground shelter)*, Dien Bien Phu, 1954, ink on paper, 20cm x 27cm, collection of the Ho Chi Minh City Fine Arts Museum.

March 15, 1954

At C119's command post (at an undisclosed location). The 120mm mortars[81] took part in the March 13 attack against Him Lam (with the 105mm cannons, the anti-aircraft guns[82] and the mountain artillery[83]). During the battle, C119 hit four enemy bunkers, one jeep, one surveillance plane and two Dakotas that were sitting on the airfield. They also blocked reinforcements going to Doc Lap hill[84], shot down paratroopers sent in from Na Keo (many of whom died) and neutralised enemy artillery positions southeast of the airfield.

"Victory at Hoa Binh[85], February 22, 1952, means certain victory at Tra Dinh!" read an inscription that was carved into one of the mortars. I asked one of the artillerymen how they had won such a tough battle (as Hoa Binh) against the French when the company was made up of young recruits, just off the farm, with little or no training. "We fought with the mortars at Hoa Binh in the final days of the 1952 campaign," the artilleryman said. " We had captured the mortars from the French during the Northwest campaign of 1950, one at That Khe[86] and the other one at Dong Khe[87]. When we got the mortars in February 1952 (we were called up the second day of Tet[88]), they had been hidden for almost two years and were in terrible condition!

We were then joined by some recruits from Cao Bang[89] . They were healthy and strong but had never fired a mortar! On our way to battle in Hoa Binh, we stopped in Thuc Luyen (20 miles from Hoa Binh)[90] for training. Comrade Tao, who was in charge of the new recruits from Cao Bang, had two days to train them. He tried to appear confident. In fact, he was very anxious. We started training the next day. Tao showed the new recruits how to load the guns, to find the right elevation, to aim, and to pull them using ropes.

We were four batteries and we only had two mortars (instead of four) and two sets of munitions and we were missing a mortar base. The men with the battery with no mortar spent all day making the ropes that would be needed to drag the guns up and downhill. They cut the bamboo (*hop*) for the stakes, replaced the camouflage made of ivory bamboo (*truc*) with a tougher strand (*nua, neohouzeaua*) and wove camouflages of acacia wood (*phen*) to hide the mortars while they were being transported on the roads in open trucks. On February 21, two nights before the battle, we had target practice all afternoon. Then, after eating rice, at dusk we started marching. We had to cover 20 miles to reach our battle position near Hoa Binh. Our orders were to get the mortars into position that night, February 21. We hadn't got very far, when the truck that was transporting them broke down within 100 yards of its starting point! It took us two hours to fix it! We didn't think we were going to get into position in time. Once the truck was repaired, we loaded the mortars. For the last mile, we manhandled them from the road to the ridge where our firing position was. It was lucky we had the ropes and at least ten new recruits per mortar to help. Our hands were covered in rope burns. Through tick undergrowth, we inched up the hill in silence; we couldn't sing or chant because we were too close to the French positions and feared being detected. We reached the top of the ridge at 11am, the next morning on February 22nd.

We had orders to open fire the following morning on February 23rd, at 7am. We received the order late in the day because our communication line had been cut! We spent the next few hours preparing and checking the guns. Mortar number 1 wouldn't fire! I had to rig it up to the main trigger to get it to work. It was missing a base; we built a cross out of bamboo to prop it up. Mortar number 2 needed oiling and wouldn't recoil.

Then, when we fired some blank shots, they all went up in smoke.

'They must be mouldy!' we reported to the political commissar.

We checked the box. It was so old you could hardly read the specifications. They were smoke bombs, five or six of them. Luckily we had some M3 shells[91] for the 105mm M2 that we could use instead. We couldn't fix the stakes into the ground for mortar number 2. The hill crest was too narrow, the rock too hard. We hauled the mortar all the way back down the hill onto route 41. After setting it up on the flat road, we practised with some blanks. Luckily the thing recoiled even though it needed oiling. We still didn't have an accurate location of targets. The survey team of army engineers from regiment 675 were having a tough time. The terrain was extremely rough and covered in scrub. They had to cut their way through the undergrowth and push back the bushes every 30 yards while trying to measure the target distance. At 6.50am, ten minutes before the order to open fire, a messenger ran up the hill drenched in sweat to deliver the target distance.

With one of the mortars at the summit of the hill and the other mortar down on the road, it was impossible to co-ordinate our fire and we didn't expect to have very good results. One mortar opened fire. Then, the second one opened fire. And one of the two shells hit a French post! Immediate congratulations came from the command post of our division F. Every time we fired a round, the French disappeared into their trenches. Whenever

there was a pause in the firing, they jumped out of the trenches, picked up their weapons and, running as fast as they could, made for route 41 in the direction of the delta. Our attack seemed to have terrorised them. This went on for hours. At some point during the battle, they must have asked for air support from Hanoi or Haiphong. Planes started bombing our position. Fortunately we were well camouflaged and the bombings were not very precise. The artillerymen kept their cool and kept firing.

Engineers repairing lines of communication, 1954, signed Huynh Biec, graphite sketch on paper, 10cm x 14cm.

The battle had started at 7am[92]. At 1pm, we started shelling the dock at Ngoc on the Black River. (The French were evacuating their military base at Hoa Binh; landing craft were ferrying truck loads of munitions, equipment, food and combat troops across the river to reach route 41 that would take them to the safety of the French controlled zone in the Red River delta). We set our range from the survey map; we hit the part of the main road along which the enemy was withdrawing! Our infantrymen were being pummeled by heavy fire from enemy artillery and infantry. When they saw our shells hit the road, they started cheering[93]! When they heard the shouting, the French must have thought our infantrymen were launching another assault; they scattered and ran down the road. The battle ended shortly after. It had lasted five hours. It had been short but ferocious.

We were filthy dirty but relieved and happy that it was over and that we had won. At 3pm, we finally ate the rice that had been served up for an early breakfast. Since there wasn't enough rice to go round, only 6 *lang* per person (8oz), the cook bought some cassava in one of the villages and mixed it in with the boiled rice. He served it with pickled scallions, a specialty from Hoa Binh. It tasted delicious!

The following afternoon, we received an order to withdraw to the Thuc Luyen district to prepare to fight at La Phu[94]. On our way there, we unexpectedly met General Vo Nguyen Giap. We were ordered to fire the mortars on the blockhouses at the Ba Vanh[95] post to see how effective they were at demolition. We succeeded in hitting every target. Mortar number 2 in particular performed above form! As we marched towards La Phu, we received a counter-order to withdraw and regroup. The two mortars were hidden in a field of reeds where they stayed until April 1953. On April 4, 1953, we joined up with regiment 45 in Yen Bai and officially merged with the first heavy artillery regiment in Vietnam! That was a great day. We finally felt we belonged to a powerful artillery regiment."

Quy, Thong, Kim, Thuyet are artillerymen with battery 3 and Mich, Tuong, Diem, Lan and Van are from battery 4. Danh and Tue are the battalion's officers. Two of the four batteries received citations following the victory at Hoa Binh and were listed on the division's Golden Exploit Board.

March 16, 1954

Back at the command post of C805. I found my friends in a sombre mood, compared to a couple of days ago. The unit suffered serious casualties during the March 13 attack. They were firing on Hong Cum[96], the French defence position five miles to the south of Muong Thanh. The men here are suffering from fatigue. They have been in position for the last 25 days working day and night to help the engineers build 29 observatory towers, some in the jungle, others on barren hill summits. An artilleryman describes the preparations and the attack:

"Every night, the engineers from the infantry division went to the jungle, chopped trees and carried back the logs to build and reinforce our defences. Since we arrived here, we have been on one rice bowl a day; we lack water and sleep; our faces are caked in soil and dust. At least there is a peforming arts team (they have their own shelter) to provide us with entertainment and to keep us going! And we have built 200 individual shelters we can hide in when attacked by enemy fire.

When the March 13 order came to open fire, our eight guns were aimed at Hong Cum. We were ready to attack when, suddenly, there was a deluge of fire! Napalm bombs burnt down our entire fortification! The bombers dropped every different type of bomb they had on us! Phung, who was manning the radio, was buried under the rubble. We pulled him out alive. He had kept the connection while he was trapped under the debris. The napalm had burnt down the telephone line. Toan got out of the trench to unearth the line from the debris and fix it. He was groping around looking for the wire when he touched a shell fragment that was scalding hot. He was lucky and survived with burns to his hands. He is still in shock: he saw his friend Tru killed when he touched a shell that exploded. Comrades Bang and Giang, our radio operators, were killed when their shelter was hit by a bomb and collapsed on top of them. When we finally dug them out, they were still hanging onto the receivers. Throughout the battle, enemy artillery shelling was so fierce that most of us stayed hidden in our underground gun shelters. The guys who repaired the telephone lines had real guts to get out there without being ordered to do so or without an officer going with them!

After the battle, we captured a Vietnamese soldier fighting for the French. When questioned, he admitted that his unit only has one big gun left that fires. There was no damage done to our guns."

A pause follows the intense fighting of the first general offensive and the Viet Minh's unexpected victory at Him Lam and Doc Lap hills. During the lull, a badly shaken Tam reflects on the death of his friends. When a theatre company is sent from HQ to entertain the troops, young Tam falls in love (or lust) with the beautiful Miss Ty. Too shy and self conscious and aware of his inferior rank in the military, he dares not declare his love to her. When he meets her again after the war, she has married Tuyen Kinh, the political commissar he refers to in his diary notes.

March 17, 1954

At C119's command post (120mm mortars, at an undisclosed location). Today, we received orders to relax to celebrate the victory at Him Lam. First thing this morning, a voice came over the radio: "Hello! Am I speaking to battery 3? Can you hear me? I want to report that yesterday your five rounds of artillery fire hit their targets: a colonel, a captain, some sergeants and a large number of soldiers were killed!" The line crackled. Then the voice added: "Time for some well deserved R&R. Stretch out by the cannon's wheels and flick through some Russian and Chinese magazines."

Soldiers took time out to share combat stories. "The French counter-attacked Doc Lap hill (March 15)," volunteered Kien, a young infantryman. "Their counter-attack failed. During their retreat, some soldiers were blown up in mid-air when their jeep exploded. Others ran as fast as they could from Doc Lap hill towards Muong Thanh to take cover. As they reached the airfield, our artillery started shelling. They fell to the ground, one on top of another. Sadly, when we saw them 'resting' on the airfield, we felt a sense of immense relief: at the time we were being pilloried by the French artillery and this meant fewer reinforcements!"

Thang, another soldier with C804, described the devastation on the battlefield: "Him Lam hill was destroyed, the earth was scorched. There was total desolation. From my position, I could see many French wounded and dead on the airfield in Muong Thanh. A Dakota tried to land to evacuate the seriously wounded, it came under artillery fire and quickly pulled up.

Following pages: *Caring for a wounded soldier*, Dien Bien Phu 1954, ink on paper, 10.5cm x 16cm.

The plane didn't come round to try again. Then an ambulance sent to collect the wounded on the airfield came under our artillery fire and turned back. Some of the dead left on the runway were covered in the French flag, probably officers."

As for Thu, the bearded officer from the watchtower and a part-time poet, when our artillery started shelling Muong Thanh, he was humming a tune, *From the watchtower, I contemplate the horizon and I smile*, his way of keeping calm before the battle. Another officer looked on as some French officers on the runway struggled to get onto a helicopter that was too small to take all of them. How we laughed when he described the scene to us! For his part, Khu, the company deputy political commissar, was viewing an exhibition of drawings and listening to music when the attack was launched. He ordered the musicians to stop their performance at once and directed the artillerymen to prepare to open fire.

Ho and Thanh explained how they set up artillery positions with fake cannons, to divert enemy fire away from the real ones. During the attack, they moved from one position to the next, detonating explosives to simulate cannon smoke and attract enemy fire. It was probably such an effective decoy because the French artillery is situated in a valley and cannot see our artillery, whereas we overlook them from the surrounding hills. This is a useful subterfuge since their artillery is much stronger than ours, they have far more ammunition than we do and they have great military strategists and modern science on their side.

In the afternoon, Comrade Tuyen Kinh, the political commissar, paid a visit to the command post and organised a game of chess. As a former teacher, he knows how important it is to restore calm and order among the young men after a tough battle – for some, their first.

On a personal note, I received some bad news from Mong (battery 2). Two of my closest friends were killed in a truck accident. The truck was carrying ammunition to the front and fell into a gorge. My friends were crushed under the boxes of ammunition. I am only 22 years old and a reporter attached to a division but I now understand how it must feel for a unit commander to lose two of his men. I feel as if I have lost my own brothers.

Since the battle started, I have been getting so much sad news of friends dying. Each time, I can't help crying. Another close friend was killed during our operation on hill 6 . He stepped on a time bomb as we were crossing the minefield and it exploded. It was the first time I had seen a friend blown up in front of my eyes. When I was back at the command post, I broke down, weeping uncontrollably. I mustn't go on like this. This is war. I must concentrate all my energy into fighting and beating the enemy. I talked to Mong about this. He says he finds it easier at the front than he did during training. In the heat of the action there's no time to think or hesitate. It's a life-and-death situation in which he tries to stay focused on winning. The main thing, he says, is to be ready to die for the cause so that our army is victorious and the enemy pays for their crimes against our people.

Food : mostly wild vegetables, sometimes a little buffalo meat, some salt, pepper and sticky rice. The rice is mouldy and full of grit. The bicycle carriers must have run into some bad weather on the way from the northwest for the rice to be that awful. One of the young recruits said to me, "I am really sick of this rice." To cheer him up, I replied, "I think it's delicious!" As for Tang, C806's cook, he was so proud when he heard of our victory at Him Lam, that he loaded boiled rice (without grit!) onto his shoulders and climbed all the way up the steep hill to serve up his company's artillerymen. No wonder they call him "adopted brother"!

Later:
Performers from one of our best theatre companies were sent by HQ to entertain us, Minh Trien, Ty Lanh, Vinh, Long, Ngoc and others. They improvised a stage between the two mortars. They were about to start the performance when we noticed that Tuyen Kinh had gone missing. He was in the watchtower further up the mountain slope. Miss Ty spoke to him by radio: "Tuyen Kinh, I am dedicating this song to you." I was told that Tuyen Kinh listened attentively as she sang, even though he pretended to be listening to a military report! I then joined in to sing a melody on a text by To Huu[97], *On the road to the Viet Bac, we visit Uncle Ho.*

After the evening meal, we shared our tobacco and sugar rations and had a party with the singers. They are spending the night at the command post.

"We wanted to tell you that we admired your cannons firing their shells on the airfield and on Him Lam," Miss Ty and Miss Linh said in voices as melodious as the song of a nightingale.

"Watching shells, just like us?"

"Yes, we could see that your shots hit their targets."

We all felt very flattered and started to laugh, out of embarrassment more than anything.

"Just stay cool. Think of them as little sisters," one of us said.

"I'll try, but I've never heard my little sister talk to me like that!"

Even Do, one of the section officers, who never said a word, had a smile on his face.

Back to the situation on the battlefield. According to the company commanding officer, three French and Vietnamese (*nguy*) companies[98] capitulated at Na Keo – fewer enemy reinforcements for Dien Bien Phu. The enemy is besieged. Their planes cannot land or take off. Their fighter bombers are having to drop their loads at higher altitudes. The bombs are exploding in mid-air. Day and night, our infantry is digging the new network of trenches. Reportedly, they are halfway to the French posts in the middle section (hills D and E)!

March 18, 1954

At the command post of C119 (the 120mm mortars, at an undisclosed location). "We were two small hills away from the enemy, still within firing range," said Phuong, an artilleryman who participated in the attack against Him Lam. "At 3pm we tried firing and the infantry started advancing, secretly (this was before the general attack order, which came an hour or two later).

'I just want to fire one shot. After that I can die happy!' an infantryman said before going into battle.

He then jumped out of the trenches with a smile on his face! Shortly after the infantry started their advance, we received the order to fire. Phung had carried the radio with him.

'Open a ferocious barrage of fire in four minutes,' said the commanding officer over the radio transmitter.

We opened fire, we could see that we were hitting our targets. Our artillery fire had demolished the blockhouse. Then, when our guns went quiet, we heard the commanding officer give the following order to the infantry:

'Let's go! Storm the blockhouse!'

The infantry assault on Him Lam hill had started. The men threw explosives to blast open the French barbed wire fences. I was told that Comrade So was the first at the summit and had the honour of planting

Uncle Ho's flag on top of Him Lam hill! Our unit captured three French soldiers and some Vietnamese and Thai fighting on their side. The prisoners were surprised to be well treated."

Later:
Him Lam is considered an important strategic point by the likes of Navarre[99], Cogny[100], Nguyen Van Tam[101] and the American advisor[102]. In honour of our victory, Phong, the instructor in charge of the division's music band and comrade Vien, a Party[103] member from a poor rural background and a great lover of traditional music, composed new lyrics to a traditional melody :

One heart and one land, united we stand
To free our country from the Western soldiers
Who will perish at our hand!

Tam returns to company 804's command post. When he arrives, he discovers that three of his friends have been killed. As he promised in the March 17 entry of his diary, he does not confide the sadness he feels at the death of his friends in this next entry. His drawings of a soldier embracing a wounded friend depict the pain he has chosen not to express in words.

March 19, 1954
Today I returned to see my comrades at the C804 command post (at the rear, close to HQ). When I arrived at their shelter, I was told that an enemy shell exploded at the entrance of their underground. Ty, Loc, and Giao were killed instantly. Ngo from battery 2 was severely wounded. The cannon's carriage was completely demolished.

March 20, 1954
At the command post of C804, Da, the political instructor, outlined the three phases of the campaign. He explained how the first two phases would lead to the final attack. He said to those who were impatient to fight that the trench network was not yet in place. Da also reprimanded those who had disobeyed the battlefield rules. They will be required to write a report to explain their behaviour. Then Xong read out the name of the officer who would be in charge of enforcing discipline on the battlefield.

Between March 20 and March 30, the campaign enters its second phase. This is the longest and most arduous phase of the battle. To reach the French HQ, the People's Army needs to overrun the next barrier of well fortified French defence positions. The French posts are positioned on hills fortified with a deep barrage of barbed wire and minefields. The diary describes how for ten days and nights, the soldiers of the People's Army build a 60 mile long network of trenches and tunnels that reaches all the way to the bottom of the fortified hills. The trenches are to enable the People's Army infantry to approach and assault the French positions without being seen.

At the same time as the network of trenches is being dug, new roads are being built to move the heavy artillery closer to the French positions and new gun pits are being dug to camouflage the 105mm cannons. In preparation for the second general attack against the French camp, Tam joins the artillerymen in another dangerous operation. Over several nights, under the cover of darkness, their mission is to move the two-ton cannons to a new command post, on a mountainside opposite the French defences on hill D.

March 21, 1954

Late morning, with C804 at a campsite on a riverbank. Last night, we were ordered to move the cannons closer to the central zone of Muong Thanh. Hung, an experienced soldier who was deputy commander of one of the battalions of regiment 675, is the new battery commander (battery 2). He restored calm and discipline after the death of our three friends (Ty, Loc and Giao). Army engineers came to repair the carriage of the cannon that had been damaged in the attack. It is a rusty old piece of metal that dates from the 1950 Northwest campaign and the battle of Doan Hung. "Use it for now, until we can get you a brand new one in Muong Thanh!" they said.

The officers held a meeting to brief battery and company soldiers on our mission. I recited some of my best poems to get the men fired up.

Then, at 1am this morning, the order came.

"Order to leave at once!" said Kieu Van Tich, the commanding officer.

I got up in the dark, folded my canvas blanket, and packed my backpack. Kieu Van Tich then gave the order to haul the 105mm cannons out of the shelters. First the men carried out the boxes of ammo and spare parts, then they hauled the two-ton guns out of the ground, pulling them up with ropes. Their stick-like figures, bent under the strain, were silhouetted against the Dien Bien Phu skyline. A translucent white fog floated along the mountain slopes down to the fields below. Flares lit up the dark night at regular intervals. I could hear Tich saying: "One, two, three... pull!" Our progress through the night was very slow. The men pulled hard as they went uphill, guiding the cannons, turning the wheels from right to left, chocking quickly. And then, "Two, three..." Downhill. The windlass at the top of the hill groaned. The men were nearing the bottom of the hill when, suddenly, the windlass let go and the cannon thundered down, dragging the men with it. Artilleryman 4 ran ahead of the cannon and chocked it. For a moment he was caught between the carriage wheels and the chock; he jumped aside and narrowly escaped being crushed as the cannon came to an abrupt halt!

"Poor Vietnamese comrade, your suffering is as great as your Russian comrades at Stalingrad[104]!" one of us said, when we realised he was out of danger.

Officers standing on the battlefield, Dien Bien Phu
1954, graphite sketch on paper, 27cm x 20cm,
collection of the Ho Chi Minh City Fine Arts Museum.

Towards dawn, we dragged the cannons onto the road where ten Molotova trucks[105] were waiting and hitched them to the trucks. We jumped in the back and the vehicles drove off in the direction of Muong Thanh. When the trucks reached the riverbank (where I am now), we unhitched the cannons and manhandled them to nearby shelters. We have spent the last few hours cutting bamboo and weaving the branches into camouflage nets to hide the cannons during daylight hours.

March 22, 1954

At midnight we were waiting for the moon to rise. It was pitch black. I couldn't even see the man standing right next to me. Ru, the political instructor, gave us a pep talk. I wrapped myself in some straw to protect myself from the freezing cold. I must have dropped off to sleep. Then, at 1am the order came to start marching. The trucks were being used to pull the cannons. They followed behind us, moving very slowly in convoy, pulling their heavy loads. The track was steep and dark, the drivers kept their eyes peeled, two men on each side of the track waved white handkerchiefs to signal the way forward. Then a truck broke down. We all stopped, waiting while it was being repaired by the engineers. I don't know how long it took. It seemed like a very long time. We took the chance to catch up on some sleep, some of us standing up, others leaning against the guns, as if they were embracing them. I could see company deputy leader Thang, pacing up and down the road. He was anxious that it was taking such a long time to repair the truck. He then ordered us to camouflage ourselves and push the truck up the hill. The convoy set off again in the bright moonlight across flat ground and rice fields. The French planes roared above us, but our trucks kept going!

Some infantrymen were so weary they lay down on the side of the track to sleep. We kept moving on through the night. Then one of the trucks got stuck on a muddy track. We placed chocks under the wheels to prevent the truck from sliding back any further and chopped wood by the side of the road to make planks. The truck moved back and forth over the planks as we pushed. By the time we got it up the hill, it was morning! We arrived at our campsite a few hours later.

We have been up for two nights with hardly any sleep. The soldiers are worn out. Morale is holding up. Today's activities included digging and building shelters for the cannons, carrying the ammunition from the trucks to the shelters and hiding the trucks. We had some rice and the men settled down to get some sleep. Suddenly, a new order came through! An order to leave the campsite immediately to dig trenches for five days. Completely without rest, the men set off again. This time, I stayed behind with the battery leader and artilleryman number 1 to look after the cannons.

Later:

Meeting to review the situation. The building of the trench network is proceeding on schedule. There are some problems with morale. Some men are showing signs of anxiety and are becoming impatient. Section 2 of the heavy artillery regiment is concerned that some of the 105mm are too close to the road (where they can be easily spotted by the enemy). Officers reassured section 2 and confirmed that the 12.7mm machine guns will be positioned on the hilltops to cover the 105mm cannons.

Mention was made during the meeting that comrade Xuan has been showing signs of weakness ever since the singers' performance. He misses his family, he is distracted and has lost interest in everything. I am not surprised. He is a student and from a bourgeois family, unlike most of the others who are from poor rural families. It must be hard for him, coming from a protected background, to adjust to these terrible conditions in these difficult times. His mood swings have probably been triggered by the beautiful young singers: source of intense pleasure and suffering all at the same time.

March 23, 1954

Early this morning, Tuy and Ty (the driver and his assistant) arrived at our campsite after having driven all night along winding and dangerous roads. They were delivering munitions for our guns. It was so dark, everything had an air of unreality, almost as if they were dreaming. Tuy was so afraid that he might drive over the edge of the precipice that he scraped the entire side of the truck against the rock face. He was more concerned for the truck than for his own life!

I feel anxious for my friend Ngo. He remains in critical condition after the operation he had to treat the mutiple wounds to his arms, head and chest. His spirit is incredible, though. He refused all anaesthetic during the operation and was joking with the surgeons.

"Don't tell me you've removed one of my ribs, I don't believe you!" he said.

March 24, 1954
Waiting for orders. The General issued a new directive:

The harder we work today, the less blood will be spilt tomorrow.

Prepare the battlefield to besiege and attack the enemy!

We should not expect a quick victory, we must be patient and our main motto remains: Steady attack, steady advance.[106]

We are being encouraged not to overestimate the French or, on the contrary, to be overconfident – during the battle of Him Lam, for example, soldiers jumped up on top of the trenches to cheer whenever a plane was shot down or whenever our targets burst into flames.

Our long-term objectives are the success of the agrarian reform[107] and a victory at Dien Bien Phu in order to influence a favourable outcome at the Geneva Conference[108]. Our battalion is preparing for the second phase of the campaign: to advance to encircle the French camp in the central zone. We are ready to fight to avenge the deaths of our comrades!

March 27, 1954
Early evening, the order came from the C804 commander to move camp to our new fighting position. "Two batteries have already left! Hurry up, the rest of you!" he shouted. We drove through a landscape on fire. The enemy had been pouring napalm on the jungle throughout the afternoon. At dusk, the hill was still burning. A heavy fog rolled in; the sky was sombre. Fire bombs exploded in mid-air, surveillance planes circled above us. Their planes roared, so did our trucks. How dare they try to intimidate us? We came to a bridge that had sustained bomb damage. Army engineers had finished repairing it. "Come on the 105mms, get those bastards!" they cheered as we crossed the bridge.

As the trucks advanced slowly pulling their two-ton load, Te, one of the artillerymen, and a nice fellow, who was following on foot reached for the end of the cannon and wrapped his arms tenderly around it as if embracing it, swinging around the sharp bends and U-turns. Suddenly, the trucks came to an abrupt halt by the large river that flows into Dien Bien Phu. The hill crests were ablaze with fires. I could hear machine-gun fire in the distance.

Caring for a wounded soldier, Dien Bien Phu 1954, ink on paper, 10.5cm x 16cm.

Then, there was a sudden burst of heavy artillery fire. The French guns were shelling in our direction! Suddenly everything was quiet again. I don't think they had detected us. They were carrying out routine firing on this stretch of road.

Tonight, we reached our new command post. We are positioned on a mountain slope opposite the French stronghold on hill D.

March 28, 1954

A quiet day. At the command post of C804. Our new position is about a mile and a half from the French position on hill D and two and a half miles from Muong Thanh. We transferred munitions (made in China) from the trucks to the undergrounds. There were so few incidents today that it felt like a holiday. At times like this when little is happening, you have to watch that you don't become too complacent. Having delivered us safely, Ty and Sang, our drivers, took their leave. We all shook hands and said our goodbyes.

"We are off to camouflage the trucks! Good luck to you! Take good aim and make sure you hit those targets!" said Ty.

"Thanks. You are the legs of the infantry, so keep yourselves ready for us!" replied Thanh, artilleryman number 8.

I was asleep when Quy's voice woke me with a start.

"Wake up! A truck hauling cannon number 4 is stuck down by the river, we have to go and help!"

Then, during the night, the enemy attacked with mortar fire and the shells fell dangerously close to our fortifications. When I woke up this morning at dawn, the hills all around us had been scorched bare by napalm attacks. The deputy commander showed us a special type of camouflage that will blend in with the desolate terrain. Handkerchiefs were then distributed to the soldiers. They are gifts from hamlets behind the lines to remind the young soldiers that the people back home remember them and are waiting for them to come back. The women have embroidered the cloth in bright colours with messages such as, "I am from the hamlet of Chi Luong. This is a present for a soldier at the front. Come back soon."

Later, a letter from the General arrives:

"Advance, destroy and attack as effectively as the wind. When one soldier falls, let the one behind take his place. Each worker and Party member should follow this rule and each one of you should be an example to others. Do not expect it to be easy. Do not fear hardships or difficulties. Do not fear injury or death and you will strike fear into the heart of your enemy. Be determined to conquer the enemy and to plant the flag of victory on the enemy posts in honour of Uncle Ho!"

March 29, 1954

At the command post of C804, on the eve of the second general offensive. A smell of sulphur and wet earth, powerful yet fragrant. I keep banging my head on the ceiling of the shelter: earth trickles down my neck, mud sticks to my hair. Last night, soldiers delivered more munitions, slept for a few hours and left again at dawn. The watchtower had predicted thunderstorms for today, which is keeping the enemy planes away. We took advantage of the rain to prepare our target range. We chopped down some big trees and dug some holes for latrines and for bathing.

Through the artillery lens, Tuat could watch enemy movements on hill D and in Muong Thanh. He described how French soldiers ran for cover when our artillery started shelling. They had been digging new tunnels when the shelling started. Engulfed in huge clouds of dust, they scattered all around to dive into the nearest trench, like crabs looking for holes to burrow into.

On the horizon, I can distinguish the outline of the mountain chain that borders Laos. The Nam Ron[109] flows through the plain, peacefully unaware of the conflict. A fog is descending over the valley, like a white shroud over the enemy camp and the villages nearby. Tomorrow the weather is supposed to be beautiful and we should have a clear view. Take heart, artillerymen, our infantrymen are digging tunnels so close to the French positions they link up with enemy trenches! They can hear the French running above their heads: the enemy must wonder whether they are living on top of a void! One of our units has cut across the road running between Muong Thanh and Hong Cum[110]. Another unit has dug tunnels that reach right to the back of the airstrip! There are reports that the enemy is running out of wood and has to rely on parachute drops or re-use wood from collapsed fortresses.

Our artillery has prepared a novel strategy for the second offensive. Comrade Nam Thang has trained newly-formed artillery units to attack the enemy, commandeer their posts and then deploy their cannons from that position. (As the second general offensive approaches,) Uncle Ho and Truong Chinh[111] are waiting for news from our regiment 45. We are determined to plant Uncle Ho's flag on top of hill D[112]!

Facsimile of diary pages dated 31/3 and 1/4, 1954.

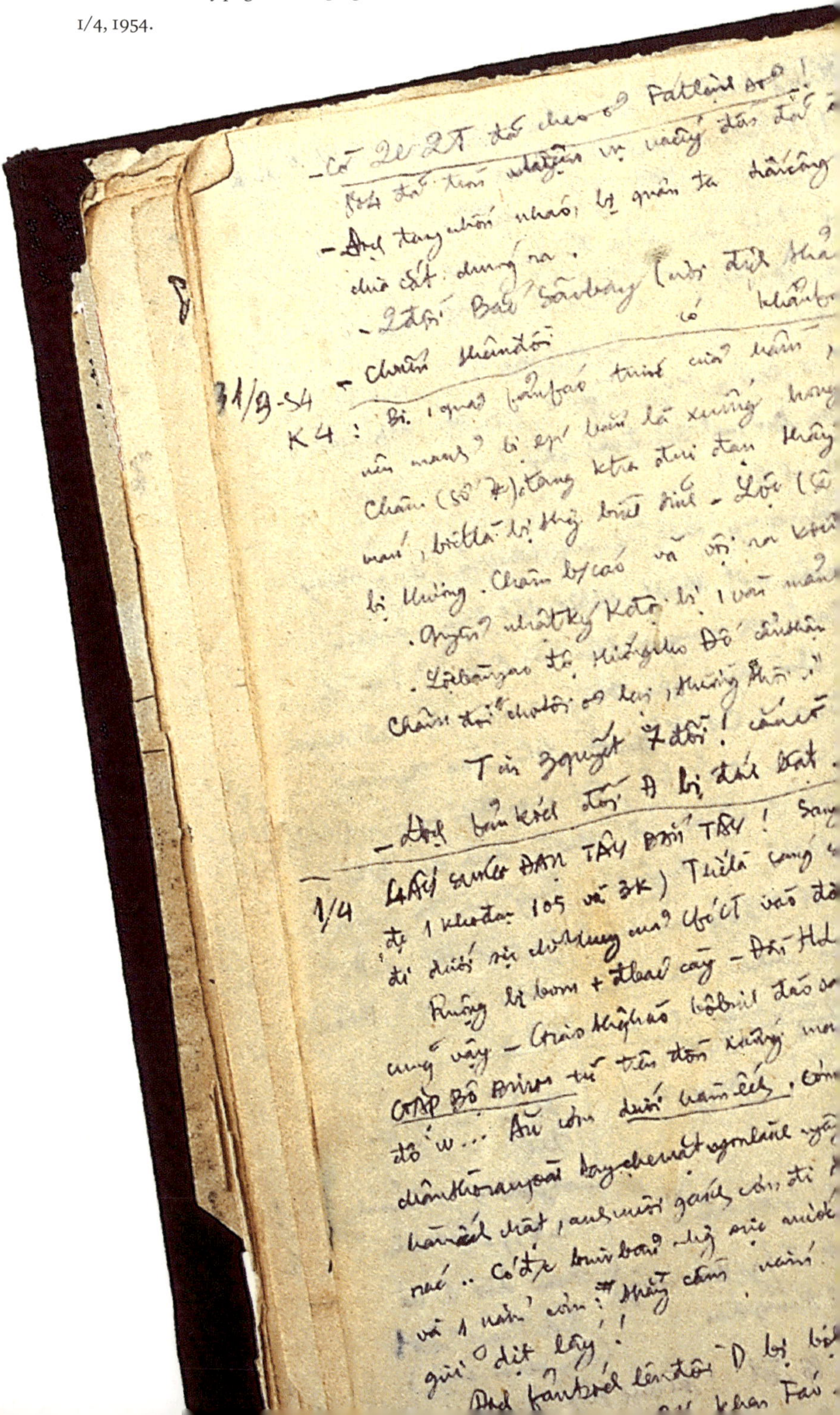

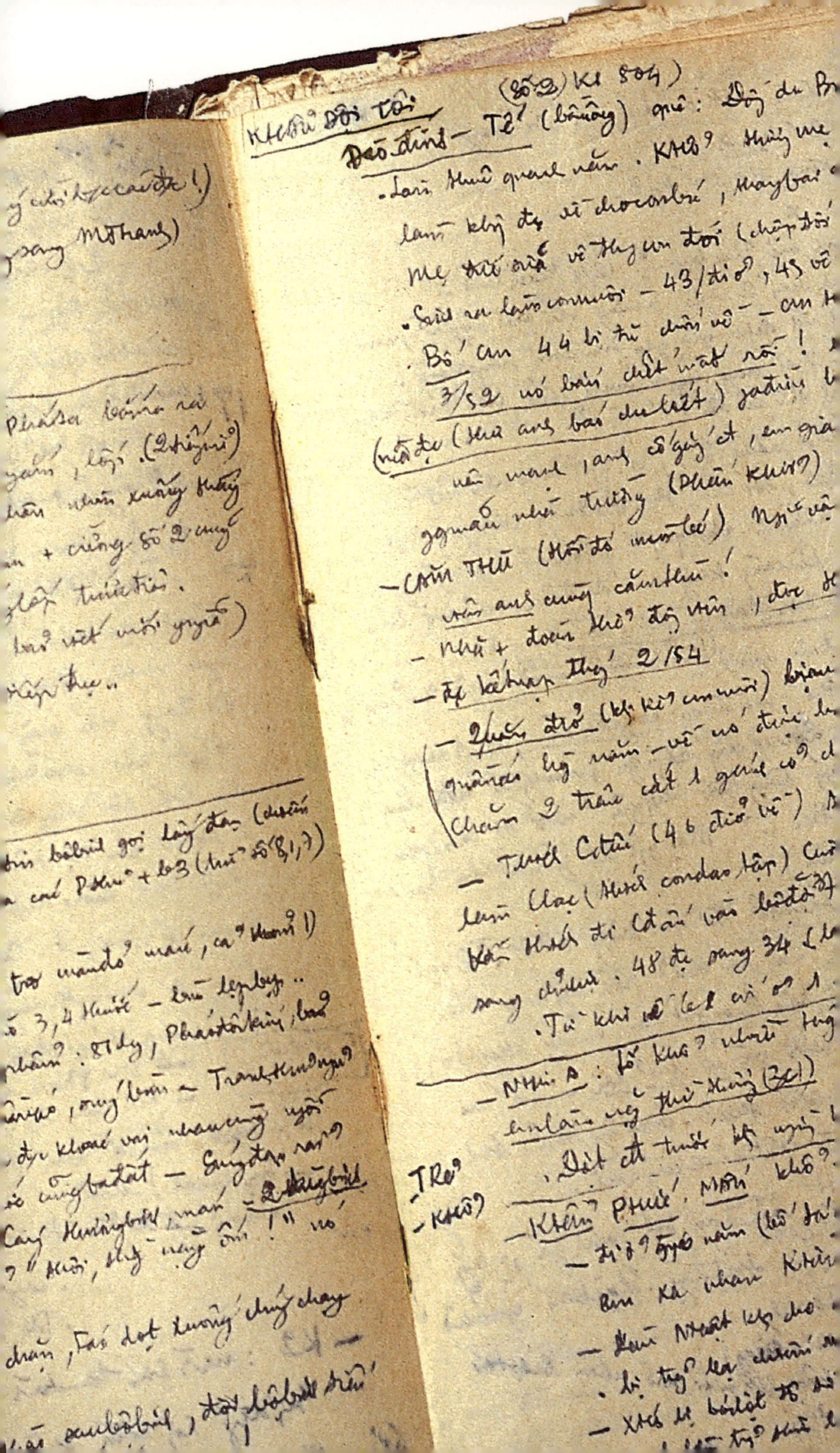

The second general offensive starts at 5pm on March 30, a short but violent burst of fire. Tam is with the artillerymen from C804 on a mountain slope facing the French defences on hills D and E. Simultaneous attacks are launched against the French strongholds on hills A and C.

March 30, 1954

At the command post of Company 804. Today, we had orders to open fire at 1pm. A couple of engineers arrived to chop down a huge tree that was still blocking our firing range. The massive trunk was the size of six people embracing each other and far too large for us to take down yesterday! Artillerymen from an anti-aircraft gun unit wearing iron helmets passed by and complimented the engineers with "these nice men wearing green uniforms who so patiently and so skillfully chop down trees!" A few minutes before we were supposed to open fire, the tree came crashing down and everyone cheered. Then the rain started. Shortly afterwards, a counter-order arrived to hold our fire. The engineers took refuge in our shelter.

"Can we stay and watch you fire the cannons?" they asked.

"With pleasure. Thanks to your help, we are sure to win Uncle Ho's flag and at least a few medals!" answered the head artilleryman in his booming voice.

We waited several hours for the rain to stop. At 5pm, the order came to fire seven rounds. Thundering blasts against the enemy followed. Muong Thanh was on fire!

"Fight to avenge the deaths of Ty, Loc and Giao!" shouted Comrade Te.

Then came the order to open fire on hill D.

"Turn right 3, rear sight 235, two shots, fire!"

"Battery 1 hits the top of hill D! The blockhouse is demolished! Bravo!"

Two Thai battalions on position 201 were wiped out. The enemy started to surrender.

"A shell is blocking the tube! Unblock it immediately!" someone shouted.

Quite suddenly, once the blockhouse was hit, the attack was over. "C804 has succeeded in its mission to destroy the posts as ordered!" Quy shouted. "Enemy soldiers are scrambling down the hill and making a run for the steel bridge across the Nam Ron (to get back to central camp). Our snipers have isolated them into small groups." Satisfied that he had accomplished his mission, Quy hung the victory flag up on the trench wall.

March 31, 1954

At the command post of C804. Battery 4 suffered heavy casualties during the attack against hill D yesterday. An enemy shell exploded at the opening of the shelter at the same time as the cannon opened fire. The twin blasts were so powerful that fragments of shell blew deep into their underground chamber. The wheels and range finder of the cannon were damaged. Three artillerymen were wounded. Cham, number 7, was checking the ammunition to see if it was damaged, when he saw blood. He was in shock and did not realise that it was his own blood. Although his leg was badly hurt, Cham stayed in position. Loc, the number 8, and Cuong, the number 2, the other two who were wounded, were evacuated. As for the log book, it had been torn by shell fragments. Tuan suggested they should keep using it, since it "now had even more meaning!"

We have just received some good news: Uncle Ho's flag is flying on seven hills! This morning, the French led a counter-attack against hill D. They held the position until the evening when they were forced to retreat!

April 1, 1954

Early this morning we received orders from the deputy political commissar to bring munitions back from hill D. During their assault, the infantry had seized an ammunition depot and three 105mm cannons. I accompanied the artillerymen from battery 4 (except for artillerymen numbers 2, 7 and 8). The rice fields were ploughed under with bomb craters and littered with shells. As I passed by Him Lam hill, it was bare and sombre. Arrived on hill D; it was scarlet with blood. The trenches our infantry had dug brought us to within ten feet of the barbed-wire fences. We were sinking into the mud. Infantrymen were coming down hill D, loaded with munitions, guns, 81mm mortars and maps. I stopped at the vaulted entrance to a trench to have something to eat with the soldiers there: rice balls wrapped in banana leaves. Their clothes and guns were covered in mud. They were so weary they fell asleep as soon as they finished eating, wherever they happened to be, their heads in their hands and their black toes sticking out of the rubber-soled sandals that they didn't have the strength to take off. Two of them slept shoulder to shoulder, right there, at the entrance to the trench.

A cook, nice face, about 30 years old, had made his way here from behind the lines to bring hot water and cooked rice to his officers and men.

The water arrived full of grit and dirt in spite of his efforts, but the men were so thirsty they drank every drop of it, every drop that had been sweated over by the cooks who do their best to supply the trenches. No wonder they are given the nickname "adopted brothers". Guns and munitions from the depot are brand new. Some of the young soldiers stank of perfume they had found in the French parachutes! We loaded the wounded onto stretchers. There was blood everywhere you looked. One of the prisoners gobbled down a whole rice ball without giving any to his compatriot: he claimed that the other prisoner was too sick to eat.

Young soldiers coming down the hill congratulated us. "Are you with the artillery?" they asked. "Good work! We don't know what we would have done without you!" They were carrying grenades, munitions, guns and K50 machine guns. Others carried 105mm shells. "Here you go," they said and transferred the shells from their shoulders to those of the artillerymen, who formed a human chain all the way down to the trench. "Keep hitting your targets!" they added. "And send some shells onto Navarre's head while you're at it so we can storm Muong Thanh!" Then they climbed back up the hill to fetch more supplies from the depot. Later on, we came across some infantrymen cleaning machine guns who were overjoyed to see us. "These brand-new machine guns are for you," they said. "Your battery really defended us during the enemy's counter-attack. Leave your old machine guns here; they must still be spent from the last attack!" It was getting dark and we made our way back through the trenches to our command post. The cannons fired once more and then were quiet.

Ah, here comes Bich, the cook! Bich dished out some sticky rice, still hot, filled with beans.

"This is your reward for having repaired the cannon in time to open fire!" he said.

When the enemy led their counter-attack against hill D yesterday, they seemed bitter and vengeful. Three infantry divisions, 312, 308 and 316 sent their congratulations to C804 for their defence of hill D. We control two of the four zones in Muong Thanh and we are preparing to attack the third!

Soldiers carrying ammunition through the trenches on hill D, graphite sketch on paper, 25cm x 20cm.

In the trenches

April 2, 1954

A quiet night at C804's command post. The French parachuted five hundred 105mm shells into the hands of Big Brother (infantry division 308)! They are being kept in a depot as reserves. They were dropped at the right time; all our batteries are short of ammunition.

At today's meeting, the officers gave their progress report.

During the last three days of combat, our objectives were to occupy strategic enemy positions; to intimidate the enemy with surprise attacks; to repel counter-attacks and to neutralise enemy artillery.

We have had some good results, but it is not enough. Hill A1[113] remains in enemy hands. The position is even tougher to overrun than hill D and is extremely well fortified with secret tunnels and underground chambers. Our artillery has to be more ferocious and our officers more aggressive. We need to keep up troop morale, by organising chess, card games and other distractions.

We need to economise on ammunition. K, the deputy commander, admitted that he wasted ten shells! He will have to write a report that will remain in his file. Xich confessed he did not double check the target range. He was distracted and negligent and made a mistake in the readings.

April 3, 1954

A quiet night at C804's command post. Taking to heart to economise on munitions, The and Phuc are banging old shells back into shape. Dang tried fitting one of the shells into the cannon, it worked. Thang, the company deputy commander, told him to make a note in his report of how many shells were fixed.

As for Tao, he has been composing poems. As I write, close by, artilleryman number 8 is admiring the blue and green reflections of the French flares on the polished steel surface of the cannon, like a fanciful dance of fireflies.

April 5, 1954

Another quiet day at C804's command post. I talked to artilleryman Phieu who survived the assault against hill D. "We controlled one side of hill D, the French controlled the other side," he said. "Their soldiers didn't dare leave their trenches to go to the bathroom. They crapped in cans they then threw over the trench walls. When we fired, the shit splattered all over the corpses. Between us and the French was an ammunition depot and parachuted supplies. The French were afraid to move up the hill from their position because of the minefield. We were ordered to storm the depot. We climbed up the eastern face of the hill. During our ascent, several men were blown up by mines and killed, including the deputy commanders of the company. Cong, lost a leg. When we arrived at the top of hill D, we seized the depot which contained 105mm shells. Meanwhile, an enemy company was leading the assault up the western flank of the hill. They were backed up by tanks[114]. Armed with our bayonets, we ran through the trenches to cut off their ascent. At the same time, our artillery was shelling their rear and their front. Then, one of the French tanks burst into flames, hit by a shell from one of our 82mm Russian cannons[115]. After several waves of attack and under heavy fire from our guns, the enemy soldiers started withdrawing to Muong Thanh. Some Thais (belonging to a Vietnamese battalion fighting for the French) then ran towards us, their faces caked with mud, shouting that they wanted to give themselves up. They were hit in the back by friendly fire.

The following night, we occupied hill 105 just north of the airstrip. Our artillery destroyed nine tanks. The French artillery counter-attacked the following day. Their fighter bombers dropped their loads all day and all night long. The exploding bombs sounded like howling dogs !"

After talking to Phieu, I went up to the watchtower at Long Bua[116] . The tower was built in four nights, in time for the attack on hill D (March 30). "The night before the attack, nobody slept a wink. We were anxious that we wouldn't be ready in time," one of the watchmen said. "The next morning, we felled some trees: With only a mile between us, we could see the French and they could see us. When it started to rain, the order to open fire was pushed back. We ate some cooked rice at a kitchen three miles away and then fetched some fresh water half a mile away. We filled the three canteens we had between us. It was enough to hold out for two days, even if the hot wind blowing from Laos followed the rain. We carried the water back through the trenches. They were crammed full of soldiers standing in the pouring rain, bare headed, feet in the mud, soaked to the bone. They had used every scrap of nylon they owned to cover their guns.

Back at the watchtower, the order to open fire came. According to a radio message we intercepted during the attack, the French sounded surprised that our infantry kept advancing through the trenches in spite of such heavy fire! Throughout the battle, we stayed in the watchtower with enemy artillery shelling us from four different directions. When we finally heard that our troops had won hill D, we cheered with joy!" As I prepared to head back down the mountain, the watchman said: "Send us newspapers and books, that's what we miss most up here!"

Notes from my conversation with Duc who took part in the assault against the French post on hill C1[117]: "Our artillery was pounding Muong Thanh. Everything was burning. We fought all morning. We were completely outnumbered. We were fighting with one squadron against an entire enemy company! When the enemy retreated, they jumped into vehicles that sped away so fast, they left behind supplies that had been parachuted in! I was surprised since they are running out of everything. As we advanced, the French forced our blood brothers to fill in the trenches they had just dug."

April 6, 1954

At C804's command post. Today marks the end of the second phase of the battle. According to our estimates, 2,000 enemy soldiers and officers have been killed and 3,000 wounded. Officers are in short supply. The wounded are left lying in trenches and, from what we can observe from our positions, bandages for dressing wounds are being changed only every five days.

Food rations per day are down to a loaf of bread and one can of food for 6 soldiers; one packet of biscuits per legionnaire; a ration of salted fish, no alcohol for each Moroccan; and one bowl of rice soup per Vietnamese.

Other supplies are becoming very scarce. They are running out of wood and are re-utilising beams from bombed out shelters to build their new fortifications; two of their oil depots, several munitions and arms depots and four cannons have been demolished during the second phase of the battle.

On our side: We control strategic positions. We have tightened the siege around the French camp and neutralised their planes. We have fought on all fronts to prepare conditions for the general attack.

Keeping in mind that enemy morale is low, we need to fight any pessimistic attitudes and negative thoughts within our own ranks. We need to be well prepared, patient, and willing to endure and persevere.

Artillerymen manning an anti-aircraft cannon,
Dien Bien Phu, 1954, ink sketch on paper, 15cm x 20cm.

Sometime over the next few days, Tam leaves the C804 command post and, through the trenches, walks the two to three miles to Doc Lap hill. He arrives at the command post of an anti-aircraft gun unit. Meanwhile, French resistance is strengthening. In a counter-attack on April 11, the French win back hill C1, one of their key defence posts.

April 12, 1954

At the command post of Company 828 with the anti-aircraft guns, on a mountainslope near Doc Lap hill (occupied since March 15). During the day, C828 shot down a B26. It was the 50th plane shot down at Dien Bien Phu! Yesterday, the General had encouraged the anti-aircraft units to compete against each other. The blackened fuselage of the aircraft was in one piece. The bodies of the four pilots were burnt beyond recognition. We retrieved from the wreckage six heavy machine guns, some helmets, uniforms and rifles. A lone wallet and its contents had survived the engulfing fire. In the wallet, I found a photograph of one of the pilots. In the photograph, taken in France, the pilot was standing next to two women, I imagine they were his

wife and his mother. There was also his identity card and some local currency. The artillerymen have been in this position since the end of March. When they arrived, the mountain was bare. There was not one single tree and the surface was covered in bomb craters. The earth was red in places and chalky white in others. The villagers had fled, abandoning the rice fields, which were dry and yellow. The anti-aircraft unit built gun nests and shelters to blend in with the bombed terrain of the hill and used dried rice stems as camouflage. They even covered their steel helmets with soil so they wouldn't reflect the sun. Both the men and officers are exceptionally young. From poor peasant families, they are used to toiling the soil and they have the ruddy complexion and rosy cheeks that come from outdoor living. Many are from Hai Duong[118] and volunteered to join up. They imagined themselves sitting high up on the gun platforms and reading newspapers while they waited for the planes to fly past! When they saw how big the guns were, they were afraid!

"After military training," one of them said, "we thought it would be easier to hit a plane that was flying horizontally than one that was in a nose dive. After the first few attacks, we changed tactics. We wait for the plane to nose dive and when it is right in front of the cannon, we open fire: it is a real test of nerves between the enemy pilot and us. When the 50th plane was spotted, we were sitting on the gun platform; we had just finished firing a round of artillery and we were re-adjusting the direction and length of our aim, when the alarm was raised.

'Plane alert!' someone shouted.

The planes roared out of the sky: direction 12-speed 190. We took aim at the one in the middle as it was gunning for us. We aimed. Then, at the signal, we opened fire! When the siren started wailing,we knew we had shot it down!"

Later:
Early evening. The Dakotas dropped a dozen or so parachutes that landed on our side of the battlefield. In the fading light, I could make out from the odd shape that weapons and ammunition boxes were hanging from the parachutes. When the guns crash-landed, they left huge craters in the red soil, like a trail of blood stains that stretched down the mountainside to the fields in the valley below.

April 13, 1954

At Ban Tau village[119] after a bombing raid. There are bomb craters everywhere. Houses on stilts are in ruins; thatched roofs have been torn off; beams burnt. A mortar for grinding rice bakes in the blistering sun. Broken pots, scorched mango trees, a delicate bracelet on the fleshless wrist of a very young girl. The remains of what were jack-fruit trees, orange trees, peach trees, lettuces and sweet potatoes are the only evidence that there ever was a village here. On the ground lie scraps of dirty clothing, shreds of an indigo jacket, the remains of a quilt and, close by, a fragment from an American napalm bomb.

April 14, 1954

Back at the command post of Company 828, near Doc Lap hill. Today, Loc, one of the battery commanders, suggested to the men that they write letters to their families[120] to let them know they have shot down another plane. Before closing the envelope, one of the soldiers gave me the letter he wrote to his wife to read.

"Letter from Gien on the battlefield to his beloved Cam,

Dear Cam, I haven't written to you since I left home. I am writing to give you and our son, Thien, some news. I am so happy to know that you are both in good health. I am at the battle of Dien Bien Phu. I have learnt how to operate the anti-aircraft guns against enemy planes. Perhaps you have already heard the good news from the battlefield. Have you heard about our unit's success? Please look after Thien for me. I will tell you more when we see each other again. I must leave you now as I am writing on the battlefield. Look after yourself, my beloved.

Give my love to my mother and the neighbours."

Loc read his letter out loud as he wrote it, half in verse, half in prose.

Nhu was under the gun platform, all that could be seen of him was his behind.

Following pages: During a pause in the fighting, soldiers from an anti-aircraft battery play cards and write letters home.

Battery 4 playing cards, 16/4/1954 (*Khau doi 4, 16/4/1954, Tu-lo-khe),* ink on paper, 20cm x 18.5cm, collection of the Ho Chi Minh City Fine Arts Museum.

Dua was on one of the seats of the gun platform, with the letter writing paper resting on his thigh as he wrote. Others were perched next to the wheels. Duc's letter was humourous, so was Giang's. His started with: "My dear wife…" Another with: "To the mother of my children…" Tu, who is from Bac Gang, wrote a very touching letter, especially considering that he knows nothing of the Party programme to mobilise the masses.

"To my father and mother,

I want to thank the Party and Uncle Ho for having brought me up. I used to live in total poverty. Today I have food and clothing. Our family suffered because of the enemy. Now I am the one to make the enemy suffer on the battlefield. I will never stop, even when I am dead. Please do not worry about me. Think of yourselves, your fields and how to produce enough to feed the family."

I asked one comrade why he wasn't writing. "I don't want to talk about it," he answered. "My family lives in occupied territory, in Hai Duong. I wrote to them once but I didn't get a reply. I am afraid that something has happened to them." I encouraged him to write, since I knew it would make him feel better.

In the letters the soldiers receive from home, their families all ask the same questions: "How many French fighter bombers have been shot down at Dien Bien Phu?" and "When are the French going to stop bombing us?"

"Father and Mother," one soldier replied, wanting to reassure them. "The greatest honour for me is to fight at Dien Bien Phu. I stay calm and take aim when the planes attack, to protect the infantry. We are shooting down as many fighter bombers as possible so that none will be left to bomb hamlets and villages at the rear."

I am often asked by the soldiers I meet in the trenches to read their letters before sealing the envelopes. It is not because I have a "key to open people's souls," like the commissar in the Red Army in the Russian film I saw a few days before leaving for the campaign. They give me their letters to read, out of friendship and camaraderie. Here, on the battlefield, we all know we can die at any moment, killed by a shell or a bomb. This brings us close to one another, like one big family and nation, whether we are Meo, Thai or from any other ethnic minority. In every trench, gun nest or shelter I go to, I feel close to every soldier I encounter. Despite the fact that we have never met before, it is as if we have always known one another and we are ready to pour our hearts out to each other. From the letters the soldiers receive from their families and share with me, the people are anxiously waiting for our victory. Perhaps the entire democratic world is watching our historic struggle and counting on us to defeat the colonial aggressor.

Later:
At C828's meeting later in the day, we received words of encouragement from the General.

Let us consolidate and increase our successes.
Let us be determined to fight.
Let us create the necessary conditions to destroy all the enemy forces in Dien Bien Phu!

The officers gave a mixed assessment of the situation on the battlefield.

On the enemy side: Two fifths of enemy soldiers (5,000) have been wounded or killed; five tanks have been blown up and 50 aircraft have been shot down; a large number of cannons of different calibres have been destroyed; communication between Muong Thanh and Hong Cum has been partly severed; enemy morale and supplies are low – Navarre and de Castries[121] have been requesting to have the seriously wounded evacuated.

On our side : The Central Committee of the Party has made the right choices and our army is fighting with courage. Our infantry continues to advance steadily and to attack. The digging of trenches and tunnels is proceeding according to plan and the underground network is tightening around the enemy's toughest strongholds!

However, our preparations are not yet in place for the final attack. One reason is that a number of our officers and units have not completed their assigned tasks. The other reason is that the French remain strong even if their position has weakened. They still have 7,000 troops and a powerful artillery. Regular parachute drops are providing them with sufficient ammunition and food supplies. Some supplies are getting through to them by road from Hong Cum. Then there is the question of hill A1, which is still firmly under French control.

Our objectives are to continue building the network of trenches and tunnels, to re-occupy positions (lost in counter-attacks such as hill C1), to tighten our stranglehold on the valley plain and to cut all their supply routes (men, food, ammo and weapons, both by air and by road from Hong Cum).

To meet these objectives, our strategy is to attack and destroy the enemy as we move forward; to counter-attack any assault launched by their tanks and artillery; to control the air space above Dien Bien Phu day and night with our anti-aircraft guns; to seize all parachuted supplies; to occupy and destroy both airfields, one in Muong Thanh, the other in Hong Cum; to organise crack units of marksmen, mobile heavy artillery units and mobile artillery units for assault (headhunters); and finally to attack the strategic enemy stronghold number 1 (hill A1), destroy the enemy command position and resist all counter-attacks. The officers reported that, in order to improve the performance and morale of our troops, we have taken a number of measures which include mixing new recruits with seasoned and experienced fighters, improving the men's living conditions and rations, introducing preventative measures against disease, economising on munitions and maintaining discipline. Lastly, we are careful to analyse our experiences on the battlefield and draw lessons from them.

Our motto is: "One step forward after each battle!"

We must be determined to fight without anxiety about hardship and fatigue. If we respect these principles, we can proceed to the final attack!

The People's Army is preparing for the third phase of the battle. As he wrote in the April 14 entry of his diary, Tam is aware that, at this stage of the battle, some high-ranking officers doubted whether victory against the French was possible after all: the troops have been fighting the French for a month; they have suffered huge casualties and are physically and mentally exhausted. If Tam himself had any fears about the outcome of the battle, he does not share them with his diary. It is at this time, that he comes under a direct double attack from French artillery and fighter bombers.

April 15, 1954

At the command post of Company 827, near Doc Lap hill. Writing during the day shortly after a terrifying attack against us. We were digging our shelters and building the gun nests when we intercepted the voice of a French pilot over the radio. He was alerting the central command post in Muong Thanh: "The Viet Minh artillery is very close to Gabrielle (Doc Lap). Request that our artillery counter-attack." We dug even faster to camouflage the anti-aircraft guns. We were still shovelling when the enemy artillery shelling started. The French fired at us seven times. Dien, our captain, was wounded. He kept calm and encouraged the men to keep their nerve and get ready to fire back. The artillerymen adjusted the optical instruments and target aim. We were finally ready to open fire.

Then, a squadron of French planes headed straight for us. I counted 28 planes altogether – eight Hellcats, two B24s, eight B26s! The bombings started, intense and ferocious.

"Stay calm," shouted Luong (from the observation tower).

Hien and Chung, two new recruits, kept reloading the guns.

"Think of your families. Think of your friends who were killed. It's time to take revenge!" Loc yelled over the explosions.

Nhuan, the battery 1 commander was hit, no, he has been killed! The sky was a clear blue but the smell of sulphur from the cannons and the bombs was suffocating. The sun was in our eyes. We were blinded. The fighter bomber pilots took advantage of it and came at us from the direction of the sun. The gunners opened fire with their machine guns. We could only see

Entrance to a tunnel or shelter, 1954, graphite sketch on paper, 20cm x 24cm.

them when they were right above us. We were in real danger. We were losing our nerve. The fighter bombers came in for a second attack. Bombs, bullets, smoke, flames, earth and dust blew up into huge clouds that covered the whole battlefield. The range finder was covered in dirt; Nhien and Chung (numbers 3 and 5) couldn't see the cannon tubes pointing upwards towards the sky. One cannon stopped firing; two others were blocked. Numbers 6 and 7 jumped onto the platforms to clean them. Then the medium-sized cannons were blocked. Only one cannon was firing!

"Stay calm!"

" Nothing to be afraid of!" we kept reassuring each other.

"Let's get out of here," someone shouted.

"No. We're staying, our duty is to stay with the guns," answered Loc.

For five hours, from noon to 5pm, we fought with that one battery. The political instructor dug out the comrades buried under the explosions. Tran, who took over when Nhuan was killed, was suffocating from the smoke and pressure from the explosions. He kept on giving orders.

And then I heard sounds of cheers. A fighter bomber had been hit. It was a Hellcat! It turned back, black smoke escaping from its tail! After the Hellcat was hit, the bombers did not return. It was getting dark and the French planes must be headed back to Haiphong. All was suddenly quiet. I counted more than 300 bombs that had exploded around us! We were awarded two medals, one for Loc and one for the company. The captain was right to tell us not to leave the guns!

Later:

Throughout the campaign, our soldiers have shown incredible spirit. This is due to the training they receive. During their instruction, they are trained to compete to show bravery. They are also motivated to fight. They know that victory over the French will improve their lives and that of their families. During our long struggle, there have been so many examples of courage. Hoang Van Phuc's shoulders served as a bridge for lorries to pass over (on route 13 in 1953). Here in Dien Bien Phu, To Vinh Dien perished after throwing himself in front of a cannon, using his body as a wedge to prevent the gun from falling into a ravine! As I write, a lone French fighter bomber roars out of the sky. We fire, the plane is hit, wait, so is the bomb it unloaded, at exactly the same moment. The bomb has exploded in mid-air!

April 17, 1954
At the HQ of my division, F351. I was ordered to report back to headquarters. We are facing a serious new challenge: The rainy season is about to start and it is going to be increasingly difficult to get supplies to the front. We need 65 tons of rice a day to feed our troops! We are also short of men. The strongest and healthiest soldiers are being sent to supplement new units. Actors, singers, musicians and dancers have been drafted in to help build bridges and roads and carry the wounded.

The singers from infantry division 312 (Ben Tre) have composed a new song on the accordion that describes the situation on the battlefield: *The siege is tightening*. Our infantrymen have reportedly dug a trench across the enemy airfield. As they inched their way, crawling and digging, the enemy deployed every kind of firepower at their disposal. They shot at them with rockets and laid time-delayed detonating devices. Their fighter planes bombed them from the air. Our infantrymen were caught in violent explosions that shrieked all around them and engulfed them in black smoke. As they advanced across the airfield, they seized at least half of the parachuted supplies that litter the runway. If we win, it will be thanks to the young farmers in the infantry who, using only their pickaxes and shovels, have dug an entire network of tunnels under the barrages of barbed wire that surround the enemy positions. These tunnels have opened the way that will soon take us right to the heart of the enemy headquarters in the central zone of Muong Thanh.

Another report that was just in: We have seized control of hill 105, the French position defending the north of the airfield. The French counter-attack on the hill failed. We cut off the reinforcements that were coming from Muong Thanh!

Later:
I left HQ with Ly Thai Bao to walk down to the main road (route 41). Bao looked back towards our post, 2,000 feet above us. “Maybe the day will come soon,” he said, “when we won’t have to go up there anymore.” He’s right! One day soon the steep path that leads to the command post will vanish under thick undergrowth and remain only in our minds as a distant memory of the Northwest campaign. The road will be open, filled with people, bikes, trucks. All the villagers will return home. Water buffaloes will

Facsimile of diary pages dated 17/4, 1954, with a sketch of soldiers.

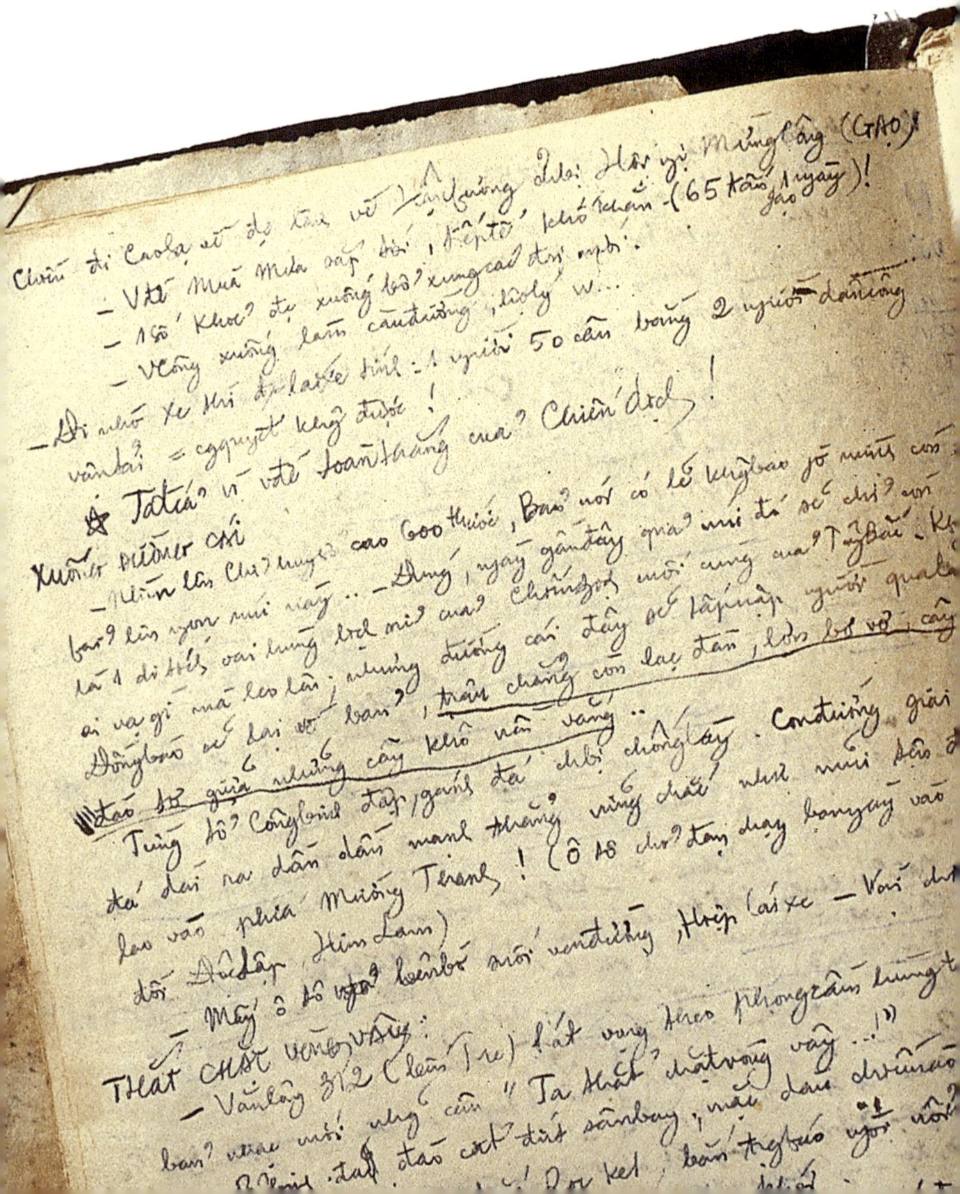

— Đến C2 Trung Tuyến — Đường số mới, — cây dâu chín ngọt

Gặp đơn vị mới thành lập lên tuyến.

[illegible] vẫn trong, hoa sim tím đỏ — ve sầu kêu. Càng xa hoa

[illegible] càng thấy chim hót nhiều! [illegible] đến Thượng Cam [illegible]

Hố bom vẫn đầy cả cánh đồng, nhiều hố đã thành [illegible] nước to

Đường qua đỉnh nhà Napalm ở đây mà hôm nay lại thấy vẫn

bay xa trong rồi lại [illegible] trong không khí..

— C2 Đội Đại: Mới đầu vào công binh mở đường tiến vào Him

Lam, tối bị napalm cháy xém cả, giờ đây có lá mọc xanh

lại các khu đồi mà C2 vẫn còn nuôi 2 toán 2 ([illegible]

(Gg xấu: [illegible] [illegible] + [illegible] quan [illegible] hạn chế CH [illegible])

— Gặp đ/c Dân công ở cùng với Cung cấp.

"Đi C2 mọi năm phải dọc gánh, năm nay được Mang gánh!"

— Hằng mấy [illegible] đi đến Nà Sản gặp bom [illegible] bị đa

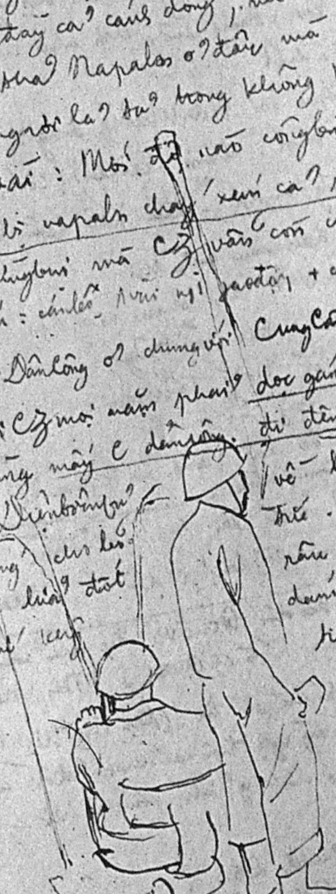

giải ở Điện Biên Phủ [illegible] bom đường [illegible] đất [illegible] kêu [illegible]

về [illegible] lại rất đông bắt nạt [illegible] có mấy anh [illegible] có [illegible] đau [illegible] rồi [illegible] dân công [illegible] là [illegible] là cơm! Bộ [illegible] dân công, [illegible] lại càng [illegible] dân công [illegible] chúng dấu mặt. [illegible] công [illegible] lại đến nói bộ đội [illegible] cũng bị ít. Cán bộ dân công [illegible] bộ [illegible] tập hợp thì [illegible] ấy người [illegible] cho bộ [illegible] [illegible] làm thơ

[illegible] lên [illegible] [illegible] cái anh [illegible] đi [illegible]

be reunited with their herds, pigs will no longer wander alone under fruitless peach trees in this desolate landscape.

Sappers and labourers are repairing the road, in preparation for the onset of the rainy season. The stones from the quarry half way up the mountain are being ferried to and fro in bamboo baskets. With most of the French planes flying over Muong Thanh, the trucks are able to circulate freely throughout the day. Several have stopped by the river. I soon realise why when I hear laughter from the river bank. Women who are helping to build the road are splashing water at each other, playing as they bathe and wash their hair.

I ran into "doctor Thu" at Long Chau. We were very happy to see each other again. We hadn't seen each other since we crossed the Red River together on our way to the campaign (on February 22). He seemed strange though. I know he believes singlemindedly in this battle and this campaign, but I don't think his heart is truly in it. Maybe it's because he spends his time behind the lines and hasn't been at the front, face to face with the enemy.

I picked some delicious strawberries that tasted very sweet. The *sim*[122] flowers are a deep red, almost purple. The cicadas are crying their endless lament. I am still far enough away from the battlefield to hear the birds singing. Now that the rains have started, the bomb craters have been transformed into peaceful ponds all across the fields. Last night, the enemy must have dropped napalm again. Black dust is left hanging in the air. I take heart in the fact that our hills do not stay bare for long. Him Lam, which was burnt by napalm only a month ago, when there wasn't a single blade of grass left, is thick with green foliage again. Nature has its way of reclaiming the barren hills, and restoring harmony to this land ravaged by war.

Today marks the end of the second phase of the campaign. I know that some of our officers are no longer confident of our victory, which is why we have still only had limited success[123].

To my great joy, I have been ordered to report back to the battlefield in the next few days!

Soldier aiming a bayonet, Dien Bien Phu 1954,
graphite sketch on paper, 20cm x 28cm.

April 18, 1954

Today, I was on route 41 when I met some workers who had hitched a ride from Na San (the former French military airbase) with a truck.

"We were used to trekking up and down steep and narrow paths, but this year, there are a lot of 'baskets' (trucks)!" one of them said.

While they were in Na San, some French prisoners were being held there. It seems that some of the workers insulted and maltreated the prisoners. The women pulled their ears, while the men burnt their beards and pulled their noses. The French soldiers didn't dare insult them back. One woman, who knew a few words of French, called them *chien* (dog) and *salaud* (bastard). The prisoners just hid their faces until one of our officers intervened.

"We ask our brothers to stop acting this way towards the prisoners!" he said.

He then ordered the perpetrators to raise their hands and do their self-criticism. At which point, all the workers raised their hands together, in support of the guilty parties!

"If that's the case, then each one of you will do your self-criticism, not only the guilty ones! What you did is against the rules!" said the officer.

"That's just the point. I didn't want to disobey the Party rules so I pulled the prisoner's hair. What I really wanted to do is to have all of the prisoners tied up and shot!" replied a feisty individual.

Not an edifying story. Prisoners should not be maltreated. Yet it seems that the people want revenge.

April 20, 1954

Another day at the rear. Walked down to route 41 where I met labourers from Muong Pu[124], a village in the district of Tuan Giao. The French had burnt their village. "We did not want to give ourselves up to the French," one of them said. "We knew that if we left our mountains we would die of hunger! So, when these French brought war to our village and burnt our rice fields, we fed ourselves with the rice from our land further afield that had been spared. Once we ran out of rice, we ate manioc from our small patches in the jungle, but it was not enough to survive on for long."

Labourers from Vinh Phuc went to Na Muong to teach our Thai brothers a faster technique to remove the husk from the rice. These kinds of activities increase the goodwill between our people.

April 27, 1954

At HQ. Today[125], Lan informed us that Mr Molotov[126] raised the question of conflict resolution in Korea and Vietnam in his speech at the Geneva Conference. Lan then reported on the situation on the battlefield.

My summary: We are starving the French of supplies. Two thirds of parachuted supplies are falling into our hands (including a large number of 60mm mortar munitions). We have seized French stocks of cereals and canned foods. Their wood supply is nil. By comparaison, our wood supply is plentiful although far away – three or four miles away on foot.

We are gradually tightening our siege through our network of tunnels and trenches. The central zone of Muong Thanh under French control has shrunk to a third of a square mile! Our new network of trenches and tunnels is dense. It covers hill D and reaches all the way down to the central zone of Muong Thanh (in the valley). The trenches and tunnels have kept casualties down, which is heartening for the soldiers and has given them confidence.

A few days ago, we occupied position 206 (on April 22; it was the first French post to be overrun, west of the airfield). One tank and two enemy companies were destroyed during a surprise attack. From position 206, our anti-aircraft guns control the airfield. Our scouts are doing some excellent reconnaissance work.

Our trenches are getting closer and closer to Hong Cum (the French defence position five miles to the south of Muong Thanh).

We will soon besiege the whole of Dien Bien Phu!

After spending a few days at HQ, Tam goes back to the front, through a bombed out lunar landscape. Suspecting the order for the final general attack is only days away, our young reporter moves in as close as possible to witness the battle first hand. Crawling through mud filled trenches, he reaches the command post of the mountain artillery situated on hill E within a few hundred yards of the French artillery.

The evening of May 1, which, in peacetime, is a day of celebration for both sides, the People's Army launches their third general offensive. The artillery attack lasts three hours, the longest and most ferocious of the battle. Tam's narrative becomes less consistent.

May 1, 1954

At the command post of Company 755, on hill E[127], a few hundred yards across from the enemy airfield and artillery. Comrade Hoang Cao came by to wish us luck.

"Remember, comrades, that today is May 1st! I hope you will have new exploits to celebrate," he said.

At 7pm, I was still playing cards. At 7.22pm, we received the order to open fire. The first shell fired by one of our units hit an enemy position.A plume of black smoke gave away their position and all our batteries fired on the same target. Our officers are on edge, the orders have become extremely exact. The operation was co-ordinated and timed down to the last minute. During the firing, Mung, artilleryman number 2, who is from a transport unit and does not know how to fire a cannon, remained calm, paying close attention. During the course of the attack, we transported an 82mm Russian mortar to the observation post. We then moved munitions to the foot of Him Lam hill (half a mile away), wading through a swamp infested with leeches.

Back at the command post, enemy fire tore across the dark sky, like red hot coals, throughout the night. A dense fog rolled in. It started to rain and thunder rumbled on the horizon. It is becoming increasingly difficult for the enemy transport planes to make their parachute drops, even under cover of night. They are under constant fire from our anti-aircraft guns.

The other morning, I went to explore behind hill E. I discovered a small stream that flows into the Nam Ron, by the iron bridge. It is a place of tranquillity amongst the carnage and remains untouched by enemy fire. Willow trees sweep the surface of the water. Some of the exhausted men

Soldiers by the stream behind hill E, 1954, watercolour on paper, 39cm x 35cm.

were resting under the trees. They come here after the long arduous hours of fighting and digging. They have a swim and wash away the mud and the dirt. They have some rice, share a loaf of bread found in a French parachute, and divide up the parachutes to use as protection against the rain. Then they sleep. In the evening, after their meetings, the infantrymen set off for the night battle in the central zone.

The mountain artillery men have been on hill E for a month. So close to the French and with a wide field of view, they are firing directly at each other. Sometimes the French open fire first, sometimes we do. When the French tanks attack, we shoot first. The artillerymen have reinforced the defences against the French 155mm cannons[128].

Being so close to the enemy position, the men are under a terrible strain. The shelters are constantly being demolished. And yet, when they rebuild them, the shelters are well kept. They bother to cover the mud walls with white parachute cloth and enemy flares to brighten them up!

Tonight, we haven't had time to rebuild our shelters. I am sleeping outside, head on the ground, lying in the fog, listening to the sound of the guns. Enemy fire has been relentless. They know we are building new defences so they deliberately aim to demolish them. So far, we have all crawled out alive through the small holes, smiling and swearing, determined to keep rebuilding!

Sometime between May 2 and May 5 (the diary is not clear), under the cover of darkness, Tam makes his way down the eastern face of hill E, through barbed wire, unexploded mines and bomb craters. Out of view of the enemy, he crosses route 41, and crawls along the narrow mud-filled trenches to the C753 command post on hill D. Writing under extreme duress, Tam reports in his diary how the battle fatigued soldiers fight on. The French stronghold on hill C has fallen. The formidable French A1 position holds fast.

May 5, 1954

At the command post of Company 753, on hill D. The men and their guns are 900 yards from the enemy. Casualties are extremely high. Even more men are being killed building defences than they are during the attacks. Comrades Lien, Dac, Chuc and so many others have died. Many more have been wounded. Dac, an artilleryman, stepped on a mine and both of his legs were blown off. ("I have been assigned to this mission by the Party. Please help me finish it!"he said, after he was wounded.) The men promised they would fight for him. They were so fired up that, during the next attack, they destroyed three enemy fortifications, three 120mm mortars and one machine-gun post.

"Despite the fact that I have been here with this company for a month and have been evaluating the soldiers' moral strength (bad, good, average) on a daily basis, I feel that it is only now that I really understand them," Huyen the political instructor commented. "It is in ferocious times like these, that you get to know what you and your men are made off."

A few days ago, we recaptured hill C. "We received orders to wipe out the enemy artillery so the foot soldiers could launch their attack," said Quy. "For three or four days we shelled enemy positions non-stop, firing 3, 4 up to 26 shells, one after the other (our targets were numbers 3,4,7 and 8, along with the flagpole). At one point, our two guns fired 56 times in four hours.

The next day, the enemy anticipated the time of our attack and counter-attacked. Part of the wall of the gun pit collapsed. One of the shells that exploded released a toxic gas. We rushed down the hill to escape the gas and wait for it to clear. Luckily no-one was hurt. Six hours later, that evening, we received orders to go back to our position at the top of the hill to repair the damaged fortifications. We had orders to fire early the next morning to cover the infantry assault.

Huyen, the political instructor, went up first to check whether the gas had cleared. The wind had changed direction and was blowing in the direction of the enemy. Huyen thought it was safe for the rest of us to come up. We improvised gas masks and covered our faces before we climbed back up to the gun pit. We repaired the fortifications in time for the attack the next morning. The following morning, we received orders from the infantry to fire for 15 whole minutes and to destroy three enemy blockhouses. We hit our targets after eight shots. The enemy returned fire. Our communication lines were cut. De and Don jumped out of the pit to find the wires and reconnect them.

Then, at 7.20am, the political commissar received an order over the radio. The order came from the General himself. The voice over the transmitter said: 'The General orders the destruction of the command post on hill C.'

We were all extremely anxious, our hearts were racing. We checked our guns, they were blocked. Thang jumped out of the pit to unblock them. Two minutes later, at 7.22am, we received the order to fire. We fired four times. Then the infantry made the assault on the command post. Fierce hand-to-hand combat followed. Some enemy soldiers were killed, others taken prisoner. Frankly, I was surprised that we won. I didn't think that the men from infantry regiment 176 were up to it!"

Early evening. Huyen gave the men some advice to boost morale. "Encourage the others on the battlefield and you will give yourself courage," he said. "We learned this from the battle of Tu Vu[129]. During that battle, the situation was extremely dangerous. The artillerymen advanced on the battlefield, four by four, carrying the 75mm disassembled cannons, under a deluge of enemy bombardments. In this inferno,the three-men infantry (*tam tam che*[130]) kept shouting words of encouragement: 'How are you doing? Are you all right? What? Louder...keep moving!' The artillerymen couldn't shout, their load was too heavy. Our mountain comrades didn't say much anyway. The infantrymen were yelling over the uproar of the battlefield in order to be heard (this would not be considered polite behaviour under normal circumstances). Hearing a fellow combatant's voice can prevent a soldier from losing his nerve when a small voice inside him is asking: 'Am I going to be hit and wounded this time? Is this my time to die?' Perhaps, it is only by shouting that one can control one's own fear of death and help others control theirs, too."

Later:
At 9pm, three 105mm shells exploded. Thoi and the cannon were buried by the explosions. We dug Thoi out but had to abandon gun and shelter. Hoang's ears were damaged by the explosion. We built a new shelter. An hour later, we were shelled again. Beams, everything collapsed.

It is now 4am, and we are rebuilding yet another shelter, the third one tonight!

Sometime after 4am on May 6, Tam walked through the trenches from hill D back to hill E. During an eerily quiet pause in the fighting, Tam shares a few moments with the artilleryman, Phung Van Khau.

May 6, 1954

At C755's command on hill E. Met Phung Van Khau, who is only 25 years old and has been in every campaign since 1950. He is a soldier of exceptional courage and character. A month ago, when we were fighting for the French post on hill E, Khau was the first up the hill with a small team of men. Under heavy enemy fire, they dug the gun shelter and hauled the 75mm mountain gun up the hill. Khau:

"The French artillery had spotted us and were firing directly at us. The smoke from the explosions was so thick I lost sight of my comrades who were coming up behind me. I went back down the hill to make sure everybody was alive. We then dug shelters for three nights. We were so close to the enemy we could only shovel at night and in total silence. Our hands were swollen and covered in blisters. We dug lying down to protect ourselves from gunfire. We used small shovels and scooped away the earth with our hands. In that position, I could only dig down eight inches so I had to stand up to gather the strength to go deeper."

"What about the bullets?" I asked.

"I'm still here, aren't I?" he smiled and continued. "Getting the cannon to the top of the hill and into the gun pit was the most difficult. It had started to rain. The cannon weighs half a ton and there were only seven of us. Losing a few pounds of rice out of several hundred is not a problem, but with the cannon, we couldn't afford to lose a single bolt! Four of us usually team up to carry one part of the gun. In this case, the slope was so steep and narrow, there was only room for two men to carry each gun part. We went up and down five times during the night. It was daylight by the time we were ready to move the gun parts into our defence work. We were in full view of the French. We lay down and passed the tube, the base, the wheels, to one another, on down into the mouth of the shelter, passing them up over our heads, arms stretched high. We were drenched and covered in mud and so was the gun. We climbed back down 1,000 feet, to fetch water, then cleaned the gun and reassembled it. I double-checked it myself to make sure it was not blocked. When everything was finally in place, we were able to report back: mission accomplished in total secret!"

"How did you defend this hill, being so close to the enemy guns?" I asked.

"It was very tough and we have had very high casualties. We started with seven artillerymen, we were soon down to five. I doubled up as battery leader and as number 4 (turning the 'ploughshare', taking care of the smoke and checking the range finder).

Recently, we fought seven consecutive battles, without rest. During the first battle, we hit all our targets with 28 shots (only two fell short) and the infantry succeeded in launching their assault! Then our shelter was hit and the beams collapsed. Our officers felt we were too close to the enemy and ordered us back to the company command post at the bottom of the hill. Before leaving our position, I covered the gun's range finder with canvas to protect it. When the shooting died down, I went back to collect what was left, two pickaxes, two shovels and five cartridges.

Then, while we were at company command post, the enemy counter-attacked. Artillerymen numbers 1 and 2 were wounded. An artilleryman was sent from C752 as a reinforcement. Our battery was down one man, there were now only four of us. After the second battle, we were ordered back up the hill where we built five new shelters, with more protection this time[131]. We took it in turns to cut trees and carry wood back at night. I was promoted

to deputy commander of the section and replaced number 2 since nobody else knew how to operate the Japanese cannon[132], and I had to help out the new number 1 (from C752) who didn't know how to work the American cannon[133]. We then moved the American gun to the new gun pit up the hill.

During a third battle, we destroyed three French 105 mm guns and were awarded a third class medal. Then, the fourth battle started.We were so close to the enemy that we were staring into the mouth of their 105mm cannons! A shell hit the entrance to our shelter. Pao and I jumped out to repair it. We continued shelling and destroyed position 203. The French guns returned fire, machine gunning us with their 12.7mm weapons. When our guns rumbled, their machine guns fell silent.

A fifth battle followed almost immediately. Pao replaced me as number 2. We fired five shots and destroyed two gun positions. Then the French blasted us again with machine-gun fire. Our comrade from C752 was wounded in the arm and had to be evacuated. There were only three of us left to man the cannon, so we took advantage of a pause in the fighting to reinforce our defences during the night. The next morning, after eating some rice, we caught a few hours of sleep. Then, at noon, we were ordered to prepare the guns. An hour later, at 1pm, we received orders to fire.

'Let's not panic. Let's stay as calm as we did yesterday,' said Nghien.

Pao then opened the breech of the cannon to load a shell. I was at the range finder. Nghien, who was not used to the American cannon, had trouble pulling the string. Every time he was about to fire, I kept him steady.

'Count slowly to three, then… Pull! You've hit the left side of their gun pit! Keep it straight (the string…) and...Pull!'

Suddenly, our loophole was hit. All three of us jumped out to shovel away the dirt. We continued shelling. Our orders were to destroy five enemy positions. We wiped out three of them and were about to reload when we were hit again; this time a smoke bomb exploded right in our loophole. We were gasping for breath and we must have passed out, all three of us at the same time. When I came to, everything was dark. I fumbled around in the rubble that had fallen on top of me and stretched out my arm. I found the

Soldier with the pickaxe used for digging tunnels, Dien Bien Phu 1954, ink sketch on notebook paper; 6cm x 8cm, collection of the Ho Chi Minh City Fine Arts Museum.

range finder and unscrewed it. I crawled out from under the debris through a small fox hole. I called Pao and Nghien. No answer. I crawled back in through the hole and called out again. I waited anxiously, then I saw Pao and Ngien clawing their way out. They were covered in mud. Pao dragged himself to the trench wall and collapsed. He had stopped breathing and his eyes were shut. Both Nghien and I thought he was dead. We pumped his chest to revive him, we were crying and calling his name. After what seemed like hours, he came to. We carried him to the vaulted entrance of the shelter so he could rest, when another shell hit. This time our cannon was done for! I still had the range finder in my hand. I was worn out. I had never felt so tired and sad. I needed to regain some strength, and although I wasn't hungry, I reached for the rice ball I kept in my pack and took a couple of bites.

Then the company command ordered us to withdraw back down the hill. We refused, as we were determined not to abandon our position. Then a second order came. And a third. Finally, we obeyed orders and made our way down to the bottom of the hill. When we arrived at the company command post, we were shocked to find that most of our comrades had been killed or wounded. Our casualties were enormous. We were so overcome with grief that we broke down and started weeping.

When the order to start the seventh attack came, I was determined to avenge the deaths of my friends. Violent enemy counter attacks on our company command post continued. The breech of the cannon kept filling up with earth. Trang and Tuong kept unblocking it. Our shelters and trenches kept collapsing, we kept shovelling.

We were then ordered back up to our earlier position at the top of hill E. Our battery was assigned more men. Again we laboured uphill through earth ploughed deep from the bombs. Three of us carried the cannon parts on our shoulders, the men at the front pulled the cannon carriage up the hill while the men at the back pushed. When we reached the summit it had been stripped bare by the bombing raids. The soil was like a pile of ashes. The French had been bombing non-stop to obliterate our defences. We had finished placing the cannon in position when I was ordered back down to the company command post and Tuong was sent to replace me as number 2.

Shortly after Tuong took over the command of my unit, enemy tanks advanced. The tanks took aim at the hill summit. Tuong was killed. Immediately a new recruit was sent to replace him. I was so concerned for the men that I asked to be sent back up to the position at the top of the hill."

Khau returned to command his unit. He was then sent on to help another unit that had lost five of its artillerymen.

"When I slap my thighs, just look at that dust! That's how many days and nights I have been up on this hill! I haven't had the time to go to the bathing pool at the back of the hill!"

"What do you think of when you are alone?" I asked.

"When I left home for war, my father told me always to do my best. He also said I should take responsibility for my own actions and not expect others to take responsibility for me. I promised."

"How about some rice?" I asked.

"The last time I tried to eat, an explosion buried my rice! Let's eat!"

We sat side by side in the trench and shared some rice. A messenger from the infantry arrived with news from the battlefield in the central zone. We invited him to join us. Even though he was famished he politely refused at first, only accepting once he was sure there was enough for all three of us.

"So what is the news?" Khau asked our dinner guest.

"We have launched an assault against the French with all our weapons, including our bangalore torpedoes (DKz or *Dai-bac-Khong-Ziat*), cannons of all calibres and rockets. When we hit a loophole, black smoke engulfed the blockhouse. Enemy soldiers were hit again by our 82mm Russian mortars. They were running scared and shouting: 'Shit, shit!' We occupied four enemy posts."

Later:
On hearing the news that an all out attack is underway, Tam heads back to the command post of the mountain artillery on hill D. The command post there has a vantage point from where he can observe the attack on the French headquarters in the central zone of Muong Thanh.

Going home

May 7, 1954

At C757's command post, on hill D. Last night I was going from hill E back to hill D through the trenches and the fields when I met some soldiers with a strange weapon. It looked like two long tubes attached to each other. Then, during the night, I heard thunderbolts as if hundreds of thousands of gigantic birds were taking flight, beating the earth with their wings. The rockets smashed into Muong Thanh with deafening sounds. It was horrific! They were the H12 or Russian Katchusas[134] I had seen earlier, the very same weapons that terrified the Germans during the Second World War. This morning, I met some soldiers coming back from the night fighting. Instead of answering my questions, they pointed at their ears. "We were so close to the explosions last night that we are now totally deaf!" they said.

I heard that last night we occupied hill A1[135] and most of the hills this side of the Nam Ron. This morning our artillery continued to pound the French headquarters in the central zone of Muong Thanh. From what I learned from headquarters and from talking to soldiers in the field, this must be the final attack. From my position on hill D, I can see the central zone in Muong Thanh. Fierce fighting along the banks of the Nam Ron carried on

Flowers and damaged helmet, Dien Bien Phu, 1954, watercolour on letter writing paper, 22cm x 18cm.

throughout the day. As the day progressed, there were more and more enemy dead and the French artillery response grew weaker and weaker. Then, a few hours ago, the shooting started to die down. We were all very tense as we waited for something to happen. But what? It was late afternoon when, dragging himself up the trench, a foot soldier came towards us. He was back from Muong Thanh. He was so weary that all he could do was shuffle along, barely able to walk. Exhausted and in a state of collapse, his legs crumpled under him and he sank to a sitting position.

"It was tough but we won!" he said.

"What happened?"

"Our troops were fired up and ready to storm the French headquarters in Muong Thanh. Incredibly, they found themselves face to face with the French capitulating! And de Castries was among them!"

Later:
Tonight, writing at C753's command post on hill D. It took some time for news of our victory to spread throughout the battlefield. Little by little, cries of joy erupted on the hills, red with blood and burnt by napalm. These young infantrymen, our little infantrymen are victorious! How happy we all are! Down in the valley, enemy soldiers streamed out from the French central camp in Muong Thanh. There were Vietnamese in disparate uniforms. The French were dressed in white, some wearing only their underpants, their steel and plastic helmets left lying on the ground.

Shortly after 5pm, following a series of fires and rocket attacks against Muong Thanh and Hong Cum, the French waved a white flag[136] made from a torn parachute! Soldiers started crawling out of their holes, hands in the air, holding white handkerchiefs. They poured onto the bridge to cross the river. They seemed relieved to be out of the tombs that had interred them for weeks. One of our officers stood on a mound in the middle of the enemy camp, waving his scarf to show them which direction to go in. The enemy soldiers lined up, bowing their heads obediently. There were no attempts to escape; they knew there was no way out and that we had them surrounded.

Another officer hoisted our "Fight To The End, Victory At All Cost" banner. Using a rudimentary loudspeaker, he addressed the men: French and Vietnamese alike raised their heads to listen to him speak.

I was told that de Castries was in his underground command post when he found himself faced with our soldiers pointing a loaded gun at him. He raised his hands in surrender. Naturally, the General would have preferred to surrender at the wheel of his jeep. Instead he was loaded into a truck with all the others and driven to the command post at Hong Gang[137]. Then, according to Thanh, my engineer friend from C753 who was in Muong Thanh, swarms of enemy soldiers gathered by the bridge. A Vietnamese fighting for the French came running towards our troops.

"You saved us! It really stinks down there. We were terrified when you fired at us with Stalin's organs[138]!"

I can't help feeling contempt for my fellow Vietnamese who fought on the French side. At the same time, I have pity for our nation and for our people: how many of us have been pitted against one another, divided and encouraged to kill one another?

To the west, the sun slowly disappeared behind the Laotian mountains on the border with China. As the enemy surrenders, the Dakotas continue to parachute in supplies. In Hanoi, Navarre and the puppet government must be aware of the tragedy and keep the supplies coming. One of these parachutes landed close to our shelter. The iron box had broken open on impact and we shared the cakes and sweets it contained amongst ourselves. The young peasant soldiers refused the *chocolat* (dark chocolate) finding it too bitter. They didn't like the taste of the *fromage* (cheese) either!

Artillerymen from different units (75mm+DKz+120mm) are overjoyed to be reunited with one another. Stretcher-bearers have started loading the wounded onto trucks. There is much to do: repair fortifications, attend to the wounded and bury our dead, martyrs to the cause. We must also take special care of the enemy wounded and dead[139].

I can hear mines exploding somewhere in the distance. A translucent fog floats down over the fields and the valley. Fires burn in Muong Thanh. Fragments of parachutes, twisted iron and wood torn from the shelters and trenches are lifted up with the flames and the smoke, making it look as if the smoke is alight with dancing fireflies. To the southwest, the French arms depot in Hong Cum is burning[140]. Once in a while, brilliant fireballs explode and dazzle the horizon.

I have such admiration for the endurance and bravery of our infantry. They used simple shovels to dig tunnels and trenches from all four directions, little by little surrounding the enemy, like giant arrows targeting the centre of the airfield. The jagged steel plates of the runway, dislodged and torn apart by fierce explosions, point upwards towards the sky. Our capture of hill A1 was the most incredible feat of the entire battle! Throughout the campaign, the African French soldiers mounted a fierce defence of the hill. Then, last night, at 11pm precisely, a short, muffled blast exploded beneath their feet. Our soldiers had dug a tunnel under their hidden chambers where they planted half a ton of explosives. An entire battalion was wiped out! After numerous attacks and counter-attacks, the destruction of the French position on hill A1 cleared the final obstruction to the iron bridge. Our troops then crossed the bridge into the French camp, ready for the final assault. When they reached the other side of the bridge, they were met by the French and their commander-in-chief capitulating!

There must be hundreds of miles of tunnels and trenches in the valley. The soldiers couldn't dig standing up. As they advanced, they had to dig lying down, to avoid being shot at, using their shovels without raising their arms. When we began our final offensive, our network of trenches joined up with the enemy's maze of underground tunnels and led us straight into the French central camp. In the end, we were fighting them in their own trenches. Trapped within their own defences, their only option was to counter attack in small groups with tank support. In that sense, Dien Bien Phu is different from that other great war of the trenches, the First World War (1914–1918), where there were two distinct fronts; when the adversaries launched their attacks, they could clearly see the other side advancing.

Back to the present and Dien Bien Phu. The night is black. Some comrades open a box of flares. Flashes of green and red light up the sky like fireworks. Cheers and laughter rise from the hills. My friend Thanh plays a tune on his harmonica. At our command posts around the battlefield, units receive their new orders. After a while, a silent darkness falls on the valley. The only source of light is the headlights of trucks on route 41 that intermittently light up de Castries' command post and the iron bridge over the Nam Ron river. I was looking down over Muong Thanh.

"Can you imagine how happy the people at the rear are going to be when they hear of our victory!" said Huyen, the political instructor (C753).

"And what about the participants at the Geneva Conference? Do you think they will be surprised?" I asked without looking for an answer. We both knew some would be overjoyed and others disappointed!

A crescent moon rises on the horizon. The C753 committee members, officers Cat, Huyen, Phuong and Dinh held a meeting at the entrance of the shelter to organise the departure of men and cannons. Then the cook laid out a feast, having first stretched out a piece of parachute as a tablecloth. By the light of our electric torches, we ate rice balls, cans of food (from the French supplies) and fresh water.

It is clear now that we occupy most of the hills around the valley of Muong Thanh. As we looked back on the battle, we agreed that of all our assaults, taking hill D was not only the most daring but the most surprising! It was incredible that our artillery hit all their assigned targets. Once we occupied hill D, we could actually see each other through our respective loopholes. The mood is so friendly and relaxed, soldiers stand around, some resting one hand on another's shoulder, laughing and joking, saying things like, "Hey, look over there, I can see some guys watching us from that hill!"

After we finished our modest feast, the C753 committee ordered a newly created team to depart immediately for Muong Thanh and start evacuating the wounded. Another team was sent down the hill to the valley to recuperate enemy equipment for the company. From our current position, we can see electric torches being switched on in Muong Thanh as soldiers from different units inspect the weapons captured from the enemy.

One young idiot, who was fooling around with a 105mm, fired off the last shell by mistake and terrified everybody. He was severely reprimanded. Soldiers were accosted by curly haired prostitutes and turned them away telling them to "Get lost!" Trucks have been ordered to hitch up two enemy cannons that are still fairly new and many more cannons were seized in Hong Cum.

What a wonderful day this has been. Even the sun was shining after several days of rain. How can I ever forget the sun setting over Dien Bien Phu on this day, May 7! A few enemy planes flew over the valley. We practised aiming the anti-aircraft guns for fun. We didn't have to fire at them since they are only parachuting supplies and no longer dropping bombs!

Tonight, as I lie down at the top of hill D, under a star-filled sky, I feel calm and excited, all at once. I try to forget those nights of bombing when shells exploded so close to me that they shook my entire body. I have no doubt I will fall asleep immediately: I am utterly worn out and I am utterly grateful to be alive.

Barbed-wire fence after the war, 1963, signed Huynh Biec, watercolour on paper, 14cm x 25cm.

May 8, 1954

This morning, I left the C753 command post on hill D to walk down to Muong Thanh to see for myself the valley that we fought so long and hard for! Throughout this violent battle, with all the anxiety, all the waiting and the fear, I felt as if time had stood still. Now that victory is here it is hard to take it all in. I am one of the few to have been given permission to roam the battlefield freely and I immediately set off for the central zone. I went to the French headquarters and then walked over to the airfield. Wrecks of airplanes, tanks and cannons damaged by our artillery; parachute strings, dented steel helmets riddled with bullet holes; corpses decomposing in the muddy trenches that are full of excrement and barbed wire.

The enemy wounded were gathered at a central point in Dien Bien Phu to facilitate medical care. They were dirty and in rags, it was a pitiful sight. The supplies that are being parachuted in for the enemy wounded are being seized by our side. Our labourers who worked so hard to supply the front have been given access to the central zone and permission to take what they choose. They are so happy they sing day and night. Young soldiers were running around, shouting slogans and jumping up onto enemy tanks to have their pictures taken. Trucks go to and fro. Once in a while I could hear a mine exploding: Khac Thinh, the head of the political section, stepped on a mine but I don't know what happened to him.

I didn't have time to investigate further, as I was summoned back to the command post. All units are being given orders to clean the guns and prepare for marching. The soldiers due to leave tonight used their remaining free time to bathe and clean the dirt from their mud-caked faces, in which their eyes are the only recognisable feature. At the evening meeting, C753 officers reported that we captured one General (de Castries), 16 lieutenant colonels and 1,749 officers, destroyed 62 planes and totalled 16,000 enemy dead, wounded and captured[141]. There is no doubt that this is the greatest victory our army has ever won! They also went over the battle, which went according to plan. The first phase began with our March 13 attack when we pierced the hard core of Him Lam hill. Then we moved into the second phase and after our second offensive on March 30 we occupied hills 1,2,3, and 4 in the eastern zone. During phase two, the enemy planes could no longer land on the central airfield and their supply route from Hong Cum was cut off. In phase three, after our May 1 offensive, we occupied four enemy positions

my face, hands and feet and fill up my bamboo tube. (You had to remember to bring your own bamboo to carry water; most of us did not have any actual water bottles.) It was a small oasis like the one at the back of hill E that remained untouched by the bombing raids and the artillery fire.

Later:
I set off for my journey back to the rear. In broad daylight and by truck! Trucks are moving freely during the day, transporting weapons, munitions and supplies captured from the enemy. The road was full of people, activity and noise. Green parachutes flapped in the wind and you could hear the thud of new boots on the tarmac. Prisoners in rags were carrying rice sacks. They came to Vietnam by plane, now they too are having to endure some of the hardships we suffered during our long marches. They are still fortunate by comparison: they do not have to hide in the jungle from fighter bombers, worry about food or fear being attacked, since they are escorted by our soldiers. Perhaps they feel equal amongst each other for the first time: whites and blacks, foreigners and Vietnamese, soldiers and officers, all marching together in one line. There is no preferential treatment.

The morning was bright and fresh. A strip as white as snow covered the blue mountain on the horizon. As we drove through the countryside, the landscape had been transformed. Corn is starting to grow. Rice fields will soon sprout new shoots. Everything seemed green and blossoming. What a contrast with the red of the blood-soaked earth, the black of the napalm and the chalky white of the hills and valley of Dien Bien Phu where we fought these last months. At a pit stop by the road, we met some Thai. They had left their jungle refuge to join in rebuiling the road. A nearby village was coming back to life, people were returning home, smoke was rising from the rounded thatched roofs and the huts on stilts. A villager stood by the bombed-out site of his old house showing his children how they were going to rebuild. Village women were embroidering handkerchiefs to offer as gifts to the young soldiers returning home. At dusk, actresses improvised a song-and-dance act while the trucks provided the lighting. Everyone was excited and able to have fun at last: for so long all we had been able to talk about were weapons, soldiers and cannons… Dong and Long are being sent on ahead to make the preparations for the division's victory party. I am spending the night here by the roadside.

May 13, 1954
Arrived at Hat Lot for the night. I am travelling with the stenographers and the weakest soldiers. We call them *damoiseaux* (young ladies) to tease them. We are being sent ahead to the Tuyen Quang base[142], to organise the camp for the troops' arrival. In the Molotova, we are jammed together like watermelons in a field. The ride is very bumpy. Do I care? Anything is better than those long marches along never-ending roads, carrying a heavy backpack!

Today we drove through Tuan Giao where people on both sides of the road cheered as we went by. We were greeted by an arch of triumph and a banner celebrating our return, "Hurray for the combatants of Dien Bien Phu!" After Tuan Giao, the truck climbed up the Pha Din pass. I could not believe how wide and straight the road is now! At the top of the pass, workers and youth brigade volunteers, wrapped in pieces of nylon, were sleeping soundly by the road in the pouring rain.

We passed Son La where youths built a temporary bridge over the Ngam river so we could get across. We then had a clear run to Na San and arrived in Hat Lot for the night.

May 15, 1954
Today, arrived at the military camp at Tuyen Quang. At the Ban Chen pass[143], we waited for hours behind a long line of vehicles. The road had been cut off by landslides. It is no wonder that the high command was anxious for victory before the rainy season. It would have been almost impossible to supply our troops at Dien Bien Phu during the monsoon season. As we were sitting in the back of the truck, my friend Hoang, who was next to me, was visibly moved . "This road will soon be a route for silk, sugar and salt," he said. "When you think that our country has thousands of miles of sea coast, yet the people of the northwest were so much in need of salt that they were reduced to burning reeds and licking the ashes to get salt! They suffered from terrible diseases. It sickens me that the French profited from their misery and used salt to barter with them!"

We were travelling along the edge of a gorge when suddenly the road gave way and torrents of water rushed down. It gave me butterflies in my stomach. We waited there for two days for repairs to be done. It was far more dangerous than repairing the road after the bombings! We finally started moving again at night at 11:30pm! Further on, we stopped again. This time, the road was flooded. Boys as young as 15 and 16 from Thanh Hoa worked until nightfall to repair it. They built new dykes to channel the water to irrigate the rice fields further below. I was surprised to see how many civilians from all parts of the Viet Bac were on their way to the northwest to join in the reconstruction effort, from traders from Thai Nguyen to farmers. A young man of 20, from a poor family in Moc Chau (a town in Son La province, 100 miles southwest of the Pha Din pass) was wearing one of the new blue uniforms being distributed by the government. Very shy, he introduced himself in a soft voice as "younger brother" and said he was on his way to Tuan Giao and Lai Chau.

I wonder what is happening at Dien Bien Phu. Perhaps soldiers and villagers are celebrating the victory together. The units left behind have a great deal to do: clear the battlefield, the command post, hill A1, Hong Cum and Muong Thanh; take inventory of the number of tanks, cannons and planes that can be re-utilised; prepare reports and review operations; look after the prisoners; organise medical care; take care of the dead and bury the corpses left in the trenches and the shelters. Minefields need to be cleared. Above all else, the villagers in the Muong Thanh valley must be relocated back to their villages so they can get back to a normal life to rebuild their houses and cultivate their fields.

During the journey from Dien Bien Phu to Tuyen Quang, I came across numerous teams of civilian workers heading north: the reconstruction of the northwest has truly begun! I have the feeling that liberation is here and that peace is near. We are officially still at war since the French continue to occupy the country, yet the atmosphere has completely changed. Villages and towns are festooned with red flags – from Vietnam, China and the USSR, flying in a sea of sky blue banners[144]. Festivals, reunions, parties... Farmers no longer don camouflage, they have left their jungle and mountain hideaways and are out on the roads waving flags, smiling, and singing. Women and children wear colourful clothing. Markets are crowded, prices are coming down and people are buying sweets – signs of a recovery in buyers' confidence. Children flutter around soldiers like flocks of small birds, roads are so crowded with people that vehicles can't get through. Farmers are hard at work rebuilding their old villages that were demolished in the bombings. Families are talking about starting a new life. How many times have I heard the phrase from people I have talked to during the journey: "We are at peace! No more famine!"

By the roadside, an elderly mother was looking for her son asking every soldier that went by:

"Do you know where my child is?"

I knew that many units had not returned from Dien Bien Phu. How I hoped that her son was amongst them.

Tonight, at the Tuyen Quang base camp, I find myself in a magical forest of majestic trees and clear water streams. Soldiers are repairing the thatched huts and building new ones for troops coming back from Dien Bien Phu. They have constructed a spacious new meeting room, furnished with tables and chairs, out of bamboo that has been carefully selected for its strength and aesthetics. The cook is busy rounding up pigs and cattle for the celebratory festivities being organised by the division. The herds were gifts from the village and district committes.

July 28, 1954

Two and a half months later. At the Tuyen Quang base camp. Have heard that progress is being made at the Geneva Conference and in the negotiations for an exchange of prisoners. I am convinced that peace is at hand.

My great joy is that in the middle of this jungle, far from anywhere, the political section of the division has given me an abundant supply of white paper and powdered colours and a new paint brush! I have been spending my time painting.

I am comfortably settled in a thatched cottage with four comrades from the propaganda section. We each have a hammock to sleep in. Mine is suspended from four posts of perfumed wood that are solidly planted in the ground, a real luxury after all those nights spent underground! I have finished several watercolours: *Artillerymen pulling cannons*, *The defence of hill D*, *Infantry assault*, *Building roads and carrying rice to the front*. But there is so much more I want to paint, I wonder how I can ever find a way, or the time, to express all the emotions we lived through on the battlefield!

Following pages: *Thai women laying 'sim' forest flowers on soldiers' graves at Dien Bien Phu*, 1954, graphite and wash on paper, 16cm x 20cm.

August 1, 1954

I received some very good news: I have been given a position in the art section of the General Political Office, the section in charge of organising the celebratory exhibition in Hanoi!

August 28, 1954

Today, I left the base at Tuyen Quang for Hanoi. My joy is mixed with sadness at the idea of leaving my unit and my brothers with whom I shared so many difficult and terrible times.

We walked together to the edge of the jungle. It was too painful for me to say goodbye. With my backpack and my rice belt, I started my journey down to the plain. I suddenly felt very alone.

It is the month of August, the beginning of autumn. This is the season when we usually plan our spring offensives. I wonder whether we will ever have to go back to war again.

Tam won the third prize at the exhibition held in Hanoi to celebrate the victory at Dien Bien Phu. A few years later, in the late summer, the beginning of autumn, Tam left to sketch the war against the Americans.

Barefoot soldier with gun, wearing a piece of parachure as rain gear, 1960 (the beginning of the second Vietnam war), signed Huynh Biec, charcoal on paper, 34cm x 24cm.

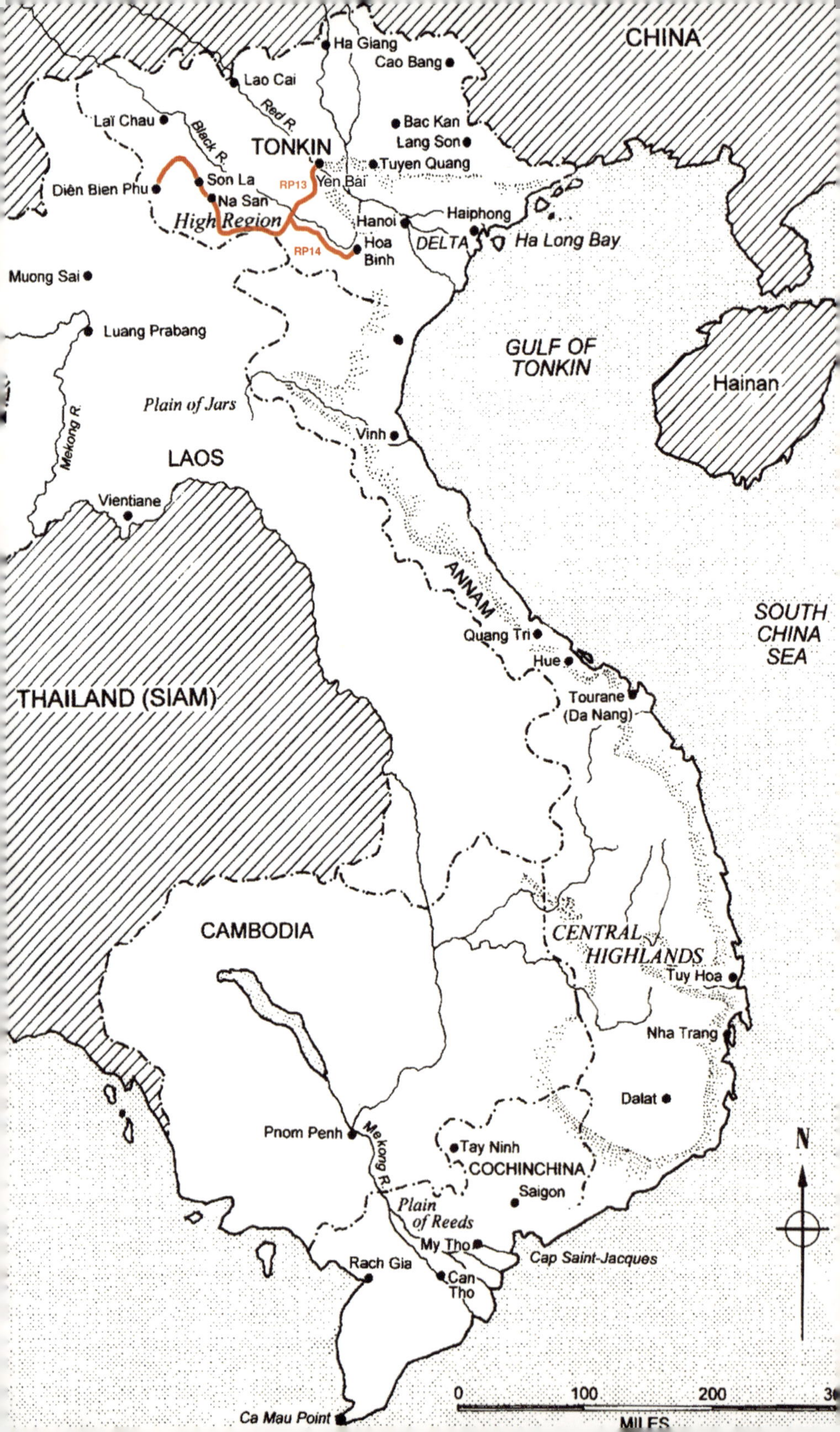
CHINA
Ha Giang
Cao Bang
Lao Cai
Red R.
Laï Chau
Black R.
Bac Kan
Lang Son
TONKIN
Tuyen Quang
Yen Bai
RP13
Son La
Diên Bien Phu
Na San
High Region
Hanoi
Haiphong
Hoa Binh
RP14
DELTA
Ha Long Bay
Muong Sai
Luang Prabang
GULF OF TONKIN
Hainan
Plain of Jars
Mekong R.
Vinh
LAOS
Vientiane
ANNAM
SOUTH CHINA SEA
Quang Tri
Hue
THAILAND (SIAM)
Tourane (Da Nang)
CAMBODIA
CENTRAL HIGHLANDS
Tuy Hoa
Nha Trang
Dalat
Pnom Penh
Mekong R.
Tay Ninh
COCHINCHINA
Saigon
N
Plain of Reeds
My Tho
Cap Saint-Jacques
Rach Gia
Can Tho
Ca Mau Point
0
100
200
MILES

Notes

Organisation of the Vietnamese People's Army (*Quan Doi Nhan Dan*)
Division, F, *dai doan*
Regiment, E, *trung doan*
Battalion, D, *tieu doan*
Company, C, *dai doi*
Section, B, *trung doi*
Squadron, A, *tieu doi*
Battery, K, *khau doi*

1 The author was a reporter for the newspaper of the heavy artillery division (*dai doan*) F351 of the Vietnamese People's Army (*Quan Doi Nam Dhan*). He travelled with an arts group that included artists, writers, musicians, singers and actors. Their function was to entertain the troops and boost morale.

The heavy artillery division F351 was of paramount importance to the Vietnamese People's Army which, unlike the French, had neither air power nor tanks and was reliant on the power of its artillery. The division included the corps of engineers responsible for building the road network leading to the French entrenched camp at Dien Bien Phu and four artillery regiments made up of 105mm howitzer cannons (estimates vary between 24 to 36), 120mm mortars, 37mm anti-aircraft guns and 75mm mountain guns. In comparison, the French artillery numbered twenty-four 105mm howitzers, four longer-range 155mm cannons and light artillery. The French had fighter bombers, reconnaissance and transport planes as well as tanks. The People's Army was supplied by the People's Republic of China after Mao's victory in 1949, the French Expeditionary Corps, by the United States. "In late December 1953...Ho Chi Minh and the Politburo decided to destroy the vital enemy base in the northwest.

Opposite: Map of Indochina at the time of the war. In red, the 200 mile itinerary from Yen Bai to Dien Bien Phu that Tam describes in his diary. Before the start of the diary, he had covered 100 miles on foot from Lao Cai, a town on the Chinese border.

The historic Dien Bien Phu campaign was about to begin. On January 1, 1954, the Politburo nominated the supreme authority and campaign command. I was concurrently chief commander and secretary of the battlefront Party Committee. More troops were deployed to the northwest. Division 351, with its newly formed artillery and 37mm anti-aircraft units, crossed the Red River for the first time to join the campaign." Giap, *Dien Bien Phu.*

2 Ben Ngoc: ferry crossing on the river Chay for men and munitions on the way to Dien Bien Phu in the province of Yen Bai where the author starts his diary. It was one of the strategic road points bombed by the French Tactical Air Command (GATAC or Groupement Aérien Tactique) in their efforts to disrupt the supply routes to Dien Bien Phu.

3 Song Chay: river in the north of Vietnam.

4 Red River or Song Hong: 745-mile-long river in the north of Vietnam, starts in the Chinese province of Yunnan, and flows to the Gulf of Tonkin.

5 Yen Bai: capital of the mountainous province of the northwest of the same name, a strategic point on the way to Dien Bien Phu.

6 Route 13 or RP 13: *route provinciale* or French provincial road, main road for the troops of the People's Army advancing from Viet Minh controlled territory to Dien Bien Phu. RP 13 (and RP 13 bis) joined up with the RP 41, the only road into the valley of Dien Bien Phu. The RP 13 and 41 were key targets for French bombing raids.

"Targets for these [bombing] missions were scattered along the whole supply route from the Viet Bac, the main resistance area of the Viet Minh, to Tuan Giao and beyond, but priority was given to RP 13 bis and RP 41, between the Red River crossing at Yen Bai and Dien Bien Phu." Windrow.

7 Dien Bien Phu: name of the district, town and valley, 11 miles long by 5 miles wide, in the province of Lai Chau. Site of the fortified air base chosen by General Henri Navarre to defend the French-held territories of Laos and the Red River Delta around Hanoi against the People's Army which controlled the area north of Dien Bien Phu, all the way up to the Chinese border. The French camp was defended by 11,000 men under the command of Colonel Christian de Castries, heavy artillery, air power and tanks. Two airfields supplied the camp. Fortified outposts on hills around the central command post, situated in the valley west of the river Nam Ron, were: to the north, Gabrielle (Doc Lap); to the northeast, Béatrice (Him Lam);

to the east, the Dominiques (hills D and E) and the Elianes (hills C and A); 5 miles to the south, Isabelle (Hong Cum) and to the west, Anne-Marie and the Huguettes. The French high command thought the camp impregnable.

8 Lung Lo pass: pass on the RP 13 and one of two supply routes from the Viet Bac, the Viet Minh's resistance base, leading to RP 41 and Dien Bien Phu. "Enemy planes struck repeatedly at important sections of road, mostly on the high passes and at ferries. The Lung Lo Pass and Ta Khoa and Co Noi, junction of two roads from Hoa Binh and Yen Bai in the northwest, became huge bomb craters. Flares were dropped all night long onto key locations." Giap.

9 Youth brigade volunteers: auxiliary forces that numbered women amongst them. They built and repaired roads after the bombings. Interview with the author.

10 Collapsible bridges: bridges made of wood and bamboo. They could bear the weight of heavy military trucks and be dismantled once the convoy had passed. Bonnet.

11 Ho Chi Minh (1890–1969) or Uncle Ho, as he was affectionately named by the people: Founder and leader of the Viet Minh (*Viet Nam Doc Lap Dong Minh*), the National Independence Front, he was the first president of the Democratic Republic of Vietnam, from September 2, 1945, when he declared independence, until his death in 1969. Poetry, intrinsic to Vietnamese culture, was commonly used by Ho Chi Minh and other Viet Minh leaders to address the people.

12 Vinh Phuc: province of the Red River Delta, under French control since the 1951 battle of Vinh Yen.

13 Civic worker: one translation from the Vietnamese term, *dan cong* (another, is conscripted labourer); also designated as "coolies" in English and French. A coolie is "an unskilled native labourer in Eastern countries" according to the Chambers 21st Century Dictionary. "33,500 civic workers supplied the battlefront at Dien Bien Phu. Using 2,724 pack bicycles (*xe tho*), 2,673 junks and 17,400 horses, these workers transported 20,584 tons of rice to the front, in addition to munitions and other materials. Between January and May 1954, they contributed 5 million work days to the resistance against the French." Dinh Van Ty, "The iron-horse brigades," *Etudes Vietnamiennes 3* (1965): 47–61, cited by Pierre Asselin.

14 Morane 500 Criquet: surveillance plane used by the French to take aerial

photographs and to alert their fighter bombers of enemy positions. In Vietnamese, they were known either as planes with two seats or *may bay hai minh;* or *ba gia*, which means "old lady," because they flew so slowly.

15 *ibid*, footnote 13.

16 Frog drum: In the north of Vietnam, children hunt frogs, considered a delicacy, and make small drums out of their skin. Interview with the author.

17 Song Da: Black River, see footnote 93.

18 Pack bicycle or *xe tho*: bicycle that was also used during the second Vietnam War (1964–1975), that could transport two sacks of rice weighing 220lb each. The bicycle porters covered on average 12–20 miles a day. The bicycle was reinforced with bamboo to steady the load.

19 Bac Giang: province to the east of Dien Bien Phu. From Bac Giang to Yen Bai, the bicycle porters had travelled a distance of 87 miles.

20 Thai Nguyen: province and town in the Viet Bac. The Viet Bac was the centre of the Viet Minh resistance against the French. Ho Chi Minh and his government took refuge there, when the French troops returned to Vietnam in 1945, at the end of the Second World War.

21 Meo: one of several ethnic minority groups in the north of Vietnam, they cultivated opium poppies. During the Vietnam wars, both sides enlisted the help of minority ethnic groups.

22 Art, music, theatre and dance groups followed the soldiers and performed for them in the evenings. Their repertoire varied from the comic to the revolutionary heroic style.

23 Co Noi: valley at the crossroads of RP 13 and RP 41 that was a strategic point on the road to Dien Bien Phu and one of several strategic bombing targets for the French Air Tactical Command Group. The bombings temporarily closed the road in December 1953 but it was quickly repaired by the People's Army engineer corps.

24 Na San: French military airbase and precursor of Dien Bien Phu, 12 miles from Hat Lot, that was evacuated by French troops in August 1953 and left in an abandoned state.

25 Son La: town 28 miles from Tuan Giao. At the time the author was marching on the road in early March, army engineers had been working on the road for three months. Interview with the author.

26 Pha Din: 20-mile-long strategic pass, also named the Meo Pass, regularly

bombed by the French Air Command. The two points "at either end of the Meo Pass, were attacked by a total of 58 sorties dropping 135 tons of bombs, which had only temporary effects on motor traffic." Windrow

27 The Thai: ethnic minority group in the north of Vietnam. The three thai kingdoms were consolidated into a federation under the French colonial administration. Several battalions of the French Far East Expeditionary Corps, the French troops in Indochina, were made up of Thai.

28 *Ban* flowers: The latin name of this tree that flowers in spring in the northwest of Vietnam is *bauhinia variegata*. The flowers that resemble orchids are a symbol of young love and often decorate the sculpted roofs of the houses on stilts that are typical of the region inhabited by the Thai. Interview with the author.

29 Engineering corps: engineers belonged to the regiment 151 of the People's Army's heavy artillery division 351. They were in charge of building roads and bridges and of reconstruction and repair after bombing raids. They were also responsible for detonating unexploded bombs and for building the casemates and the underground fortifications where the 105mm howitzer cannons were camouflaged. Tam estimates 1,000 kilometres of roads were built during the Dien Bien Phu campaign.

30 B24: American bomber nicknamed "liberator" during the Second World War, supplied to the French by the Americans, with a maximum bomb load of four tons and altitude of 13,000 feet.
B26: American bomber, used by the French Resistance against the Germans during the Second World War, with a maximum bomb load of two tons. During the Indochina War, B26s dropped butterfly and napalm bombs. They were equipped with eight manned heavy machine guns for ground attacks. They flew from mostly from Cat Bi airport in Haiphong. Interview with the author.

31 Hellcat or Grumman F6F: main American bomber during the Pacific war, it was supplied to the French forces in Indochina by the Americans. Equipped with machine guns fixed to its wings for ground attacks, it had a maximum bomb load of close to a ton.
Interview with the author.

32 Butterfly bomb: anti-personnel bomb containing a large number of smaller 4lb bombs fitted with variable fuses that made them particularly dangerous for the teams detonating unexploded bombs who could not

foresee the timing of the explosion. Wounds were either deadly or difficult to treat. Interview with the author.

33 Vo Nguyen Giap (1912–): a founding member of the Viet Minh, he became Minister of the Interior, then Minister of War in Ho Chi Minh's first 1945 government. When the 1946 Franco-Vietnamese agreement collapsed, he was named President of the Defence Committee of the Viet Minh in charge of preparing the general insurrection. Promoted to General in 1947, he directed the operation against the French during the Indochina War and the battle of Dien Bien Phu. From 1960 to 1980, he was Minister of the National Defence of the Democratic Republic of Vietnam and Vice Prime Minister until 1991. He is the author of several books about the conflict, including *Dien Bien Phu*, The Gio, Hanoi, sixth edition, 1999.

34 Calm mind, strong mind: popular concept derived from Buddhism to describe the strength of mind achieved through meditation, used by the author to describe the strength of character of Viet Minh soldiers and artillerymen under fire.

35 *Khong loi*: *khong* means air, *loi* means thunder or thunderbolt. As the bomb explodes in the air, the fragments reach and kill a large number of soldiers on the battle field. Interview with the author.

36 Tuan Giao: a town 53 miles from Dien Bien Phu, on the RP 41. When the French chose Dien Bien Phu as a military base, it was inaccessible except for the RP 41, the road from Tuan Giao. The "road" was a small track across rugged mountainous terrain. Part of the challenge the People's Army faced was to build a road for trucks hauling heavy artillery in a little over three-months. General Giap had to push back the start of the campaign by over a month to enable his army engineers to finish building the new road.

37 Route 41 or RP 41: *ibid*, footnote 36, *route provinciale* that went from Hoa Binh to Dien Bien Phu. The last miles into Dien Bien Phu were only a track and the road had to be built by the People's Army's engineer corps.

38 Company (*dai doi*) 804: the author was in military training camp in China with the artillerymen from C804 and counted many friends among the artillerymen. C804 had four batteries (*khau doi*) and each battery, one 105mm howitzer cannon. Interview with the author.

39 105mm howitzer cannons: Heaviest artillery of the People's Army. Each 105mm cannon weighed two tons, a shell, 33lb. Most cannons were supplied by the People's Republic of China. The PRC had received them from

the Soviet Union to fight against the forces of Chiang Kai Shek. Interview with the author.

40 Withdrawal order: the order came directly from General Giap himself. "I phoned the artillery units to inform them: The enemy situation has changed. Our determination to destroy Tran Dinh (the codename for Dien Bien Phu in this campaign) remains unchanged. Our plan of attack has changed. I therefore order you as from 17:00 hours today to haul the heavy guns out of position and back to re-groupment areas for new preparations. This order must be strictly executed. No explanation can be provided." Giap.

41 Artillerymen were in charge of steering the cannons, the infantrymen were in charge of the ropes and the windlass. Interview with the author.

42 Withdrawal order: *ibid*, footnote 40.

43 Napalm: napalm bombs were banned by the 1949 Geneva Convention; they were first used against the People's Army in 1950 and throughout the Indochina War, including at the battle of Dien Bien Phu. General Ely (Chairman of the French Chiefs of Staff) raised the question of obtaining authorisation to use the C-119 transports to drop napalm at Dien Bien Phu. This was approved by the US Joint Chiefs of Staff on the condition that "no US crews were involved." *The Pentagon Papers*.

44 The political commissar: the commissar was appointed by the Party. They were often former school teachers. They chaired committees and self and group criticism meetings, kept up morale with praise and encouragement, supervised relations between troops and local civilians and monitored officers and men through a system of internal informers. Depending on the circumstance, the decision of the political commissar decisions overrode the decision of the combat commander. "From the few (inevitably censored) accounts we have of life in the ranks of the People's Army, an impression of genuine admiration for the commissar usually emerges." Windrow.

45 Artillerymen Ty and Loc of C804: friends of the author from military training camp in Yunnan who were killed by a shell explosion during the battle of Dien Bien Phu.

46 Casemate or *ham*: underground shelter built by People's Army engineers, artillerymen and infantrymen for the 105mm cannons. Usually on mountain slopes, eight feet wide, under 15 to 20 feet of packed turf, held up by

wooden beams, with a loophole for the cannon tube, making them very difficult to locate, they are credited for the superiority of the Vietnamese artillery at the battle of Dien Bien Phu. Most of the French 105mm cannons were positioned in the valley in open pits making them easy targets. The Vietnamese cannons were so well camouflaged that, before the battle, the French had no reliable intelligence on the emplacements of the Vietnamese cannons, despite aerial photographs from their surveillance planes. The commander of the French artillery commitsuicide on March 17, 1954, four days after the first Vietnamese general offensive and artillery attack.

47 Inhabitants of the region thatched their roofs with the dried rice stems once the grains had been removed. Interview with the author.

48 Withdrawal order: *ibid.*, footnotes 40 and 42.

49 Regiment 675: regiment of the heavy artillery division 351. This regiment had 3 battalions, eighteen 75mm mountain artillery and twenty 120mm mortars. Windrow.

50 Upper Laos: The People's Army launched an offensive against the French in Upper Laos, part of the French Union in Indochina. According to some sources, this was mainly a diversionary tactic away from the build-up around Dien Bien Phu.

51 Dakota or Douglas C47: US-made plane used for the evacuation of the French wounded and for airlifting and parachuting supplies to the French troops at Dien Bien Phu. Dakotas, leaving from Hanoi and Haiphong airports, were used for daily air lifts of tons of food, munitions, paratroopers and weapons to the French camp. The planes even airlifted four 155mm cannons. One of the objectives of the Vietnamese artillery at Dien Bien Phu was to cut off the French air supplies. When Dakotas could no longer land on the airfield, all supplies were parachuted in.

52 *Lang*: Vietnamese measurement. One *lang* equals 1¼ oz.

53 Jungle spinach (*rau tau bay*): food supplement for the troops when rice rations were running low or could not be cooked because of enemy planes. Interview with the author.

54 Viet Minh rules of behaviour: On joining the army, a Viet Minh soldier swore by an honour code which, among other things, regulated behaviour towards civilians. The rules included not entering a civilian house without being invited, cleaning quarters that had been lived in by

soldiers and only accepting food if the family had enough of their own. Interview with the author.

55 Muong Sai: French military airbase on the plateau of the same name, in Upper Laos, 31 miles southwest of Dien Bien Phu. The People's Army was preparing to launch an assault against the airbase when a withdrawal order came on February 20–21. The author refers to Muong Sai as a victory, supporting the idea that the Laos operation was a diversionary tactic to distract the French from the Viet Minh troop formations that were marching to and surrounding Dien Bien Phu.

56 Souvanaphong: Laotian prince, founder of the Pathet Lao, nationalist and anti-colonial party allied to the Viet Minh. His half-brother, Souvanna Phouma, was the founder of a rival party, the Lao Issara.

57 American pilots: The American pilots worked for CAT, a CIA owned air fleet, and they piloted Dakotas, the transport planes that airlifted and parachuted supplies to the French Expeditionary Corps in Dien Bien Phu. The American technicians on the ground were US Air Force personnel. "Summary of Action Agreed Regarding Urgent French Requests. It was agreed: a) To provide a total of 22 B26 aircraft as rapidly as practicable. b) To provide 200 uniformed US Air Force mechanics who would be assigned as an augmentation to MAAG, Indochina. These mechanics to be provided only on the understanding that they would be used at bases where they would be secure from capture and would not be exposed to combat. c) To send the CAT pilots, with CIA arranging necessary negotiations." "Memorandum for the Record, Meeting of the President's Special Committee on Indochina, January 29, 1954," *The Pentagon Papers*, Gravel Edition, Volume 1, Document 21.

58 Regiment 45: artillery regiment of the 105mm howitzer cannons, the People's Army's most powerful artillery. The regiment had 24 105mm cannons. Interview with the author.

59 Ben Tre division: Division 312 was one of the infantry divisions of the People's Army. Ben Tre is a rice-producing province, with a provincial capital of the same name, in the Mekong Delta in the south of Vietnam and a traditional centre of Vietnamese resistance to French colonial rule.

60 "Steady attack, steady advance": On January 26, 1954, General Giap and the Politburo decided to push back the beginning of the first general offensive against the French camp in Dien Bien Phu to March.

"Given the essential principle of "attacking with the certainty of victory', it is imperative that we change our guiding philosophy from 'swift attack, swift victory' to 'steady attack, steady advance.'" Giap.

61 Company (*dai doi*) 805: heavy artillery company with four 105 mm cannons. In the People's Army, an artillery company was made up of four batteries. Interview with the author.

62 Position of the People's Army artillery: The artillery was positioned on the mountain slope facing the French positions. This was an unconventional tactic chosen by General Giap . By the time of the Indochina War, thanks to new technology allowing artillerymen to calculate the firing range, artillery was usually positioned on the inner slopes, hidden from the adversary. Even though they were facing the French positions, the People's Army artillery was so well camouflaged it was not detected by the French prior to the battle. "Our cannons were three to four miles away from their targets. Usually 105mm can fire six to seven miles. Being closer to the enemy fortifications, they could fire directly, so used up less ammunition," Hoang Minh Thao, professor, General of the People's Army. www.vietnam.vnagency.com.vn

63 Company 757: artillery company.

64 Muong Thanh: name given by the People's Army to the French headquarters at Dien Bien Phu. It was the name of the Thai village displaced by the French troops to set up their camp. Once the centre of the French opium trade in the northwest of Vietnam during French colonial times, Muong Thanh was then held by the People's Army until the French chose the valley of Dien Bien Phu as the site for their new air-defence base and occupied Muong Thanh.

65 Pathet Lao: books on the Laotian party allied to the Viet Minh.

66 Eastern targets: People's Army targets to the east of the French central headquarters that included Him Lam, the French stronghold Béatrice; hill E, the French stronghold Dominique 1; hill D, the French stronghold Dominique 2; hill D2, the French stronghold Dominique 3; and hills A1 and C1, the French strongholds of the Elianes. Interview with the author.

67 Battalion 954 (*tieu doan*): the heavy artillery battalion was divided into three companies (*dai doi*) C801, C802, and C803. The battalion had a total of twelve 105mm cannons. Each company had four batteries, each battery, one 105mm howitzer cannon. Interview with the author.

68 12.7mm machine guns: heavy machine guns.

69 The French command had 200 trucks.

70 Wooden cannons: Subterfuge by the People's Army to attract French artillery fire onto false artillery positions. Artillerymen positioned by the wooden cannons set off explosions to simulate the smoke effect of artillery fire. Interview with the author.

71 Helicopters were used for the evacuation of the seriously wounded from the French camp to Muong Sai, the French airbase in Upper Laos.

72 Position 201: probably Eliane 10. "Under cover of night on 12 March three of (the 155mm) had been towed forward to pits east of the river in location Eliane 10, less open to enemy observation. The late move to Eliane 10 had not been spotted by the Viet Minh." Windrow.

73 Hill D: this French stronghold was made up of several hills. One of the D hills had six heavy mortars backing up French forces on Him Lam hill (Béatrice). The 105mm batteries of the Colonial Artillery Regiment of the French Expeditionnary Corps were positioned on hill D2 (Dominique 3), one of the D hills that resisted until May 2, 1954.

74 Regiments 209 and 149: these infantry regiments belonged to the Ben Tre division 312; regiment 149 carried the explosives used to blast through the French barbed wire defences. Interview with the author.
Infantry assault: "At about 3pm on March 13, Regiments 141 and 209 – inspired by an order of the day from President Ho Chi Minh – left their forming-up areas in thick forests and moved forwards to their jumping-off points. By this time three trenches had already been pushed to within about 50 yards of the wire, hidden by scrub; one of the RCL positions was within 100 yards of Béatrice 1." Windrow.

75 This Vietnamese adjective translates literally as subjective; the term is used to denote a negative attitude among officers and soldiers who over-estimate or underestimate the strength of the French defences. Interview with the author.

76 Three French posts: three of the four French fortified posts on Him Lam which included three hills. All four French posts were overrun by regiments 209 and 141 during the first general offensive of the People's Army against the French (March 13, 1954).

77 Easternmost enemy stronghold: *ibid*, footnote 76. The fall of Him Lam allowed the People's Army to move their artillery forward to positions

closer to the French central command post. During the first general offensive, the People's Army also seized the French stronghold of Doc Lap (which means independence in Vietnamese), or Gabrielle, the northernmost French fortification. The French counter-attack against Doc Lap hill failed on March 15, 1954.

78 "300 prisoners": estimates of the number of French prisoners captured after the battle of Him Lam vary. "More than 200 prisoners." Windrow.

79 *Cam thu*: the translation is hate or vengeance and is used several times to describe the rallying cries of Viet Minh soldiers before going into battle . It was also used in Viet Minh war propaganda to describe revenge for the crimes committed against the people by the French during their colonial administration of Vietnam. These crimes included political imprisonments, torture and "unjust" executions . One "crime" was the man-made famine that killed an estimated one to two million people during the French administered Japanese occupation between 1944 and the summer of 1945. The famine rallied popular support for the Viet Minh.

80 Hill E: French defence position known as Dominique 1.

81 *Co phao*: Vietnamese term for the 120mm mortar. The 120mm mortar had a shorter range than the 105mm howitzer. However, the mortar was almost as powerful as the 105mm and was used to reach positions in valleys and trenches behind hills.

82 *Phao cao xa*: Vietnamese term for the People's Army's anti-aircraft gun at Dien Bien Phu, characterised by a very long tube. A French-US report concluded before the battle of Dien Bien Phu that the anti-aircraft guns would be easily destroyed by French fighter bombers because the long tubes were too difficult to camouflage. Windrow and Rocolle.

83 *Son phao*: Vietnamese term for the 75mm mountain cannon. This gun was lighter than both the 105mm and the 120mm mortar and could be dismantled into separate parts and carried up hill, making it easier and faster to move than the 105mm cannons. It also fired at a steeper angle than the 105mm. This meant that it could not be hidden in underground shelters and the artillerymen of the 75mm were more vulnerable to enemy fire than the 105mm artillerymen. Interview with the author.

84 Doc Lap hill: *ibid*, footnote 77.

85 Hoa Binh: name of a town and famous battle. The term means peace in Vietnamese. At the beginning of the Franco-Vietnam war, the town

served as a base for the People's Army. Captured by the French, the People's Army counter-attacked during the Hoa Binh campaign of 1952 and won back their base after a ferocious battle. The heavy casualties on both sides led the battle to be remembered as the "hell of Hoa Binh."

86 That Khe: town and strategic French post on the colonial road, RC4 close to the Chinese border that was captured by the People's Army during the 1950 Northwest campaign. French troops evacuated in a hurry, leaving behind "13 cannons, 120 mortars, 450 vehicles, 240 machine guns, 850 rifles, 10,000 shells and 130,000 gallons of petrol." www.membres.lycos.co.uk/Indochine/vm/vmlogistics

87 Dong Khe: town and strategic French post along RC4 evacuated by French troops during the 1950 Northwest campaign.

88 Tet: Lunar New Year or Chinese New Year, usually in early February. In the north of Vietnam, the month of February is the beginning of the dry season and is traditionally chosen by the People's Army for their winter campaigns.

89 Cao Bang: town and key French post on the Chinese border that was captured by the People's Army during the 1950 Northwest campaign.

90 Thuc Luyen: town 20 miles north of Hoa Binh.

91 M3: shells for the 105mm cannons which could be used in the larger calibre 120mm mortars.

92 An eyewitness account by a French journalist recounted the following: "At 6am on the following morning, the French combat troops began to cross the river and go back to Xom Pheo under a constant umbrella of artillery and fighter bombers. More than 30,000 shells were fired in support of the salient between February 22 and 24 (1952). Apparently the enemy had been taken by surprise, for its first reaction occurred only at 8am." Fall, *Street Without Joy*.

93 Battle of Hoa Binh: see footnote 85.

"Seen from a long-range viewpoint, however, the French once more had been the heavier losers, for while the Viet-Minh used the battle for the Black River salient as a sort of dress rehearsal for a future showdown battle, the French apparently failed to consider the operation as either a dress rehearsal or as a portent of things to come." Fall.

94 La Phu: French fortified camp near Son Tay province.

Interview with the author.

95 Ba Vanh: French fortified camp near Hoa Binh captured by the Vietnamese during the battle of Hoa Binh. Interview with the author.

96 Hong Cum: French defence position 5 miles to the south of the French central headquarters, with a second airfield.

97 To Huu (1920–2002): official poet of the Communist Party and cultural czar who held many important posts in the Democratic Republic of Vietnam including that of Deputy Cultural Minister in 1955. One of his most famous poems was a eulogy to Stalin written on the occasion of the death of the Soviet leader.

98 Vietnamese companies: the Vietnamese fighting on the French side made up 20% of the French forces and included one Vietnamese parachute battalion. The Viet Minh considered them to be collaborators.

99 General Henri Navarre: commander in chief of the French Expeditionary Corps in Indochina. His strategy, known as the Navarre Plan, was to build entrenched camps such as Dien Bien Phu in anticipation of an international negotiated settlement in Indochina.
"Salan (Navarre's predecessor) was known as the 'mandarin' for his superior knowledge of Indochina. He was replaced by Navarre who had never served there." Dalloz.

100 General René Cogny: commander of the French Armed Forces in the Tonkin, the northern region of the French colonial federation.

101 Nguyen Van Tam: head of the French-installed Saigon government in 1952, he had been Minister of the Interior and Governor of North Vietnam.

102 American advisor: Lieutenant General John W. ("Iron Mike") O'Daniel, the head of the US Military Assistance Advisory Group (MAAG). MAAG was created in August 1950 in Saigon to disburse military and economic aid estimated at US$ 2.6 billion at the time, or 80 per cent of the war effort, to the French Expeditionary Corps and provide them with technical expertise. The first shipment of material to the French forces, under the Mutual Defense Assistance Program, consisted of Grunman F6F Hellcat fighters and was made in October 1950. A number of American advisers including O'Daniel made several visits to Dien Bien Phu.
"On February 2 (1954), General O'Daniel led a large group of American officers to the valley (of Dien Bien Phu); neither he, nor any other US officer, put in writing any fundamental misgivings about the Dien Bien Phu

plan or the position itself." Windrow.

103 *Dang Lao Dong Viet Nam* (DLDVN): The Vietnamese Workers Party was created in 1951 to replace the Communist Party which had been dissolved in 1945.

104 Stalingrad: siege and battle that lasted from August 19, 1942 until January 27, 1943. The Soviet Red Army defeated Hitler's forces at a huge cost of human life. Dien Bien Phu has been compared to the battle of Stalingrad and called the Stalingrad of the East.

105 Molotova: 600 Soviet trucks weighing 550lb each were used to transport the weapons, munitions and supplies of the People's Army to Dien Bien Phu. The troops usually advanced on foot.

106 "Steady advance, steady attack": *ibid*, footnote 60.

107 Land reform: part of the Workers' Party program "to give the land to those who work the land."
"After planning the Dien Bien Phu campaign, Party leaders decided to strengthen the land reform program to win support from poor peasants." Duiker, *Ho Chi Minh: A Life.*

108 Geneva Conference: at the initiative of the USSR, the four great powers met in Berlin on February 18, 1954 to set a date for the Geneva Conference to settle the conflicts in Korea and Indochina. The Soviet Union insisted on the participation of a Viet Minh delegate. This had been initially opposed by France and the United States.

109 Nam Ron: river flowing through the valley of Dien Bien Phu. The French headquarters and central camp were on the western bank of the river; the People's Army positions were on the eastern bank. An iron bridge known as the Bailey bridge and a wooden foot bridge connected the two banks.

110 Hong Cum: *ibid*, footnote 92. French stronghold Isabelle, five miles south of Muong Thanh. It resisted until the French capitulation on May 7.

111 Truong Chinh (1907–88): member of the Politburo during the Dien Bien Phu campaign and General Secretary of the Vietnamese Workers' Party (DLDVN). He was the Party's theoretician and the author of a practical guide on revolutionary guerrilla warfare read by new recruits in the Viet Minh training camps. Entitled *We Will Win*, it was published in 1947. Interview with the author.

112 Hill D: *ibid*, footnote 72.

113 Hill A1: French stronghold Eliane 2, to the east of the central zone. It was attacked during the second general offensive, the night of March 30, at the same time as hills E and D and hill C1 or Eliane 1. The People's Army captured hills E and D. Hill C1 resisted until May 1.
"On hill A1, after 107 hours of uninterrupted fighting, the People's Army withdrew on April 4. Hill A1 resisted all further attacks until May 7 when a Viet Minh commando dynamited the French command post from a tunnel." www.dienbienphu.org

114 Tank: "Ten M24 tanks Chaffee, weighing each 18 tons, were parachuted into Dien Bien Phu." Windrow.
"Only the Expeditionary Corps has tanks and fighter planes which gives them an undoubted superiority (over the Peoples' Army)." Dalloz.

115 82mm Russian mortars: their presence in Dien Bien Phu is confirmed here.

116 Long Bua: People's Army observation facing the French-held hill D.

117 Hill C1: *ibid*, footnote 113. French stronghold Eliane 1; hill C2, French stronghold Eliane 4. French defence positions attacked by the People's Army during the second phase of the battle on the night of March 31. The French counter-attacked with battalions, artillery, tanks and fighter planes on April 10 and 11 and re-occupied the position until May 1 when it was overrun once again by the People's Army. Windrow.

118 Hai Duong: territory occupied by the French and headquarters to one of four territorial divisions of the Expeditionary Corps in the Tonkin. The commander in chief had been General René Cogny who later became commander of the French troops in the Tonkin during the battle of Dien Bien Phu.

119 Ban Tau: Thai village in the Dien Bien Phu valley, north of Doc Lap hill.

120 Keeping the mail flowing to the troops was important for morale.

121 Colonel Christian Marie Ferdinand de la Croix de Castries (1902–91): Commanding Officer of the Operational Group North-West (GONO), one of the divisions at Dien Bien Phu. His command post was situated in the former village of Muong Thanh, west of the Nam Ron river and south of the airfield. Letters from his wife were found in one of the French parachute drops by the People's Army. Interview with the author.

122 *Sim* flowers: Myrtle flowers traditionally left by young girls on the tombs of their lovers killed in war.

123 Limited success: this was blamed on "a rightist tendency" during the second phase of the campaign among high ranking officers who doubted that victory was possible. The Political Bureau instructed the Party committees to suppress all "subjective" tendency through sessions of self- and group criticism, from the division level down to individual units.
"A negative tendency appeared among some of our officers and men, in various forms: fear of casualties, losses, difficulties and hardships, as well as fatigue, underestimation of the enemy, subjectivism and self-conceit." Giap.

124 Muong Pu, or Muong Pon: village near Tuan Giao that was burnt to the ground during a battle between the French and the Viet Minh in December 1953. Interview with the author.

125 April 27, 1954: day after the opening of the Geneva Conference.

126 Vyacheslav Molotov (1890–1986): Minister of Foreign Affairs of the USSR and delegate to the Geneva Conference. It was Molotov who insisted that the People's Republic of China be included as the fifth participant at the Geneva Conference. (The United States, the United Kingdom, France and the USSR were the four great powers). And it was Molotov who invited a delegate from the Democratic Republic of Vietnam (Viet Minh), agreed to by France and the United States after initial opposition.
"At the beginning of April, the USSR, the People's Republic of China and the DRV were looking for a diplomatic success in Geneva over a purely military solution." Woodrow Wilson International Centre for Scholars.

127 Hill E: French stronghold Dominique 1 and 2 that was overrun by the People's Army on March 30, at the same time as hill D .

128 French 155 mm cannon: The four 155mm cannons at Dien Bien Phu had a longer firing range of nine miles than the 105mm and their shells were more destructive. They were air transported to Dien Bien Phu by the Dakota transport planes. Dominique Lemaire.

129 Tu Vu: fortress of the French Expeditionary Corps, situated on the Black River, north of Hoa Binh and the site of a ferocious battle during the 1952 Hoa Binh campaign.
"The tanks of the (French) platoon, guns depressed to minimum elevation, fired into the screaming human clusters (of Viet Minh) crawling over the parapets into position…" Fall

130 *Tam tam che*: Vietnamese term meaning teams of three men.

"They (the political commissars) tried to follow the Chinese model of internal surveillance: each platoon was divided for tactical purposes into teams of three men or *tam tam che*, and one of these soldiers – whose identity was kept secret – was also supposed to be a Party member, tasked with both encouraging and spying on his comrades." Windrow

131 Gun pits for the 75mm cannons: Unlike the 105mm, the 75mm fired at a higher angle and were positioned in open gun pits which gave them a wider firing range. The pits were dug by artillerymen without the help of the army engineers. The gunpits were shallow and had no cover. As a result, they offered less protection than the underground shelters for the 105mm cannons.

132 Japanese cannon of 75mm, 94 series: cannon weighing half a ton with a projectile weighing 13lb. It was one of the cannons that was probably seized by the People's Army at the end of the Second World War when the Japanese surrendered to the Allied forces in Indochina. Unlike the 105mm, this cannon was built for mountainous terrain and could be dismantled into separate parts and carried. Interview with the author.

133 American cannon: "Artillerymen and infantrymen of the People's Army dragged 200 cannons through mountain passes and over hills, including 24 howitzers 105mm of US manufacture, which had been captured in Korea by the People's Liberation Army of the People's Republic of China." Doan Khue, translated by Pierre Asselin.

134 Russian Katchusha: rocket launcher developed by the Soviets towards the end of the Second World War, nicknamed "Stalin's organs" by the German troops who likened the thundering noise of its firing power to the sound of a church organ.

135 Hill A1 or Eliane 2: *ibid*, footnote 113.

136 White flag controversy: To avoid official humiliation, the French High Command in Hanoi did not want a capitulation with an official white flag. Authors and accounts differ on what happened that day in Dien Bien Phu. A number of personal accounts, including this one, maintain that a white flag made from a parachute was hoisted on the French central command post and that soldiers emerged from their shelters waving white pieces of cloth.

137 Hong Gang: General Giap's command post, 39 miles northeast of Muong Thanh, on route 41.

138 Stalin's organs: *ibid*, footnote 134.

139 Prisoners at Dien Bien Phu: Estimates vary with sources concurring that, by international standards, a very high percentage of prisoners died during the forced marches and in the POW jungle camps once the prisoners had left Dien Bien Phu.

140 Hong Cum on fire: After the capitulation of their forces in Muong Thanh, the French blew up their own munitions depot in Hong Cum (Isabelle) so it wouldn't fall into enemy hands.

141 Official Vietnamese estimates cited by General Giap in his publication on the conflict, Dien Bien Phu. According to French sources, Rocolle estimates that out of 15,090 French troops, including those who were parachuted in, 7,984 were killed and wounded. According to Dalloz, 3,000 people were killed during the battle.
There are no official Vietnamese estimates of the number of their dead and wounded at Dien Bien Phu. The French official estimate puts the figure at 8,000 Vietnamese dead (12,000 according to other sources) and 15,000 to 20,000 wounded.

142 Tuyen Quang: town and military camp over 300 miles from Dien Bien Phu, on route 13; on the banks of the Clear River, it is approximatly 25 miles from the town of Yen Bai, where the author started his diary and his journey to Dien Bien Phu.

143 Ban Chan pass: mountain pass on route 13.

144 Light blue flag: flag with the light blue background of the United Nations flag, created in 1949. The white dove in the centre, modelled on a Picasso drawing, was a symbol of peace and harmony between nations. The flag was adopted for festivities and celebrations by the Viet Minh and other socialist countries.

Chronology

1887 France creates the Indochinese Union that includes Cambodia.

1890 Ho Chi Minh is born in Central Vietnam.

1930 Ho Chi Minh creates the Indochinese Communist Party in Hong Kong.

1939 The Second World War begins as Germany invades Poland.

1940 Japan occupies Vietnam leaving the French Vichy government in place.

1941 Ho Chi Minh creates the Viet Minh (*Viet Nam Doc Lap Dong Minh*) to fight for Vietnamese independence.

1944 A famine kills an estimated one to two million Vietnamese.

1945 Japanese coup and takeover of the French administration throughout Indochina (March 9). The Viet Minh launches the August Revolution and calls for the mobilisation of the people against the Japanese and the French. Japanese capitulation (August 15) after Hiroshima and Nagasaki. Ho Chi Minh proclaims the independence of Vietnam (September 2). French troops land in Saigon (October 5).

1946 France recognises Vietnam as a "free state" within the French Union. French troops authorised to land in Haiphong to replace the Chinese (March 6). Negotiations in Fontainebleau between Ho Chi Minh and the French break down. Amid growing tensions, French warships bombard Haiphong (November 23). Viet Minh forces leave Hanoi to set up the resistance in the Viet Bac. The Franco-Vietnam war begins (December).

1949 Establishment of the People's Republic of China (PRC) (October 1).

1950 Creation of the Vietnamese People's Army. The USSR and the PRC recognise the Democratic Republic of Vietnam (DRV). North Korea invades South Korea(June 26). President Truman signs legislation granting military aid to the French for the war in Vietnam (July 26). The PRC supplies the Viet Minh. During the Northwest campaign, the French are defeated at Cao Bang, Dong Khe and That Khe, keyposts on the Chinese border (October 3–8).

1951 The Viet Minh are defeated at the battle of Vinh Yen in Vin Phuc province (January 17). Ho Chi Minh creates the Lao Dong, or Workers' Party to replace the Communist Party dissolved in 1945 (March) .

1952 Campaign of Hoa Binh (February). The French evacuate Hoa Binh. Dwight D Eisenhower is elected US president (November 4).

1953 Joseph Stalin, the Soviet leader dies (March 5). The Viet Minh launches the agrarian reform (May) and an offensive in Laos (December). General Henri Navarre is named Commanding Officer of the French forces in Indochina (May 8). Following the Navarre Plan (July 24), the French set up a new air defence base at Dien Bien Phu. Christian de Castries is put in charge of French forces at Dien Bien Phu (Nov 30). Ho Chi Minh and the Politburo plan to attack Dien Bien Phu (late December). Infantry and artillery divisions of the Peoples' Army march to Dien Bien Phu.

1954 Giap becomes Commander in Chief of the People's Army (January 1) and leaves for Dien Bien Phu (January 5). Agreement by the US, the UK, France and the USSR to hold a conference in Geneva on Korea and Indochina (February 18). The battle of Dien Bien Phu begins (March 13). Second general offensive by the People's Army (March 31). The Geneva Conference opens (April 26). Third general offensive by the People's Army (May 1). French capitulation at Dien Bien Phu (May 7). Ngo Dinh Diem becomes Prime Minister of the Saigon government (June 16). The Geneva Accords (July 20) call for the provisional partition of Vietnam at the 17th parallel pending national elections in 1956. The People's Army march into Hanoi (October 11). The United States pledges to give US$100 million in aid to support Diem in south Vietnam.

1955 Diem rejects the Geneva Accords and refuses to participate in nationwide elections (July 6) and proclaims the Republic of Vietnam in the south (October 26) with himself as president.

1960 In Hanoi, the DRV creates the National Liberation Front for South Vietnam, to support the Viet Minh insurgents in the south, called Vietcong by Saigon (December 20).

1964 Gulf of Tonkin incident. American B 52s bomb the DRV. The second war in Vietnam begins.

1975 End of the Vietnam War.

2005 Thirty years of peace in Vietnam.

Sources: VO NGUYEN GIAP, (GENERAL), *Dien Bien Phu*, sixth edition, The Gioi, Hanoi, 1999; KARNOW, STANLEY, *Vietnam: A History*, Pimlico, Random House edition, London, 1994; WINDROW, MARTIN, *The Last Valley: Dien Bien Phu and The French Defeat in Vietnam*, Weidenfeld & Nicolson, 2004; DALLOZ, JACQUES, *The War in Indo-China, 1945-1954*, Rowman & Littlefield, 1990.

Select Bibliography

Given the abundance of publications on the Franco-Vietnam war, the historical bibliography was chosen to represent the best sources as well as authors who were participants in the battle of Dien Bien Phu. Recent memoirs in French by former combatants published to commemorate the fiftieth anniversary of the battle of Dien Bien Phu, even though not translated into English, have been included. A significant number of autobiographies, memoirs and historical accounts that have been published only in Vietnamese are not represented here .

Art and the Vietnam Wars

AGUSTONI-PHAN, NHUNG, *L'Esprit du Viet-Nam: croyances, culture et société*, Genève, 1997.

ANDRÉ-PALLOIS, NADINE, DAYDÉ, EMMANUEL, DO PHUONG QUYNH, MÉNONVILLE CORINNE DE, and NGUYEN TRUNG: *L'aventure de l'art moderne au Viet Nam*, catalogue for the exhibition, *Paris–Hanoi–Saigon* at the Pavillon des Arts, Paris Musées and Art Books International, 1998.

BUCHANAN, SHERRY, *Tran Trung Tin: Paintings and poems from Vietnam*, Asia Ink and Thames & Hudson, 2001.

"Artists and the Role of Propaganda," in *Vietnam Behind The Lines: Images from the War, 1965-1975*, British Museum Press, London 2002.

"Drawing Fire", *G2, The Guardian*, 10 June 2002.

"Silent Warrior", *The Independent on Sunday*, June 2002.

"Rebel With A Cause: The Violent Past of Southeast Asia Still Haunts Artists And Their Work", *Asian Art News*, May/June 1996.

"Buu Chi: Bittersweet Hope of A Vietnamese Artist", *International Herald Tribune*, 25 November 1994.

BUI THANH PHUONG and TRAN HAU TUAN, *Bui Xuan Phai: Life and Work*, Hanoi, 1999.

CLARK, TOBY, *Art and Propaganda in the Twentieth Century*, London, 1997.

FAST, HORST and PAGE, TIM, *Requiem: Photographers Who Died in Vietnam and Indochina*, Random House, 1997.

HARRISON-HALL, JESSICA and BUCHANAN, SHERRY, "The Unseen War", *British Museum Magazine*, Summer 2002.

HARRISON-HALL, JESSICA, BUCHANAN, SHERRY and STERN, THU, *Vietnam*

Behind The Lines: Images from the War, 1965-1975, The British Museum Press, 2002.

JAMIESON, NEIL L., *Understanding Vietnam*, University of California Press, Berkeley, 1993.

QUANG PHONG, *Art in Vietnam: 1925–1945, The Fine Arts College of Indochina and the epoch of painting prior to the Revolution; 1945–1954, Painters volunteer to fight for national salvation; 1954–1995, From socialist realism to the after-war multiform tendency*, Association of Fine Arts, Hanoi, 1995.

RIDING, ALAN, "The Vietnam War , As Seen in Art From the Other Side", *The New York Times*, October 22, 2002.

SINAIKO, EVE (edited by), *Reflexes and Reflections,* Harry N. Abrams and the National Vietnam Veterans Art Museum, Chicago, 1998.

TAYLOR, NORA ANNESLEY, "Contemporary Vietnamese Painting: Past and Present," *The New Asia Review*, New Haven, Fall 1994.

The Artist and The State: The Politics of Painting and National Identity in Hanoi, Viet Nam 1925–1998, PhD dissertation, Cornell University, January 1997.

THAI BA VAN, *Masters of Vietnamese Painting: To Ngoc Van, Nguyen Gia Tri, Nguyen Sang, Bui Xuan Phai*, Hanoi, 1994.

THOMAS, DAVID C., *As Seen From Both Sides: American and Vietnamese Artists Look At The War*, Boston, 1991.

VAN TAM, *War Sketches*, Truong Dai Hoc My Thuat, Ho Chi Minh City, 2001.

Dien Bien Phu and the Indochina War

ARGENLIEU, THIERRY D', (ADMIRAL), *Chroniques d'Indochine*, Albin Michel, 1985.

ASSELIN, PIERRE, "New Perspectives on Dien Bien Phu", Explorations in Southeast Asian Studies, *Journal of the Southeast Asian Studies Student Association*, University of Hawaii Manoa, Vol 1 No 2, Fall 1997.

BODARD, LUCIEN, *La guerre d'Indochine: l'enlisement, l'humiliation, l'aventure*, Grasset, 1997.

The Quicksand War: Prelude to Vietnam, Faber, 1967.

BONNET, GABRIEL, *La guerre révolutionnaire du Vietnam*, Payot, Paris, 1969.

BORTON, LADY and THOMAS, DAVID C., *Hồ Chí Minh: Môt chân dung*, Thanh Nien, Hanoi, 2003.

BRANCION, HENRI DE, (GENERAL), *Diên Biên Phu: Artilleurs dans la fournaise,*

Presses de la Cité, 1993.
"Diên Biên Phu – le choc de deux artilleries", *Revue Historique des Armées, 1992/4.*

CHOMSKY, NOAM, *At War with Asia: Essays on Indochina*, AK Distribution, 2004.

CURREY, CECIL BARR and KEEGAN, JOHN, *Victory at Any Cost: The Genius of Viet Nam's Gen. Vo Nguyen Giap*, Brassey's Inc., 1999.

DALLOZ, JACQUES, *The War in Indo-China, 1945-1954*, Rowman & Littlefield, 1990.

DUIKER, WILLIAM, *Ho Chi Minh: A Life*, Hyperion, New York, 2000.

FALL, BERNARD B., *Street Without Joy*, Stackpole, Harrisburg, 1961.
Hell in a Very Small Place: The Siege of Dien Bien Phu, Philadelphia, 1966.

FOX, ROBERT, *Vo Nguyen Giap*, Weidenfeld and Nicolson military, 2005.

GRAS, YVES, (GENERAL), *Histoire de la guerre d'Indochine*, Denoël, 1992.

GUILLAIN, ROBERT, *Diên Biên Phu: La fin des illusions*, Arléa, 2004.

HO CHI MINH, *Prison Diary*, Bantam Books, 1972.
Poems From the Prison Diary of Ho Chi Minh, Small Press Distribution, 2004.

HO CHI MINH, *On Revolution: Selected Writings*, 1920-1969, ed. Bernard B. Fall, Westview Press, 1984.
Patriotism and Proletarian Internationalism, University Press of the Pacific, 2003.

KARNOW, STANLEY, *Vietnam: A History*, Penguin Books, 1997.

LANGLAIS, PIERRE, (GENERAL), *Diên Biên Phu*, France Empire, 1963.

LOCKHART, GREG, *Nation in Arms: The Origins of the People's Army of Vietnam*, Allen & Unwin, Sydney, Australia, 1989.

MARR, DAVID G., *Vietnam 1945: The Quest for Power*, Berkeley: University of California Press, 1995.

NAVARRE , HENRI, (GENERAL), *Agonie d'Indochine,* Plon, 1956.

ROUSSEAU, SABINE, *La colombe et le napalm: des chrétiens français contre les guerres d'Indochine et du Vietnam*, 1945–1975, CNRS, Paris, 2002.

ROCOLLE, PIERRE, *Pourquoi Diên Biên Phu ?*, L'Histoire Flammarion, 1968.

ROY, JULES, *The Battle of Dienbienphu*, Carroll & Graf Publishers, 2002.

SAINTENY, J., *Histoire d'une paix manquée*, Fayard, 2ème éd., 1967.

SIMPSON, HOWARD R., *Dien Bien Phu: The Epic Battle America Forgot*, 2004.

TASSIGNY, JEAN DE LATTRE DE, (GENERAL), *La ferveur et le sacrifice, Indochine, 1951*, Plon, 1988.

(including hill C1) in the central zone and one position in the southern zone (Hong Cum – a quarter of a mile from the enemy command post in the southern zone). During our final attack on May 6, we launched a general assault that lasted all night and most of the following day. The enemy capitulated on May 7! Our victory has been so sudden that everyone seemed paralysed when they first heard the news, not knowing how to react. But after the meeting we all started hugging each other and shouting for joy. We are so happy!

Phung Van Khau and the other artillerymen of division F351 were cited for their contribution to the battle of Dien Bien Phu.

Tonight, I watch the trucks leaving the battlefield in long convoys, transporting the cannons along the winding roads.

May 12, 1954

At the command post of my division, near route 41. Today the time has come for me to say goodbye to the shelter where I spent my first night at Dien Bien Phu! Within a month the jungle will have reclaimed this isolated and wild place! If there hadn't been a military command post on this hill, nobody would have ever wanted to come here. Before we boarded the trucks, the cook prepared a far better feast for us than the one we had never actually got to eat on May 1. He served rolls of roasted meat on large banana leaves, with banana flowers and jungle spinach (*rau tau bay*). We joked around and wrote the word "victory" with the juices from the meat. That cook deserves a medal for the numerous times he carried food up to the men at the division. The kitchen was at the bottom of the hill with an 80-degree slope! The cook carried food to those with key jobs at headquarters who had no time to leave their posts – in intelligence, information, radio communication, map drawing, stenography and document printing. Then there were those who were simply too lazy to get their own food. They got caught out eventually since they had to bring their mess bowls back to the kitchen for the preparation of the next meal or go hungry! I didn't mind going down the hill because there was a clear water stream shaded by trees where I could wash

Following pages: *Tractor, mountains and fields after the war*, 1956, watercolour on paper, 26cm x 38cm.

TRUONG CHINH, *The August Revolution*, Foreign Languages Publishing House, Hanoi, 1958.

Primer for Revolt, Praeger, New York, 1963.

VO NGUYEN GIAP (GENERAL), *Art of The People's War: Selected Writings*, ed. Larry Jagan, Pluto Press, 1989.

Unforgettable Months and Years (translated by Mai Van Elliott), Southeast Asia Program, Cornell University, Ithaca, New York, 1975.

Dien Bien Phu, sixth edition, The Gioi, Hanoi, 1999.

Mémoires 1946-1954, Tome 2: Le chemin menant à Diên Biên Phu, Anako, Paris, 2004.

Mémoires 1946-1954: Tome 3, Diên Bên Phu, le rendez-vous de l'histoire, (translated by Huu Mai and Nguyên Van Su) Anako, Paris, 2004.

"The Most Difficult Decision," *Memoirs of War: Dien Bien Phu*, The Gioi,2004.

WINDROW, MARTIN, *The Last Valley: Dien Bien Phu and The French Defeat in Vietnam*, Weidenfeld & Nicolson, 2004.

Memoirs

AINLEY, HENRY, *In Order To Die*, London, 1954.

ANAPI (ASSOCIATION NATIONALE DES ANCIENS PRISONNIERS D'INDOCHINE), *Notre histoire*, Atlante, 2004.

BRUGE, ROGER, *Les Hommes de Diên Biên Phu*, Tempus, 2004.

DANG VAN VIET, *Highway 4: The Border Campaign (1947-1950)*, Hanoi: Foreign Languages Publishing House, 1990.

EINAUDI, JEAN-LUC, *Viet-Nam ! La Guerre d'Indochine, 1945–1954*, Le Cherche-midi éditeur, 2001.

GALABRU, ANDRÉ, *La Victoire avortée*, André Galabru, Atlante, 2004.

GALARD, GENEVIÈVE DE, with BRAZIL, BÉATRICE, *Une femme à Diên Bên Phu*, Editions les Arènes, 2003.

GRAUWIN, PAUL, *J'étais médecin à Diên Biên Phu*, France-empire, 1956.

JOURNOUD, PIERRE and TETRAIS, HUGUES, *Paroles de Diên Biên Phu: Le Témoignage des survivants*, Tallandier, 2004.

LEONETTI, GUY ed., *Lettres de Diên Biên Phu*, Fayard, 2004.

LONG, PEDRO NGUYEN with WALTER, GEORGE, *La Montagne des Parfums, Une Saga Indochinoise*, Robert Laffont/Phébus, 1996.

NGO VAN CHIEU, *Journal d'un combattant viêt-minh*, Le Seuil, 1955.

NGUYEN, KIEN, *The Unwanted: A Memoir*, Little Brown, 2002.
PELISSIER, PIERRE, *Diên Biên Phu, 20 novembre 1953–7 mai 1954*, Perrin, 2004.

On line

The Vietnam Project, Texas Tech University, www.vietnam.ttu.edu/
DOMINIQUE LEMAIRE, *Encyclopédie des canons de la deuxième guerre mondiale*
www.dienbienphu.org ; www.vietnam.vnagency.com.vn

Editor's acknowledgements

In Vietnam, I am grateful to the author and war artist, Pham Thanh Tam for authorisation to proceed with this project and for allowing me unrestricted access to his diaries and his collection of war drawings as well as for giving so much of his time in an atmosphere of friendship and trust. Our frequent meetings took place at his house in Ho Chi Minh City and I would like to thank his wife Lanh and his youngest daughter Ly for their warm and unfailing hospitality throughout the project. My thanks to his daughter Hoa Pham and to Chau for interpreting and for spending many days and evenings placing stories and anecdotes in their cultural and historical context.

In Ho Chi Minh City, my special thanks go to the artist Tran Trung Tin who started me on this adventure. My gratitude to Tran Thi Huynh Nga, the director of the Blue Space Contemporary Art Gallery at the Ho Chi Minh City Fine Arts Museum, who introduced me to Mr Tam and who shares my passion to bring modern and contemporary Vietnamese painting and literature to a wider audience. I would like to thank Nguyen Toan Thi, a war artist and the director of the Ho Chi Minh City Fine Arts Museum, who gave me unrestricted access to the museum's collection of war drawings that he has put together over the last ten years. I would like to thank the staff at the museum, who were unfailingly helpful, in particular Phan Huu Thien and Mrs Cao. For facilitating my research, my thanks go to Huynh Phuong Dong, a war artist and the former minister of culture for Ho Chi Minh City, Quach Phong, a war artist and the former director of the Fine Arts Association in Ho Chi Minh City, Nguyen Thanh Chau, a war artist and the director of the Fine Arts Association in Ho Chi Minh City. In Hanoi, my thanks to Nguyen Duy, a war artist and the fomer director of the Hanoi Institute of Fine Arts and to the war artists Van Da and Thanh Ngoc.

I would like to thank the photographer Hans Kemp, who photographed Pham Thanh Tam's collection of drawings as well as the Ho Chi Minh City Fine Arts Museum's collection. His expertise at bringing to life and capturing damaged Vietnamese works on paper is not as simple as it might appear.

This project would not have been possible without Nguyen Van Ha, of the department of English Linguistics and Literature of the University of Social Sciences and Humanities in Ho Chi Minh City. My thanks for her meticulous translation of the diary into English, which she managed to do in record time. And I would like to thank Phan Anh Tu for his contribution to the translation. For their computer skills, speed and accuracy, my thanks go to Hoang Minh Duc who organised to have half of the manuscript typed overnight in time for my departure back to London and to Tran The Doanh, Nguyen Dinh Vu and Tran Huy Cuong, who spent an entire day and night transcribing the other half of the handwritten diary onto disc.

In London, my special thanks to Misha Aniskt for his sensitive design, inspired from his closeness to the subject through his own father's letters from the front at the battle of Stalingrad. I would like to thank Jessica Harrison-Hall of the British Museum, for contributing her wonderful preface and for sharing this adventure with me, and Thu Stern for her support and counsel. My thanks go to Clémence Jacquinet, the project editor for the French text, who through her perspicacity gave the diary its chronological rigour and accuracy and paved the way for the English text found here and to Yvonne Worth, the project editor of the English text, who offered advice for the content of the introduction.

For their interest and support my thanks to Do Thi Phan, director general of the SCPC and to Pham Phi Hong of Fahasa.

I would like to extend my thanks to all those who contributed their help to this project in different ways: Pierre Saulnier d'Anchald, Anthony and Marie-Laure Aris, Martine Berthéa, Béatrice and Jean-François Buisseret, Dieu Thuy, Do Thu Huong, Pier Laurenza, Nguyen Dam Thuy, Nguyen Thi Tam, Nam Nguyen, Fabrice Pataut, Robert Ogburn, Sarah and Christian Thun-Hohenstein and Jonathon Waugh.

My greatest thanks go to my husband William Spurgin for his constant and unfailing support. From a long line of soldiers who fought for the British Empire, his firm belief that bringing a Vietnamese side of the war to the fore was long overdue supported me throughout.